REAL
EASY

REAL EASY

MARIE RUTKOSKI

Henry Holt and Company
New York

Henry Holt and Company
Publishers since 1866
120 Broadway
New York, NY 10271
www.henryholt.com

Henry Holt® and ⒽⓄ® are registered trademarks of
Macmillan Publishing Group, LLC.

Library of Congress Cataloging-in-Publication Data

Names: Rutkoski, Marie, author.
Title: Real easy / Marie Rutkoski.
Description: First edition. | New York : Henry Holt and Company, 2022.
Identifiers: LCCN 2021020446 (print) | LCCN 2021020447 (ebook) |
    ISBN 9781250788245 (hardcover) | ISBN 9781250788252 (ebook)
Subjects: LCSH: Stripteasers—Crimes against—Fiction. | Women detectives—Fiction. |
    GSAFD: Mystery fiction. | LCGFT: Novels.
Classification: LCC PS3618.U789 R43 2022 (print) | LCC PS3618.U789 (ebook) |
    DDC 813/.6—dc23
LC record available at https://lccn.loc.gov/2021020446
LC ebook record available at https://lccn.loc.gov/2021020447

Our books may be purchased in bulk for promotional, educational, or business use. Please contact
your local bookseller or the Macmillan Corporate and Premium Sales Department at (800) 221-
7945, extension 5442, or by e-mail at MacmillanSpecialMarkets@macmillan.com.

First Edition 2022

Designed by Kelly S. Too

Printed in the United States of America

1   3   5   7   9   10   8   6   4   2

for Alexandra Machinist

REAL
EASY

SAMANTHA

(RUBY)

"You're so pretty it makes me want to go home and punch my wife in the mouth."

Samantha smiles and asks if he wants a dance. He smells like a kid, like sweat and juice boxes, and has a stubby body with one hunched shoulder. He skims a big palm over the silver bristle of his hair and says, "I sure do."

She leads the way to the leather sofas under the main stage, where the bass throbs through the low plexiglass ceiling. Next to her, Violet dances for a bearded guy who looks like a teacher, her dark brown skin shiny in the pink light, her lipstick tangerine. Samantha wishes she could trade places with her. Samantha's client, settled into the sofa, leans forward to say, "I remember you, from before you got your fake tits. Flat as a popped tire."

She shouldn't be annoyed. He's right, for one, and for another it's not the worst thing she's heard. She peels down her dress. "How do you like me now?"

"What I wouldn't give."

Samantha reaches for the tiny see-through hook of her V-string and lets the scrap of red fabric fall. She cups her breasts, which still feel alien even though she got them many months ago. They have the density of chewed bubble gum. "Want to come with me to the champagne room?"

"Maybe later."

The song ends. He gives her a twenty.

He leaves, and Violet's client does, too. Samantha hooks her V-string back into place. Violet wobbles on her heels as she steps into her dress. She grabs Samantha's arm for balance and whispers, "Check out the new girl."

The new girl has plopped bare-butt onto the sofa to wiggle her thong up over clunky shoes. Samantha can't remember her name. Skinny thing; pale, doughy face. Violet sucks her teeth.

Samantha almost tells the new girl what should be obvious, but Morgan, a tan brunette with librarian glasses and breasts that are fake yet judiciously small, beats her to it. "Don't sit on the seats," Morgan says.

The girl glances up.

"You'll get germs in your cookie."

THE EARLY-MORNING LIGHT is smoky when Samantha pulls into the parking lot of her apartment complex and parks next to Mrs. Zace's car, which the neighbor lets them use in exchange for picking up groceries. Nick says that Samantha wants the world to be like a Hallmark card, but what's so bad about that? Mrs. Zace likes to play grandmother to Rosie, and occasionally babysat her before Nick lost his job. Mrs. Zace's sedan looks gray in the mist, like it has been breathed on. Samantha's sneakers make no sound on the asphalt. Her tight jeans feel cozier than pajamas. Her loose hair smells like cigars and the sour apple of sweat and body spray.

She is glad she wiped off her makeup at the club. Rosie is up, much too early for a Saturday morning, watching TV.

"Your daddy awake?" Samantha says.

Rosie sucks the ends of her blond hair. "No."

Samantha joins her on the couch, which is new: a nice, sage chenille. Some dancers talk about moving to Chicago to make more money, but she can afford a better life in Fremont. The schools are good, and there's a playground a block away. Fremont has a cute main street with antique stores, a used CD and DVD place, and a former theater converted into a cinema. The red velvet seats are itchy, but the ceiling is painted like the sky and Rosie loves when the lights go down and tiny stars appear above. Fremont is the right kind of city: not too big, but big enough that a nightlife centers around the club and a casino on the Des Plaines River. Fremont has a Costco and a Best Buy and tracts of unincorporated land interrupted by silos of farms that grow corn and soybeans.

Samantha melts into the couch. Her feet ache beneath the double layer of tube socks. The curtains are still drawn. "Come here, baby."

Rosie doesn't move. She is dappled by the shifting light of the television. A commercial becomes another commercial.

"What're you watching?"

Rosie shrugs her slim shoulders, then leans into Samantha, curling up against her. "How come you're always late?"

"Not always."

"I was waiting for you."

Samantha slopes a hand over Rosie's hair, down to the spiky wet tips. "I'll take you out for breakfast. Silver dollar pancakes with chocolate chips." She feels the possibility of becoming a perfect stepmother, wholesome and lovable, ready to make any moment special.

"Okay." Rosie's voice is muffled against her side. "You smell bad."

That sense of possibility crinkles up inside her like cellophane, like something that can't return to its original shape even after it is smoothed out.

NICK IS AWAKE when they get back from breakfast, and thanks her when she hands him half the cash. "Let's see a movie tonight," he says.

Rosie lights up. "I want to choose."

"I have to work," Samantha says.

Rosie doesn't like that. "We'll go without you," she threatens.

"You should. Go have fun." Samantha reaches to tuck a lock of Rosie's hair behind her ear, but she squirms away.

Later, after Samantha gets out of the shower and Rosie is playing in her bedroom, Nick says, "I wonder if those assholes you dance for can tell that you're part boy."

THERE IS STILL daylight when she pulls into the Lovely Lady's parking lot. She can guess by some of the cars who is working tonight: Skye's yellow Hummer, Morgan's blue Taurus. There is a fancy black Caddy Samantha doesn't recognize, whose black paint holds the sunset the way dark hair can, with hints of red.

She walks into the club through the backstage door and past a row of lockers. Hers bears her name on a simple strip of masking tape, but other girls have elaborately decorated theirs, like Paris, whose locker is lacquered inside and out with pictures of her daughter, also named Paris. Many lockers have photos of the dancers' children. One of Rosie is taped to the inside of Samantha's locker door. Even Sasha, who seems far from maternal, has a picture of a quiet-looking, dark-eyed girl whose name, Melody, is written below the photo against a musical staff, the *d* transformed into an eighth note. A few lockers have fake flowers poked into the air vents, which is not allowed because the flowers eventually fall onto the floor, and so many girls work here, several dozen, their schedules written over each other's in arcane patterns, that things get messy fast. Dale, their manager, has said it a million times: "The Lovely Lady stays clean." He is fussy but a good boss. He says his door is always open to them, and it is true. Anyone can walk into his office anytime.

Samantha spins her lock, feeling that jammy give around the right numbers, and remembers how Nick saw what her face did when he called her part boy. She couldn't respond at first because of the tight pressure of what she wanted to say, the way words bunched up in her throat. Nick said he was sorry. He knew that what he had said wasn't true. She was a girl. He knew that.

"Think about how hard this is for me," he said.

"It's just a job."

"It makes me feel small."

She did not care. She did not forgive him.

"Samantha, come here. I said I was sorry." He brushed hair away from her wet face. "Beautiful girl. Like JFK Jr.'s wife." Nick always said that, and Samantha used to be flattered until Carolyn Bessette Kennedy died earlier that summer in a plane crash, with her husband flying the plane in the dark. Samantha wished Nick would stop comparing her to a dead girl. Nick said, "How did I get so lucky?" When she remained stiff, he added, "Don't be like this," clearly wounded, close to anger, so she forgave him, because if she didn't she would quickly be blamed. Although he had hurt her, she would be made to feel guilty for being hurt.

It is important that he apologized, she decides. They are not married but they almost are, and she is sure they will be one day. Marriage takes work, everyone knows that. Samantha opens the locker, stuffs in her purse, and grabs a red dress trimmed with feathers.

Violet sits before a mirror in the dressing room, blow-drying her thin braids, which have all been braided into two thick braids. The new girl is doing her own makeup, which she should know by now is a bad idea. She should pay Bella to do it.

Bella is counseling Rhiannon to get a real estate license. Rhiannon has pulled her dress down to her waist and rubs orangeish foundation into the curves of her meager cleavage to make it look bigger.

Violet meets Samantha's eyes in the mirror. "Hey, Ruby." Her accent is creamy, almost British. It's not even fake. She was born in Trinidad.

"Hey," says Samantha.

"Cut the string after you put the tampon in," Morgan tells Desirée. "A string is the last thing they want to see."

"Some do," Gigi says around a forkful of homemade, gourmet-looking risotto.

"Shut up."

"Once, I leaked right down my thigh. This guy asked to lick it off. Said he'd pay extra."

The dressing room howls. Gigi laughs, her belly trembling, her light brown skin rippled with the stretch marks of someone who used to weigh more. She still loves to eat, just like anyone, she has said, but she is choosy. The food has got to be good.

Rhiannon leans back to study her breasts and says she wishes she could leave her panties on so she didn't have to worry about tampon strings. Oh no, you do not, they tell her. Full nude means it's against Illinois state law for men to touch them. No lap dances, no beard rash. Panties means pasties, too, or cut-up strips of clear Band-Aids taped around the nipple, because in those states, the law says no holes.

"Titties ain't holes."

"The fuck you think the milk comes out?"

Violet turns off the hair dryer. She unbraids the big braids, then finger-shakes the mass of little braids, curly now. Samantha changes into her red dress. The new girl roots through her makeup bag, clearly having paid no attention to anything anyone has said, which makes Samantha prickle with irritation so intense it surprises her. What could you do with someone so clueless, so helpless, someone who doesn't even try to learn?

SAMANTHA DOESN'T SEE the new girl again until later, when she steps off Stage 3, the smallest stage, which is tucked into a corner on the second floor. Stage 3 is a desert on slow nights. No one likes Stage 3, or so they say. Samantha complains with the rest of them, but the truth is that she has scored big there before, so when she hears girls gripe about Stage 3, she wonders whether she knows something they don't or if they are faking, too.

Jimmy offers Samantha a chivalrous hand. Bouncers have been instructed by Dale to do this so the girls don't trip in their heels. She carefully descends the plexiglass staircase and makes her way to the main floor. Every hour on the hour there is a two-for-one special, and everyone knows they must be backstage in time to get the T-shirts. The new girl is still dancing. Samantha catches a glimpse of her below the main stage. She jumps a little in her heels, a swing to her hips. The guy on the sofa is lanky, with a pale, lantern-jaw face and a baseball cap marked with the letter Z. Samantha has danced for him before. No deep pockets there. She sees the new girl's expression: familiar, smooth, glowing. It bothers Samantha. Its familiarity feels misleading, out of place, which makes her recognize the expression as frank pleasure.

The girl is late for the twofer, of course. She is last in line, hugging the XXL T-shirt emblazoned with the club's name to her chest. Buy one dance, get the second free. Plus a T-shirt.

"Look at all of our Lovelies!" the deejay calls through the sound system, his voice extra deep, buzzing at the bottom of his range, and they file out onto the main stage and descend to spread across the club floor, coyly waving shirts. Samantha hates selling them, but the twofer is as good a means as any to finding a man who will pay two hundred dollars for an hour in champagne.

SKYE IS ON the main stage when Samantha gets lucky. The man Samantha is dancing for can see the main stage over her shoulder, and later she thinks that maybe his offer had something to do with the contrast between her and Skye, who has opulent hips, pebble eyes, and a lot of ink. Skye's boob job had gone badly, her new breasts shaped as though molded by basket coffee filters. She has sex for money after hours. Most girls know this, but Dale doesn't, or he would fire her. "I got a kid," she said once, loudly, so they keep their mouths shut.

"You're fun," the man tells Samantha as the song comes to an end. He is gray-haired and middle-aged, maybe fifty, but fit, with a hard, super-hero chest. He slips another twenty into her garter, and she rubber-bands it to the rest. "Keep going," he says. "Sweet little ass. Altar-boy hips."

Normally this wouldn't bother her. She knows she has a boyish body, except for her new breasts, but his words recall how Nick knew exactly what would hurt her most.

The man says, "How much for champagne?"

"Two hundred," she answers breezily.

"I hate champagne. Gives me gas."

"I'll drink it for you."

"And what do we get to do there?"

"Talk."

He makes a face. "Talk?"

"The bouncers keep an eye on us."

"Do you like to gamble, Ruby?"

"Sure."

"Come with me to the casino after closing. I'll pay you the same you'd make in the champagne room. By the hour."

She keeps the smile but her voice is serious: "I don't do that. I don't hook."

"It's just gambling, I swear. I want a pretty thing on my arm while I play. Maybe two. Ask your best girl to come. Same deal for her." He leans back, opens his muscled arms wide as if to encompass the size of his innocence, then tries on a canny smile and pulls out his wallet to show a spread of cash. "I got it. I'll give you extra to play with, too."

"Look, I like you, and I wish I could."

"I'm safe as houses."

"I can tell," she says, because it is always wise to confirm a man's good opinion of himself. "But I can't."

"You're smart. Gotta be safe, I respect that. Why not get a bouncer you trust to join in? I'll pay him."

Samantha glances across the room at Jimmy and calculates the potential haul from such a night. She thinks about calling in sick tomorrow to skip her Sunday double shift. Tonight she could slip into Rosie's narrow bed and breathe the balm of Rosie's breath. She will wake when Rosie wakes.

"No tricks," the man says. "On my honor."

"I can take a bouncer."

"Yes."

"And a friend."

"Hell yes!"

THE CASINO IS furred with smoke. Slot machines flicker. Their symbols vanish and return, *flippety-flippety*, but roulette is Tony's favorite, so that's what Samantha and Violet play, with Violet cashing out every few rounds and slipping most of her winnings into her purse. "Such a grandma," Tony says. Violet laughs like she is supposed to, her teeth very white. A few bottom teeth slant just enough to be cute. Her slender hand rests on Tony's sleeve.

Jimmy rubs his chin. The roulette spins its white ball. Jimmy is large in a puffy way, and Samantha realizes his chubby body and ruddy cheeks have always made her assume his sweetness, but now he looks unhappy, even unfriendly. Samantha has a miniature fortress of chips. She slides him a stack, which makes the corner of his mouth lift. But he loses, and keeps losing.

Tony strokes Samantha's hair and tucks a lock behind her ear, brushing the small pearl earring and fingering its diamond stud, then turns to bury his face against Violet's neck. "My girls."

Violet meets Samantha's gaze. They don't stiffen or pull away, although Samantha wants to. The money is too good. Tony's hand slides to the small of Samantha's back, and Violet and Samantha agree with their eyes to say nothing. A little touching is okay, so long as it is nowhere that matters. Anyway, they are safe. They have each other and Jimmy.

Before they left the club, Samantha caught Morgan's attention and pointed out Tony, who waited at a distance by the exit. Some girls would have been jealous. Others would have believed Samantha and Violet were tricking themselves out. Bella would have said, "Bank it, bitch!" Morgan pushed her glasses up her nose and said, "What're you telling me for?"

"It's like, when you go for a hike you should say where you're going, just in case."

"He'll expect more from you."

"I'll be fine. Jimmy and Violet are coming."

Morgan's shiny brown hair spilled over her shoulder as she bent to fuss with a stiletto strap. "Call me when you get home."

"Place your bets," the dealer says.

Samantha, glad for an excuse to lean away from Tony, sets a stack of chips on twelve.

"Lucky number?" Tony says.

"My birthday," she says, but it is Rosie's birthday.

She wins.

Violet squeezes Samantha's arm and shakes it. "Cash out! Cash out!"

Samantha is wobbly, her blood carbonated. She places all her chips on the layout and is given a light blue chip spoked with white, plus a few pink chips and some green ones, some red. Thousands of dollars.

"Can you walk?" Violet teases. "Are you going to faint? Do I have to carry you to the cage?"

"I'll carry you," Tony offers, but Violet swats him. Jimmy follows the girls to the cashier's cage, heavy-footed. He falters when Samantha gives him a pink chip. He rolls it over his knuckles, looking like he might give the chip back, then captures it in a fist. "Thanks."

Later, in the ladies' room, Violet flips her braids over one shoulder and leans into the mirror over the sink to reapply lipstick as Samantha wets a paper towel and runs it under her smudged eyes. Violet's gaze doesn't leave the mirror. "We look good together," she says.

"Yeah," Samantha says. "Nice haul, huh?"

Violet drops her lipstick into her purse and zips it shut. "We look like queens."

TONY PEACEFULLY DRAINS his beer, then licks a thumb to count out cash for her, Violet, and Jimmy. When he is done he sighs, satisfied to see how slender his wallet has become.

Violet and Jimmy head out the door, which lets in the dawn. Orange light washes Tony's face, illuminating an old scar, thin as thread, that cuts through his right eyebrow.

Samantha says, abruptly, "You've spent so much on us."

Tony's brown eyes go slow. He is looking at her, but also at something else inside of him. "I got nothing else to spend it on."

SAMANTHA IS HONEST with Nick, and that is a mistake.

"This fucking job," he says.

"But look."

He swipes the cash away. It feathers the floor.

"Nothing happened," she says. "I was safe the whole time. I had Violet. You've met her. Her real name is Catherine, remember? You like her. A bouncer came, too."

"He wants what they all want."

"You don't know him."

"And you do? How well?"

"Jesus, Nick."

He touches her neck as if checking her pulse. It feels tender, surprising, like they are going to make up. "Quit," he says.

"No."

For a moment, his thumb stays light against her throat, then squeezes. She backs away. His hand hardens. Her head thumps against the bedroom wall. "Nick," she tries to say, but can't. She thinks of Rosie's new bedsheets, crisp and bright, the print of her favorite princess, and Nick's job, which is no job, which they pretend is a job. She swallows against his thumb and remembers how she knew him in high school, sort of, from afar, and how when prom was coming he dressed in a tux and passed out flyers. Years later he told her he had done it for the free rental, and had been ashamed. Why? she said. You were handsome. It made me shy, you looked so good. His eyes got shiny. There's something I haven't told you, he said. It was their fourth date. I have a daughter. Her name is Rose. She's eight.

She can't breathe. His grip hurts. That's great, she told him.

It is?

I love children.

Yet even though he had told her his secret, she didn't tell him hers, not then, and when she eventually did—that she had a chromosome that she shouldn't, a rare genetic condition—he said, Why didn't you tell me before? You could have told me.

I thought you wouldn't like it, she said. He said that it didn't matter.

His hand loosens. She sucks in air. "Okay," she whispers.

He releases her, but she isn't sure he heard her. His mouth is slack. His gaze is interior, as if he cannot see her, only a trick mirror that bends the light and shows himself distorted. "Okay," she says again. "I'll quit."

He pulls back, horrified. He tells her he didn't mean it. He takes it back, all of it. He tells her to work, if that is what she wants. She should do what she wants. He is so sorry. She tries to make him feel better for having hurt her.

DALE RARELY COMES to the dressing room, but the girls pay little attention to his surprise appearance. They are busy getting ready for what promises to be a lucrative Friday night. Gigi kisses Dale's hollow cheek with a loud smack. Desirée yanks down her dress to flash him, and he smiles indulgently.

"Feeling better, Ruby?" Dale's eyes are lime green, practically glow-in-the-dark. Scalp satin, face handsome, teeth a clutch of gravel. He was in the army. You can still see it in his shoulders. "I heard you were sick." His voice is light and smooth and noble. Dale's voice is on the club's answering machine, inviting callers to leave a message, informing them of directions and hours.

"Yeah," she says. "Just a bad cold."

"Come talk with me."

"Uh-oh!" Bella coos. "Ruby's going to the principal's office!"

Samantha follows him not to his office but, oddly, to the club's unused lower level, which smells of sawdust. Raw wooden frames split the room into incomplete compartments. Dale unfolds a couple of metal chairs with fabric seats, the kind used in churches that can't afford pews, and invites Samantha to sit.

"We missed you last Sunday," he says.

"I'm sorry. I didn't feel good."

"How long have you been with us?"

"Two years."

"So you know the rules."

Three shifts minimum per week, and one must be either a weeknight or Sunday. Samantha doesn't work during the week. She picks Rosie up from school, helps her with homework, and tucks her in at night.

"Of all the girls"—he smooths his suit—"you're one of the smartest." She takes the cue. "Actually."

"Yes?"

"I wasn't sick."

He tips his head, considering her. "Why did you lie?"

He is curious, not upset, and she wants to keep him that way. Dale is nice enough. Unlike many club owners, he doesn't try to sleep with his dancers. Plus, he is reasonable. Gigi misses shifts all the time, and he overlooks it because her mother is dying. Samantha says, "My boyfriend wants me to quit."

"Do *you*?"

"No. I said so. He got rough." Samantha lets her eyes fill with tears. "I wasn't sick. I was too embarrassed to come in looking like I did." Yet Nick had left no marks. He had never done this before, and has been so gentle with her since that even if she told Dale exactly what had happened, it would have felt like a lie, too.

Dale says, "Do I need to worry about you?"

"No, it's fine now."

"You sure?"

"Yes. I'll make the Sunday up."

"Forget about that."

It's what she hoped. She hides her satisfaction behind a brave smile.

"We need you, sweetheart," he says. "Especially on slow nights. You're my star. When these VIP rooms are finished, when the walls are up and this room looks the way it should, this club will be a legend, a destination. Men will come from Chicago, from all over. Bankers, lawyers. Money. You want to be a part of that, don't you?"

Samantha looks again at the blind studs of the unfinished VIP rooms. Uneasily, she realizes that each room will be a box, closed off, in the club's basement. Anything could happen in one of them, and while an important reason she works at the Lady is that Dale enforces the rule that no one touches his dancers, rules can always change. Before she thinks better of it, she says, "Are you sure these rooms are a good idea?"

Offense flickers across his face. "I've been in this business a long time."

"Oh, I'm in," she says hastily. "It's going to be a big moneymaker. I just meant that maybe it'll cause conflict between the girls. They'll fight to get into VIP."

"They?"

"I mean *we*."

For a moment, his mouth looks tight, like a little sealed envelope, like he might make her work that extra shift after all. Then he smiles and says she can go.

HER TALK WITH Dale has cost her time, but she waits her turn backstage to get her makeup done, because Bella is worth it.

Bella slaps the seat of a barstool. "Hop on up." Bella is hot in a sporty way, her reddish hair cut shaggy and short, arms slender and tight with muscle. She is the only one of them who actually looks like a real dancer. She calls herself a dyke, and maybe that's true, or maybe she says it to appeal to a certain kind of regular. "Sweet or smoky?"

"Smoky," Samantha says.

Bella dabs foundation in a sticky vibrato over Samantha's forehead, her cheekbones, a swipe down the nose. A plume of powder. "Close."

Eyes shut, Samantha hears the click of a cosmetic brush tapped to rid excess shadow. The brush push-pats her eyelids, firm and soft.

"Open."

Samantha sees the new girl watching them. Bella follows Samantha's gaze, and the corner of her mouth lifts. Bella's skin is dusted everywhere with freckles, even her lips. "Up." Samantha looks at the ceiling. Liquid eyeliner slides on cool. "Close. Did you hear?"

"About what?"

"Cops found a girl by the side of the road. She'd been dead awhile. They ID'd her real easy, though, on account of her tits."

Samantha opens her eyes. Bella protests, so Samantha shuts them quickly, but not before she gets a glimpse of the new girl's shocked face.

"What?" says the new girl. Her name is Jolene, Samantha remembers. "What do you mean, her tits?"

Bella's hand keeps busy. "Implants, duh."

"I don't get it."

"Implants have serial numbers. Police traced them. Better than dental records. Open."

The first thing Samantha sees is Bella's freckled smile. To Jolene, Bella says, "Guess that means that if you end up in a dumpster, you'll be SOL." Jolene's breasts are nothing to write home about, but big enough, and real, with one slightly inverted nipple. Bella looks gleeful. "Who knows?" she says. "Maybe the killer is outside the club right now, waiting to get in. Maybe he'll ask you for a dance." She slicks gloss over Samantha's mouth. "All done."

Samantha tips her. "Where'd this happen?"

"In the woods by the highway, near Hodgkins." A few towns south. "Anytime you need a touch-up, you know where to find me."

When the girls gather behind the curtains for the opening number, during which they will be introduced one at a time, pageant-like, by the deejay, Samantha gets stuck next to Jolene despite careful maneuvering. Jolene has huge, frightened eyes, and starts to remind Samantha of one of those lemur-eyed troll dolls, so Samantha says, "Bella's messing with you." She adds, "Bella made that up," though she is not totally sure.

Jolene blinks rapidly. "Why?"

"You never pay to get your makeup done."

"I can do my own makeup."

"You do a crappy job, and it shows."

"I'm not like you," Jolene mumbles. "I don't make a lot of money."

"You don't know what I make."

"It's more."

"So what. Get your makeup done. It's an investment," she adds, using the word she used with Nick when she booked the boob job.

Desirée scoots by, grabbing Samantha's ass ("Hello, gorgeous!") along the way.

"You think it'd help?" Jolene asks.

"I think you need all the help you can get."

The deejay's voice booms. Violet tells all the girls to shut up, and the noise backstage briefly dips, then goes right back up. Rhiannon, ahead of Samantha, turns to the mirror along the stairway, hikes her dress, and spreads herself. "Toilet paper." She sighs, picking it off.

Jolene looks defeated. "What I mean is," Samantha says, "you'll get more dances with better makeup, and Bella will like you. It's win-win."

"What does it matter if Bella likes me?"

"You need everyone to like you."

Broken bits of stage lights whirl through the slightly parted curtains and scatter.

"So it's not true?" Jolene says. "She said that to scare me?"

"Trust me," says Samantha. "Just a stripper ghost story."

Still, Samantha thinks about it throughout the night. It comes to mind when she finds the hunched man from last week, who is starting to be a regular and can be counted on to buy five dances in one go. She thinks about the guy who took her to the casino and has not been back to the club since. Bella's story creeps in when a college couple pays double the cost per dance, though then the thought comes because the boyfriend and girlfriend look so happy and dopey that she decides, Not them. Never in a million years. As the night ages and her feet turn into bags of blood, the story drones in and out of her head.

She doesn't ask around about it, in case it turns out to be true.

"MY MONEY!" JOLENE is naked except for her heels and stands in front of her open locker, body tight, fingers tucked into fists. Then her hands go wild, beating around inside her locker, searching for what everyone in the quiet room knows is no longer there. "Someone stole my money!"

The locker to the right of hers is shut; Angel doesn't work today. To the left is Sasha, who, half dressed, plants hands on hips and says, "It wasn't me. Go ahead. Search me." Sasha—dry marigold hair, messy teeth—probably takes home a couple hundred on a Friday night if she is lucky. She stands defiantly, wearing track pants and a leopard-print bra, and has a temporary butterfly tattoo on her belly. It looks freshly applied; it shines in the light.

"I bet she shoved the money up inside her," Violet says.

"No one's searching *that*," Rhiannon says.

"Nasty."

"Joley can do it."

"Jolene."

"Whatever," says Desirée. "Let's take a look."

"Ha-ha," Sasha says, but she is nervous now. Jolene weeps.

"I'll do it," Skye says.

"You wouldn't!"

"Who's gonna hold her down?"

Dale arrives. Someone must have gone to get him. The tension drains from the air, and Jolene's hitched gasps are sharp in the sudden quiet.

Dale calls a meeting. Lockers slam. The girls tug on jeans and head out to dump themselves into the leather chairs surrounding the main stage and listen, sullen, to Dale's lecture about looking out for each other. "You might not all be friends," he says, "but you're sisters."

Jolene is a mess of tissues and snot. Her shirt is inside out.

Dale holds out a glass bowl. "Each and every one of you. We take care of our own."

Sasha drops a twenty into the bowl for Jolene. They all do. When it's Samantha's turn, she wants to put in more but doesn't.

A DOZEN ROSES stand on the kitchen table. Red, just opened. The same bouquet Samantha's father would give for her birthdays. He gave her one on the day her mother drove her home from the doctor's office with the diagnosis.

The refrigerator hums in the dark apartment. She reaches for the note. It says that Nick dropped off his résumés earlier today. It says that he loves her.

THERE'S A BACHELOR party, which is great for the club but not necessarily for the girls. Many dances will be bought, but no one dancer will hold anyone's attention for long enough to make real cash. A man hails Violet as she passes ("Gimme some of that chocolate"), and when the party reserves the champagne room without naming any girl in particular, it's a free-for-all.

Samantha keeps her distance. The sudden rush of girls into champagne means less competition on the floor. She makes a hundred off some Irish tourists who hired a limo to drive them in from Chicago, then notices Jolene sitting with a customer. Jolene's makeup is impeccable. She is sipping a drink.

The emotion Samantha feels thicken in her chest is close to pity but feels more personal, as though in being embarrassed for Jolene she experiences the aftermath of some shame from her own past, an unnameable moment that fills her with regret and the desire to revise. She decides to swing by the table to slink an arm around Jolene. "Can I steal her?" She nuzzles Jolene, and the man's mouth parts in childlike wonder. Men love the lesbian act. They love to think all the dancers are getting each other off backstage. Samantha says, "I'll bring her back when I'm done with her."

She tugs Jolene along by the wrist. Jolene stumbles ("You're going too fast"), but Samantha drags ("*You're* wearing the wrong shoes") until they are backstage in the empty dressing room.

"What were you doing?" Samantha demands.

"Having a drink," Jolene says. "I can have a drink."

"Did he pay you to sit with him?"

"He bought the drinks."

"Guess how much I make a night."

"You brought me back here to make me feel bad about myself."

"A thousand," Samantha says. "*At least.*"

Jolene's mouth crumples.

"Don't you want that?" Samantha says.

"That's not fair. It's easy for you. Everyone wants you."

Gently, Samantha says, "Everyone feels out of place at first."

"Not you."

"Yes, me."

Jolene's shoulders soften. She bites at a hangnail and stares at her feet. "What's wrong with my shoes?"

"You went to a regular shoe store and bought the highest heels."

"So?"

"Look." Samantha's platform shoes are clear Lucite and elevate her several inches without torquing her feet. The heel is mostly an illusion. Cinderella stripper slippers. "You probably sat down because your feet hurt."

"I didn't have anything better to do." Jolene's light hair hangs in her face. "No one wants a dance."

"You need regulars. What about that guy in the baseball cap? With the letter Z. I saw him earlier, by the deejay booth. You dance for him sometimes."

"That's Zack. He's my boyfriend."

"Oh."

"I mean, he was. He dumped me."

"Sorry," Samantha says, though she wants to roll her eyes. Dating a patron is, without exception, a bad idea.

Jolene shrugs. "He just wanted to tag a stripper."

"You deserve better."

"Yeah." But Jolene is looking at the door.

"The club is packed," Samantha says. "You could make big money tonight. I'll tell you how."

An expression slips over Jolene's face, almost iridescent, a little fish of supple happiness, so fleeting and lovely that Samantha pretends she does not see it. She gets right down to strategy. When she is done giving advice, her throat is dry, and she finds that she is nervous. It is because of Jolene's silence. It is because of her adoring face. She is not bad, Samantha thinks, when she looks like this. Then Samantha wishes, suddenly, that she hadn't said anything. She feels possessive—or rather, possessed by possession, curled into its damp warmth, held by the way she wants to hold on to Jolene's transient beauty, the buttery skin and sloppy mouth, silver-fair eyelashes, devoted smile, all something that seems to belong only to Samantha for the very reason that it will be shared with everyone else.

"I bet you're a good mom," Jolene says.

"I can't have kids."

THE BOUNCERS CLEAR the parking lot of all clients at closing. The girls aren't allowed to leave the building until the bouncers give the okay. This is a new rule. There is a rickety cheer in the girls' voices as they call good-bye, walking out to their cars, that makes Samantha think that they

have heard Bella's story, too. The lot lamps cast a medicinal light and
make the wet blacktop gleam like metal. The big bouncers try to look
bigger. Keys jingle, car doors open and close. Jolene bops along to her
car and gives a booty wiggle of triumph before she gets in.

Samantha's window is down, the air washed and smelling of earth-
worms. She hadn't meant to tell Jolene that she couldn't have children.
It's not even strictly true. Someone else's baby could grow inside her. She
could get a donor egg. She used to set money aside each month. Then
Nick said, Isn't Rose enough? Samantha said yes, and meant it.

Samantha thinks about calling her parents, who live in Florida now,
when she gets home. She thinks about how her pediatrician called it
a syndrome. She had been just a nervous kid, only fifteen, and had
heard "sin dome," and was afraid to ask what that meant. The doctor kept talking. He was kind, but his kindness was worn out, the way
fabric gets thin at the elbows and knees. *Karyotype, dysgenesis.* Time
has chiseled the words, clarifying their slur, revealing how acutely she
had listened to what she had not really understood at the time. Her
mother interrupted. They had thought she was a late bloomer. No, not
quite, the doctor said. A never bloomer. Or a maybe bloomer. Things
could be done. Hormones could be taken. A beautiful young woman. A
misplaced chromosome, XY instead of XX, but she was in all outward
respects female, organs normal, fully functional. But not the ovaries, her
mother said. The doctor's smile was win some, lose some. Well, he said,
in many ways she is fortunate. True, instead of ovaries she has streaks
of gonadal tissue. Yet when you consider the symptoms of most intersex disorders, this is, ah, I won't say minor. Preferable.

She sat with her mother in the car for a long time after. A storm was
muscling in. Clots of navy clouds were edged by yellow sky. It was tor-
nado season. If the sirens went off, they would have to go back inside
the clinic and shelter in the basement. XY is for boys, Samantha said.

You are a girl, her mother said.

But not really.

You are *my* girl.

Samantha is sick of watching bouncers pace the club's perimeter.
She starts the car. She feels tired, but it is a tired inside. She won't call

her mother. Telling people you miss them just makes you miss them more.

JOLENE'S EYES BRIGHTEN when Samantha enters the dressing room the next day. Violet has her feet up on the beauty bar, calmly painting her toenails, but the other girls are visibly annoyed with Jolene.

Jolene bounces up to Samantha. "Guess what!"

"Um, what?"

"I changed my name."

They all have stage names. To tell another stripper your real one is kind of a big deal. Samantha knows a few: Violet is Catherine, Morgan is Rachel, Paris is Paris. Name switching isn't common but happens. Dante, a college student, became Titania, then Althea, then Molly, and then she quit.

"I bet you already know what it is," Jolene tells Samantha.

"I really don't."

"Think."

"Spit it out, Joey," says Bella.

"See?" Jolene says. "That's my problem, right there. I went with Jolene because it's kinda Dixie, kinda cute."

"Kinda Dolly Parton," says Gigi.

"Dolly does have big starter buttons," says Bella. "I bet she at least *thought* about becoming a stripper."

"But everyone gets my name wrong," Jolene says.

Violet selects another nail polish and rattles it.

"My new name is much better."

"We can't wait to hear it," says Bella.

Jolene says, "Green."

"Hoo-boy," says Gigi.

"Yeah, that ain't gonna work."

"That's your name?"

"That's not my name," Jolene says. "It's a hint."

"I think you should just tell us," Samantha says.

"Lady Jade." Jolene makes a flourish. "I am *Lady Jade*."

"Okay," says Samantha. "That's nice." But Jolene is holding a breath that has alchemized into an explosive agent. She blurts, "Because we're a team."

Samantha meets Violet's hooded eyes in the mirror. "I don't know what you mean."

"You and me," Jolene says. "Red and Green. Ruby and Jade."

"Oh."

"I could've picked Diamond, but"—she shrugs self-consciously— "I'm not, like, *that* special. Ruby's the best, of course. The prettiest."

"Lady Jade's a great name," Samantha says. "Royal."

The girl hugs Samantha tight. "I knew you'd love it." Her skin smells nutty, her hair like a sugary latex glove. "I gotta pee! See you on the floor, sister," she calls as she heads for the toilet. The door bangs behind her.

"Well," Violet says to Samantha. "Aren't you sweet."

IT'S MIDWEEK. THE evening is lavender and layered with dryer-sheet clouds when Nick pulls into a Portillo's drive-thru and they discover that Rosie has fallen asleep in the back. Nick reaches behind the seat to set Rosie's meal beside her, then passes the rest to Samantha. The odor of hot dogs and fries rises from her warm lap.

He drives steadily, clicking every turn signal. The model homes of a new subdivision float along the passenger side. The houses' lit windows show their perfect contents. Nick doesn't take his gaze off the road, but Samantha senses the car drift toward the homes, and she wonders if he, too, imagines the three of them as a family framed in one of those golden windows. She bets those houses have huge backyards. Kids need grass, they need trees. Samantha has a nice home, but she is sure that one day they will have an even nicer one. Nick wants that, too, and although he had hurt her, wasn't it because he was committed to her? Wasn't jealousy a form of love? He knows her inside and out. Samantha has never told anyone except Nick about her syndrome. She is grateful to him for loving her anyway.

An oncoming truck approaches in the opposite lane, one headlight dark. Nick squints and straightens out.

Later, when Rosie is in bed and they are watching TV, he lifts Samantha's large feet onto his knees and massages the soles, one for much longer than the other. She thinks that he is remembering the truck's headlights, one on, one off, and the phototropic glide of their car toward the homes. He switches back to her other foot a little too quickly, like he knows what she is thinking, like she has caught him doing something wrong.

THIS NIGHT WANTS to bend into itself. Some Saturday nights do. Men buy because others are buying, then buy because they have already bought, then hide from what they are doing by doing it again. The club has no windows; there are no clocks. She is used to not knowing what time it is. She dances for a man with four kids. He shows her a photo from his wallet and is deeply pleased when she compliments the family portrait, the fluffy-headed children, his wife's studied smile.

Then the hunched man, Ron, who had been in construction, whose back was broken on the job, buys a bottle of champagne, and the waitress jots down when his time in this room will end. Though he pays Samantha immediately in two starchy hundreds, plus extra per dance, and doesn't care that she fake-drinks the champagne, which he has poured into flutes with strawberries at the bottom, he is difficult company. He shifts from skepticism that, in fact, no touching is the rule and the bouncers will enforce it, to cheated belief, to seeking compensation by talking dirty. Does she know what he would *like* to do? He knows she wants to hear.

It's gross but also boring. There is nothing original about what men want to do to women. Listening to Ron makes her appreciate Nick more. He is a good man. He is the kind of man who keeps other men in line.

When the hour is up, the waitress pulls the champagne bottle from its slushy bucket and tells Ron he must buy another if he wants to keep the room. He reaches for his wallet. Samantha is relieved when Gigi interrupts, stepping into champagne even though she is not supposed to. "Your chia pet's got a problem," she tells Samantha.

"What kind of problem?"

"The kind that gets you fired."

Ron is not smiling. He taps his watch. Samantha ignores him, grateful for the excuse to leave, and follows Gigi backstage. A cold creek of worry runs through her. What did "you" mean? Jolene? Or *her*, Samantha?

Then she sees Jolene floppy in Bella's makeup chair, tears leaking from shut eyes, and forgets to worry about herself. "Hey," Samantha says. "Honey. It's me. What's wrong? Come on, don't cry."

The girl opens her eyes. They are deep blue, the kind of blue that crayons get named after. "I am so happy."

Gigi blows out a breath. "Lollipops."

"I kept her back here soon as I realized," Bella says. "She's as high as a kite."

"Dale's gonna lose it. He's gonna put her out on her ass."

Samantha shakes her. "What'd you take?"

"Must be X," Gigi says. "She keeps saying she loves everyone."

"I do." Jolene shivers. "I love you."

Gigi rolls her eyes, one false eyelash askew. "We can't hide her here forever. The twofer's coming up. People will notice she's missing."

"We say she's sick," Samantha says.

"You say you did not find her with me," Bella says.

"This won't work," Gigi says. "She does not look sick. She looks ready to fuck the chair."

"There she is. I thought you'd want to know."

It is Violet, with Dale right behind her. She meets Samantha's flung-up gaze, and there is something about Violet's expression that makes Samantha wonder what her own shows. Betrayal? How had Samantha come to feel so protective of a girl she didn't even like?

Dale's dress shoes clap the concrete floor as he approaches the chair, the girl's prone form, her billowing chest, open mouth, open eyes, tear-streaked cheeks.

"She didn't take any drugs," Samantha says.

Gigi gives her a cynical look.

"I mean, it's not her fault," Samantha says. "Someone must've put it in her drink."

Dale's gaze doesn't leave the chair.

"She's new," says Samantha.

"Not that new," says Violet.

"Trusting," says Samantha.

In the uneasy silence, Gigi turns to a mirror and tries to nudge the loose eyelash back into place, then catches Dale watching her. "Lady Jade's got pennies for brains," she says.

A hot hand slips into Samantha's. "I want to go home," Lady Jade says.

"I'll drive her home," Samantha says, though she doesn't know where Lady Jade lives.

"Come with me, Ruby," Dale says.

In his office, high up on the third floor, with an interior window overlooking the club, he pulls a manila folder from a wooden filing cabinet and sits at his desk with its blotter and an old-fashioned green library lamp that makes his hands look out of proportion to the rest of him. The club music is muted here. A large fish tank burbles, fish sliding behind the glass. He consults the file, writes a few lines on a pad of paper, and rips the paper from the pad. "Her address."

Samantha takes it. She knows more or less how to get there. "Are you going to fire her?"

"No drugs at my club."

"She didn't mean to take it."

"Maybe she didn't, maybe she did."

"Please."

Dale smiles. "Lady Jade's lucky to have you as a friend," he says, a polite way of telling Samantha not to push it, and lifts the phone from its cradle.

She calls Nick and imagines him turning over in bed, burying his face into the pillow, and Rosie, who sleeps like the dead, sleeping on. She hears her voice echoing from the answering machine as she explains the situation, sort of ("another dancer has a stomach bug, poor thing"). Dale's smile becomes one of amused confederacy.

A bouncer is summoned to carry Lady Jade. Samantha goes back-stage and is changing in front of her locker when she hears, "Ruby." She turns. Violet has a bar receipt in her hand. "That man in champagne was looking for you."

On the back of the receipt, in delicate script, Ron says he under-stands why she never came back. He always runs his mouth. He says things he shouldn't. He just hasn't been the same since his accident. He has left his number.

Samantha folds the note. She looks at Violet, who doesn't look sorry she betrayed another dancer. Samantha says it calmly: "Fuck off."

THE LOT IS armored with cars. The club will be open for another few hours. The packed lot reminds Samantha of what leaving early will cost her. Four hundred? Five?

Jimmy carries the girl, who, while not exactly unconscious, is defi-nitely not all there. Dale had the lock on the girl's locker cut off, and Samantha has Lady Jade's—not Jolene's—earnings from the night, bifolded and rubber-banded, and keys. Although Samantha wiped off her makeup and changed into jeans and a T-shirt, Lady Jade still wears her slithery dress, which spills like mercury down Jimmy's pants.

After Samantha's in and the bouncer has strapped the slumped girl into the passenger seat, he pats the hood of the car, solidly, twice, instead of saying goodbye.

IT'S NOT CLEAR when Samantha notices the car behind them.

It's late, but there are other cars on the road, at least at first. Since nothing comes from the passenger seat but murky breathing and iso-lated words dropped like laundry no one is going to pick up, Samantha chews gum to keep herself company. She snaps and pops. She fiddles with her pearl earrings.

Maybe it's after she gets off the interstate. Maybe that is when she notices. This road is nothing special. Strip malls, mostly, strange only because everything is so empty, and that's not actually strange—it is expected at this time of night.

And there is that car, that same dark car. It has been behind them all the way from the club.

The tank is three-quarters full. Samantha stops at a gas station anyway and takes longer than she needs to pay. She asks the man behind the counter for directions, though she is not worried about how to get where she is going. The attendant spits a long brown stream of tobacco juice into a paper cup and gives an endearingly detailed answer.

For a while, after Samantha drives off again, she is relieved. She takes a turn. Then she hears, "The lights."

Jolene/Lady Jade is right. A set of headlights is following them. Samantha switches on the radio, keeping only one hand on the wheel. "It's nothing." There is always a car behind another car. This is a road. That is a car. This is what cars on roads do.

"I'm sleepy."

"Go to sleep."

"You—"

"Yes?" Samantha turns off the radio to hear better, yet there is nothing to hear.

The road is darker now, headlights brighter. Open land pours around them: prairie, probably. Or—a low crossbuck fence zips past—horse farms. Maybe the land has been bulldozed for building. It is too dark to tell.

A spongy anxiety makes Samantha say, although she has just said the opposite, "Hey, wake up."

She doesn't wake up.

They are not far from their destination. All Samantha has to do is drive, and it will not surprise her if the car behind her takes the next turn she doesn't, and the rear windshield goes black, and her fear is wiped away.

She imagines the sleeping woman beside her as a child. Blond braids, the part in her hair as white as the spine of a feather.

Light slices into the car. Samantha's heart goes fast. She reaches for the girl's hand. Samantha wants to say her name, but isn't sure what to call her. She is still holding her hand when the car behind hurtles into them, running them off the road.

SAMANTHA OPENS HER eyes in the jolting dark. Her head hurts. It feels broken. Her body is jammed into itself, her cheek pressed against rough, wiry carpet. The constant hum of the carpet makes no sense until she realizes that she is in the trunk of a car.

The motor accelerates. The car hits a hard bump. Her head rings with pain, the pain pushing her far away from here, until she forgets where here is, and then is nowhere at all.

GEORGIA
(GIGI)

Georgia opens her locker and rubs her body down with baby wipes, even her bare feet. She gets in between the toes.

"Why bother," says Bella, pulling on a sports bra. She has small, rosy nipples and a keloid scar shaped like a cocoon on her right shoulder blade. Her tight belly is less freckled than the rest of her. "We all smell." They smell like cigars and beer and cooking oil from battered chicken wings. They smell like Secret and sweat and candy-scented body mist.

"I don't want my mom to guess where I work," Georgia says.

Bella jerks the hair out of her eyes. "It's two a.m. Won't she be asleep?"

Before Georgia can lie, Violet clips past in pink-heeled Pleasers. The locker room gets quiet and mean. Maybe other dancers can't believe Violet would rat out Lady Jade, but Georgia is not surprised. Violet has been cold to Georgia from the start, even though (or because) Georgia is the only other Black dancer at the club. Half Black. Which, as far as anyone who looks at Georgia is concerned, means Black, until the moment her skin means something else, and people get nosy and ask where her parents are from.

Earlier that night, the dancers watched as Jimmy carried Lady Jade out the back door, her body slopped in his arms, legs dangling. Her silver dress made her look like a dead fish. Ruby followed the bouncer, face firm and responsible, like a nurse's. Now the club is closed and it has been hours since Ruby drove Lady Jade home. Dale won't let Lady Jade come back to work, that's for sure. Other girls did drugs—more than once Georgia had heard, through the bathroom door, Desirée snort a bump of coke—but as long as they did their job and Dale didn't know, it couldn't hurt him. Lady Jade broke one of Dale's many rules. Violet broke a different one, a backstage one adjudicated by the dancers. They had only two rules: don't mess with my money, and keep your mouth shut. Even if the other dancers can't directly punish Violet, they can still resent her.

Violet, still in one of her club outfits, a sticky latex dress as pink as a tongue, hits the breaker bar and walks out into the night.

ONCE, WHEN GEORGIA first started working at the Lady and couldn't make enough to cover house fees, she agreed to meet a customer after hours. She drove to the Walmart parking lot and got out of her car and into his. She gave him head, the gearshift jabbing her ribs. Tell me you like it, he said. She said that she did and he came and she didn't want to swallow it. She spat into her hand and took the cash. What shames her most is that she carried his semen with her out of his car, feeling an unquestioned instinct to clean up after herself, even though she was really cleaning up after him.

THE PLAN HAD been college. The plan had been student loans, because her mother's main source of income was working in the high school as a lunch lady. That will add to your application, said the guidance counselor, who was white and had tiny fingers and huge, light eyes, her streaky hair styled in a hard way. She said, Be sure to talk about that in your essay. You will make an excellent affirmative action candidate. When Georgia, hands laced tightly across her knees, was quiet for too long, the counselor, emboldened and mistaking Georgia's silence for shy gratitude, said, Look at your grades. Look at your scores. You check the right boxes. Georgia, a college admissions board will eat you *up*.

Georgia had tried, but when her mother got sick, she postponed her applications. She accepted her diploma. Next year, she thought. Then next year came and her mother had only gotten worse. She couldn't remember who Georgia was half the time, and Georgia thought, My aunt and uncle will help. But they said, Your mom needs full-time care. They said, We wish we had the money. They said, Kaitlyn will be applying for college this fall. We have been saving for years. It wouldn't be fair to your cousin, would it? Her aunt said, This is hard for me, too: my only sister vanishing before my eyes. Georgia's uncle said, She made her choices. She should have known what she was getting into, with your father. We helped her with the down payment on your house years ago. We have helped all we can.

Georgia worked as a waitress. She worked night shifts while her mother slept, or was supposed to be sleeping. Sometimes she would get calls from the police that her mother had been found wandering in her nightgown.

Who are you? she demanded when Georgia came to claim her at the station.

I'm your daughter.

Her mother's eyes narrowed. She said, You can't be my daughter. I'm white.

TECHNICALLY IT IS Sunday morning now, creeping toward dawn, but it still feels like Saturday night. It is dark when Georgia lets herself into her apartment. The building is a new development, the lobby strung with the sails of ships, the walls decorated with nautical posters. The Atlantic is eight hundred miles away, but Lake Michigan is so large that it swells with waves. Georgia often drives to Chicago to visit Kaitlyn, a freshman at DePaul University, and sees the tipping triangles of docked sailboats along the lakefront. Farther off, white scraps chart their course across water almost as rough as an ocean. When her mother died and Georgia walked away from the mortgage on their worn little house, she saw the sails in the apartment building's lobby and imagined them bellied out. What is a sail without wind? Georgia had been working at the Lady for six months then. She was supposed to be twenty-one, but she showed Dale a fake ID when he hired her, and she will be twenty-one soon enough.

She showers. Robe belted, she opens the fridge, takes out the shrimp she left to marinate, and sets it beside the stove. The windows show a sky puddled with pink. It will be a nice Sunday. The marinade is lime and garlic, cumin and turmeric and green habanero sauce. She clicks on the gas.

It is too late to go back to where she was as a high school senior. She is where she is. A sail without wind is an image of what is gone. It is a liar, it is a fake. It is a canvas corpse.

Dale was sympathetic when she explained her mother's dementia. You're a good daughter, he said, and never made her pay extra house fees when she was late or missed a shift. It was easy to pretend that her mother hadn't died. Now Georgia always has the perfect excuse. Her mother is a blank check Georgia keeps cashing, though that is not why she pretends.

Lady Jade must be sleeping off the molly now. The spicy shrimp stings Georgia's throat. It burns her eyes. The apartment is quiet. There is no one here but her, and when the sun rises she will sleep, the only sounds her breath, the shift of sheets.

It would hurt too much to say it. My mother is dead. She died in the worst way. Her mind was a small white stone. I have to take care of her, Georgia said instead, to anyone at the club who listened. She needs me.

Hey, honey, it's me, Georgia remembers Ruby saying as Ruby shook the drugged girl. Lady Jade is lucky, but Ruby is, too, Georgia thinks, to have someone to protect. I love you, Lady Jade said, and that was not nothing.

DETECTIVE VICTOR AMADOR

Victor has his windows down. His patrol car smelled like ass from the first whiff of his late-Saturday-night shift. Then a DUI pissed himself in the back seat right before Victor dumped him at lockup, which made things extra awesome. A few hours later, it is clear that a fistful of disinfectant wipes has not helped much. The radio is quiet, so he parks near a forest preserve, one of those new, curated affairs with a bridge over the marsh, and listens to the gulping frogs while he reads his *National Geographic* and tries to enjoy the fresh air.

Being a detective is supposed to be the better job, but Victor likes occasionally working overtime in patrol, paying down the mortgage on his mother's house, and West Cover isn't bad, though he prefers Central, with its dime bags and domestic abuse, where calls come in a steady patter, making it easier to stay awake. The other detectives rib him about working overtime, but since Tess dumped him, he doesn't have anything better to do. "He *loves* the uniform," says Backyard. "I get hard just thinking about how much he loves it," says Pradko. Holly, though, never says anything, only lifts her dark gaze from her paperwork to consider him. "She's spooky," Tess said after she met Holly. Tess would have pitied Holly if Victor had explained, which is why he hadn't.

A gray predawn halo hovers over the fringed water, and there are only a few hours left to his shift. It will be a nice Sunday. Victor cranks his seat back and gets cozy with its humid grime, scooching over a patch of duct tape on a hole worn into the fabric. His finger tracks the yellow frame on the magazine's cover, corner to corner. It is the latest issue. He has read most of it already. He likes the story about Marco Polo in the desert, sucking on a pebble to forget his thirst, and he likes the crazy-looking birds of paradise. He admires a spread of wild orchids and huffs, recalling a question on his psych eval when he was applying to the police academy: "I would like to be a florist. AGREE or DISAGREE." Afterward, Victor asked the examiner what was up with that. He was told that sociopaths like the idea of being a florist.

"But I said yes." Victor was worried.

The man smiled.

Victor gets it: the trimmed stems, arrangements, water-laden green foam collapsing beneath the touch, refrigerators like glass coffins. The tricks of the trade. Forcing an orchid stem to grow erect, clipped to a stake. Peonies, his mother explained, can be cut in the bud, when the bloom is compact yet marshmallowy. Go ahead, squish it, she added in English, her Cuban accent heavy. She often spoke in English about the flower shop, proud to show that she had learned this country's language and could do anything to take care of him. They had taken a bus from the town where he was born to Cuba's northern coast, where she paid a fisherman to take them across the bay to Miami. He had been little, and can't remember that bus or the boat. He remembers playing marbles in the sandy dirt beneath an almond tree outside his grandfather's house the day before they left. He remembers taking a Greyhound bus from Florida to Illinois, where his mother's second cousin said he had a job for her. The bus window grew colder as they drove north. He saw his first snow. Being a florist is good work, his mother said. All that beauty, every day. He said, One day, I will buy you all the flowers you want. When he became a cop, he told her to quit her job. I'm taking care of you now, he said.

At the time of the police academy exam, he felt fooled by the question, like it wasn't a general question everyone had to answer but had been tailored to him so that he would fail. "So I like flowers—so what," he told the examiner.

Victor got into the academy anyway.

His stomach is sour from his last cup of coffee. He drinks the cold dregs and reads. It feels almost as good as sleep. A woodpecker is typing in the trees. The sky gets pink as he reads the article he had been saving, the one about woolly mammoths.

"West Cover," says the radio, "we got a 10–50, single vehicle, unknown injuries. Do you copy?"

Victor rolls the magazine into a baton. An hour ago, he would have been grateful for something to do. Now he is on the cusp of going home and going to bed. His supervisor, Sergeant Rabideaux, should overrule dispatch. Rabideaux should come onto the radio, take this job from Victor, and reassign it to the day shift. Plenty of fresh patrol officers have just started work, and one of them could—*should*—handle this. Rabideaux, though, is saying nothing—if he is even paying attention.

"Do you copy?" says dispatch.

Silence.

"Copy that," Victor says, rolling his eyes.

Dispatch says the abandoned car was seen in a ditch on US 6. Victor runs his lights. Years ago, when he was new to the job, Victor would have tried to predict what he might see at the scene. Now he keeps his head clear. Nothing he can do. Not for an accident. Not until he gets there, and even then, not always.

"Advise me when you're on scene," Rabideaux says over the radio.

Oh, so *now* he's got something to say. Rabideaux used to be a friend—a mentor, even—in Victor's early days in the Fremont PD. Now Rabideaux is snide and lazy, lively only when he complains about his ex-wife, and steals time from the department by clocking in earlier and out later than his actual shift.

The sun is up. Victor sees the glint of the wreck down the long, straight road. He can smell it, too: oil and fuel and blown airbags. The road is sequined with smashed glass.

His pulse raps at his chest. His mouth tastes like tin. The red car lies in the ditch on its side.

Victor throws his car into park and he is out, shoes crunching glass. He jogs up to the vehicle. He expects to see blood greasing the street, but there is none. He skids into the ditch and glances into the windows. His breath sags out of him, and he is, all at once, sleepy again, bottomed out, and pretty fucking annoyed.

He gets on his handheld. "This is West Cover. The vehicle's unoccupied." Typical. He has seen a lot of these, though it rarely looks this bad. The story here is clear: a drunk crashed his car and walked off to avoid arrest for a DUI. "Run the plates. See who comes up."

"10–4," says dispatch.

He snaps on his blue search gloves, primarily out of caution for his hands. There is glass everywhere, even on the seats. The car is wedged onto the driver's side. Victor never likes to look at the underbelly of a car. It feels wrong to see it exposed to the sky, all its snaking, arterial parts. The vehicle is cool; the crash happened at least a few hours ago. The door on the passenger side is open, tilted up like a dog's lifted leg. He pushes back the airbag on the passenger side and reaches for the glove compartment.

There is blood. It is on the dash. The airbag, he sees now, is spotted, too. The old coffee bubbles in his stomach.

He flips open the glove compartment. The registration is there, sealed in a Ziploc bag.

The radio clicks. Dispatch says the plates came up clean, no record. They match what is on the registration: a Nicholas Sullivan, whose address is the old Fremont button factory that has been converted into apartments. A nice part of town. "Send someone over there," Victor says into his handheld. "See who should be driving the car." He pauses. "There were two people in it. Unknown injuries." Then he sees the seat belt.

It's cut. The seat belt is cut. The driver's side, too.

He skids a rubbery blue thumb down the surface of the cut. He drops the strap and pushes in the red button on each buckle. The seat belts release nice and smooth.

Dimly, he knows his shift should be over. But he sees his future. He will not be going home now, not for a long while. He sees his day aging, how his eyes will scum over with fatigue. Close encounters with higher-ups. The paperwork. He wants to call Holly, but he shouldn't. Not today. She has taken this day off, same as she does every year.

"Send an ambulance," he tells dispatch. "An evidence tech. And an accident reconstructionist." Though it kills him (he does not want to deal with Rabideaux), he adds, "I need a supervisor on scene. I got a possible 10–35."

"Will-all, Lincoln-all, do you copy?" says dispatch. The dawn is quiet, but the radio makes its own kind of birdsong. *Will-all, Lincoln-all.*

Victor is aware that he must have contaminated evidence, might be contaminating it even now, but he goes through the car, looking for signs of a struggle, of knife cuts to the seats. He finds a purse—no, two purses, the contents spilled—and the license of a pretty woman with large, straight-ahead eyes. Samantha Lind. Her wallet has a school picture of a gap-toothed girl smiling one of those smiles that tries so hard it hurts you a little.

He finds money, two fat folds of cash, on the floor of the car. He holds a wad in each palm, feeling their chummy weight, then carefully puts the money back where he found it.

He ducks out of the car. He looks at the bright sky like it is not the sky but a photograph of it, something from the magazine he was reading. He has the feeling of *This is a place I will never see* even as he is seeing it.

Up on the back slope of the ditch, the high grass is flattened. Not very noticeably, just a dip in the line of green.

He feels slow as he walks the slope into the grass, up to his hips. Grass hisses against his wrists. His numb, blue-gloved hands push his way into the field. He thinks about his unfinished article, the woolly mammoth frozen in a cave, the cold hulk of it.

He does not need to part the grass when he finds the body. The body has created an open space around it with its own weight. She is lying on her back, her silver dress slit open. There is a piece of glass embedded in her cheek. It winks at him like ice.

DETECTIVE HOLLY MEYLIN

"Paper or plastic?"

Holly squints. "Paper." It seems like the right answer, or at least what the girl behind the register expects. Holly thinks of a horse she saw as a child at a state fair, long before the idea of becoming a cop had occurred to her. The horse could stamp the answer to simple arithmetic problems. She thought it was magic. Her father lightly rapped the top of her head and said it was a con. He explained how the horse sensed that everyone held their breath when the hoofbeats reached the proper number. Smart in one way, he said. Stupid in another.

She didn't call him after it happened. She knew what he would say. *Forgot? What do you mean, forgot? How stupid can you be?*

"Even the eggs?" The checkout girl raises her brows. A hoop pierces one of them. The piercing is infected, pink and scaly. It is a Sunday morning and the grocery store is busy. From the next register over come the steady blips of items scanned, the sound like droplets falling into a tin can. A child wails. A long line stretches behind Holly. "The eggs?" the cashier repeats.

"What?"

"You want the eggs in paper, too? If they break and leak, it'll get gross."

"Bag it how you want."

The checkout girl scans a sack of sugar. "Baking?"

"Just give me the goddamn groceries."

"O-*kay*," the girl mutters. The paper bags rattle as she stuffs them.

Holly made herself come here. It was her choice to walk past cut watermelon with studded black eyes, the freezers of popsicles and Klondike bars, the boxes of pasta with their small, hollow bones.

She avoids grocery stores when she can. Too many kids. A Sunday means even more kids than usual. But today she had to go.

She pays the bill quickly, scrawling her name on the check. The girl at the register asks to see two pieces of ID, just to be a pain.

Holly sets her police badge on the counter and the girl shuts up.

When Holly gets home, she pulls into the two-car garage until the nose of her aggressively new Jeep touches the tennis ball strung from the ceiling. The unmarked police vehicle alongside, a gray Ford Taurus, looks dingy. As Holly brings in the groceries, she eyes the old library card catalogue repurposed as an organizer for nails, bolts, and screws. She thinks, as always, about junking it. She thinks the same thing when she drops her keys in the blue dish that waits on the kitchen counter. The tennis ball and card catalogue and dish had been her ex-husband's doing. Matthew had believed that little things could improve their life.

The house listens to her unpack the paper bags. She takes the dusty mixer out of the cupboard and creams butter and sugar, enjoying how the smell of electricity mingles with the sweetness. Eggs (not broken en route; she was careful, she is always careful), vanilla extract, and, because she thinks that four years probably means a passion for chocolate, clouds of powdered cocoa.

It is one of those gorgeous September days. She opens the kitchen window and hears children playing in the park two streets away. It sounds almost like the beach: wind and happy voices. The sun is bright. Trees twinkle in the breeze. She indulges in a sort of pretending as she makes the batter, the pretense a parachute dropped through time. She floats in the moment. This will be a good cake. It will be the best cake yet.

She left out a stick of butter to soften (she was organized, she is always organized), so it is no trouble to make frosting as the cake bakes. While the timer runs, she watches *Jeopardy!* and then *The Golden Girls*, imagining herself forty years from now: missing teeth and with thin hair and plastic pillboxes. She is sad to hear the timer ring. It makes her throat ache, makes her think of the magic fish in the fairy tale, and how, if Holly could not have her greatest wish, she would ask the fish to make her old.

When the cake is ready, she can't do the candles. She sweeps the cake into the trash.

THE CELL PHONE rings first: a chunk of black plastic with a nubby antenna. The other detectives make fun of her for it. Most people in the department have Blackberries or sleek silver clamshells, but they feel slippery to her, easy to lose. It is a concession on her part to have a cell at all. Normal people get by fine without them.

When the cell stops, the home phone begins. Giving in to the inevitable, she answers. "It's my day off."

"We got a body." In a voice gentle enough that she would like to punch his face, Victor Amador says, "Do you really want to be off today?"

WHEN DANIEL WAS newly born, Holly had bad dreams. In one, a pediatrician recommended that she have the baby's head removed. Holly could put it back on whenever he needed to nurse. It's standard procedure, the doctor said. Holly held her headless child, touching the blank skin from shoulder to shoulder, with its small protrusion of a spine where the head fastened. She wondered why she had listened, what had she done? She would wake and go to Daniel's bassinet and see him sleeping, faceup, swaddled tight, a drool of milk on his lips. He had a thick head of silky black hair. When he got a little older, he liked to twirl it. Daniel's velvet slug of a body shuddered with a sigh. Holly went queasy with relief. She had done nothing wrong, and never would.

———

"STRANGULATION," AMADOR SAYS on the drive over. The cell heats her sweaty ear. "There were two people in the car."

"But just one body?" Holly cruises through a red light, wishing the Taurus had more horsepower.

"The owner of the car says his girlfriend was driving. Her name is Samantha Lind. No sign of her so far."

Holly skims past a field of high, glossy corn. There are still a few fields left, untouched by development, at least in this part of Fremont. "Any evidence of struggle?"

"Why don't you see for yourself," Amador says.

ONE MUST HAVE a mind of winter. Holly remembers the first and last lines of the poem, though little of the rest.

"This one's perfect for you, Holly," her teaching fellow said. "It's as though Wallace Stevens wrote it with you in mind. *Junipers shagged with ice.* A winter poem for someone with a wintry name."

"My name is Hollis," she said, especially annoyed because he had the roster right there in front of him on his desk. It was one of the few times she willingly used her given first name, which was also her father's. She regretted this later, when her college classmates assumed that her name's disregard for gender placed her in a moneyed class of people whose privilege was writ large in baby names like Winthrop, Bitsie, and Grier, as if no one could possibly tease their children. Since Hollis was also the name of Harvard Library's card catalogue, rumor had it that she had gotten in because her family was a prominent donor, a rumor that only solidified when she denied it. Holly was too proud to explain that she was that other cliché: the charity case, a diamond in the rough plucked from the cornfields of southern Illinois because of her perfect SAT score and an essay she had written about her mother's greenhouse. Although it did not occur to her at the time, her downstate drawl during the admissions interview had probably helped. It made her sound poor.

"The syllabus doesn't say anything about memorizing poems," she told the teaching fellow.

"And reciting them."

This class had only two redeeming qualities: it met a requirement and fit her schedule. "I'm prelaw," she said.

He was smug. "Wallace Stevens was a lawyer."

She thinks about the poem's first line when she crouches in the grass, sun heading toward noon. She has thought about it before, on calls where the body had decomposed so badly that it sprung a leak, and that time when a foot fell off from the ankle at the touch of her gloved hand. She remembered it when maggots squirmed beneath the skin. One must have a mind of winter. For her, it is a mantra, it is resignation. It is purpose. She will think of it later during the medical examiner's autopsy, when the woman in the grass, identified as Kimberly Campana, who worked as a stripper named Lady Jade at the local club, has her chest cracked open. But Holly thought of nothing, nothing at all, the nothingness a loud void, when she learned that Daniel, two months shy of his first birthday, in the full ripeness of summer, had been left, forgotten, in the back seat of Matthew's closed car.

SAMANTHA

(RUBY)

Her head hurts. Her mouth is full of dirt. She spits it out. The nauseating pain is so bad that she whimpers. Then she bites off the sound, suddenly aware that someone is with her in this enclosed dark. Someone stands behind where she lies on her side, her wrists bound at her back.

She hears the scuff of a foot. Fear spouts up inside her. She has never been so afraid, has never heard her breath come in this keening animal panic. Footsteps draw closer. She is okay, she tells herself. Maybe she will be okay.

"Hello, Ruby," he says.

DETECTIVE VICTOR AMADOR

The evidence techs are still searching the field, the sun low and red behind them. They duck into the grass and come up again like swimmers. Victor has been awake for more than twenty-four hours now. It's Sunday. It's late. He should have spent the day napping and watching baseball. His brain is jigsawed, so that when he glances at the patrol officers there to secure the scene, he gets vertigo, and seems to be standing where they are standing.

Pradko, Backyard, and the dogs are far-off shadows, expanding the perimeter. A dog whines, but it is a frustrated sound, not one of discovery. Holly bagged the greatest find hours earlier: a pearl earring, smooth as bone, that she had lifted out of the grass. When Holly found the earring, she straightened out of her crouch, pale face intent, the lines of her body hard. She was always smaller than he expected.

The body's gone. Holly went with it to the morgue to explain the case to the medical examiner. Victor had offered to go, but she ignored him, closing the bagged earring in her fist and shutting the car door behind her to follow the silent ambulance. The accident reconstructionist is gone. The LT, too. Sergeant Rabideaux stayed longer than Victor expected. He was there first, after Victor. He nosed around the dead girl's car and then stood over her naked body, stiff-legged. Rabideaux wasn't old, exactly, but police can retire after twenty years of service, and Victor wished Rabideaux would seize his opportunity. The sun lit Rabideaux's gray hair yellow and glinted on the wedding ring he wore even though his wife had left him. Like a lot of white guys, Rabideaux loved to talk about the origins of his last name. French, Victor remembered. The last syllable of his name was said like the word *dough*, but the guys called him Deuce, a nickname Rabideaux tolerated, possibly because it was better than Douche.

Rabideaux stared down at the dead girl in the silver dress. His pocket looked fuller than before. It bulged. Victor remembered the two wads of cash in the crashed car, and how Rabideaux had inspected the vehicle. Victor had the feeling that if he looked inside the car again, the money would be gone.

"Now that's a damn shame." Rabideaux's gaze was still on the girl's face.

"Yeah."

"So eloquent. Thought you spoke good English, *Amador*." Rabideaux exaggeratedly rolled the *r*. "Need to go back to ESL?"

You couldn't exactly tell your supervisor to go fuck himself.

Rabideaux one-eyed her, wrinkles creasing. "She reminds me of someone. Can't think who."

That's what happens around a dead body. Everyone thinks about what's not there. Later, on the ride to HQ, Victor will listen to the wind flutter the pages of his magazine and realize, though it is a realization that will leave him as soon as he presses his face into his pillow, that the closed expressions on his ex-girlfriend's face when she broke up with him and on Holly's face when she showed up at the crime scene were akin to the dead girl's: the look of someone who is long gone.

Pradko and Backyard follow the dogs in from the field, having turned up nothing, and head back to the station to interview Samantha Lind's boyfriend. The evidence techs are now shooting the shit, so Victor calls, "Hey, you still need this scene?"

"Nah, you can close it down."

The patrol officers pull out after the techs, and then it's just Victor and a lot of lonely yellow tape.

Victor gets in his car, fatigue sparkling all over his vision. His sense of time is strange. Each thought is oiled, sliding away as soon as it comes. The missing girl. The earring. Dawn on dead skin. He needs to sleep. He needs to find her. He shouldn't have called Holly.

He steps on the brake to start the car but then stops, frowning. Something is jammed beneath the pedal. He reaches down. His fingers go still with surprise. It's a fold of cash, the thinner of the two he had found in the dead girl's car.

EARLIER, AROUND MIDAFTERNOON, Victor noticed the accident reconstructionist packing up. Dolan was sipping coffee from a green thermos. Watching him drink made Victor's head ache with ice-pick precision. Victor said, "So what happened?"

Dolan was slovenly: patchy neckbeard, loose shoelace. His appearance surprised Victor, given how painstakingly the man had surveyed the skids and yaws in the road. "Pit maneuver," Dolan said.

"Someone ran her off the road?" It wasn't hard to do if you came up behind at a good angle and nosed the rear bumper. Really, anyone could do it.

With the hand holding the thermos, Dolan raised two fingers. "Them. There were two girls in the car."

"Right." Victor thought about how his fingertip had dented the dead woman's skin, like it wasn't flesh but Silly Putty. He thought about the eerie, bloody mark he had seen on the sole of her bare foot. "Them. I forgot." He hadn't. It was more that he had said *her* to include the missing girl, too. Samantha Lind. He rubbed his head.

With a smile, the reconstructionist tipped the thermos toward him. Victor closed his eyes with need.

"Say please," Dolan said.

"YOU DIDN'T CALL in the other dicks?" Victor had overheard Lieutenant Carson say that morning to Rabideaux when Carson arrived on scene ("You don't really call detectives *dicks*," Tess had said. "Do you?").

"The fuck, Deuce. That body's getting older by the second. We need more than Amador on this case. We need more dicks, we need dogs, we need techs, we need your head out of your ass."

As he listened to Carson chew out Rabideaux, Victor stayed quiet, though he had noticed the way Rabideaux had, at first, kept the crime scene to himself and Victor.

"Christ," Carson said, "what were you waiting for?"

"You, sugar," Rabideaux said.

"WHAT A WAY to start the day," Rabideaux had said after he got out of his car that dawn. Morning birds sang riotously.

"Whoever did this was a fit guy," Victor said. "She was carried, not dragged." Otherwise, the grass would be flattened in a path.

"What about the other girl?"

Victor remembered the pretty face on the license. "Samantha Lind. Our man over at the boyfriend's says she wasn't supposed to be anywhere near here."

Rabideaux shrugged his shoulders and let his arms flop at his sides. His mild dark eyes and scarred eyebrow made him look scrappy yet friendly, when he was in fact just your average prick. "Maybe there is a second body we haven't found yet."

"Lind could have fled the scene. Better get a search unit, more people on this."

"I'll let the LT decide," Rabideaux said, which wasn't *un*standard procedure, and Rabideaux outranked him. "Carson will be here soon." Rabideaux crouched to examine the collar of bruises around the girl's neck, then craned around to study the bare feet. "You can tell by her feet that she didn't walk here from the crash site. The feet are clean. Except for that."

———

WIND RUFFLES VICTOR'S hair. On the ride back to HQ in the growing dark of Sunday night, the air soft and warm and sweet, Victor listens to the magazine flip its own pages in the back seat, and sees the bloody zigzag behind his open eyes, marking his vision like a migraine's aura. It was on the sole of the dead girl's left foot. "What is that?" Victor had said. "A *W*? *M*?"

"It's a crown," Rabideaux answered.

SAMANTHA

(RUBY)

She knew him. The horror of knowing him filled her throat. She cried out, the sound echoing. Her face was against the dirt, but she was somewhere inside—a garage? Cellar? When she escaped, she would tell everybody where she had been and what he had done. She would be okay. The light in the rear window had been bright. The car had slammed into her. Her head was swollen with pain. "Please let me go. This isn't you."

He was quiet behind her. "This is my most me."

She twisted her wrists against the bindings.

"You'll bleed if you do that," he said. Her wrists were damp.

"Rosie." The name was a plea. "I'm her mother. I'm a mother."

He took her shoulder and turned her onto her back with slow ease. It was too dark to see the face that she knew.

"A mother?" he mused. She felt the flat of a blade against her stomach, then he cut the button from her jeans. He grabbed the waist of her jeans and underwear and yanked down. He spread his hands all over her belly, her perfect skin. Her mind went mute with panic. He already knew that he would find no stretch marks, no pucker of birth. He had seen her naked before.

"No, you're not," he said, and stood, and left.

———

SHE DOESN'T KNOW when that was. She doesn't know how long she has been here. Her stomach has stopped growling with hunger. She doesn't know where Jolene is. She is afraid to know. Her jeans are still down at her thighs, her hands numb under her back.

Rosie, she thinks. Tears slide hot into her hair.

I will be okay.

MELODY

Every awful situation has one special thing, Melody chose to believe, and this belief, on more than one occasion, had been as necessary as her inhaler: an artificial gasp of *This is not so bad*. No computer? At least she could do homework at the library. A doctor's appointment? Okay, but at least it was Sunday, so hey, no school. As for herself, she liked her eyelashes. "Asthma *and* a hunchback, poor kid," her mother said once, looking at her as if she'd never seen her before. "But, Lord, would I kill for your lashes."

Even the apartment had its one thing. Melody sometimes pretended that she had a little sister whose diapers she changed, cloth diapers. Gennifer at school said her mother had done cloth for her. A cleaning service would whisk away the dirty ones and leave a fresh stack. It was sort of not normal to explain exactly how your mom kept your butt clean, but that obliviousness was why Melody couldn't hate her, despite Gennifer's heart-shaped face and her huge home in Saint Andrew's Woods, where an elm grew out of the porch that had been built around it.

The imaginary diapers that Melody used on her imaginary sister were held together with old-fashioned safety pins that Melody made certain never pricked. After the baby grew older and Melody fixed her hair with twin bead ponytail holders and slept on the floor so that her sister could have the sofa, because the little girl had grown too big for them to share, Melody would point into the kitchen and say, See that?

It was a round window of frosted glass. It glowed with marmoreal light. *Marmoreal* was a word she had found in a library book. Although her teacher, who first questioned the word's existence and then grudgingly looked it up, said it was a word for stone, Melody thought: *mammary*. Milky. When her sister grew yet older, Melody would teach her that the word meant "marble" or "resembling marble," and would explain how she collected words, especially the unusual kind, because sometimes a word could be the one thing she needed.

She rubbed her cheek against the sheet, not minding the scratch of the sofa beneath the sheet's thinness. Morning light came softly from the kitchen. It was going to be a nice Sunday. She got up, folded the sheets and put them away, and unloaded the dishwasher. She sponged cigarette ash off the drop-down table affixed to the kitchen wall and poured a bowl of cereal.

Her mother came out of the bedroom and into the kitchen, wearing a too-big T-shirt from the club where she worked. She rubbed a hand through her blond hair. The dye job was growing out; Melody could see the roots. Her mother opened a drawer, dug through piles of delivery chopsticks they never used, and came up with Pixy Stix, which she ripped into and poured down her throat. Candy was her mother's coffee. She had terrible teeth.

"Mom?"

"What."

"Can I have some money? For laundry."

"I don't have any."

"I don't have any clean underwear."

"Turn the dirty ones inside out."

"Mom."

"Mel, if I had it, I'd give it to you."

Melody sucked her spoon.

"I work today," her mother said. "I'll have money tonight. You can do laundry then." Sometimes her mom had a good night at the club, like a couple of weeks ago when Melody saw her counting out a big pile of cash on the kitchen table. Her mom bounced on her toes as she counted, her crop top riding high to show a temporary tattoo of a butterfly on her belly. Melody could tell that it had been freshly applied; it shone in the light. Since then, the butterfly had flaked away, and money was tight.

"Morning, babe," said a man's voice, startling Melody so badly that she spilled her cereal. "Hey, sorry," the guy said to Melody as he walked into the kitchen. "Didn't mean to scare you." He was wearing boxers and a baseball cap that was marked with the letter *Z*. He got close to her mother and kissed her neck, slipping a hand under the shirt that must, Melody realized, belong to him. Then he put on a smile and leaned to offer his hand—the same hand—to Melody. "I'm Zack."

She ignored the hand and pointed at his hat. "Zack with a *Z*?"

He liked that. "That's right."

"We gotta get a move on, Mellie." Her mother's voice was singsong, presumably for Zack with a Z's benefit. She fired a finger-gun at Melody. "You have a doctor's appointment. I better put some clothes on. Can't show up looking like this." She laughed as if it was the doctor's loss. She and Zack left the kitchen. There was some muffled giggling. Melody stirred her cereal. Then the man came back and it was just the two of them. He had his Lovely Lady shirt on. Not unkindly, he said, "Don't you need to get ready, too?"

Melody was wearing a long flannel nightgown her grandmother had given her. It was too hot. September nights were cold but the days were warm. She stayed where she was.

"Here." He slid a five-dollar bill over the table. "For your laundry."

She felt her ears burn. She slid the money back toward him. "I don't need it."

"Come on, kid, take it. Sasha can always pay me back."

"My mom's name isn't Sasha." Melody stood, edged around him, and got out of there.

SHE WASN'T A *hunchback*. She had scoliosis. *Mild* scoliosis. Her right hip cocked higher than her left, one shoulder drooped, and every six months a chiropractor measured the curve of her spine to make sure Melody didn't need surgery or a brace or both. Melody's grandmother, with whom she'd lived for a few years, paid for the doctor. Her grandmother prayed to God every night that Melody wouldn't become a cripple. "I'm okay," she would tell her grandmother over the phone. Melody didn't like prayers. If God was listening, maybe the devil was, too. Maybe it was a bad idea to say what you wanted out loud.

Melody's mother fidgeted in the waiting room, watching the clock. "Dale will make me pay double house fees if I'm late."

"Won't he understand? It's a doctor's appointment." Melody stared at the boyfriend quiz in *Seventeen*.

Her mother blew out a long breath. "Yeah, but he won't believe me."

"Get a note."

"He'll think I faked it."

Melody closed *Seventeen* and set it back down with the other magazines. She didn't have a boyfriend and couldn't focus on pretending that she did.

"Melody Tillson?" called the receptionist.

"About fucking time," muttered her mother, but made no move to get up when Melody did.

"Aren't you coming with?" Melody's mother always came with her.

"Jesus Lord, Mel, you're not a baby anymore." Then she looked at Melody's face and said, "Sure, okay. Not like it's a barrel full of money hanging around here."

A broth of relief and gratitude warmed Melody's chest. She resisted taking her mother's hand.

In the doctor's office, Melody undressed down to her socks and underwear—which, she now realized, was her oldest, ugliest pair. She put on the paper gown, open to the back, while her mother fiddled with a jar of tongue depressors, peeked into the biohazard box, and finally settled into a chair. Melody hopped up onto the paper-covered examining table. She thought that the paper in a doctor's office should be called something other than paper. It didn't really seem like paper. It was as loud as a poltergeist. It was the loudest thing in the room.

The doctor came in. He was newish to Melody. She had seen him for the first time a year ago, when she was eleven. He was short and had an accent. "Some kinda Oriental," her mother had said. Melody thought maybe Indian or Pakistani. "Hello, Melody," he said. "Hello, Mrs. Tillson."

"Ha!" said her mother, who wasn't Mrs. anything.

"I wonder," he said, "I may have a favor?" He spoke formally, as though each word were a precious object he set down with care, in a particular arrangement, so that even if he made a rare mistake in English, the tone of his voice insisted everything was intentional and perfect. "I have a student with me today. Sundays are my student days. My student wants to be an orthopedist, too. He wants to observe. Do you give permission?"

"Um," said Melody.

"Why not," said her mother. "Mel?"

"I guess."

"Thank you," said the doctor. He opened the door, and a young guy with floppy brown hair came in. He was cute in a sheepish way, like he had a hidden tattoo of a dolphin and only some girls got to see it. Melody clasped the paper gown to her. The room felt too small. The doctor told her to get off the table and bend over, something she was used to at these appointments, but she had no bra, not even a training bra, and her butt was in the air. She pictured the flower pattern of her ratty underwear. The student's hands were cold as he measured the curve of her spine. She stared at her bare knees. She thought that maybe she needed her inhaler.

"You may stand up straight," said Melody's doctor. When she did, she saw that her mother was looking appreciatively at the student.

The doctor was pleased; the curve had remained stable. He showed her X-rays from over the past year. He asked if she was getting exercise ("sort of"), and then he said, kindly, "Did you bleed yet?"

"What?" She thought he had said a word in another language. He repeated the question. When her mother started laughing, Melody understood. She glanced at the cute student. His eyes were averted. He was biting his lip.

"Did you—"

"*No*," she said. "I haven't gotten my period."

On the way back to the car, Melody's mother reenacted the scene, laying the doctor's accent on thick. "Did you *bleed* yet? Did you *bleed*?"

Melody wished that shame were a contagious disease so that everyone would die of it. "It's monkeys," Melody said, slamming the car door.

"What?" Her mother stopped laughing. The key was in the ignition, the key chains clicking against each other.

"It's a barrel full of fucking *monkeys*," Melody said. "Not money."

"Watch your mouth," her mother said.

"FUCK." HER MOTHER punched the gas. "Fuck fuck fuck."

Melody said nothing.

"I'm going to be late," her mother said.

Melody was glad.

"Look, Mel, I can't take you home first. No time. You're going to have to come with."

"To your *work*?"

The car vibrated from increased speed.

"No," Melody said. "No way."

WHEN THEY PARKED in the back lot of the Lovely Lady, Melody said, "I'll stay in the car."

"I'm working a double shift."

"I can wait."

"With all those perverts who come here? What kind of mother do you think I am?"

HER MOTHER PUSHED her into a low leather chair at the back of the club, behind the bar. The club wasn't open yet and was empty except for the bartender and a couple of bouncers by the stage. She guessed that most of the dancers were backstage getting ready. "Just stay out of sight," her mother said. "Okay?"

"Mom, please."

"It's nothing you haven't seen before." Her mother went to the bar and must have made a deal with the bartender, because when she returned with a jar in hand, she said, "Rob will keep an eye on you. Here." She handed the jar to Melody. It was full of maraschino cherries. "In case you get hungry."

MELODY SCRUNCHED AS low as possible in the chair. She kept her gaze fixed on the open jar, poking a finger into the syrup. The club thudded with music. The smoke made it hard to breathe. A few men had tried to talk to her, but, true to whatever his word had been, Rob leaned over the bar and said, "Touch her and you're out on your ass." He sounded chivalrous the first time but annoyed the second. The third time, Melody realized he was annoyed with her.

"Whoa," someone said. "You can't be here."

Melody glanced up. It was one of the dancers. She was what her grandmother would call a "real woman," someone with "meat on her bones." "Not like your mother," her grandmother would say. "She was made with a chisel and file."

The dancer had large, light brown eyes and a viciously red mouth, her hair a dark cloud of loose curls. She was Black but could almost be white. A strappy dress squeezed and pushed up her trembling breasts, which held a bouquet of dollars in their cleavage. "How old are you?" the woman said. "Ten?"

"Twelve."

"You are so illegal. You better leave before someone notices you."

"I can't. My mom told me to stay."

"Shut the front door," the woman said. Melody wondered if she was mocking her. "Who is your mother?"

Melody scanned the club. The nakedness was disorienting. It made her think that she wouldn't recognize her mother. Then she saw her dancing topless for Zack with a Z. She had a hard body except for her breasts, which were floaty, like soap bubbles. They made Melody's insides go quiet. She thought of the word *virga*, for rain that vanishes before it reaches the ground. "She's there," Melody said, "with her boy-friend."

"Sasha, huh?" The woman looked tired. "Baby, our boss will lose his mind if he sees you here. He's already mad because two dancers didn't come to work, didn't even call in sick. If he finds out your mom brought her underage daughter to hang out at the bar while she took her clothes off, he'll fire her. Do you want that?"

Melody gave her a look.

"Wrong question," the woman said. "Don't you want to get out of here?"

Sometimes, instead of crying, Melody used her inhaler. She gave herself a good blast. When she spoke, her voice sounded thin. "I don't have a ride home."

"Can you call someone?"

Melody thought of Gennifer with her tree-porch house. She found herself saying, stupidly, "My grandmother lives in St. Louis."

"St. Louis! That's no help."

"I know."

The woman fished money out of her breasts. There were several ones, a few fives, and one twenty. She gave the twenty to Melody. "Take a taxi back to your place. The bartender will call one for you. I'll tell Sasha. If you get in trouble with her, say I made you do it. I'm Gigi."

The twenty was damp with boob sweat. "Thanks," Melody said, and almost said more, but didn't want to use her inhaler again.

SHE USED PRACTICALLY all the money getting home. She had enough left for a pitiful sixty-five-cent tip. She kept one nickel of it, then got out of the cab fast, though the driver just looked tiredly at the apartment building and back at her, closed his fist around the change, and drove off.

Her hair stank of smoke and she was ravenous. As soon as Melody entered the apartment, she went to the fridge. There was leftover spa-ghetti with meatballs and a bunch of little vials that hadn't been there before Zack had spent the night. Melody nuked the spaghetti. As she ate, she looked at the bright nickel in the late-afternoon light of the kitchen window, pushing the coin around the table with one finger. The nickel and the light suited each other. Melody wondered what word would describe their likeness. She thought, in a way she hadn't before, that naming something might make it less than what it was.

After she finished eating, Melody squeezed dishwashing detergent into the dispenser of the empty dishwasher. She loaded her dirty underwear and socks onto the racks, shut the door, and pressed start.

GEORGIA
(GIGI)

Georgia was out of soymilk, so she went to the grocery store early. Sunday mornings were busy, but they beat shopping at 4 a.m. at some twenty-four-hour place after her shift at the Lady. Convenience stores don't carry good food, and they make bad food seem too good.

When she got her cart, with one stuck wheel that occasionally whipped itself around its axis, she heard, but did not see, a woman being rude to the cashier. "Just give me the goddamn groceries," the woman said. Georgia wanted to say, That cashier is doing you a service. She is *serving* you. She wants to make sure your eggs don't break and make a mess. Georgia had no patience for people who disregarded goodwill. Or worse, people who thought that just because they paid for something, they could behave as if no one had taught them any better. Georgia almost stopped and turned around to speak. But she knew how it'd be. It'd end up seeming that *she* was the problem.

She walked the aisles, loading her cart with quinoa and extra-virgin olive oil. She got sushi-grade tuna, Tellicherry pepper, jasmine rice that smelled faintly like Bella's body lotion, and stiff, bright asparagus. All healthy healthy healthy. And it would not come cheap. Corn was on special, though, six for a dollar. As much as Georgia liked feeling rich, she was also her mother's daughter. She was peeling back the husks—not

far, just enough to see the corn's pearled teeth—when she heard someone say, "What are you doing?"

Georgia looked up. It was a white woman wearing flip-flops, her
straight, light brown hair in a ponytail. At her temples, fine baby hairs
stood out like cat whiskers. To Georgia, it seemed fairly obvious what
she was doing, so her guard went up, because she didn't know what this
was going to become. Then she glanced at the woman's cart and saw that
she, too, had ears of corn. They were tightly sealed. "I'm checking the
corn," Georgia said.

"Oh," the woman said.

"If you don't check, you might pay for corn with smut, or earworms,
or sap maggots."

"Oh."

"No one wants bad corn. Do you want bad corn?"

"No."

"See." Georgia peeled back a pale sheave. It made the squeaky sound
of packing tape. "Like this."

SUNDAYS WERE DOUBLE-SHIFT days for Georgia. She liked Sundays
because fewer girls worked them, and although that meant she had less
time between stage sets to sell dances, she did better onstage than most
people thought. There were dollars, sure, but some guys tipped fives and
tens, mostly because they wanted to see her pick the bills up from the
tip rail with her tits or ass. ("Six inches, Gigi," Dale told her. "Take the
cash how you want, but there must be *six inches* between you and a customer or we're not legal."

"Like I want to get close," she told him. "Like cops come here."

"You'd be surprised.")

Plus, Sundays were game days. The Bears were playing the Packers
and men would take their afterparties to the club.

"You're late," Bella sang when Georgia entered the dressing room.

"Yeah," Angel said. "Where you been?"

Georgia unbuttoned her dress, a cute blue-and-white gingham, and
shimmied out of it. "Grocery shopping."

"Don't say that to Dale," said a sleek blonde.

"Who are you again?" said Georgia.

"He is in a mood," said Angel.

"Totally on the rag." Bella opened her cosmetic kit and went to work on Georgia.

"I'm Lacey," said Lacey.

"Sometimes I can't keep you all straight," Georgia said.

"I'm the hot one," said Bella.

"Just watch yourself," Violet told Georgia, which was surprising given her backstabbing last night. Violet had betrayed Lady Jade *and* cheated Ruby, since Ruby was nice enough to drive the girl home and miss out on the club's best hours.

"Tell him you're sick," said Bella. "Not a lot. A little. Like, *just* under the fucking weather."

"Tell him you had to take care of your mother," said Angel.

"Can we not talk about my mother?" Georgia glued on her lashes.

"You were supposed to be on the main stage already," said Violet. "You were up first. Sasha covered for you."

"You're gonna owe her," said Bella.

"Fuck me," said Georgia.

"Ruby didn't show," said Angel.

"She will," said Violet.

"Her sidekick bailed, too," said Angel.

"More for the rest of us," said Bella. "Am I right?"

Skye clomped in, naked except for her heels and a garter wreathed with ones. She pulled off the bills to neaten them, then folded the airy stack over her garter and rubber-banded them tight. "They're fucking ghosts," Skye said. "They didn't even call in. *I* call in."

"Are they *fucking* ghosts, or fucking *ghosts*?" said Bella.

"Ghost fuckers?" Angel offered.

"Whatever," said Skye.

"All right, all right, I'm ready," said Georgia.

"Naked as a baby," said Angel.

"Au naturel," said Bella.

"In the flippy floppy," said Angel.

"In the nutty," said Lacey.

"In the butty!"

"I don't know what the fuck y'all talking about," Skye said.

"Ta," said Georgia.

IT WAS PRETTY slow. After apologizing to the house mom and taking a turn on Stage 3 (she hated Stage 3), Georgia worked the floor with little luck beyond managing to avoid Sasha, then stopped backstage to get CDs from her locker.

At the deejay booth on the mezzanine above the main stage, Eric sipped the pillowy Starbucks that he brought every day. He chatted up Paris, who, word had it, was sleeping with him. Georgia didn't approve. Eric was a redheaded scrub. She didn't see what Paris got out of it beyond total control of her tunes. After Paris finished a conversation Georgia didn't particularly want to overhear and wiggled off, Georgia gave Eric her CDs. He flipped through them, then held up her Lauryn Hill CD. "I can't play this," he said.

"Track five. It's good, I promise."

"No Black music. You know that."

"You play Prince."

"Prince is beyond Black and white."

"Now, that's just dumb."

"Prince is the patron saint of strippers. Prince is jizz for your ears."

"You play Hendrix. You play James Brown."

"I am not going to debate this. It's not my rule. Dale wants to cultivate a certain clientele. So, sorry, but no." Eric handed back the CDs. "Now go shake your moneymaker."

He played Britney throughout her entire set.

LATER THAT AFTERNOON, Georgia watched Sasha dance for a familiar-looking guy in a baseball cap marked with the letter Z. "Her boyfriend," said Sasha's daughter, which made Georgia wonder how the money worked. Was Sasha dancing for free or was the boyfriend paying her, and if so, did he tip extra? And wasn't he Lady Jade's regular?

Georgia sent Sasha's kid home, wobbly chin and smart eyes and all. Then she tracked down Sasha, whom she found coming out of the bathroom backstage. "Hey, Sash," she said. "It's never Take Your Daughter to Work Day at the strip club."

"There's pee all over the seat," Sasha said. "It's disgusting."

"I sent her home in a cab."

"You think I'm a shitty mother, don't you."

"I am not thinking anything."

"I got a number in mind tonight."

"Sasha, we all got a number."

"I'm going to make it. Then I'm going to go home and buy Melody clothes, and buy her food, and pay my rent, because she's *mine*. You don't know what it means to be a mom."

"I'm not saying I do."

"I covered for you."

"And I covered for *you*."

"You're welcome," Sasha said, and went out to work the floor again.

RUBY AND LADY Jade never showed. Georgia expected it of Lady Jade (the girl was probably still off her face), but Ruby was a professional. She was a force of nature with an easy beauty: tall and blond, her face delicate, mouth vulnerable. She came in and cleaned up. Everyone knew she took home much more money than they could hope to make, but she never acted like she was any different from them, and played by the rules. If she missed a shift, which was rare, she always gave a reason.

Dale mostly stayed in his office, but you could feel his subsonic anger, and Georgia knew that payout would take forever. He was going to lord it on the main stage, lecturing them about responsibility and professional courtesy.

The postgame crowd came in and things picked up, but not for her. Some days were like that. She got shut down. A lot of "Not nows" and

"Maybe laters". Even "You're not my type," which pretty much meant "not white." She felt a leaking balloon in her chest, and wondered if she'd make house fees or go home in debt to the club.

Then one guy, a loner, said, "You look tired." There was a space of quiet around his table. Georgia knew she was supposed to say, "I can go all night." Instead she said, "My feet hurt."

"Sit with me."

"I'd rather dance." She ran a palm down his back.

"I got you." He opened his Velcro wallet and gave her a twenty. "Sit for a song."

"Do you live around here?" A man who paid for a stripper to sit would make a good regular.

"I live all over." He blew out smoke. "Just finished a job in Brazil. They treated me so good there. I have never been treated so good. I build towers. Communication towers. Thousand feet tall. I build a level, climb up with what I need to build the next one. I do that, level by level, until I'm high in the sky."

"It must be beautiful, the view."

"Not as beautiful as you."

She believed that he meant it. He took out another twenty. "One dance."

As she pulled her strappy dress down, Georgia wondered whether Ruby would have sat and talked with him. Sometimes Georgia watched Ruby work. Ruby was all business and few words, which Georgia respected, but as she watched the man's expression change, slacken, she envisioned him building a tower in another country and was glad she had talked with him. It made what she did easier. She pretended he was there instead of here. She didn't know whether this was a good thing or a bad thing, the way people got inside her, how she imagined their lives. She wondered whether she'd always be this way: someone who just had to see, had to know.

DETECTIVE HOLLY MEYLIN

After the identification of the body, Holly promised Kim Campana's mother time to talk, though the woman gave no sign of needing it. When Patty Campana saw the body in photographs at the station, she shook her head, not in denial but disapproval, as though she might take the body to task. She showed no visible grief, which made things easier for Holly.

Still, there was department etiquette to follow. Holly waited one precise day before driving twenty minutes to Buffalo Hills, past the church that had been part of a nineteenth-century pioneer settlement near the newer main street with its shuttered movie theater and a pet shop whose green-tinted windows made it look like one of its own aquariums. Holly sees the concrete bunker of what had probably been Kim's high school.

The mother lives on a street that displays an array of personality or maybe just a difference in income. One house has an apron of autumn flowers: sedum and foamy, long-lived alyssum. Pots of geraniums, each blossom a bright spatter, mark the steps leading up to a porch that dangles wind chimes. *FAITH is the only WEAPON*, says a laminated sign on the door. The neighboring house has a scrubby lawn and a noisy tethered dog. The slow resonance of wind chimes follows Holly down the uneven sidewalk after she parks and locks her car. People have their windows open, savoring what might be the last warm day. In Illinois, fall has a way of slamming straight into winter. She hears the blare of a television. Farther off is the mellow lift of a trumpet, a fluid scale, someone practicing, someone good. Dime-sized pine cones lie underfoot, the sidewalk chalked with hopscotch.

Patty Campana's house is pistachio green with a crooked downspout, the windows fringed with lace. A butterfly suncatcher has improbable green wings. Holly knocks.

It's midafternoon, but Patty comes to the door wearing a robe that looks like what happens when you drop scoops of sherbet into fizzy fruit punch. She greets Holly with a polite, "There you are," then lets Holly in and shows her to her daughter's childhood room, which has a New Kids on the Block poster on the door and a bookshelf holding rows of fashion magazines, plus three thick yearbooks. "She dropped out senior year," Patty says, following Holly's gaze, "to have the baby."

Holly doesn't like what the words do to her. They remind Holly of how it was to feel her baby flicker inside her. She is made aware of her belly's flatness. She pulls the 1993 yearbook off the shelf and finds Kim: blond bangs, hairband, a smile with all her teeth.

Patty sits on the twin bed, whose pine headboard shows the phantoms of stickers peeled away. "Maybe it's my fault."

Holly, fallen into the slick pages of the yearbook, looks up. "What do you mean?"

Patty doesn't mean her daughter's death. "I kept her back a year for kindergarten. She was small. I'd heft her, she'd weigh about as much as a sack of kitty litter." She has a thick downstate accent. Holly wonders which county the woman is from, whether she grew up in the floodplains of the Mississippi River, or east, near Shawnee, where cream-and-copper cliffs roll into Ohio and miners dig into seams of coal.

"Kinda slow, too," Patty says. "I thought it'd be good for her to start late. Give her an edge, you know? I wanted her to do better than me. That worked okay at first. Then in high school, her chest came in before the other girls. Boys noticed. She goes, You worry too much. But I go, A girl like you makes one mistake and you're done. That baby weren't nothing to me. Get rid of it. Have it and give it up, like she did. Keep it. What got me was, she didn't listen. I told her how it'd be. Guess you don't know till it happens."

"Until what happens?"

"Some people get chance after chance, but you get just one. You lose that, you lose it all. Ain't no kind of life, a one-chance life."

"Was there anyone who would have harmed Kimberly?"

"Weren't no harm in her."

"What about the father of her child?"

"Gone. His family moved out west. He was only too glad not to deal with the situation. Anyhow, that was four years back."

"Did you see her often?"

"She'd come by to take me to Aldi's, get my shopping done." Patty looks down at the backs of her age-yellowed hands, their ropy blue veins. "She'd pay. I knew what she did for it. Said she was working as a waitress at a titty bar, but she was always telling that kind of lie—skidding, like, alongside the truth. Kim said she kept her clothes on, served drinks, no different than Hooters, but who am I? I knew. She been showing herself since she was fourteen."

"Did she mention anyone she was close to?"

"She had a friend, a good one, from church. Ruby. But that's no Christian name."

"Do you know who this is?" Holly holds out a photo booth strip found at Kim's place, not far from the crash. She had lived in an extended-stay motel stocked with boxes of mac 'n' cheese, perfume samples, nail polish, and extra-large white T-shirts apparently used as pajamas. The evidence techs were not happy. There was no trace of someone other than Kim beyond the many stains on the mattress—expected for a motel, and not necessarily connected to her. The menstrual blood, dollops of semen, and yellow amoebas of sweat or urine could have been there long before Kim checked in. Nevertheless, the stains had been cut out of the mattress and sent to a lab. The main prize was the black-and-white photos: Kim, giddy, kissing the cheek of a skinny-faced man with clear eyes, a baseball cap with a Z, and the expression of someone who wants praise for good behavior. In the last of the four photos, Kim is a blur, her mouth open, laughing.

"Her boyfriend, I guess," Patty says. "She was dating a nice guy named Zack. So she said. A doctor." Patty's gaze drifts to a shelf lined with My Little Ponies, including baby ones with translucent wings and dusty cotton-candy hair. Sea Ponies lie tilted onto their seahorse sides. Holly thinks that maybe the woman will cry, but she doesn't.

Later, walking back to her car, Holly imagines Kim's four-year-old child, the same age Daniel would be now. She imagines the child as a boy, then corrects herself. She sees a towheaded girl who burns easily in the sun. Holly wonders if the adopted girl, wherever she is, has a one-chance life, or two, or three. She thinks about Samantha Lind, whose face is on flyers all over the department, hair a natural brown although it was dyed blond when she went missing. It was the best picture of her, Nick Sullivan insisted.

Holly thinks of Kimberly Campana's mother, of the weight of a child ready for kindergarten. Daniel never grew to weigh that much, but he would be close now, if he were alive. She remembers the soft, small beanbag weight of his infancy, and later, his sturdy struggle to escape her arms. She had been lucky, for a time. She had thought she always would be. Some people seem to have so many chances, only for them to be eaten, all of them, as though by a whip-bodied weasel, a mink with its dense shine of fur and barbed mouth, an animal you never noticed because it slunk long in your shadow, waiting for its moment.

SAMANTHA
(RUBY)

He has left her alone. She is hungry but afraid of him coming back, even if he brings food. She grows colder as the day outside ends. Her head aches—a little less than before, but she is confused enough to hope that her confusion means that none of this is real. She is clearheaded enough to know that it is.

She was going to marry Nick. She had had it all planned out. A strapless dress, satin, so that she would look like a pillar of light. No veil. She wanted to see everything perfectly: Nick waiting at the end of the aisle, Rosie scattering petals. Red, Samantha's favorite, and pink for Rosie, hers. White for Nick, for what she would be for him: pure. Love is patient, love is kind. It keeps no record of wrongs.

But that is not what love is, not what love does. Not for her and Nick. It had never been that way. A different verse suited them better. For where you go, I will go. Your people will be my people, your God my God.

ROSIE

$\int$amantha's voice woke Rosie up. It was dark. Her mouth was spitty, and her eyes had grit in the corners. Rosie couldn't tell what Samantha was saying. It sounded like she was reading from a book, but not one that Rosie would enjoy. "Stomach bug," Samantha's voice said. "Poor thing." Rosie got out of bed and pulled up her loose socks, which she always wore when she slept because they kept away bad dreams. "Samantha?" she called, but Samantha ignored her, so she followed the voice into the living room. "I'm going to drive her, make sure she gets home safe," Samantha said. "Love you, bye." There was a click, and the answering machine beeped. Rosie felt dumb. A little strange in her belly, too, as if Samantha had hurt her feelings, as if Rosie had said *wait* and Samantha hadn't.

Of course Samantha wasn't home. It was Saturday night. Samantha always worked Saturday nights.

Rosie was on her way back to bed when the phone rang again. She picked it up. "Sam?"

There was a long silence that went down deep. Rosie thought no one was there after all. But someone said, "No." He was a grown-up.

Rosie said, "Who are you?"

He said, "Who are *you*?" in a fun way, like a game, so Rosie said, "I'm

Rose." Then they talked until Rosie didn't want to anymore, and hung up fast.

She went to her father's room, afraid that he might not be there, but he was. Her hand on the doorknob was slippery. "Dad?" He made a noise that meant he had heard her. "There was a phone call," she said. He lifted his shadowy head.

Her throat hurt. She thought of the man on the phone. She told her father that Samantha had called and left a message. Then Rosie returned to her bed, yanked her socks up to her knees, and tried to fall back asleep. Her loud heart filled her whole body.

She thought that she heard the front door open and close, but when morning came she was not so sure. Too early, when it was barely light out, the doorbell rang. The sound got mixed in her head with the answering machine's beep, and how the phone had jangled in the dark. The doorbell rang, the front door opened. The phone rang, the front door opened. Bells and doors echoed through her head, so that when Rosie realized it was morning and someone was at the door talking to her father, she was sure—in a hard, freezing way, like the feel of a flagpole in winter—only of what the man on the phone had said.

A POLICEMAN WAS at the door. Behind him was a nice, bright day. As Rosie came into the living room, she saw her father talking to him and heard the man introduce himself as Officer Schrader. Officer Schrader was shorter than her father, which made her feel better. "Your daddy is a big man," Samantha always said, so Rosie knew that was something to be proud of.

"It's a Sunday morning," her father told the policeman. His voice was mad. I'm not mad, her father would tell her, I'm cranky. But Rosie knew the difference.

"Are you the owner of a 1996 red Honda Civic?" the policeman asked.

Rosie couldn't see her father's face but could tell from his shoulders that he was frowning. His sandy-brown hair stuck up in all directions, and he was wearing sweatpants and a T-shirt, which meant that he, like Rosie, had just gotten out of bed. "Yes. Why?"

"Do you know where your car is?"

Her father turned, looking around the living room as if he expected to see the car parked in it. His gaze fell on Rosie, and she didn't like what she saw. He looked afraid. "My girlfriend has the car. It should be out front. Samantha should be here."

Rosie felt tight and bony.

"Any reason she would be over by Route 6?" the policeman said.

"No."

"Was she with someone?"

"No."

"Your car was involved in a crash."

Her father's voice rose, and Rosie's ears roared. The officer kept repeating the same thing, cutting through her father: they didn't know much more right now, calm down, he should calm down.

A new, crackly voice cut in. "Are you 61 for 43?" It came from the mini microphone on the officer's shoulder. The man held up a flat hand to Rosie's father, so that the police officer looked like a drawing of a police officer, the one on signs that say *STOP*. The officer put a little thing in his ear and said, "I'm clear." He listened, and whatever he heard changed his face so that Rosie, who had wanted to approach her father and lean against him, didn't want to anymore. She didn't want to get close to the men at all. The officer said to her father, "You're going to have to come down to the station," and then, for the first time, noticed Rosie. He put on a nice face, which made Rosie realize that the officer was not nice, and that whatever he had heard or was thinking was bad. "Hello there," he said. "What's your name?"

But Rosie, who had learned her lesson last night, refused to speak.

LAST SUMMER, THEY had driven to Lake Michigan in Indiana, where sand dunes burned Rosie's feet until she cried and her father carried her. He set her down by the water. There, the dry pebbles were warm until they darkened in the lapping water and became as cool as mirrors. Rosie brought one to Samantha, who lay in the sun, her skin shiny with lotion.

"It looks like an arrowhead," Samantha said.

Rosie brought another. "This one?"

"Like a thundercloud."

It became a game. "A sea otter floating on its belly," "A tree with a princess sleeping in its branches," "A skinny, hungry horse that wants to nibble you." This delighted Rosie, until it began to bother her, because she couldn't think up anything as good as Samantha could. Rosie was a little angry when she brought the last find, a piece of green glass made smoky and smooth. She thought glass would be harder to figure out than stone. "What about this?"

Samantha held it up to the sun. It cast a small, green beam. She was quiet for a while. Then she said, "It looks like you."

"HELLO, ROSE," THE man on the phone had said. "Are you a big girl, or a little girl?"

"A big girl."

"How big?"

"I'm eight."

"Since you're such a big girl, I want you to do me a favor."

Rosie was suddenly not so sure she should be on the phone.

"We're friends now," he said. "And it's a little favor, as little as you."

This confused her. It made her feel like she didn't know what she was.

"Don't tell anyone I called," he said. "Promise?"

There was a silence. Rosie knew that she was the one making the silence, but it seemed more like he was making it, or making her make it. She twisted the telephone cord tight around her finger.

"Promise," he said, his voice no longer friendly, "or I will come and play with *you*."

HIM

He liked the girl. He liked the long, echoing ring before she answered, his breath light and cool and fast in his throat as he wondered who would pick up. And for it to be her. Rose. Rosie. A treat. He shouldn't have called, of course, but it felt good to thumb the numbers. Good to feel the soft click of each button under his pressure. Then the pretty ring. He wasn't sure anyone would answer, and had liked the uncertainty.

Don't you know, he asked, what can happen to girls like you?

Didn't your daddy teach you not to talk to strangers?

Where is your daddy?

Is he sleeping?

Do you like to sleep with him?

Do you get under his blanket?

Oh, I see. You are a good girl. Well, then, Rose, I apologize.

He slid the cell phone, the number untraceable to him, into his pocket. She might not know it now, but he was doing her a favor. He was telling her about the world. Someone ought to teach her. He could be the best of teachers.

His mind returned to Ruby. She was a light he had left on at home, red as the name she had chosen for herself, aglow, waiting for him.

DETECTIVE HOLLY MEYLIN

Before Daniel died, Holly had loved home-delivery catalogues. It was an old allure. The thick Sears, Roebuck catalogues of her childhood had been talismanic with power, especially in September, when her mother allowed her to choose one item of clothing for the first day of school. Holly would choose something plain, such as a green plaid jumper dress, and feel filled with goodness to see her mother's faded smile.

"This house came from a Sears catalogue." Her father looked out over the lawn and into the fields. He had a southern twang in his voice, just like Holly did, but she didn't realize it then, because it was the way everyone she knew spoke. People think of Illinois as the Midwest, but where Holly grew up, in the southernmost tip of Illinois, men had defected to the Confederacy during the Civil War. "It was a kit," he said. "All the lumber arrived precut in a train car. My grandfather built it, my daddy with him. I held a can of nails." The words had made Holly, for a moment, see her father as a boy. Then her mother flitted him a hooded look and Holly remembered exactly who he was.

She had chosen Matthew because he was different from her father. Matthew was a junior high school science teacher who refused to do dissections. They had met through a college-loan relief program that waived Holly's debt when she enrolled as a patrol officer. Matthew had grown up in northern Illinois, in a town near the Wisconsin border called Harvard that was full of dairy cows and held an annual Milk Days parade. In the fall, leaves turned the color of butter—out of pride, townspeople said. There was not one red leaf. The trees were burnished gold. Matthew had gone to the University of Wisconsin at Madison, consternating his parents, who objected to paying out-of-state tuition, though in the end they had helped the best they could, which was better than Holly's father had agreed to do for her. Matthew graduated with debt anyway, and shared Holly's fear of it. When Matthew, who had chosen to teach in an underserved school district, met Holly in line at the debt-relief program's local office, he said, wide-eyed, "A cop? I couldn't do what you do." Holly explained that she wanted to become a lawyer and thought that working in law enforcement would help her better understand the justice system. She didn't add that she liked being a cop, and that becoming a lawyer had been her father's plan for her, not her own. "It's just for a year," she said, sensing that Matthew's gentleness might be the kind easily spooked. "Maybe two." But in two years Holly was ready to be promoted up the department ranks. Matthew graded schoolwork at the supper table, hands long and soft, with purple half-moons at the base of each nail. His long lashes smudged his glasses, and he was forever cleaning the lenses. He liked walks after supper, which he called dinner, the way people did up north. "We both went to Harvard," he liked to tell people, in a way that elevated Holly and diminished himself as he explained the joke, which had never been funny yet retained its sweetness as she listened to him describe Harvard High School and his hometown's Milk Days in June.

After Daniel's death, sales catalogues piled up on her doorstep, some with Matthew's name on the label. The mailman dropped them there because the mailbox was too full; it shed envelopes like feathers. These days, catalogues huddle against the door, swollen by rain. They hold nothing she wants.

Holly thinks that Owen has a catalogue in his head when he autopsies. It takes a certain person to be a medical examiner. Owen is good. He doesn't bother with a Vicks VapoRub mustache even when dealing with the most oozing of corpses. For him, the woman found in the

grass is easy. "Cake," he tells Holly and Amador. "Fresh as they come."
Owen is big yet moves nimbly around the cadaver carrier in the small
morgue, his skin a lively pink. Holly sometimes gets the sense that as
he opens and cuts and swabs, Owen feels what she felt when she used
to hold a sales catalogue: a repository of possibilities. He hums while
he works. "I thought I'd have a boring Monday morning with some
dead junkie. Little did I know that you'd bring me a murder vic. I love
an interesting body."

Amador gives her a look that she ignores.

Owen eases the paper bags off the woman's hands, which were mit-
tened on scene. He scrapes beneath the fingernails and examines them
for defensive wounds, scrapes or broken nails. There appear to be none.
Kimberly Campana's nails are nibbled to the quick, cuticles ragged.

Amador is not wholly paying attention to this. "Her foot."

"I'm not ready for her feet," Owen says.

"It's fucked up," Amador says, but Holly wonders where he has been
his whole career, his whole life, if a mark cut into the sole of a woman's
foot as though by a sculptor on his statue rattles him. He looks away
when the body is swabbed for semen. "Doesn't it bother you?" Amador
once asked her. His voice turned accusatory. "How can it not bother
you?" She didn't know how to express the expectedness of sexual violence, how it felt nearly inescapable. It is so common that a warning
might as well be stamped on the birth certificate of every newborn girl.

Amador gets like this only during autopsies. He might be like this
only around her. Maybe he imagines Holly in the body's place. Maybe he
looks at the body and looks at her looking at it. But for her, there is only
one body. She doesn't understand how Amador doesn't understand this.
Then she almost hates him, because she realizes that he *must* understand,
must at least guess how Daniel's body had been too small, marooned on a
metal examining table as huge and bright and flat as the moon.

She says, "You're such a little girl, Amador."

Amador blinks, but before he can speak, Owen proves he can be as
much of an asshole as Holly. "Mom, Dad, please don't fight. I'll examine her foot."

The cuts are postmortem, done by a steady hand. Rabideaux said the mark looked like a crown, and Holly doesn't disagree. Owen measures the cuts and probes them for DNA. There is none. "Elegant," Owen says.

The silver dress, leaden under fluorescence, is examined for stains. The woman's organs are unpacked, her stomach opened, her bladder sampled. The bruises on her neck bear no trace of nails dug into the flesh. There are no signs, none that Owen can find, that she fought back. It is cold in the morgue, but Holly already feels the warm September day she will step into after this, and how, out of everything, what will stay with her is that the hip bones show the wear of childbirth. Kimberly Campana gave the child up for adoption at the age of nineteen. For a moment, as though under a malignant spell, Holly feels certain that if she were to look for the child she would find Daniel. She pats her pockets and feels a reassuring pack of cigarettes, but leaves them where they are. She quit when she was pregnant. Now there is no point. Sometimes, though, she likes to resist smoking, because it reminds her of when there was a reason to try.

Owen puts the time of death between 11 p.m. and 2 a.m. The sperm samples, he says, are about three days old. He observes, his face scrunched and eyebrows raised, head ticktocking as if he is doing math that doesn't add up, that there is also evidence of recent vaginal penetration that has left no trace of DNA. Possibly consensual, more likely assault. "I don't think she was awake after the crash," Owen says. There's some head trauma, which explains the blood found in the car.

Owen promises toxicology reports. Later, the reports will give Holly and Amador their first lead. "A fuckload of GHB," Owen will say over the phone the next day. "Not my personal date rape drug of choice, but it does the trick." Owen's laugh comes quick into the phone. Holly lets her irritation ice the line.

"What?" Owen says.

"You're not as funny as you think you are."

"Come on," he tells her, "don't be such a little girl."

———

PRADKO AND BACKYARD, the other two detectives on the case, questioned Samantha Lind's boyfriend at the station the day before yesterday, while Holly and Amador continued searching the field where Campana's body was found. Holly came in at the end of the interrogation, after dropping Campana's body off at the morgue to be stored for autopsy, Amador still on his way from the crime scene. She saw Gina, a clerk, with Nick Sullivan's daughter in the waiting area. Gina was trying to talk to the girl and not getting much of a response. Rose Sullivan wore Little Mermaid pajamas the color of a tulip, but she had underground eyes. The sight of her made Holly hesitate before stepping into the interview room, but the girl wasn't her concern, at least not then.

Backyard let Holly into the box.

Pradko was nursemaiding Sullivan, saying, in soothing tones possibly intended to make Sullivan lose his shit, that Samantha Lind's information was put on NCIC. "It's a national database," Pradko said. "It stands for—"

"I don't give a fuck what it stands for." Sullivan swigged from a bottle of water Pradko must have given to him. "I want to know why you're talking to me and not to her boss, the other girls."

Holly gave Backyard a look. His face didn't change except for his mouth, which squinched slightly at the corner. He was tall and broad and generally gave the impression that he was not someone to be trifled with, which had earned him the nickname Not in My Backyard, even though he had pointed out that that was a real white lady sort of thing to call a Black man.

"Don't worry," Pradko told Sullivan. "We plan on talking to Samantha's coworkers." When he wanted to, he could pretend to be kind. His blue eyes were earnest, and the overhead light gave his pale, prematurely bald head an angelic look, as though he had a small halo. "I promise you, we are doing everything we can."

Sullivan shrank into his seat. "I don't know what to do," he whispered to his hands.

Holly sat down across from him. She slid an evidence bag across the table. "Do you recognize this?"

Sullivan looked at it. Fear rose off him. It mushroomed into the room. "Where did you get this?"

Holly had found the pearl earring in the field, backless, nestled into the grass like a tiny egg. It had a spark of a diamond stud. "So it *is* Samantha's."

"It was a gift from her parents. Where did you find it?"

"That's not information I can share."

"I have given you everything. I have told you everything."

"Not a whole lot," Pradko said. "You must admit."

"I was asleep," Sullivan hissed. "I was fucking sleeping."

"It's interesting," Backyard told Holly. "Mr. Sullivan told the patrol officer who came to his apartment that he had no idea where his girlfriend was. But he told *us* that Samantha Lind called to say she was driving a sick coworker home."

"I'm not lying." The water bottle crackles as Sullivan's grip tightens. "It's on the answering machine."

"Why didn't you mention the call in the first place?"

"I didn't remember."

"You didn't remember?"

"It was the middle of the night. I listened, I went back to bed. It didn't feel real. None of this does."

"Mr. Sullivan," Holly said, "where was your daughter last night?"

"Why are you asking about my daughter?"

"I just want to know where she was."

"With me."

"In your room?"

"In her room. She has her own room."

Pradko shot Holly a warning look, but she thought of Rose Sullivan in the waiting area, fear lighting her up like a candle. Holly said, "I wonder if you'd mind if we asked her a few questions."

"Yeah, I fucking mind."

"Not alone. A social worker would be present."

"No."

"We'd need your consent."

"You are not talking to my daughter."

Backyard said, "We'd like to take your DNA sample." He held out a buccal swab. "Just routine. Very easy. Run this around the inside of your mouth, against your cheek and gums."

Sullivan ignored the swab. "You know what? How about you guys do your job and stop treating me like a criminal."

"I guess that's a no," Backyard said.

"You guess right."

They could have held him down and swabbed him by force, but they didn't have to, not anymore.

"I need that back." Holly pointed at the evidence bag that held the earring. Sullivan's hand tightened around it; then he tossed it onto the table as though he had emptied his pocket of trash.

Outside the interview room, where they left Sullivan alone, Holly said, "You got enough to keep him here?"

Pradko and Backyard exchanged a look. "No," said Pradko.

"Then cut him loose." When they groaned, she said, "Thanks for the water bottle." She would send it to the lab to be processed for DNA. Technically, they were supposed to get a court order to collect Sullivan's DNA, but they could (as Pradko liked to say) piss backward: get the lab report on Sullivan's sample and use the information to solve the case. If they eventually arrested Sullivan, it would be easy to claim the DNA was inevitable evidence and get a judge to issue a court order after the fact.

"Hey," Backyard said, "you'll never guess where Samantha Lind worked."

"Works," Holly said.

"Listen to our lady dick." Backyard nudged Pradko. "She thinks Lind's still alive."

"Aw, how sweet," Pradko said.

"Go on," Backyard said. "Guess where."

"Frankly," Pradko said, "I look forward to questioning her coworkers."

"Mm-hm."

"A little friendly interrogation."

"A little good cop, bad cop."

"A little show you mine, show me yours."

"Do I *want* to know where she works?" Holly said.

"Get yer glitter on," said Pradko.

SAMANTHA
(RUBY)

She wakes up because he has hauled her upright. She screams, and keeps screaming until she realizes that her screaming fascinates him.

She wants to be asleep again. She was safe when she was asleep.

Something is offered to her in the dark. He raises the narrow, upright object to her face. "You must be thirsty."

Her throat is dry. "Please," she says. Although she can't see his expression, she senses his pleasure. Is this the way? If she does whatever he wants, behaves the way he wants, will he let her go?

He touches the cold glass to her lips. She gulps, then coughs. It is not water. It is sour. It bites.

"I thought you liked champagne." He brings the glass to her mouth again. She drinks. Something thick and light bobs against her lips. She chokes in revulsion. Champagne burns her nose, it burns her eyes. He keeps tipping the glass. The round, fleshy thing tries to get into her mouth.

"It's a strawberry," he says.

Champagne fizzes down her neck. She tries to scoot back from him, her heels scrubbing the dirt, the waistband of her jeans down at her thighs, her legs bound together by the denim.

"I thought you were a lady. A *lovely* lady." He presses the glass to her mouth.

He hasn't touched her, not since he stroked her stomach.

Maybe he won't. Maybe he won't hurt her, if she's good.

The glass clicks against her teeth. Bubbles sting her lips.

"Drink," he says.

"Okay," she says, and does.

GEORGIA
(GIGI)

She comes in again on Monday, having signed up for an extra shift even though Mondays are slow. She covered her Sunday house fees with some left over, but hadn't made her number. This makes her think of cold fried food, and how it used to be that the only way she could hide it from herself was to put it down her throat, how shame grew on her like a waxen second skin. But today, she thinks, will be different.

It is.

When Georgia arrives (early, as penance for prior behavior), Heidi says, "Dale's office, Gigi. Right now."

"Better hustle, little chicken," says Bella. Other than Bella and the stage mom, the dressing room is empty. There are only seven girls on the schedule tonight.

The woman sitting across from Dale at his desk has tired eyes and no makeup. She is white in an unhealthy-looking way, with a yellowish undertone. Georgia's first thought is that this is a new dancer, and she will be asked to show her the ropes. Her second thought is that this woman needs a serious makeover to work here. She's not *not* pretty, but flat, with pencil bones, hair short. Likely to appeal primarily to the pedophiles. Nakita has already cornered that market, though it is possible that this new girl could wrest some regulars away while Nakita is suspended for having hit a client with her shoe ("You can't do that," Dale said. "It makes our girls look bad." Nakita said, "He *came* in his *pants*. I ain't here for that shit").

"Georgia," Dale says. It takes Georgia a moment to notice that he has used her real name. "This is Detective Holly Meylin. She has some questions."

Georgia is glad she's still in her street clothes, yet is conscious of not wearing a bra. She folds her arms. "Why?"

"There's been an accident," Dale says.

"Homicide," says the woman. She doesn't look like police. She looks like an old-fashioned black-and-white photograph of someone who can't smile because she has to sit too still for too long or else she'll blur.

Dale says that Lady Jade is dead and Ruby is missing. He calls them Kimberly and Samantha. "Kimberly's body was found yesterday," the woman says.

Fear creeps through Georgia. She thinks of Bella telling that horrible story about a stripper killer. Georgia says, "Lady Jade OD'd?"

"Drugs weren't the cause of death," Meylin says. "I understand that you were with Kimberly and Samantha that night, before they left the club."

"Not really."

Meylin looks at Dale, who doesn't move. She says, "I want to talk with Georgia alone." This is the only time Georgia has seen Dale on the other end of an order. He says, "I have a duty to my entertainers."

"You have a duty to the law, and I say you need to leave."

"This is my office."

"Thank you for letting me use it while you arrange for the rest of your workers to meet with me."

Dale still doesn't move. He keeps one palm flat against his polished oak desk. His office looks like a rich man's office, with heavy furniture and leather-bound books that she certainly has never seen him reading and were probably bought because they looked nice on a shelf. She spies some classics, a guide to playing chess, an atlas, a *Farmers' Almanac*. She doesn't blame him for wanting to impress. People like a good show. Plus, she is touched that he thinks his dancers are worth impressing. But as Dale hesitates to obey the cop's order, it occurs to Georgia that his fancy office and suits could indicate real, not pretend, wealth. He might be laundering money through the club, not that it's any of her business.

"I would like to review your liquor license," the woman says. "I'd hate to see it revoked."

Dale leaves. Georgia can't quite believe it, nor is she especially happy with this turn of events. She does not love being left alone with police. "I'm sorry for Lady Jade," Georgia says, "but I'm not involved."

"Samantha's car was run off the road," Meylin says. "Kimberly was pulled from the car and killed in a field. We don't know where Samantha is."

Georgia's chest goes oceanic, and she hates Meylin's quiet, direct voice, she hates how her own large breasts rise and fall so visibly with the tide of her breath.

Meylin says, "Don't you want to help find your friend?"

Friend is not a word Georgia would have used, but she sits, her feet tucked beneath the chair, one hiding below the other. She likes Ruby. Everyone does. "I don't know her," Georgia says. "Not really. I didn't know her real name until you told me."

The detective lifts a loose hand, fingers relaxed into their natural curve, almost as if she might whisper a secret instead of being in the business of extracting them. "I just want to know about Saturday night. Your manager says you found Kimberly first."

"Bella did."

"I'll speak with her later. How would you describe Kimberly?"

Georgia blew out a breath. Lady Jade. What a mess. "You mean, how she was that night, or how she is?"

"Start with how she is."

"Kind of girl always getting kicked to the curb. You see these women. They come here, they get in bad with the house—"

"What do you mean?"

"You have to cover fees to work here. Every night, no matter what you make, you pay sixty to the house, forty to the bouncers, twenty to the deejay, twenty to the house mom."

"You pay to work here? One hundred and forty dollars?"

"It's not so bad. Some places make you pay a percentage of your entire haul."

"What do they do, the women who don't cover their fees?"

Georgia looks at her—pale, thin, alien—and is no longer afraid, at least not of her. "You don't want to know."

"Yes, I do."

"They blow the bouncers. They trick themselves out. They go into debt with the house. They disappear." It feels eerily natural, expected almost, that Lady Jade is dead. It is just another way of disappearing. "They leave the club. They don't come back. Not in a good way." Georgia thinks of girls who claim they'll quit and never do, and girls who quit and make you wait, wondering if they'll return. Usually they do, but sometimes they don't and you think, She made it. She is never coming back. And you feel left behind, but glad, a little, too. "Some girls, when they're gone, it's a good thing, because they either stopped stripping or found a better club. Others, you know that wherever they are, it's worse. Lady Jade was like that. Not yet. Not exactly. She was, like, waiting to happen."

"How was she Saturday night?"

"High."

"On what?"

"E, I guess."

"Did she take it or was it put into her drink?"

"That," Georgia says, "was the big question."

"Did you see her drinking with anyone? Backstage?"

"None of us would have put something in her drink."

"Then with customers."

"I didn't see her on the floor much. She has one regular, though. Skinny white guy, scruffy face. He's Sasha's boyfriend."

"Sasha who works here."

"Yeah."

"So he's with Sasha, but got dances from Lady Jade."

Georgia shrugged. "He wears a baseball cap with a Z. I don't know his name. I don't know if he was there Saturday night. It was busy."

"What about Samantha? Anything you can tell me."

"Ruby has a *Rolodex* of regulars."

"Who was she with that night?"

"Bunch of guys. She was up in champagne with one when I went looking for her about Lady Jade."

"Can you tell me his name?"

"It's not like I see credit cards. Or IDs. I don't know their names. First names, sometimes, but no guarantee they're real."

"If we brought you down to the station, would you be able to describe him and Kim's regulars to a sketch artist?"

She is not going to the station. "No."

The detective hands her a business card. "If you think or hear of anything, let me know. Maybe Samantha ran. Maybe she is hiding somewhere . . . or someone has her. We just don't know, and our priority is to find her."

Dale's fish tank burbles in the quiet. Georgia almost gives the business card back but doesn't want to be rude, so slips it into the back pocket of her jeans to throw away later.

"Also"—the detective offers a small Ziploc baggie—"do you recognize this?"

It is a backless pearl earring with a diamond stud. Georgia wouldn't have recognized it if Ruby hadn't worn those earrings constantly, in the way of jewelry never removed, not even to shower or sleep. She tells the cop this, thumbing the pearl through its little sack.

"You're smart, Georgia. Attentive."

This flattery is not designed to go nowhere. "So?"

"I hoped that you could be my CI. My informant. You could watch what happens at the club, and report anything interesting to me."

"You want to make everyone here hate me? Dancers don't snitch on each other."

"Then give me information about men who come here. What if

you could save Samantha's life? No one has to know what you're doing but me."

"Ask someone else to be your CI."

"I want you."

Despite herself, Georgia is pleased. No one has recruited her for anything before. No one asked her to be a stripper. She drove past the Lady a few times on her way somewhere else, noticing the sign advertising amateur night and a cash prize. One day she thought, I could do that. And she needed the money. Simple as that. It makes her impatient, the way people think that a stripper must be some cracked-out whore, like no good woman ever took off her clothes for practical reasons. What is marriage, half the time? Women have sex they don't want in order to keep the peace and avoid the calamity of divorce, yet everyone thinks that's perfectly acceptable. Georgia doesn't tell her cousin about her job because Kaitlyn will assume that something must be wrong with her. Some trauma, some flaw. I could never do that, Kaitlyn would say, her eyes as green as a meadow.

The detective says, "Samantha needs you."

Georgia thinks about the men who empty their wallets, knowing they are being manipulated, letting it happen. She has an image of Samantha folded in half, shrunk small, and shoved to the blind bottom of someone's pocket. Georgia feels guilty, but more than that, scared, because she is not stupid. She doesn't want to be wherever Samantha is. She doesn't want to end up like Lady Jade. "Finding Samantha is your job."

Detective Meylin gives Georgia a smile that is disappointed yet not dismissive, one designed to tempt Georgia to live up to expectations. "Think about it. You have my card."

Later, when Georgia looks at the detective's card again backstage, it is warm and curved to the shape of her butt. She flicks the card into the trash, which bubbles with clear plastic cups. There is a bouquet of flowers, too, that some sad loser brought in for a girl: pink roses, the blossoms like rolled slices of ham. An empty deodorant stick, candy wrappers, spores of baby powder. The card rests on top, name up.

"Will Ruby be okay?" she asked in Dale's office.

The detective held her gaze. "I hope so."

Georgia retrieves the card from the trash. She sticks it into her locker through the air vent.

GEORGIA IS NOT on the schedule until later that week. Meanwhile, she stays close to home, usually venturing only so far as her building's mailroom. She sleeps until midday, waking sometimes on the couch although she knows she fell asleep in bed. Once, her eyes open to the horizon of the living room carpet, its fuzz damp beneath her cheek.

She dresses simply, with UGGs and lip gloss as final touches, and takes her cousin shopping.

"Mani-pedis!" Kaitlyn cries over the blunted song of birds trapped in the mall. The escalator carries Kaitlyn and Georgia up through canola-colored light that brightens Kaitlyn's blond hair. Her eyes are the delicate green of pea shoots.

"Not this time." Georgia leads her instead to the new cell phone store with a dotted map of America on the wall. Georgia is aware that because Kaitlyn is white, everyone in the store thinks they are friends and not cousins. "You need one, too."

"Mom said no. She says cell phones are a fad."

"I'm buying," Georgia says, and sets them both up with Nokia phones and one-year contracts. "A girl's got to be careful."

WHEN GEORGIA ENTERS the dressing room, Bella is holding court, her short, fox-colored hair pulled back tightly. "I'm just saying, *they* didn't believe me when I told them. It's a curse, like Bloody Mary."

"Mirror magic," Rhiannon says. "You look in a mirror and say Bloody Mary's name three times. Then she says, 'I'm here.' Bloody Mary does mirrors. She has nothing to do with car accidents."

"Bitch, please! We are talking about the undead. They can do anything."

"The car's rearview mirror," says Lacey. "Bloody Mary used that."

"Exactly," says Bella.

"You said before that it was a serial killer," says Angel. "Now you're saying it's a ghost."

"Maybe," says Bella, "it's *both*."

"It's not a ghost," Georgia says. "It's someone who comes to the club."

"I bet they find Ruby with her eyes sucked out," Bella says. "Or like, hog-tied in a refrigerator."

The dressing room falls silent.

"Bella," says Georgia, "shut the fuck up."

Bella licks her middle finger and points it straight at Georgia. "You can do your own makeup tonight."

IT'S MIDNIGHT WHEN he slides a hand around Georgia's wrist.

It's the man from champagne, the one who had been with Ruby that night. He is squat, like a bullfrog. One shoulder hunches. He has a gray buzz cut and smells slightly fermented. "Where's Ruby?" he asks.

Georgia has gone still. He holds her wrist firmly, but this is not a big violation of club rules. She has her dress on. It is only her wrist. And this man can't have had anything to do with Lady Jade and Ruby if he just asked where Ruby is. Wouldn't he know the answer, if he'd been the one to attack them?

Or *would* he, if Ruby got away?

"Ruby doesn't work today," Georgia says.

"You'll do." He lets go of her to reach for his wallet.

Below the main stage, he sinks into a leather chair, and it is only moments after the next song starts that he narrates her every move, telling her to turn around, show him this, spread that. Georgia's throat tightens. She understands why Ruby left champagne without a backward glance. Georgia is down to her V-string when he says, "What are you?"

She knows that he means her race, but she says, "Your wildest dream."

"Take it off," he tells her. This is the job. This is what she is here for. Yet this time she doesn't want to. She thinks of Ruby. She thinks of the detective's business card. She thinks of how Lady Jade held Ruby's hand. Georgia thinks that maybe she can do one thing, a small thing, to help. She unhooks her V-string.

He sucks in his breath. She braces herself against the arms of the chair and leans in from the waist, letting her breasts swing slow. "What's your name, baby?"

"Ron."

"Ron what?"

"None of your business. Now turn around."

She does, grateful that the song is almost over. She knows the club's songs by heart. They last only three to four minutes.

He says, "Skunk me."

"Excuse me, what?"

"I want you to fart in my face."

This is the moment when the Gigi that Georgia knows and half loves would demand her twenty, flag a bouncer, and get Ron thrown out. Instead, she glances over her shoulder. Ron holds a hundred-dollar bill folded lengthwise. "I know how it is," he says. "Do it, and this is yours."

She remembers the detective's words: *I hope so.* She thinks of what it might mean to give the detective Ron's full name, if she had it. She says, "How about champagne?" Champagne lasts an hour. She could manage to get the police here within an hour. Then Ron would be their problem.

"I don't want champagne. I'm leaving in five. That's my offer. Do it or don't."

"If I do, will you come back to the club to see me?"

He smiles.

AFTER THE CLUB is closed and the girls dress, groaning about how Dale is sure to go over new safety measures *again* during payout, Georgia tells them what Ron wanted.

"Ew," says Morgan.

"Did you do it?"

"Sick fucking puppy."

"You could not make this shit up."

"Of course she didn't do it."

"I would never, not even for a hundred bucks."

"I would," says Bella.

"Did you, Gigi?"

"Hell no," Georgia lies. "Like I can just do that on command."

SAMANTHA
(RUBY)

This barn must have housed cars or tractors after it stopped holding animals. There are empty milking stalls, and she can smell traces
of motor oil. Whenever long needles of daylight appear between the
boards, she calls for help. She imagines a passerby, a hero who stops
and listens. He follows the sound, his horror growing. That is no animal. He will cut the sharp binding on her wrists. He will have a blanket.
There is no logic to this. No one carries a blanket on a walk. Unless for
a picnic. Yes, he is on a picnic. He will have food, miraculously warm.
Baked chicken in foil, hot milky tea, soft bread and runny butter. And
the blanket. She wants one badly. She keeps calling. Her jeans are still
down at her knees. He will have a picnic blanket and look away as he
gently covers her.

"Ruby."

She swallows her cry. The sky behind him is the color of grapefruit.
The barn door slides across the sky and shuts, clucking as it settles.

She won't look at his face. She won't look in the direction of the milking stalls. Maybe he will drag her there. She is terrified of everything.
She is afraid of him leaving her lying in the open of the barn, she is afraid
of him taking her somewhere else, she is afraid of what he will do, she
is afraid of him forgetting her.

"Please let me go," she says.

"Why?" He sounds genuinely curious.

She has tried appealing to his kindness. She has said she will do whatever he wants. She has promised that she will never tell. She will keep everything a secret. She hasn't reminded him that he could be caught. She is afraid of threatening him, and doesn't want him to think that getting caught will be less likely if she is dead.

He says, "Why should I let you go?"

It is useless but she tries. "I was nice to you."

"Not nice enough."

DETECTIVE VICTOR AMADOR

The office phone on his desk rings. Victor, pencil between his teeth as he types up a report, glances at the caller ID and sees a Florida area code. It's Samantha Lind's mother. "Hey, Hol," he says through clenched teeth, "can you get that?"

Holly, at the adjacent desk, cuts him a look that says she knows why he's asking. "No."

"Come on."

The phone continues to ring.

Victor takes the dimpled pencil from his mouth. "I got this report."

Holly isn't even looking at him anymore. She is typing up her interview notes.

Victor answers. "Detective Victor Amador," he says, very friendly. There is nothing from the other end but a loud swallow. Victor falls down the line into Maryann Lind's grief and fear.

"I thought of something," she says.

"That's good," he says. "Tell me. Anything might help."

"You said you had—have—surveillance."

"That's right. We canvassed the gas stations, convenience stores all along the route Samantha drove to her friend's house. There is a witness, with video. A gas station attendant says she topped up and asked for directions."

"It's been five days."

Holly's eyes are on him again, dark and deep.

"And there is nothing," Samantha's mother says. "You have found nothing."

A cold dread grows inside him, sharp at its bottom, like an icicle. "I promise you, we are putting every available resource into finding your daughter."

Pradko, listening from across the aisle, gives Victor a thumbs-up.

"You need to check the pharmacies. She—" The line muffles, as if the receiver on Maryann Lind's phone has been covered by a palm, or let fall from her chin. Placed, maybe, against the breast. The connection clears. "She wouldn't want you to know, but you need to know. She has a condition. She would never *not* take her pills. I mean, she did once, when she was a teenager, because it was so hard for her. She needed to take them and she didn't *want* to need to, do you understand? Since then, she takes them every day. She promised me. Samantha doesn't lie. Not to me." The woman's voice deteriorates. "So you need to go to all the pharmacies, all of them. I know she will go somewhere to get more pills."

"What kind of condition are we talking about?" Victor listens to her explain that her daughter needs hormones for a syndrome whose name she says too fast and he makes her repeat. He makes affirmative sounds as he scrawls on scrap paper, though he does not fully understand what is being said.

Pradko wheels his chair over. Backyard has stopped eating his lunch. "Thank you, Mrs. Lind. We will check all the pharmacies in the area." He says nothing about the eerie implausibility of Samantha Lind breezing into a pharmacy to fill a prescription. He saw her car. He saw those seat belts. He was there at Kimberly Campana's autopsy. "This is very helpful."

"We're on our way," the woman says, just as she said earlier that day, and the day before, and the day before that. "We got the earliest flight we could. There was a big storm here, in from the sea. The airlines, the planes, we called and we couldn't get through, we said it was an emergency and it was as if I had said nothing. They asked if there had been a death and I said, No. I said, Who are you to even ask that, how dare you."

Victor remembers how he had tried to help Holly when she lost Daniel, how badly that had gone. His palm against her cheek. The way she flinched at his touch. Victor finds his voice and tells Samantha Lind's mother to call him anytime. He regrets it the instant he hangs up.

"What's up?" Pradko says. Holly and Backyard are listening, too. Victor tells them.

"So Lind's what, half man, half woman?" Backyard sucks ketchup off his thumb.

"Freaky," Pradko says.

"I don't think it's like that," Victor says.

"Run by the pharmacies," Holly tells Backyard.

"What makes me your bitch?"

"She and I are lead on this case," Victor reminds him.

"Only because the chief dick wants a woman's velvet-soft touch," says Pradko.

"Lucky me," says Holly.

"Hey," says Backyard, "how about instead, Pradko and I interview more of those dancers?"

"Ladies," Pradko corrects. "*Lovely* ladies."

"You *said* there are a million of them. You *said* it was a metric shit ton of work. Send me over to the club. I am willing"—Backyard lays his wide hand over his heart—"to fall on this sword."

"Pharmacies." Holly smiles, her teeth even and small. "Now."

VICTOR DECIDES TO swing by Amy Tillson's place, a shitbox in Central. The apartment building has little stalactites of concrete and pollution rimming its ledges. An expanse of dirt that frames the building was once a lawn. A few strands of grass grow, overlong, like something that needs tweezing. The low afternoon sun drizzles the courtyard and gets Victor good in the face, washing his vision and warming his mouth as he listens to the *pop* of someone playing handball, the shuffle-shout of kids, a basketball's twangy bounce. When he reaches into his coat pocket for the slip of paper with the right apartment number, his fingers bump against the wad of cash Sergeant Rabideaux left in Victor's car, and his resentful guilt is immediate and pointless. He can't explain to Holly or the other detectives what he is doing with that money without denouncing Rabideaux. Victor might not like him, but he doesn't want to get him fired. Victor stuffs the address back into his pocket alongside the cash and takes the apartment building's middle staircase to the second floor.

Holly flagged Amy Tillson as uncooperative. Holly said that the dancer, whose stage name was Sasha, denied that she was dating anyone. "'And for damn sure,'" Holly echoed Amy Tillson, "'I wouldn't touch someone who'd been with Lady VaJayJay.'"

Samantha Lind sits badly with Victor. The whole thing gives him a heavy feeling: the way this case is going, sightings that turn up nothing, woods searched, bright leaves exhaling duskily underfoot. He is relieved it isn't his task to go from pharmacy to white-lit pharmacy. That cut on Kimberly Campana's foot read as a promise. "That's some wacked-out serial shit," Pradko said.

For Victor, dead is easier than missing. Probably because missing almost always means dead, just not yet. It's the *not-yetness* that gets him. Victor remembers when he first understood what *missing* meant, how, as a child growing up in a nearby town, he heard at school about Jessica Anders: his age, abducted while riding her bike. For days he imagined finding her. He looked for the car described on the news. He sat on the blue rug at school, making his *E.T.* hologram sneakers *scritch*, the Velcro ripped and fastened, and thought maybe Jessica was hiding somewhere, that he would find her in the hollow of a tree, afraid but miraculously safe. She would be hungry, of course, so he carried a box of Sun-Maid raisins in his pocket to lure her ("Víctor," his mother said, extracting a melted mass of raisins and a fuzzed red carton from his freshly laundered corduroys. "¿Otra vez?"). Come out, he would say to Jessica. He stared into faces of strangers. One day he heard, from the back seat of the car, the radio say that police had found her body and her dress, but not the necklace she wore the day she went missing, a gold chain that dangled ballet slippers. "They found her!" he said, only a little disappointed that he hadn't been the one to save her. "They found Jessie!" His mother switched off the radio. She stopped at a stop sign and stayed there. Victor couldn't see her face, only the way her right hand loosely held the wheel, then fell to her knee. In English, she said, "*Body* means dead."

Victor knocks on the door of apartment C. The brassy letter has been shined. Fresh air comes in from an open window at the end of the building hallway. When the door opens, a kid is behind it, her eyes widening, so he gets out his badge fast. "Sorry to bother you," he says, and introduces himself with the smoothest, most trustworthy smile he can muster, though he, too, is unnerved. He didn't know Amy Tillson had a child. It is unsettling to think of strippers as mothers. "Is your mom home?"

The space made by the door narrows. "No. Why?"

"Actually, I'm hoping to talk to her boyfriend."

"Zack?"

"That's right," he says, though the name is news to him. The girl's eyes remind him of Holly's despite differences in shape and color. Holly's gaze is blacker, more slender, but the girl has a similar look. Of not belonging, maybe, or seeing too much. Victor has a high school diploma and a few hours of community college, but Holly has a golden pedigree. "Fucking serious?" he said in their early days in patrol, when he found out where she had gone to college. "You could be anything, a degree like that. How come you're a cop?" She took a drag on her cigarette and tossed it, unfinished, out the patrol car window. She smoked a lot back then. She said, "Because my father wanted me to be a lawyer."

The girl says, "Zack's not here." Her rounded shoulders come up, the gesture of someone remembering to correct her posture. She lets go of the door to fold her arms across her chest. "But he has drugs. You should arrest him."

Victor squints at her in surprise, like she is a sudden, bright light.

"I don't want him around," she says.

Victor scrubs his forehead. "Listen, um." He flips a hand palm up in her direction.

"Melody."

"Melody. I can't just arrest him."

"I am telling you he has drugs. Lots."

"You're a minor. Know what that means?"

"I'm not stupid."

"I get that. But because you're a minor, I can't use what you tell me unless there's another adult present, or unless there's proof."

"The drugs are here," Melody says, "in the refrigerator."

He can see straight through the tiny living room into the kitchen. He can even see the closed fridge. "Maybe, but my hands are tied. I don't have a warrant."

Melody glances down, oddly, at about the height of her knee or hip, as though there were a small child close by. Frowning, Victor says, "Is someone else home with you? Little brother, sister?"

"No."

"Adult?"

"I told you my mom's not here."

He is now thinking domestic abuse, so he says, very low, "If someone is around and you can't say, if you are in danger, nod."

"No! God, what are you, a TV cop? I'm not, like, *SVU*." Melody rolls her eyes. "It's not like that. I just want you to make Zack go away. It's better when it's me and my mom, only us."

The door swings open with a sudden breeze. "Melody, I can't come into your apartment. I can't nose around inside your refrigerator. However," he says slowly, "if I came to the door and *happened* to see, by pure chance, something in plain view, something obviously illegal, well, I would *have* to act on it, and get a search warrant for his arrest."

Melody is silent. From the open window in the building's hallway comes the sound of the handball, far away now, muffled, like popcorn popping in a microwaved bag. The girl regains her posture. Again Victor thinks of Holly, how she upheld her husband's story. Holly had said, voice iron, that their baby's death had been an accident. She accessed the 911 tape. She played it for the room and listened without flinching to the garbled panic of her husband's pleas. "My schedule changed," she told Victor later when they were alone. Her hand edged away from his. "I asked him to take Daniel to daycare before he went to work. Usually, I did that. Daniel fell asleep in the back. Matthew forgot he was there." She used influence to make certain no charges were brought against her husband, then cut the poor bastard out of her life.

Melody turns, strides across the living room into the kitchen, and opens the refrigerator door.

NICK

"One day, I was born. My mom and dad brought me home from the hospital. 'I'm sorry,' the super said. He had a dead cat in his arms. It was their cat. The super found it broken on the sidewalk. No one knew how it happened. But when they opened the apartment it was cold because a window was left open when they went to the hospital. 'How could you do this?' my mom yelled at my dad. 'We don't know who did it,' my dad yelled, 'so stop yelling.' My dad wanted to cremate the cat. He wanted to keep the ashes forever. 'Call the vet,' he said. 'That will be four hundred dollars,' the vet told my mom. 'Four hundred dollars! I spent fifty bucks to have a baby. I'm not spending four hundred on a dead cat. I'm finished with *you*,' she told the vet. 'Let's cremate the cat ourselves,' she told my dad. 'Ha-ha,' he said. Then they remembered me and were happy, it was the best day of their lives. Now we have two dogs. The end."

The boy lowers his handmade book, which has been backed by cardboard dressed in strawberry wallpaper. The adults in the audience sneak looks at the kid's mother, who smirks behind her hand. The children, cross-legged in front of the boy like he's Jesus, are wide-eyed. "What's *cremate*?" says a girl next to Rosie.

"A baby costs way more than fifty bucks," a dad mutters to Nick. "I mean, come on."

"What a special family story," the teacher says when the applause stops. The classroom smells of cookies and glue. It's hot. The ticking radiator is on, though it's barely fall. Nick wishes he had showered.

"My publishing party," Rosie said that morning when he dropped her off at school in the rental car.

"Your what?" He did not feel, nor had felt for some time, wholly awake.

"For my family story. It's Friday. You're supposed to come at two o'clock." When he stared, she said, "Friday is today."

His chest tightened. He had that sick feeling in his bowels he's been getting lately, as if he's about to shit himself.

"I want our own car," Rosie said.

Nick turned off the ignition. "I told you, it's totaled."

"In the accident."

His hands curled around the wheel. "Yes."

"When's Samantha coming back?"

He made himself look at her. Rosie's jaw was set, her mouth pursed, chin made pointy. "Baby, I don't know."

"She said she would come today."

He didn't trust himself to speak. He nodded, then wished he hadn't. It was a stupid thing to do. He had told Rose that there was an accident and Samantha was missing. Rose's face had gotten weird, making him think she didn't understand but didn't know that she didn't. What was he supposed to say? He couldn't explain the whole thing. As it was, several nights since then, she had woken screaming. Nightmares. Something about a monster, calling her. "By your name, Rose?" But she would clamp her mouth shut and roll away to face the wall.

"Bye," Rose said, and darted out the door before he could kiss her goodbye. He had to stop himself from getting out of the car and snatching her, scooping her into his arms, holding her close like the time she fell out of a tree from high up. She had gotten the wind knocked out of her, but nothing broken, not even a scratch. Be normal, he told himself. Normal.

It is Rosie's turn to read. She gets up, thin little legs clad in dark blue jeans with a jeweled heart button. She tugs her ponytail high up onto her head and walks to the center of the space that Cat Boy has vacated. The teacher hands the book to her. Rosie's grip tightens on the book. She stares at her feet, then tips her chin up and clocks the room. Nick knows who she's searching for. The parents, shifting in their pint-sized chairs, begin to know, too. People say "burst into tears" like it's a thing, a—what? lie?—that it's not real, doesn't happen except on TV, but they haven't met Rosie. She can go from zero to hysteria in two seconds flat.

"Hey," Nick says softly, already out of his seat, but she simply opens the book, closes it, wedges it under her arm, and stalks toward him. Her eyes are dry.

"I want to go home," she says.

HE USED TO feel an itchy half pleasure when he pulled into the parking lot of his apartment building. It had been newly renovated when he and Samantha put down their deposit and first and last months' rent. It had been a button factory, part of the early-twentieth-century industrial boom, back when this country still made things. He imagines it: heaps of seashells, four-pointed drills and clamps, multicolored buttons stacked like Necco Wafers, loose disks scattered in constellations, their varied circumferences, matte, gloss. Samantha liked the building's history. She had made a game of finding pretty buttons, some vintage, at garage sales or Goodwill or antiques fairs. She bought them for Rose, who threaded them on a string and believed Samantha when she said that they had been made in their home, their very apartment. Nick remembers Samantha reading a kids' book to Rosie, the girl's cheek against her shoulder: "That is not my button. That button is thin. My button was thick."

The two-bedroom apartment (ground floor, which made it more affordable) was small but had high ceilings and oversized mullioned windows. "This is good," Samantha said when they first saw it, "for now." He didn't know whether she was saying what she meant or what she thought he was thinking. They split a bottle of champagne on their first night there. It was late, almost early morning, his muscles sore from moving furniture all day, before she brought her mouth to his. She tasted like money. He got her long bones between him and pressed her into the sofa, fingers working against her until she came (had she?). Although he knew she didn't like it, he thought it would be okay, this time, because it was a special time, to turn her over beneath him. He slid into her from behind. He was anxious after, but she said it was good, and it didn't occur to him until after she fell asleep and he almost dropped into sleep himself that maybe she had spoken in the same way that she had described the apartment.

"Daddy." Rose is staring. They are in the hallway outside their door, keys in his hand. He thinks of what he was thinking. A clod of shame sits in his gut. "Go on," he says, opening the door, "get inside the house."

"It's not a house," Rose says. "It's an apartment."

ALTHOUGH HE DOES not want to, he asks if he can read her family story. She says no. He thinks of the slim book hidden in her pink back-pack and hates her teacher, hates that Cat Boy got strawberry wallpaper and his daughter got brown pinstripes.

Rose does not want peanut butter crackers. She does not want milk. She sits at the kitchen table and cuts her sparkly nails into the pine.

"Raisins?" he asks.

She drops her jaw and widens her eyes at him in disgust, then goes back to rocking each nail into the wood.

"Doritos?" he says.

"Do we *have* Doritos?"

He opens the cupboards. "Um."

"Samantha would tell me to stop."

He looks over his shoulder at her. The table is flecked with tiny cuts. He thinks the marks should be curved, because a nail is curved, but they are perfectly straight.

He pulls up a chair to sit beside her and puts a hand over hers. "What's wrong?" he asks, though he knows what is wrong. He is a coward to pretend he doesn't know. He thinks of his hand on Samantha's throat. He pulls away from his daughter.

She says, "I want to talk to my mommy."

Jesus Christ. "I don't think that's a good idea, Ro."

Her face goes still. There has been a mistake in what he has said, though he is not sure what. She's got this greedy look to her now, not a bad kind, not like she wants something she shouldn't, but something that she *should*, something that he has not let her want. She says, clearly trying not to make it a question, "But you can call her."

"Yeah, I guess. Your mother, though . . ." *She's a crazy whore* won't fly, so he goes with, "She's got no kind of sense. What do you want her for, Rose? Best let it be."

"I need to tell her something."

"You can tell me."

"No. Her."

Sadness blows through him like dust. "Okay," he says. "Sure."

So he dials Lauri, who still lives in Tennessee, pregnant with yet another half-sibling Rose will never meet, possibly with the same guy she fucked when Nick was still with her, though he has never asked, has not seen her, nor has Rose, since the night he strapped his howling toddler into the car seat and drove north through a blizzard, across two state lines, back to Illinois. The snow came down thick, his windshield wipers caterpillared white. Rose was unrelenting. She screamed for miles. He hadn't packed enough diapers, had packed little of anything, just swept a bunch of crap into an empty cardboard box: baby clothes, toys that later he realized were the ones she liked least, half of a baby monitor. He thinks of the Winnie-the-Pooh lamp that had been his as a child, with its light-up balloons, and wonders whether Lauri trashed it or kept it for her new kids.

Samantha, even from the beginning, insisted that Rosie call her mother at least a few times a year. Samantha said, "She needs to know that she has a mother."

"She has you."

"That's different."

Lauri picks up. "Nick? What the fuck do you want?"

He imagines the conversation as if he were Rosie, listening to his side of it. *It's important. Yeah, I know you know. It's on the news. Everyone knows. I don't want to discuss it. Leave it. Will you—I said leave it. Well, this wasn't my idea. It was Rosie's. Yeah. She wants to talk to you.*

"Then what're you wasting my time for," Lauri says. "Give her the phone."

"Just," he says, "be careful."

"You asshole. She's my daughter. You think I won't be careful? Just because you took her from me doesn't make her any less mine."

"We've been over this."

"I'm hanging up."

"Wait. Wait." He hands the phone to Rosie, who curls both hands around it, her chest rising, her eyes on him wide, almost scared. No, that's not it, he thinks as she brings the receiver to her ear. It is awe, he realizes. She looks touchingly grateful. It is as if by calling Lauri he has wrought magic.

"Mom?" she says.

If he hated to hear her say "mommy" before, he hates this more, that swallowed last syllable. Already he wants to yank the phone back and rip Lauri a new one, what is she saying, that bitch, to make Rose's eyes change as she listens. They go glassy. Her little body hunches. She throws the phone. It hits the floor and yo-yos back on its cord. "Not *her*," she says. "I don't want *her*."

"Oh, Rose." He understands now. His mistake funnels down inside him to a blind point. He doesn't know where everything inside him is supposed to go. He reaches to pull his daughter into his arms.

She hits him. "Not her! Not you!" She is sobbing. "I want my mommy, I want Samantha!"

Nick's hands go to his face. He is not sure what his face is doing beneath his hands. He doesn't think he can ever take his hands away. If he does, his palms will well with phantom buttons. They will spill like large seeds over the floor. He imagines retrieving each button and swallowing them so that they stack inside his throat. He thinks of that boy's story, of coming home with something new and tender, and finding something dead. He imagines taking that stupid fucking cat and burning it: the smell of it, the stink, all over his house.

SAMANTHA

(RUBY)

It must be days since she has taken her pills. This becomes an obsessive thought. At first, that's okay, because the worry is almost normal. It helps to think about taking pills or not taking pills. Then a new worry grows inside her. When will the effects show on her face? Fuzz on her upper lip. Her cheeks. What if he wants her less, and gets rid of her? What if he wants her more? She is too afraid to know which scenario to fear most.

When he comes, she says, "May I have a favor?" He has refused everything, but he likes when she asks. He likes when she is polite. Sometimes women convince their captors to let them go. It has happened. She is sure of it. "May I have a mirror?"

He leaves. He returns with one, and a candle, which he lights as if this is a date. She is conned into sudden hope by the simple fact that he has done something for her. Then she looks into the mirror he holds and sees half of his smile behind it and realizes that he did this for him.

Candlelight licks her face. This is her face. She is here. She is nowhere else. There is nowhere else. The black ridge of her jaw. Her awful eyes. One earlobe has a brown line of dried blood. Her earrings are missing. Her pearl earrings, from her parents. Her mother. She must not think of her mother.

He lowers the mirror and her face is gone. There is only his face.

DETECTIVE HOLLY MEYLIN

"What've you got?" says Holly.

"The pharmacies?" says Pradko. "Zip."

"The Walgreens in Central says Lind usually picks up there right on the dot, the same day her script's filled," says Backyard, "but she hasn't been in to get her refill. She hasn't stopped by any of the other pharmacies in Fremont, either, or any in Glendale or Sunrise Heights."

"Amador's at the courthouse," says Pradko. "He's getting a warrant on Amy Tillson and the dead girl's fuck buddy, who, bless his skeevy heart, is a drug dealer."

"GHB?"

"If we're lucky."

It's early, but the dull gray sky outside the slatted window makes it look later. The office is bigger than it needs to be, with binders of old cases lining the walls. The three detectives sit at the central table, Pradko ripping the rim of his Styrofoam cup and dropping the pieces into its bottom inch of cold coffee. Backyard may or may not have been eating something before Holly turned up; he's stroking the black wool of his goatee with a plastic fork. Lind's Honda Civic has been processed for DNA, and he presents the report: no trace evidence was found that didn't belong to Lind or Campana except a small spot of B positive blood. They ran the blood against the DNA they had grabbed from Nick Sullivan's water bottle during the interview, and it matched, but the car was his, too, so that wasn't proof of anything. Circumstantial evidence at best. The blood could have been left there years ago. "Meanwhile, Missing Persons canvassed," Backyard says. "They distributed flyers, did the K-9 thing, checked the forest preserve and morgues in nearby towns. Nothing. It's been more than a week, so they're shifting resources."

"We got other cases, too," Pradko reminds her. He has a hectic blush high on his cheeks, which could be from annoyance or his eczema. "How long are we gonna be down on this one? Some of us care about our clearance rates."

Backyard mimes jerking off.

"Stats matter," Pradko tells him.

"Wanker," Backyard says.

"What's that? That's not English."

Backyard points the fork at him. "It's *English* English."

"Sounds Black."

"The fuck you know."

The thing about detectives, though Holly does not consider herself part of this phenomenon, is that they love to talk. Backyard and Pradko can disappear into an interview room with a suspect for hours and emerge surprised by the passage of time.

"I pulled phone records on Sullivan," Holly tells them. "The Lovely Lady, too. The 12:07 a.m. call to his residence from the club's office matches the one on the answering machine from Samantha Lind, but Sullivan's records also show an incoming call right after, at 12:15."

"Ooh." Pradko perks up. "Whose number?"

"A burner."

"Fucking prepaids," Backyard says.

On their long list of things cops would love to outlaw, fifty-dollar gas station cell phones, untraceable to their buyers, are pretty high.

"The drug dealer's phone of choice," Pradko says. "Kim Campana's boyfriend is looking good to me."

"I don't know," Backyard says thoughtfully. "There's Sullivan."

"Sullivan's being a pain in the ass," Pradko tells Holly.

"A true hemorrhoid," Backyard agrees.

"He showed up here yesterday when you were out to lunch. He's a wreck."

"Guilt?" Backyard says.

"Boots covered in mud."

Holly says, "Tell me he hasn't been searching for her by himself."

"Oh yeah."

When a family member finds a body, they touch it. They try to save it. They damage evidence even if they don't mean to. Holly would have done it, if she had been the one to smash the window and pull Daniel's body from the baked car seat. She would have known (she could not have helped but know, she was trained to know) that there was nothing she could do. She would have done it anyway. She would have forced her breath into his limp body. He would have felt like he had a fever, and she would have remembered the time he had a febrile seizure and had gone rigid, mouth frothing as he gripped her finger. He's okay, the ER doctor said later, smile easy. This sometimes happened with little children. It was frightening but not serious. Holly was doused with relief. Daniel's gaze had been filmy and unfocused in the ER, but the next morning when he called from his crib, gripping the rail with pudgy hands, his eyes were glossy, his skin fresh. He wore a onesie that her mother, whom Holly had not seen in years, had sent in the mail. It showed a John Deere tractor, its green and yellow bright.

"I hope you shut that shit down," Holly tells Pradko.

"Sure did. He was mad."

"Maybe"—Backyard raises one thick finger—"he wants to *look* like he's looking."

"Your theory is a shitty theory," Pradko says. "Sullivan was miles from the scene, at home, his daughter in the next room—"

"His alibi is a sleeping eight-year-old."

"Neighbors say they didn't see him leave."

"We haven't hit all the neighbors yet."

"You really think he left home that night? With what car? There's only one registered to him, and that was in the ditch."

"I triangulated the call," Holly says.

"That's right, the call," Pradko says. "The *evidence*." This word is pointedly for Backyard, who says, "There *is* evidence: the B positive blood in the car that matches Sullivan's DNA, which he didn't want to give us. Dude is guilty. Plus, you know and I know: it's always the boyfriend."

"Yeah," Pradko says, "the drug-dealing one."

"The call came from within about a three-mile radius of the club," Holly says.

"One day," Pradko says, widening his whey-blue eyes and panning his palm across the air, "cell phone towers will be everywhere. You will be able to ping calls down to a dime on the sidewalk."

"What interests me," Holly says, "is that the call lasted four minutes and thirty-seven seconds."

Slowly, with a glance at Backyard, Pradko says, "Someone picked up and talked."

"See?" Backyard says. "Sullivan's lying."

"Or the answering machine got it and someone left an unusually long message," Holly says. "But that tape's in evidence and only Lind's voice is on there, for that call from the club's office."

"Someone could have erased that second call from the tape," Pradko says grudgingly.

Backyard smiles and leans back, interlacing his fingers over his tight curls. "Sullivan."

Holly's father rescued a one-eyed red-tailed hawk that had been hit by a car near their land. It was summer. Stonecrop rioted in the rock wall. He kept the hawk in the barn and, at first, fed it with a dropper. She had never seen him gentle with anything before. After it healed, the hawk could not be released into the wild. It had imprinted on him. She was young enough then for that to have been the first time she'd heard that word. He said it like she should know it, so she looked it up. There was a list of synonyms in their Merriam-Webster: *stamp, mark, emboss, brand.* He checked out falconry books from the local library, which had once been a settler's stone house. She saw him reading at night after dinner as she cleared the Formica table and brought dishes to her mother, who washed them. She saw him in the field with a leather work glove, launching the bird from his fist. He walked away. The bird always wheeled back, its fingered wings spread wide, and followed him home.

Holly thinks of this as she looks at Backyard, who likes to pick his culprit early. A few weeks after the hawk healed, it wasn't in the barn one Sunday when she and her mother came home from church. "It flew away," her father said from the porch. "Finally." The sun painted the white porch bronze. The skin beneath his chin was slack and softer than she'd ever noticed, the set of his mouth sad. She was sure that if she were to find the bird, she would find it with its neck broken.

Like Backyard, Holly can be ruthless in choosing who committed a crime, but she is not so certain now. She wonders, for a moment, if she would have touched Daniel's body after all, had she been the one who had left him in the car. She wants a cigarette. An unopened pack sits in her coat pocket, hanging on the hook by the door, but she ignores it for now. The Lind case is a better distraction. "Let's bring Sullivan in."

The fact that Sullivan has no friends or family to help with his kid is a red flag that Backyard would be happy to plant in his Sullivan Did It territory. She calls and asks Sullivan to come down to the station. She makes sure it's right around pickup time at the girl's school.

"That's going to be tough," Sullivan says.

"I'm afraid that's the only window I've got," she says. "Unless you can do about twenty minutes later."

"I'd have to bring my daughter."

"No problem." Holly hears the ghost of a downstate drawl in her voice. In college, she worked hard to erase it, but now she lets it seep through when she wants to set people at ease. This works especially well with men. "She can watch cartoons with Gina, our clerk. You remember her. She's good with kids."

He is silent.

"It could help us find Samantha," Holly says.

"All right."

SHE HEADS DOWNSTAIRS past Major Crash, which used to be the accident reconstruction office until the department outgrew it. Now it is a room with a raggedy sofa and a couple of La-Z-Boys for naps. Patrol officers love to say, "Gonna crash in Major Crash," almost as much as they relish calling detectives dicks or naming their masturbating hand Jill because of the letters formed with their open fingers. "Don't look down on them," Amador would say. "Patrol is the heart of any department. You were one of them once." Then he'd catch her look and say, "Maybe not."

Dolan is at his desk in Accident Reconstruction and doesn't glance up when she walks in. He's got his untied sneakers up on the desk and is snapping a rubber band wrapped around his left wrist. There is a smear of cream cheese on his office phone and a chain of paper clips garlanding his desk, but she doesn't say anything, because their rapport is mostly based on her not giving him shit.

"It's there." He wags his crossed feet in the direction of a file on his desk. "Took me a while because I had to consult with the FBI about the paint."

"You found paint transfer?" Holly opens the manila folder. She flips through photographs of the crash and sees Dolan's precise hand-drawn map of the scene, with the road and its locations of debris.

"Don't get too excited. The paint transfer on Lind's bumper is black and"—he rolls his eyes—"the make is General Motors."

Holly gets why black is no good. Too many black cars out there. "What's the problem with GM?"

Dolan rubs his ear rapidly. "I used the skid marks to measure the chassis of the car we're looking for, but GM has several different models that use the same chassis, so I can say that the paint's made by General Motors, but I can narrow it down only to a pool of five models."

"Tire tracks?"

He spreads his hands wide. "Alas."

"Why not?"

"It was a dry night, so no tracks from our mystery car on the shoulder, though I'm inclined to think the driver didn't waver from the road. The rubber residue from his skids is minimal and he barely touched Lind's bumper. He might have been forcing her car where he wanted it to go without actual contact for some time along that road. I got flakes of chrome near the crash site that probably came off his car. No rust, so the culprit's car might be new or well taken care of, but then again the chrome is such a small sample. It could have been from a shiny patch off a beater."

"At least give me a range of models and years."

He uses a pencil to tap the file in her hands. The pencil is spaceship gray with a brassy ferrule. She is sure that it cost more than she would ever spend on a pencil. "All '90s. You're looking for a Cadillac Brougham—nice car, my grandma used to drive one—or an Oldsmobile, a Fleetwood sedan, Buick Roadmaster, or"—he passes a *voilà* hand along the window with its view of a fleet of squad cars—"a Chevy Caprice."

She closes the folder. "Come the fuck on."

"I'm just saying."

"You think it was a cop?"

"I"—he splays a hand over his heart—"am a scientist. I offer facts and hypotheses. I merely observe that GM stopped producing the Caprice for police in '96, but we've got several in the lot, and there's black on every fender and hood. Likely? No. But a Caprice is one of five models you're looking for. Police and military know how to pit maneuver."

"Was it a pit for sure?"

Dolan twirls his fancy pencil. "Let's say that if it wasn't a pit, it was done by someone who was most definitely chill. He didn't bash into the side of the car. He didn't do much more than tap it the right way. The skid marks go back about a mile from the crash, but most of them are from Lind's little red Honda hatchback. The other car glided around her, herding her this way and that. Then he nosed her rear. A 'pit'?" He does air quotes with the hand holding the pencil. "Looks that way to me, but all we know for sure is that the driver ran Lind's Honda off the road and took his sweet time doing it."

SOON BEFORE SULLIVAN is due to arrive at the station, Holly takes a smoke break. She leaves her coat upstairs and never wears a hat; she dislikes anything that confines her head. The wind is thin and sharp. The elms' dry leaves chatter. She lights up, sucking smoke into her grateful lungs, and walks the length of the lot, passing in front of each vehicle's bumper. Although she sees a few dings and scratches, there is no red transfer from Lind's Honda, nothing different from the usual beating a cop car gets.

Her breath blows white. It's cold and it's time, so she flicks the unfinished cigarette to the asphalt and heads inside.

DETECTIVE VICTOR AMADOR

Nick Sullivan looks like shit. Victor sees him in the station's commons as he drags in his sullen prize: handcuffed Zack Antonucci, picked up from a bar after Victor went to the Lovely Lady and told Melody Tillson's mother that he had a warrant for her arrest for possession of GHB with intent to distribute, as well as for endangering a minor. He might let that all slide, though, if she gave up the whereabouts of her boyfriend.

She refused to put her dress on when he showed his badge and made her get off the stage. Amy Tillson ("Call me Sasha," she insisted) had a small, tight body. Her skin was goose-bumped, her nipples hard. The air conditioning, at full blast despite the plummeting temperature outside, churned cold air down on them both. Stage lights painted her body pink and green. He didn't know if she stayed naked to make him desire her or forget her, as though she were a different person in her bare skin than the name on the warrant. Maybe her nakedness was a way to make him not know where to put his eyes. To shame him. Or to make him use her.

But his plan all along had been to use her. "Give me what I want," he said, "and I'll make it all go away."

She stepped close enough that if she breathed deeply, her nipples would graze his jacket. He became aware of how much taller he was.

"You don't know what you want." Her voice sounded like a movie voice. "Let me show you."

"The DCFS will take Melody from you. A drug-dealing stripper mom? You'll never see her again."

Hatred on her face burned, prismatic, through the stage lights. She told him where to find Zack.

Now Zack, the charmer, is whining that the drugs are Amy Tillson's, not his, no one can prove the drugs are his. Victor tells him, as he had many times on the ride to the station, that if Zack knew what was good for him he would shut up.

Nick, out of earshot, is sitting on the bench down the hall, looking at his big hands. His stubble is almost a beard, and his sandy hair is unwashed, spiky with grease. His lips move slightly, like he's whisper-ing to himself. Beyond him, through the glass windows of the office, Victor sees Holly leading Sullivan's daughter to the clerk. Holly touches the girl's shoulder, which slopes beneath the weight of a pink backpack with clip-on toys that sway with the child's every step.

The clerk glances up from her desk and catches Victor's eyes through the window. She says something to Holly. Holly's gaze meets his. She tips her chin: a question. *Who's this?* her expression asks. In answer, his grip on Zack tightens. He is sure that Holly notices; even if she can't see the tension in his hand at this distance, she must read it in the rigid line of his shoulders and know that he has brought in a suspect he wants to interrogate right away. Her gaze flicks to Zack and then back to him. Slightly, she shakes her head, so Victor brings Zack to holding and tells him he'll come for him later.

Back in the commons, Sullivan hasn't moved, but now Holly is next to him on the bench. Victor can't hear her words but knows from her expression that she is speaking softly. Her hand rests on her knee, inches from Sullivan's. As Victor approaches, Holly says to the man, "Let's bring you upstairs," as if upstairs is a place where his wounds will be tenderly cleaned and dressed.

They usher Sullivan into the nicest interview room they've got, with a carpeted floor and a window. "Just a moment, okay?" Holly tells Sullivan, and shuts the man in, leaving her and Victor outside in the hallway.

"Kid fucking gloves," Victor says. "What is this?"

He sees a glint of the old Holly. "A setup."

"For now or later?"

"Later."

"Who's on point, me or you?"

"Me. He likes them sweet. I can be sweet."

He gives her a cynical look that makes her smile. "You got something on him?"

"A phone call." She explains that a second call was placed to Sullivan's residence the night Lind went missing, a call neither mentioned by Sullivan nor recorded on the answering machine.

Victor leans against the locked weapons cabinets. "He hasn't asked for a lawyer?"

"He either thinks he doesn't need one, or he worries he can't afford it and is too proud to ask."

"We should work him over."

"Not now. Not yet."

"We've caught him in a lie we can prove. He's got no representation. He's hiding something, maybe has even tampered with evidence. Look at him." Victor nods at the video feed of Sullivan in the interview room. Sullivan has his head in his hands. "Let's break him open."

"I'd rather break your boy in holding."

"So you *can* be sweet."

"Dead girl's druggie boyfriend, right?"

"Yep."

"Good. We've got time. We play nice with Sullivan, tough with the dealer. The latter's more likely our bad guy, and I don't want the former to get wise and lawyer up."

He nudges her. "You say 'latter' and 'former' like you think I don't know what that means."

"I say it because I know you know."

"Fine, we play things your way."

"Dinosaur bones, Amador."

"Dinosaurs?"

She mimes feathering dust off fossils with a brush. He loves when she is able to forget what happened to her.

"Delicate," she says. "See what shape it takes."

INSIDE SULLIVAN'S INTERVIEW room, seated next to Holly, Victor sets a pad of paper against his crossed knee and takes notes while Holly says that they need to ask about Samantha's relationship with the dead girl. "Were Samantha and Kim Campana friends?"

"I guess." Sullivan rubs his thumb against his palm. "Samantha never mentioned her."

"Does she have other friends from work?"

"She likes Catherine. Catherine's stage name"—Sullivan's lip curls—"is Violet."

"Does Samantha spend time with Catherine outside the club?"

Sullivan hesitates. Victor has seen this before: the look of someone who has let something fall and wonders whether he should try to retrieve it. "No," Sullivan says. "I don't think so. Never."

"Has she spent time with anyone else she met at the club?" Victor says.

"She's not a whore."

Victor stops writing.

Under the table, Holly taps Victor's shoe with hers. "We meant friends," she says. "Does Samantha hang out with other dancers?"

"This job isn't her life," Sullivan says. "She goes in, works her shift, comes home. She isn't part of some stripper sorority, or a fucking naked book club." Sullivan's hands, once loose on the table, have changed. One hand grips the opposing wrist.

"Does she like working at the Lovely Lady?" Victor says.

"Yeah." Sullivan slides his arms off the table and into his lap. "She likes it."

Do *you*? Victor wants to ask. Do you like that she likes it? But Holly glides in and says, "It's possible that Samantha will get in touch with someone from work."

Sullivan has not thought of this, and does not seem to guess that Holly, who speaks so encouragingly, doubts her own words. Sullivan's eyes widen, hopeful. Then his jaw hardens and his expression narrows into resentful hurt. "She wouldn't do that. She'd call me first."

"Speaking of calls," Victor says.

"That little thing." Holly flips a dismissive hand.

"What thing?" Nick says.

"Phone records show that a second call came in on your line just after Samantha left the message saying she was driving Kim Campana home. Do you know anything about that?"

"No."

"You sure?"

"I told you before. I listened to Samantha's message and went back to sleep. I was tired."

From working all day at that job you don't have? Instead of that, Victor says, "You didn't hear the phone ring again?"

Sullivan is quiet. His eyes close for slightly longer than a blink. "Was it Samantha," he says, "who called again?"

"There's a lot we don't know right now," Holly says, which is cop talk for *We're not handing you info we might want to use against you later.*

"You didn't say whether you heard the phone ring or not," Victor says.

Sullivan says, "I don't think so."

"That was a yes-or-no question."

"Back off, Amador," Holly says, and Sullivan shoots her a grateful look.

"I sleep heavy," he says. "I remember, sort of, the phone ringing, but I don't know whether it was the first time or the second time. I don't even know if the memory is real."

"You're saying that maybe you *want* to remember it ringing again," Holly says.

He shrugs.

"Because then you'd have had a second chance to talk with her."

Sullivan tips his head back and looks at the ceiling, a trick Victor learned as a kid, to keep tears from welling out. "It could be," Victor says, "that there's a mistake with the phone records."

Sullivan is clear-eyed now. "Really?"

"Happens all the time," Victor says, which is true if "all the time" means "never." Suspects lie, but detectives do, too, and if Nick's their guy, or if there's another reason he's hiding the truth about the call, there's no reason for him to believe that they can pin him down.

"We're looking into it," Holly says.

Sullivan's got this eager look. Victor can't tell whether it's because the man doesn't want to blame himself for missing a second call, or because he heard it and wants them in the dark. Maybe he believes that this is the lead that will bring his girlfriend back.

Holly wraps things up with the typical pleasantries ("doing all we can"). She opens the door, and for a moment Sullivan doesn't move, like he wants to tell them something more. Then he shoves back from the desk. They hear the thuds of his retreating feet across Homicide's nubby gray carpet.

"What was that all about?" Victor asks Holly.

She pulls something small, fuzzy, and pink from her pocket: a unicorn with a shiny horn. It swings from Holly's finger by its plastic clip. "This."

THE UNICORN CAN wait. First they bring Zack Antonucci out of holding and into an interview box. No cushy niceties for him. They dump him into a hard chair in a tiny room with gym-floor tiles and a ceiling light fixture whose yellow plastic square shows, as though made by woodcut, the black silhouettes of dead bugs.

"That shit's not mine," Zack says. "I told you, I don't even live there."

"We know you don't," Victor says. Holly's staying quiet for this one. She's got a way of making herself easy to ignore. "We don't care about the drugs."

"You don't?"

"Nah." Victor breezes through the Miranda rights, making this seem like a boring formality. When he gets to the part about having a right to an attorney, he says, "You *could* get one, but, Zack, buddy, we should just clear everything up, right now, you and me. I don't want to book you on the drugs, but I will if you won't answer my questions about another matter. Plus, I *can* book you. Your fingerprints are on those vials. So you help me, I help you."

Zack's posture straightens, and although he's all sinew and is probably the type who puts away a quarter pounder and gets the shakes an hour later, starving again, there is a babyish quality to his face. His eyes are a pretty blue, with fair-tipped curled lashes. He has the look of someone who was once a cute kid and has never forgotten it. "Hey, man," Zack says. "You want a one-for-three? No problem. I know guys who deal big. I give you names, you get three busts, and I walk. That's what we're talking about, right? Draw it up. I'll sign, and we're all good."

"Unfortunately, a three-for-one plea deal won't fix your problem. The case I care about isn't with Narcotics. It's Homicide."

"Whoa." Zack's hands, still cuffed, go up, fingers spread like wings. "Not me. You are not looking at *me* for killing someone."

"Your ex-girlfriend was murdered: Kimberly Campana, who worked at the Lovely Lady under the stage name Jolene, then Lady Jade." This is the moment when any thinking individual would say "lawyer" and say it fast, but Zack leaps back into the conversation, erupting with denials. He is so eager to make them believe he had nothing to do with Campana's death that he does not consider, or does not know, that if a lawyer were here he would be told to say nothing at all.

"She was *not* my girlfriend," Zack says. "I heard she died, and that sucks, but I didn't know her."

Holly silently slides him the photo strip of him and Kim Campana.

Zack lets out an aggravated breath. "I fucked her *once*."

Holly writes a note on the pad of paper.

"So what?" Zack says to her. "Doesn't make me a killer."

"I get it," Victor says. "A club like that, it's for women who want to get fucked."

Zack snaps his fingers at him. "Yes."

This is how to make them talk: inhabit a pretense of shared understanding. "She knew why you're there."

"Yeah," Zack says. "Exactly."

"You walk in, you buy a dance. You don't buy a ring and ask her to marry you. If she wants to see you outside the club, that's her choice. She knows the score."

"It was one time. Couple of times. I haven't seen Jolene for weeks."

"Why'd she drop you?"

"Man, I dropped *her*."

"She wasn't any good?"

"Sure. Needy girls, they'll do whatever."

"So what was the problem?"

"No problem. I got bored."

"Bored."

"She tried too hard. Then she got all sad and shit."

"You cut her loose."

"Yeah. I mean, *no*." Zack's eyes widen. "Not, you know, *cut* her. I dumped her. I didn't kill her."

"I am on your side," Victor says, which is cop talk for *I am going to nail you to the wall*. "But it doesn't look good for you. I don't like that you're lying to me."

"I'm not lying!"

"The autopsy report." Victor holds his hand out to Holly. Treating her like his secretary will play well to Zack, who has shown, from how he talked about Kim Campana to the presence of his drugs in Amy Tillson's refrigerator, that he enjoys when women do what men want. Holly passes the file to Victor, who doesn't flip through it but holds it up, flat and closed, in front of Zack's face before he sets it on the table. Victor gives the file an emphatic tap. "Your three-day-old semen was found in her body."

Zack pales. Although Victor did not know the semen was Zack's, and would not have known without a DNA test, he knows now. "You said you hadn't seen her in weeks," Victor says. "We have physical evidence that proves that's not true. You lied."

"I meant *ballpark*." Zack's voice goes high. "I don't keep a diary of who I fuck when."

"Whom," Holly says.

"Also"—Victor raises one finger—"the toxicology report says that her body was flooded with GHB. Funny enough, the GHB in the vials you kept in Amy Tillson's refrigerator has the exact same chemical compound as the GHB we found in Kim's body." That last part is bullshit—if the technology exists to make such a match, Victor has never heard of it—but Zack clearly buys it. His parted mouth is dry, and his gaze flicks around the small room as though tracking a trapped fly.

"You slipped the drug into her drink," Holly says.

"No," Zack says, "I didn't."

"You followed the car. You killed her."

"No."

"Tell us what you did," Victor says. "Tell us where the other girl is, or you're on the hook for a double homicide."

"She *asked* for it."

There is a little leap in Victor's throat: a twinned flicker of excitement and regret. He hadn't thought this interrogation would finish so quickly, that Zack would confess in a matter of minutes. "She made you kill her."

"No, *no*. She asked me for the G. She said she was tired of being broke. That she'd make more money stripping if she was high. She was too ordinary. Like a carpet sample at the hardware store. That's what she said. Fucking weird, right? But honestly? She was not wrong. So why not give her a taste, if she was willing to pay? I was *helping* her. Some of those girls, they look bored out of their minds, like you're nothing, like you're a wallet with a dick. G makes you happy. Happy with whatever someone wants to give you."

Holly says, "That's why it's used for rape."

Zack's mouth lifts in such an exaggerated sneer it is as if he has pressed half his face against a plate of glass. "You think I did her right there in the club, in front of everyone? I was at the bar for at least an hour after I sold Jolene the G. We had a few dances. She didn't eat the

G then, not in front of me. She said she'd save it for later. I stuck around for a while after she went backstage. The bartender will remember me, 'cause I bought him a drink, 'cause I'm a nice guy."

"Clearly," says Holly.

Zack slouches in his seat with the lithe disregard of a teenager. "You ain't got shit."

"I don't?" She says it almost sweetly.

"Nah. I was in the Lady for a while. Plenty people saw me there. Strippers, too. Sasha, Skye, Paris. They're my girls. Ask them, they'll tell you. After, I went to the casino. Guess what? I used my credit card, both places, so there's proof. I came by Sasha's around dawn, even met her kid, Melody. There you go. The whole night. Bam. Alibi. You can't touch me."

Victor and Holly exchange a look. "We'll check this out," Victor says. He thinks of the box of raisins he used to carry with him, as a child, to feed the missing girl. In his mind, the raisins have turned into shriveled beads of rabbit shit. He thinks of Samantha Lind. He thinks that Zack is not lying.

"You do that." Zack's smile is full of straight teeth. Someone, long ago, paid for braces. "I have never been so glad for gambling."

Holly caps her pen.

"You like to gamble?" Zack asks Victor.

"Sure." The answer is automatic, not because it is true but because Victor is washed by a sudden fatigue that casts him back into the habit of playing pals with Zack, though the value of that particular strategy in this interrogation has fallen into doubt. "Who doesn't."

Zack's eyes rest on him, the blue of a flower Victor has seen growing wild along the road. Zack's gaze slides from him to Holly. "Yeah," he says to Victor. "I bet you are the ace in her hole."

Later, Victor thinks of how his chest filled with polar air. His sharp breath was as loud as a crack in a mirror. He thinks of how Holly leaned to speak into his ear, her hair brushing his cheek. He will not remember what she said. He will remember how her words, whatever they were, kept him in his seat, his clenched hand on the table, doing exactly what she wanted him to do, which was nothing.

HOLLY DRIVES. VICTOR watches gray buildings go by. The car dealership with its shark-tooth pennants, a White Castle advertising fried
green beans for fifty-five cents, crummy Victorian homes that make
him want to know what Fremont looked like when they were new. He
imagines neighbors pitching in to help paint the houses' gingerbread
trims. He thinks of people leaning off ladders and glancing into windows to behold someone else's life. Bill Clinton is on the radio, talking
about Kosovo. Victor turns it off.

"So what happened with you and Tess?" Holly says.

"Oh, you know. The job. I work too much." Eastside gives way to Central and big box stores. He closes his eyes. No, Tess said, it's *why* you
work so much. I know why. Do you?

Tess, please.

You don't want to be here. Not with me.

Victor says, "Tell me about the sidewalks in Boston."

Holly says, "You like that Ivy League shit too much."

He opens his eyes. Holly's got her window cracked. Cold air comes
in like water. Her short hair ruffles. She's not looking at him, but her
mouth's not hard. He doesn't say that it's easier to ask about college
because everything else in her past is charged to detonate. He says, "I've
never been there."

"Bricks are usually red, but the sidewalk bricks in Cambridge are
dark blue. It's how they're fired. High temperature, little oxygen."

"Was your dorm made of it?"

"No. It was red. By the river." She cuts him a teasing look. "You would
have loved my dorm's Junior Common Room. A black iron Tudor chandelier. Wainscoting." It's an unfamiliar word. He will look it up later.
"The House Master had paintings on loan from Harvard's art collection.
There was a Whistler on the Common Room wall that went missing. The
House Master freaked the fuck out. Then one day four sophomore
boys came to the dining hall with their pants soaked at the ankles,
faces white. I didn't know what had happened, exactly, but I knew
they did it."

"Did you bust them?"

"They confessed to the House Master. They had taken the painting back to their suite as a prank and propped it up on the toilet tank in their bathroom. Apparently one of them took a big dump and it flooded the toilet. They panicked, wading into the shitty water to rescue the Whistler. Four rich kids couldn't figure out between them how to turn off a toilet."

"What happened to them?"

"Nothing. The Master was relieved that he didn't have to tell the art department he'd lost a multimillion-dollar painting." She pulls into Sullivan's apartment complex. Victor marks two Oldsmobiles in the lot, but one is dark blue and the other is gray, so neither fits the accident reconstructionist's black mystery car. "Sounds fun," he says.

She parks. "You always think things are better than they are."

"What's that supposed to mean?"

She looks at him. He expects her to say something sharp, but she examines him more closely and says, "You're tired."

He shrugs. "I haven't been able to sleep."

"We'll find her," Holly says. "One way or the other."

He knows she means a body. He turns to look out his passenger window at nothing. He wants to go back in time, for her to say, You're tired, and for him to say, I haven't been able to sleep, and for her to say, Why?

He hears her take the keys from the ignition and stuff them into her coat pocket. "I got Sullivan," she says. "You talk with the girl."

"Me?"

"You're good with kids."

Sullivan comes quickly to the door after they knock. He looks at them as if at an incoming storm. Holly gives him an easy smile. "We found something at the station."

Victor holds up the unicorn that Holly stole off Rose Sullivan's backpack. "We think it's your daughter's. She must have dropped it."

The man blinks, uncertain. Maybe he can't recognize the unicorn when it is not attached to the girl. "Rose?" he calls into the darkened recesses of the apartment. There is no answer. He mutters, not quite to Holly and Victor, but as though to an absent fourth person at his threshold, "She won't come to the door anymore."

"Mind if we come in?" Holly says. "Since we're here, I thought you could show me some of Samantha's clothes."

"Her clothes?"

"It could help the investigation."

Which is nonsense, but Sullivan gives a short, soft nod, a duck of the chin. He's pretending to see sense in Holly's words. Victor isn't sure whether it is to seem innocently accommodating, or if this is an ingrained habit of faking comprehension out of fear of looking stupid.

Sullivan gestures them into the apartment, which is nicer than Victor expected, and leads them down a corridor to the bedrooms. Victor follows at first but hangs back when he sees a flower-stenciled door slightly ajar. He knocks quietly as he pushes it open to see Sullivan's daughter sitting in a pink polka-dot beanbag chair, reading a skinny hardback book. "Hey," Victor says. "We found something of yours." He swings the unicorn.

She barely glances up. "Put it on my desk."

"It's pretty. Does it have a name?"

"I have tons. They all have names."

Victor, who knows when he has been scorned, sets the unicorn down. The desk is full of toys: a Tamagotchi, Barbies, slap bracelets, and lots of Beanie Babies, each plush animal still bearing its heart-shaped tag. The toys are neatly arranged behind a row of painted rocks and a piece of smoky green sea glass. Victor says, "My niece collects Beanie Babies." His mother's second cousin's granddaughter, actually, but no need to get complicated. "She has a moose, a monkey, a cow, and this animal that lives in the water but it's not a dolphin or a whale—"

"Manatee."

"That's it. She's got a lobster, too."

She lowers the book to her lap. "The lobster's really rare."

"Which one should I get her for Christmas?"

She looks suspicious again, but Victor is careful to stay where he is by the open door. The bass of Sullivan's voice, words indistinct, comes in from the hallway, accompanied by the mutter of a folding closet door, the scrape of hangers on the rod. Finally, the girl says, "I like the bat."

"The black one with red eyes?"

She is impressed.

"My niece showed me a catalogue." Victor lets his gaze pivot around the room with its pink rosebud wallpaper and white canopy bed. "The bat doesn't seem your style."

She shrugs and goes back to her book.

"What are you reading?"

She heaves an annoyed sigh. "A book."

"Is it good?"

"No."

"Why?"

"It's creepy."

"Creepy how?"

"The princesses go down into the ground. They dance in the dark until their shoes fall off."

"Okay," Victor says. "That is creepy. Why are you reading a creepy book you don't like?"

"I'm not reading it. I'm looking at the pictures. The words are too big."

"My job is to find Samantha," he says. "Do you know that?"

Rose pulls her finger and thumb along the book's red ribbon until she reaches its end and it falls.

"I want to bring her home to you. Then she can read the book, or you can tell her you want a different one."

She won't look at him. She whispers, "Okay."

"Can you help me? I need to ask something about the night she got lost."

"Okay."

"Do you know that she called and left a message?"

"Yes."

"Did you hear the phone ring?"

"I don't know. Maybe."

"Did someone else call? Did you hear the phone ring again?"

Her fingers trace an illustration. It shows a man huddled under a cloak drawn as if transparent, yet with hatched lines suggesting that in the world of the book, his cloak is as opaque as skin. "No," Rose says. "I didn't."

"Did you pick up the phone? Talk with anyone?"

"No."

"Are you sure?"

"Go away."

"Do you like the bat because it can see in the dark?"

She throws the book at him. It hits his kneecap. Pain jolts up his leg.

"Get out of my room," she says, "or I'll tell my daddy you're bothering me."

Hands up, Victor makes his retreat.

HOLLY DRIVES. "HOW'D it go?"

"Don't ask." Outside the passenger window, light drains from the sky. He closes his eyes. "It should have been you."

"What?"

He meant, It should have been you who spoke with her. Already, though, he is falling asleep. His lost nights have caught up with him. He feels that he is not in a car but on the water. He can't explain to Holly, can't finish his sentence, and is finally, just before true sleep, grateful that he can't. If he were to finish his words, it would be differently and in a way she would never forgive. It should have been you. I should be with you.

It is better not to say. He sleeps. He dreams of manatees that sailors once believed were mermaids, of colonies of bats driven underground, of clothes slipping off hangers.

SAMANTHA
(RUBY)

He comes and goes. He brings champagne and strawberries. Her head aches. She is always hungry, always thirsty, always drunk. She needs water. She longs for soup: its salty glimmer of oil, corrugated bits of celery, pasta letters to nudge into simple words.

But you like this, he says, and makes her drink the champagne. She does what he asks until he grows bored and leaves.

After the door shuts, she becomes terrified at having bored him. Maybe he will never come back. She should play his game. She *would*, if she knew the rules, if she could tell whether obedience or disobedience is her best chance for survival. He seems to like that she doesn't know, and that is good, at first, because her confusion entertains him, and if she doesn't entertain him, he will never return and she will starve and die. But when he returns to the barn, she can never behave exactly how he wants. Her confusion has become tiresome. He doesn't like stupid girls. It is impossible. If she does what he wants, he is disappointed. If she disobeys, she will be punished. There is no way to please him because his greatest pleasure comes from there being no way.

How could she not have realized what he truly was from the moment she met him? She is to blame.

He must have pulled her unconscious body from the wreck. Her head must have struck the steering wheel. She remembers opening her eyes in the trunk of his car. The memory is a fracture in time.

Strands of her hair might be in the trunk. Her blood? She should have spat into the trunk's carpet. Her DNA everywhere. She should have quit her job. She should have known.

She rocks onto her side. She flips onto her belly and immediately vomits a thin gruel. The back of her throat burns. Her bound hands bob painfully against the small of her back. Despair makes her knees bunch up beneath her and push forward, chest and face against the dirt. She shoves her way toward the barn door. She tries to kick out of her jeans, can't, and is disgusted with how grateful she is to keep the clothing on even though the denim membrane binding her legs makes it almost impossible to flop across the dirt.

Her face is wet when she reaches the door. She rocks onto her back again and chokes when her weight thumps down onto her bound arms. Pressing against the barn door, she negotiates herself into a sitting position, then onto her knees. She lifts her face toward the door's long latch. Like a sheep, she nudges at it with her nose, her cheek. The latch starts to lift. Her pulse is wild.

The latch meets resistance. She nudges, hurting her face against the wood, thrusting up, but the latch won't give. Finally, she hits the latch so hard with her cheekbone that she hears a metallic thump on the other side of the door.

A padlock.

The mice in the barn listen as she pushes her face against the door again and again. They rustle as needles of sunlight between the boards melt into the dark.

HIM

She is no longer fresh. This is the problem. It is always the problem.

He thinks about Ruby all day. Same memories, same images. The other girl was forgettable, a mere pawn, but Ruby is special. He likes living inside her. He had been good to her and she had disrespected him and now she was his. His pleasure at this, though, has begun to stale. Already he watches other girls, wondering which one next. He rubs his finger and thumb over the pearl earring in his pocket. He should make himself wait, but he knows he won't.

He remembers easing up behind her car, brights on. He flicked them off, for fun. He flicked them on. He got close. She swerved. When he finally nosed her bumper in just the right way to send her off the road, he was almost disappointed.

That black car, he thinks. Ever since the night he took Ruby, the car has sat near the old barn on a plot of land he owns. He has been using a different car. He really liked his black one, but it wasn't safe to drive, not even to keep. He had better get rid of it.

DETECTIVE VICTOR AMADOR

Central's jumping. Victor can't take a call about a torched vehicle on the border of his sector and Eastside, because he's busy pulling over a car for blowing a stop sign when, lo and behold, the scared kid behind the wheel coughs up a grinder and a puny bag of weed. He looks barely out of high school.

"Listen, son," Victor says.

"Frankie. I mean, Frank Miller. Sir."

"Am I going to find anything else you shouldn't have, Frankie?"

"No, sir."

Victor calls for backup. He is going to have to search the whole car.

"You gonna arrest me?" Frankie says when the search is done, and nothing else turns up. Victor looks over at Hutchins, his backup. Hutchins shrugs with his eyes lightly closed, mouth pouched.

"You were honest," Victor decides as he writes the traffic ticket. He feels good about it. Noble. He rips off the ticket and passes it through the open window. "Honesty counts." He holds on to the grinder and weed.

"Gonna keep it?" Hutchins asks Victor after the kid, spluttering his thanks, drives off.

"Nah." Victor chucks the stuff into a nearby dumpster. Earlier, sometime around noon, he woke up in his empty apartment on his day off and microwaved a Cup Noodles soup. As he peeled off the seal and the broth heated his face, he remembered the ride home next to Holly, how tired he had been, how glad to close his eyes beside her. He didn't want to think about Holly, so he thought about the Lind case, but then he didn't want to think about the Lind case because it yielded so little. The silence of his apartment grew antagonistic. He called in and signed up for a patrol shift.

"Long day?" Hutchins says.

Long week. Long year. Victor blows into his cupped hands. He should have brought gloves. "It's fine."

"You look like hell."

"Hey, thanks."

"It's that stripper case."

"I can't talk about that."

"What's with all the overtime? Take a break, Vic. You keep pushing yourself, you're gonna fuck up."

Victor stuffs his hands into his coat pockets. His fingers nudge the wad of cash he's kept—intact, not a single bill spent—ever since Rabideaux put it in his car. The goodness he felt when he watched Frankie drive off is gone.

AFTER HIS SHIFT, Victor takes Hutchins's advice. He chucks his coat into a corner of his apartment. He gets some solid sleep, then goes to the community gym. Victor doesn't mind the odd hours of his job. On wakeful nights, he gets the sense that he is peeking under a rock, seeing what few see. Daylight makes him feel out of place in a restful way: there is no one at the gym, which is quiet but for a muttering television and the clank of his weights dropped into place. He is supposed to visit his mother, who lives in the house where he grew up, about twenty minutes from Fremont, in a town that has risen in prosperity since his childhood, with cafés and restaurants popping up around the train station that brings commuters to Chicago. In winter, kids play ice hockey on the local pond. His mother claims not to miss anything about Cuba except the way she visited friends, which was to walk through their gardens and into their houses, without knocking, and to sit down at a kitchen table as if she were in her own home. That is not the way here, she says, and anyway there are no friends.

The town where he was born, Pinar del Río, has a nice name, but Victor doesn't remember pine trees or a river. He remembers the smell of cut wood in his grandfather's carpentry workshop, a business his grandfather owned until it became nationalized and he was made an employee of the state. When Victor goes to Home Depot, he likes to walk into the lumber department and breathe deep. A lot of Cuba was still underdeveloped, and his grandfather didn't have a phone line, so Victor's mother wrote letters from Illinois. When his grandfather died, his mother did not learn about it until long after.

As Victor towels off at the gym, he thinks about driving to his mother's house. He imagines passing by the Morton Arboretum, where he went on class field trips growing up. He and his buddies hid from the teacher in the tallgrass prairie. Victor imagines driving past the enormous white balloon of his hometown's water tower and the town hall's Vietnam War memorial decorated with the shells of empty helmets he used to stick his head under for fun. If he walked through his mother's door with that cash in his coat pocket, her welcome would fade into worry. She would know from his face that something was wrong.

He drops a few coins into the gym's pay phone and tells her he can't come today. He hangs up, relieved until he realizes that now he has a whole empty day to fill.

There is a new shooting range in Fremont, not far from the casino, that he's been wanting to try. He is not the best shot, but he loves his guns: his service weapon, a rifle, a Sig Sauer, and a .45, his favorite of the four. It is a 1911, a nice pistol, pure pleasure to shoot. He had Tess try the 1911 the time he took her shooting. It has a deep voice and a cozy grip he enjoyed shaping her hands around. "Keep your front sight clear as you aim. Form your *E*. Little more forward, in from your waist." He gently pushed her thin shoulder blades.

After she fired, she hastily set down the gun, safety off. He didn't correct her although he should have. "Look at you!" he said. "See that hole?" He pointed at the paper target's abdomen. "He'll bleed slow, but you definitely killed him."

"I don't like it," she said.

The old guy behind the register—short, with a yellow bushy mustache—asks for ID. Victor gives him his commission card, and the man's expression changes as he registers that Victor's a cop. "We got a discount for you."

"No, I'm good, thanks."

"You got eyes and ears?"

Victor does. He puts on the protection before he enters the range. Inside, the air is stuffy. Victor takes his time loading his weapons. He doesn't use his duty rounds. His department gets free ammo from UPS whenever one of their packages bursts open, so he has extra 9mms to load into the magazine. Victor's wary of free, though. He doesn't want any dinged-up bullets in his piece. He checks the primer of each bullet as he loads. Some guys are cheap with their ammo. Bill Billingsley collects his casings and primes them again himself. His lips are purple from lead poisoning.

Victor shoots until the target paper has termite holes. Casings pop off around him and plink to the floor. Vaguely, in his periphery, he sees the old man sweeping them up. Victor heels them aside. Each time he shoots it's a surprise, but then, it should be. He remembers the last time he made Tess orgasm. She came against his mouth.

She broke up with him after the department's Fourth of July family barbecue. It was the first time she met the people he worked with— Backyard with his wife and kids, Pradko and his surprisingly hot sister. Holly. At the party, Victor thought Tess was quiet because she was bored. She slammed the car door. I am tired, she said, of second place.

Victor imagines going to Holly and explaining the cash from the crime scene. His chest is leaping when he empties out, and although he washes his hands with cold water after he packs away his guns and exits the shooting hall for the cottony quiet of the gun store, he is hot, irritated. He has gone through everything but his duty rounds. When he approaches the counter to buy more bullets, he doesn't reach for his wallet. He pulls the wad of cash from his pocket and, defiantly, unwraps its rubber band.

The man shakes his head. He slides the box of ammo toward Victor. "On the house."

Startled, Victor looks at the cash held in his outstretched fingers.

The man refuses to take it. "It's a thank-you," he says. "For your service."

VICTOR DECIDES TO take the problem to Backyard, who's sitting next to Pradko in Homicide, typing up a report. Victor asks to speak to Backyard in private.

"Gonna confess your love, Vic?" Pradko's blue eyes are fake sweet. "Don't mind me, I won't judge."

Backyard pushes up from his squeaky-wheeled seat and leads the way to the stairwell.

"Invite me to the wedding!" Pradko calls after them.

The stairwell stinks of cigarettes. Victor shows Backyard the cash and explains. "I didn't steal it. Rabideaux put it in my car so we'd be in on it together. So I wouldn't tell."

"Take this to IA, not me."

"Internal Affairs—"

"—would have your ass. You held on to that cash for too long."

"I haven't spent any of it. It's all there."

"Who will confirm that? The dead girl? The missing girl?"

Echoes of Backyard's words bounce up and down the steps. Victor says, "I am not afraid of IA."

Backyard slouches against the shut stairwell door. His weary annoyance shows that he gets it: Victor's record is clean, and he's doing the right thing. Whatever happens to him won't be the end of his career. It might not even be the end of Rabideaux's, but—

"Deuce'll hate you forever," Backyard says.

"So what if he hates me."

"You want to explain your loyalty, then, to a shit sergeant who stole money from a crime scene?"

"I felt sorry for him."

"You better feel sorry for your own self. I assume Meylin doesn't know about this. She's gonna flip. She's gonna make your balls into a little fuzzy purse and keep hankies in it for when your mom cries about how she'll never have grandchildren."

Victor lets out a slow breath.

"We'll keep this between us," Backyard decides. "I'll put the cash in evidence and say it turned up during a more careful sweep of the car."

"What about the rest of it?"

"Gone. Deuce gambles." Backyard must see Victor's dissatisfaction. "Do you want him suspended?"

"No," Victor says. Then he shakes his head no. He says no again.

"Then you have got to let it go."

When they return to the office, Holly has arrived. She holds a stack of papers she divides, dropping half on his desk: reports from interviews with Lind's neighbors. He pulls up a chair and finds that she has set a cup of takeout coffee on his desk. It is so hot it scalds his tongue. He sips carefully, enjoying its familiar bitterness and the heat in his chest as he and Holly sit in silence, working side by side.

GEORGIA
(GIGI)

"I can't come in today," Georgia says.

"Gigi." The stage mom, Heidi, is chewing gum. Georgia can hear it over the phone. "This is the second time this month."

"My mom's sick. Dale knows I've got to take care of her when she needs me."

"Dale's a softie."

"How about *you* change my dying mother's diapers."

"Just doing my job. Unlike some people. It's a Tuesday. We need you."

"I'll work tonight," Georgia says, "if Dale says I have to."

After Heidi hangs up, Georgia calls her cousin's cell phone. "Time for those mani-pedis."

It is not that she hates work, Georgia thinks as she pulls into the mall's parking lot later that afternoon. Once she enters the club, it's okay, or at least she has committed to believing it is okay.

Except not always. Sometimes when the sky dims and there is less of the day than there was, Georgia can't make herself go to work even though she wants the money. Nothing is going to happen, she used to tell herself. But Lady Jade is dead and Ruby is gone. Things *do* happen at the club. They happen all the time. Each night is a peculiar museum of things, some easy to understand, like when that guy breathed on her and she couldn't get him thrown out because technically he hadn't touched her. Other things are harder. Once, a woman with TV-mom hair and enormous glasses asked for a dance. "I do sex work, too," the woman said breezily, which startled Georgia. That was not how she thought of what she did. When Georgia unhooked her V-string, the woman said, "What do you think about when you're doing this?"

Sometimes Georgia just doesn't want to deal. "Mental Health Day," Morgan called it.

"Live in Your PJs and Masturbate While Watching *Friends* Day," Bella said.

Morgan stared.

"Girl," Bella said, "you know you do."

"Joey, Chandler, or Ross?" Georgia asked.

"Rachel, duh."

Kaitlyn is waiting outside the mall's nail salon, which is empty of other customers. Her cousin bounces on the balls of her feet. People always think Georgia is older than her by far more than just two years. Kaitlyn has solid limbs that make her look prairie born. Her round eyes are lucid green with pale fermata brows, her skin commercial clear.

"Georgie!" Kaitlyn squeezes her. "I love my new phone. Did you know you can play games on it? I am *addicted* to Snake."

The four nail technicians look at them and then at each other. The technicians converse in their language, and it is decided among them who will take which one. Georgia's technician looks a little like Nakita from the club, face smoothly oval, though Nakita's eyes, which are true black, darker than Georgia's, black as a clarinet, are large and round. This woman's eyes are thin, brows feathery. Her lower lip has a vertical crease deep enough to be a cut.

Georgia asks for the pedicure first. The woman's black ponytail falls over her shoulder as she shakes salts into the foot tub.

Georgia's feet are a mess. It is a gross satisfaction to watch the razor take curls of dead skin off her calloused soles. Kaitlyn, next to her, falls asleep in her chair.

"Ten-minute massage?"

Georgia agrees. After ten minutes she will be offered another ten, and she will accept. Later, she will give a fifty percent tip counted in crinkled ones. She wonders what the woman thinks of her, of her feet, this job, this mall, this town, this life. What do you think about when you're doing this?

Georgia knows not to ask. It would be better to fall asleep like Kaitlyn, or pretend, so she does.

IN THE FOOD court, Kaitlyn picks her Cinnabon to pieces and complains about her roommate, her classes. "Lydia had her boyfriend sleep over, and they were totally boning in the top bunk. Hey, assholes: *I hear you*. The bed was literally shaking. Our RA is a Classics major, and I swear she must have a statue of Athena up her butt, she is so uptight. She's always yelling at us to turn down our stereo or nagging us to come to her precious social events, which to be honest I do for the M&M cookies. Meanwhile, my English prof assigned all this boring nineteenth-century crap I can't get through without falling asleep. Oh, and I'm getting a D in bio. College sucks!"

Georgia empties a brown packet of sugar into her iced tea and stirs with the straw. Her heart feels taut, like a blown-up balloon. "You don't know how lucky you are."

"Oh my God, Georgie, I'm sorry. I didn't mean to sound ungrateful."

"It's okay."

"College doesn't *suck*. It's just hard, you know?"

"Sounds pretty great to me."

"Why don't you apply?" Kaitlyn, trying hard now to be tactful, avoids mentioning Georgia's mother. "Nothing is standing in your way anymore."

"I can't pay for college," Georgia says, which isn't true. She has saved up enough that she could pay for two years of tuition, which would be a start. She has the money. What she doesn't have is courage. She has fallen out of the habit of thinking she is the sort of person who can go to college. How would it be to open rejection letters alone? She imagines a stack of them, each envelope as thin as an electricity bill.

Kaitlyn says, "I know things have been tough."

"I don't want to talk about it."

"You should come over to Mom and Dad's. They miss you."

"Liar."

"*I* miss you."

"You see me."

"Will your restaurant need holiday help? I've got a month off for winter break."

"Sorry," Georgia says. "We're not hiring." *Waitress* is a common stripper lie. It explains the cash—all those one-dollar bills—and late hours, and since Georgia actually had waitressed when her mother got sick, it's easy enough to pretend that nothing has changed.

"Oh, okay," Kaitlyn says. "I just thought it'd be fun to work together."

Georgia takes a long pull on her drink. Across the way, a husky blond guy waiting in line at California Pizza Kitchen meets her gaze and eyes her appreciatively. If they were at the Lady, he would buy a dance, or more. Sometimes when she isn't at the club and a man evaluates her like this, she feels that he is getting away with something. She should be paid for the way he's looking at her.

Kaitlyn follows Georgia's gaze. "He's staring," Kaitlyn whispers, as if the man might overhear.

"Yeah."

Kaitlyn dusts her pink hands, relaxing into her seat. "Don't take it personally. People stare because they can't figure you out. You know, how much Black you are."

That's not why he's staring—at least, until this moment Georgia hadn't thought that was why—but Kaitlyn now has her full attention. Georgia bends her straw in half. "Their problem," she finally says.

"How does it feel," Kaitlyn says, "to be a problem?"

"Excuse me, what?"

"I mean, it's a question. Not *my* question. I read it. In a book for class."

Georgia, filled with swampy anger, sets her cup down. As she walks away, she hears, over the noise of the food court, Kaitlyn calling for her to come back. "Can we talk? Georgie, come *on*! I drove all the way from Chicago to see you!"

Kaitlyn has always been a coward. She doesn't follow. Georgia wants her to follow, doesn't want her to follow. She wants to unleash her anger at Kaitlyn. She wants to protect her from it. What kind of books has Kaitlyn been reading, that they made her think she could ask Georgia a question like that? Georgia isn't a problem. Kaitlyn is the problem. But Kaitlyn is also Georgia's only real family.

As she moves through the mall, Georgia's anger gives way to fatigue. If she got angry about everything that bothered her, she'd be angry all the time. She looks into glossy stores where the hands of dressed mannequins are lifted as if testing the wind. She passes the slow zippers of escalators, a fountain with brick planters. A Nordstrom lies not far ahead, one of the four anchor department stores set at opposing ends of the mall. The store's quiet softens the threshold like cotton batting. She goes inside.

Most of what she knows about her birth she knows from Kaitlyn, whose parents told her. Georgia tries to imagine the story from her mother's perspective. Her mother's breasts must have grown fuller, intentional, her belly a pushy curve. The taste of pineapple became an unparalleled pleasure, Del Monte rings forked golden and dripping from the can. They were the very pineapple rings that Georgia's white grandmother, according to Kaitlyn, toothpicked to an Easter ham and arranged, like so many eyes, into an Argus of an upside-down cake. Georgia imagines her mother opening a cupboard, standing on tiptoe to reach a can of pineapple, her blouse untucking from her skirt, waistband settling lower. Georgia's grandmother, standing at the gas-lit stove as coffee spat in the percolator, suddenly realized what her daughter had been up to.

She is our daughter, they said. The white parents withdrew their white daughter from the all-girls private high school she had attended since kindergarten. They purchased a crib. They drove her to doctor's visits. They fed her the best portions of every meal.

They questioned her. Georgia's mother, however, was a woman who, later, would put Scotch tape on her daughter's mouth for too much talking. She prized quiet. She kept her secrets until the baby made them impossible to keep.

When Georgia was born, she was ruddy from the long labor, face squashed. A fighter, her grandfather said, and she was named after him. Born with a cap of brown curls, Georgia had eyes the murky blue of all white baby eyes. The blue eventually became brown, and no one was surprised. Her grandmother's eyes were brown. Her grandmother, Georgia imagines, was pleased then. Yet the baby's skin, though fair after the redness faded, darkened in time. The sun, they said. Olive skin, they said. The curls grew unruly. They frizzed. It was around when Georgia could walk that her grandfather looked hard at his granddaughter's face.

If this had been a fairy tale, Georgia and her mother would have wandered after being cast out. Georgia would have become the god-child of birds. She would have lived in a cottage where her mother spun carded cat hair into thread of gold while Georgia, now a precocious child, crafted dollhouse furniture for the royal family. She would have pricked her finger on a poisoned miniature upholstery tack and slept through adolescence. She would wake in a palace so perfect she believed that it was her own dollhouse design, and would have grown tiny in sleep to fit inside a doll-sized dream.

Instead they went to her mother's older sister's home. Until you get on your feet, her aunt Carol said. Georgia remembers playing with Kaitlyn's toys. She remembers a Fisher-Price View-Master: a shark, clownfish among coral, the many white disks each ringed by shadowy squares. A trundle bed slid out from under Kaitlyn's. You were the best sleepover, Kaitlyn said once. I didn't want it to end. But Georgia's mother found a second job at the high school cafeteria, and they moved out.

Her mother met Georgia's father at Sears, where she worked after school and on weekends and holidays. Her mother started as an attendant in the women's dressing room, handing out numbered tags. Later, she manned the register, a gray metal block the size of a small dog and studded with buttons. Georgia isn't sure exactly how her mother met her father, but the stockroom, where all employees began their day by punching their cards, is the most likely place, if not in the cafeteria during a fifteen-minute Coke break.

Why didn't he marry you? Georgia doesn't know how old she was when she asked this, but she must have been little, because the memory of the conversation is faded and she thinks her intensely private mother wouldn't have replied if she hadn't believed that Georgia would forget the answer.

He didn't know about you, her mother said.

You can tell him now.

I don't know where he is. He left.

Why?

I said something he didn't like.

What?

I said that my parents would never accept him.

But he wouldn't have left, Georgia said, if he knew about me. Right?

It's easier like this, her mother said. Just you and me.

Georgia didn't see what was so easy about it, but her mother turned on the sewing machine and reached into her pile of strangers' clothes. Go play, her mother said, and began to hem a pair of trousers.

Georgia's cell phone beeps. Kaitlyn has sent an SMS. *R u mad?*

No, Georgia texts back. It's a lie, but she isn't sure what she would say even if she had the patience to multi-tap each button to get the right letter for each word. *Love u,* she taps, which is true. *BRB.*

She walks into the housewares section of Nordstrom and looks up at a rack of copper pots and pans hung so that each nearly eclipses the other. There are nice chef knives, very sharp. She touches a butcher block and thinks of Lady Jade. She thinks of Ruby. She steps back so suddenly that her heel comes down on someone, who yelps.

It is Bella, hissing through her teeth in pain. She wears no makeup and her freckles are wild. It looks like her face has been sprayed with dirt. Her hair is slightly damp, as though she just washed it and walked out the door. It is unbrushed, downy where it has dried. Bella says, "Aren't you on the schedule?"

Shit. "Aren't *you*?"

"Nope. Day off." Bella scans the department store. "Picking up something for your mom?"

What Georgia likes about lying is that it is private. It comes from within her. She is disconcerted to have a lie offhandedly bounce her way, hollow and light, a Ping-Pong ball she can lob right back. "Yes," Georgia says. "That's right. I am."

"You broke my fucking foot."

"Oh."

"Oh? How about, 'Sorry, Bella. Thanks, Bella. You're the crème de la crème, Bella.'"

"I gotta go."

"I'm picking up something, too. For a friend's wedding shower." Bella mimes shooting herself in the head. "She wants ebelskiver."

"Ebel-what?"

"I should get her a vibrator instead."

"In housewares?"

"Way more useful."

"I better go find what my mom wants."

Not looking at Georgia but off into the middle distance, Bella sketches a round shape in the air. "Ebelskiver is a pancake. But in a ball. And Danish. You need a special pan. Help me find it, and I won't bust your lying truant ass to Dale."

"Okay," says Georgia.

"Okay," says Bella, and they split off in different directions.

Surveying an array of gravy boats, some gilded, one shaped like a blue pig, Georgia wonders whether she has agreed to a one-time deal or if Bella will hold this over her forever.

Where *was* this thing? Georgia has no clue what the pan even looks like.

She never met her mother's parents. She met her father's mother when she was ten. Her mother purchased Greyhound tickets to North Carolina. Georgia remembers being embarrassed of her mother's wallet, not for its style—mauve patent leather with a gold-button snap—but for its fatness. It was so stuffed with coupons that it could not close. The motel smelled like cigarettes and chlorine and had beds that vibrated for a quarter.

Will you tell me about my father? she asked. Her mother said what she always said, save that one time in the sewing room: When you're older. This felt deeply unfair, tantamount to a trick, because why were they in North Carolina if not because of her father, even if they weren't there to see him? He has a new family now, was all her mother would say. Then why are we here? Georgia asked.

His mother wants to meet you.

Georgia doesn't remember who drove them to her grandmother's house, but she can hear the song with her name in it on the car radio. The words are sweet but sad. *Other arms reach out to me. Other eyes smile tenderly. Still in peaceful dreams I see the road leads back to you.*

Georgia's grandmother had no gray in her careful hair. She had slips of eyes, habitually narrowed, her skin the brown of an autumn leaf Georgia had glued into her science notebook. Hawthorn, she thought. Later, after she and her mother returned to Illinois, she opened her notebook to check. The dry leaf had crumbled. Flakes sifted onto her lap as she traced the raised squiggle of glue. If her grandmother knew about her existence, then her father must, too, which made his absence have a different meaning. "What have you been doing to that poor child?" her grandmother had said to her mother. "Look at her edges." Georgia, not surreptitiously enough, had touched her elbows, which seemed the edges of herself. Her grandmother laughed. "I'm going to make you a plate. Go to the pantry and choose something you like." Georgia stepped inside the pantry, pulled the bare lightbulb's string, and closed the door behind her. The shelves were lined with waxed red paper and castled with cans. There were rows of homemade jarred pickles and preserves, all kinds of vegetables and fruits, gleaming like stained glass windows.

Georgia, whose mother considered a grilled Kraft cheese sandwich a solid meal, ate the plate clean: seasoned chicken so tender it fell off the bone, fluffy rice, and pickled green tomatoes Georgia hadn't known were tomatoes but had chosen from the pantry because they were pretty, as bright as candy. They were sour and tart and sweet.

When she left North Carolina, her grandmother gave her a quarter. "In the Depression," she said, "babies slept in shoe boxes. Men played poker for turkey feathers, since there was nothing to gamble. My mother worked in an underwear factory. Bloomers. Cleaned houses, too. When I was younger than you, she sent me with a quarter to buy a soup bone. I could make a soup that would last the week. One quarter: enough for a whole week."

"But," Georgia said, thinking of the motel room's vibrating beds, "a quarter isn't worth much now."

Her grandmother pulled herself up to her full height. "Shows what you know."

Georgia's memory of the trip is like a View-Master disk, a sequence of images with no segue. She and her mother went to her grandmother's church. Georgia hadn't considered what to expect from this trip, from her grandmother, or this church, but once she was there she realized that she had expected to meet people who looked like her. No one did, not even her grandmother. Georgia felt strangely pale.

Across the aisle was a girl her age in a daffodil dress whose saddle-shoed feet did not reach the floor. Her dark skin held light the way deep water does. Georgia wondered how it would be to look like her. If she looked like her, she would look like the girl's mother sitting beside her. This thought breathed itself into a tremulous bubble beneath Georgia's breastbone. You do look like me, her mother used to say. Here, and here. She touched her chin and eyes. But at the same time that Georgia saw the likeness she also saw how no one else would see it, which made her no longer see it. This seeing and unseeing was a promise and its cheat. A wish that traps the wisher. The girl caught her staring. Georgia looked away.

"Found it." Bella twirls the pan. It is thick and has seven rounded depressions. "Some help you were."

"How much?"

"Uh, *zero*, if you're gonna make me say it."

"How much money do you want?"

Bella stares.

"To not tell Dale," Georgia says.

Bella's jaw drops, exaggeratedly, the top row of her teeth bared wide and straight. "Bitch, I don't want your money. Like I care that Dale thinks you're some angel daughter spooning SpaghettiOs into your mom's mouth. Whatever! He probably knows you're lying. You think anybody believes what we say? *Oh, baby, you're so hot I wanna fuck you on the dance floor make me your bad girl.* Dale lies when he gets all *I feel like a father to you.* Like a father who pimps you out, maybe. Sasha says she banked, and you know she made nothing. Meanwhile Morgan acts like she made only a few hundred so no one will hate her, but she stashes cash in her locker between sets. She makes plenty. Those old boys want to nail her prim ass. They fork it over for that MILFy goodness."

"And you?"

"I am not your problem."

"You think I got a problem?"

"Are you Charlie Brown? Am I Lucy? Is there a booth here that says *Psychiatric Help*? I just came here for a pan."

"So you're not going to tell."

"Do I need to write it in blood?"

"Okay."

"Okay! Jesus."

"Are other girls worried about going in to work?"

Bella shrugs.

Georgia asks, "Did you talk to that cop?"

"Yeah. I mean, I answered her questions. No one's going to be BFFs with her."

Uncomfortably, Georgia remembers the detective's business card in her locker. I hoped that you could be my CI, the detective had said. My informant. Samantha needs your help. "Ruby's been missing almost two weeks."

"Yeah, but Ruby's a keeper."

"You think he's holding on to her."

"I think that if he wasn't, there would be a body."

Georgia thinks of Ron, Ruby's foul-mouthed regular. What if she were able to give his full name to the police?

And if it *was* him? What would it mean to draw his attention to her? She tried to sign up for the busiest shifts, believing that was safer, but now wonders if that is the wrong strategy, like how zebras gather in a herd. She no longer drinks in the club. She drinks bottled water backstage. She avoids country roads at night.

But there is a compulsion. She thinks again of fairy tales. The woman who had to eat the witch's watercress. The one who touched the pricking spindle. Who talked to the wolf. The ones who had to know.

Georgia hitches the strap of her purse up her shoulder. "See you at the club," she tells Bella, and leaves to find her cousin.

RON COMES FLUSH with cash. He doesn't want champagne, but Georgia can make plenty on the floor if she keeps dancing. She has done the math. The deejay plays at least twelve songs per hour. Twelve dances at twenty each means two hundred and forty dollars. Don't take breaks, Ruby told her once. Get them to buy as many dances in a row as possible. When you're onstage and they tip you, line them up for later. I'll come find you, you say. Keep a list in your head. Potbelly. Gray beard. Army. Navy. Dot.com. Skinny tie. Work boots. Cubs hat. Sox hat. Dad. Frat boy. Find them on the floor. Don't pull them from a stage. A girl is on that stage. Take her tippers and you are toast.

After two or three dances, some men say, I'm good. Sit and drink with me.

Find someone else, Ruby said. Find someone who can't help himself and drops a hundred before he knows it, or drops it because he likes to know it.

Georgia has seen girls break the rules. They slide a leg along a man's inseam. Maybe they make more because of it. She doesn't ask. But she bets that some men pay in anticipation of a broken rule, shelling out cash, hoping for the breach. They stop paying, eventually, when they don't get it, but you still walk away with their cash.

Plus, some stop paying as soon as they get what they want, Ruby once warned. So why give it to them?

There is also the risk of Dale. Bouncers don't much care what the dancers do, but Dale does, and he has the habit of appearing out of nowhere. He can spend hours in his office and then appear at the rim of the stage as though conjured. So Georgia tries to make the rules work for her.

Ron kisses her hand. Men think that makes them look good.

She dances as they talk. He takes advantage where he can. Before he slips a twenty in her garter he strokes it down her thigh. He pokes her with it. But she is up one hundred and sixty dollars when he says she needs a drink. Normally she would pull up her dress and move on, but tonight she agrees. "A mimosa," she tells the waitress. Liz smiles as she notes the order. Mimosa is club code for plain OJ.

"Whiskey," says Ron.

"ID," says Liz.

"You gotta be kidding me."

"Club rules."

"Since when?"

Liz shrugs. "Just doing what I'm told."

"Me, underage?"

"It's because you're so handsome." Georgia touches his cheek. "Youthful."

His expression says she is full of it but he likes that she pretends. He shows Liz his license.

Later, after he has left, Georgia finds Liz at the bar. "You got it?"

"Yep."

Georgia gives her forty dollars. Liz gives her a slip of paper. It bears a name: *Ronald Needham*.

RON

Ronald Needham had about an hour after waking before the pain began. At first it pricked up his back: rat claws mounting the cracked column of his spine. Then the pain settled in and ached, denting his hips and turning his stomach. He no longer liked his favorite foods. He had a healthy appetite once. Hard, round belly. Gone now. Since the accident, he ate a steady diet of buttered mashed potatoes. Each shit left him sweaty and shaking, as though he were passing rocks. He would swear off potatoes. Too starchy. But they looked so pale and golden he would lick his fork clean.

He possessed a cane, the knob shaped into an upside-down boot. He enjoyed the friction of the boot's treads against his palm. He never took his cane with him into the Lovely Lady. He wanted the girls to see him the right way. He could be strong, sometimes. He was a big spender. His girls had never had it so good. He never got his money's worth.

On the way, he stopped at the Day N' Night to pick up a pack of Swishers to smoke at the club and a bottle of Jack for after. He glanced at girlie mags but considered buying one beneath him.

The kid at the register was pouchy-eyed and whiskery, built like a noodle. The kid didn't look at Ron when he handed over the receipt and change. Ron stuffed the coins into his change pocket, felt them slip along the wedge of his trapper knife. The receipt was stamped with the date (8 OCT 99) and the cashier's name (ASHLEY). "Is this a joke?" Ron said.

"Um?" the cashier said.

"You poor fucking kid."

"The orange stickers?" Ashley said, looking at the receipt Ron held aloft. "On your products? Those are the prices. That's what they cost. It all rang up normal."

"It's your name."

"Oh."

"Do you like your job?"

"Um?"

Ron wanted to tell Ashley to quit his job, quit his dewy name, quit everything. Ron could show him how. He could put the right tools in his hands and show him what work is. Pain climbed up him, strong as need. It was early yet. Ron shook his head and stumped out to his car.

Even when he was twelve, Ron worked. He hired himself out, illegally, for light industrial work at an Edam cheese factory surrounded by green fields. He wore rain boots, yellow rubber gloves, and a hairnet. The men wore beard nets. The factory smelled like an armpit. He manned a hose that sprayed curds and whey into a perforated metal box. He spun the box. Whey splooged onto the floor. The cheese inside the box was then pressed into hockey-puck disks and sent up a conveyer belt into a vat of brine. When he turned thirteen, he worked that end of the conveyer belt, fishing for cheese in the massive brine bath. Gloves made little difference. Salt water came in anyway, giving him washerwoman hands that wrinkled and later peeled. His mother held his hands and said, Aren't you proud? as she rubbed in Vaseline. Ron's hands were never nice again. Even when he had to stop working, when his spine fractured on a construction site, his hands were hardened paws. He was stronger than he looked, on the days the pain didn't come.

He pulled into the parking lot of the Lady, then pulled back out, deciding to go through the car wash across the street first. He let his car judder through the slapping soapy mitters and enjoyed watching Mexicans polish his car to a midnight shine.

The hostess in the vestibule at the Lady didn't recognize him. This bothered Ron, but he imagined his revenge. That was the way to show them, those careless cunts with their ironed hair and stupid eyes and plastic teeth. She barely looked at him. He paid the admission with cash, letting her see the envelope's thick, fragrant contents. He took pleasure when she noticed. Humming to the techno crap bleeding into the vestibule, Ron went inside.

He singled out Gigi. She was half-and-half. Light, though. White that had gotten dirty. Ron thought of Ruby, all tight skin and towering body, but Gigi was appealing in a different way, an old-fashioned way, if you could forget her color, which he alternately liked to forget and to remember. She had folds fit for fingers. "Dark nipples," he said out loud. "Like someone bruised them." She didn't say anything back. He stored her silence inside him.

When a waitress asked for his ID, he decided Gigi should be rewarded for pretending that he looked young. Her garter flowered with his cash. He wanted to instruct the girl in the vestibule. Study your model, he would tell her. Gigi listened to him complain about the wife he did not have. Gigi ignored the neat poverty of his clothes. Gigi did not know how he cashed his monthly workman's comp check in a series of bills calculated according to the club's increments of attention and respect. He did not intend for her to see his house, a brick one-story with holly bushes planted by his mother, leaves dark and martial. He hunched. Pain harpooned up his back.

When he returned home, his house smelled like him. He swallowed pills and whiskey. He unscrewed an empty jelly jar and leaned against the kitchen counter. When the pain got bad, it hurt more to sit than to stand. The pain was luminous, fluorescent. His breath sped. He revisited the club. He started with Gigi, then reached instead for the girl in the vestibule, blond as Ruby was blond. He hardened. He pulled her into the center of the club. The music was gone. Everyone watched. He unzipped himself and held her to the floor. The head of his penis touched the cool glass interior of the jar. He curved, coming into the jar.

Peaceful, Ron screwed the lid on. He stuffed himself, still glistening, back into his pants. He labeled the jar and put it in the refrigerator with the others.

IT IS BRIGHT when he wakes, the morning light lapidary. Cold breathes from the windows. The year is getting late. He will have to Saran Wrap the windows for winter.

There is a man outside looking at Ron's car. Ron is still mostly dressed from the night before, clothes stale and smoky. Deliberate, unhurried, he neatens his appearance. He touches the knife in his pocket and reaches for his cane.

The front door squeals open as Ron steps out onto the concrete walk. "Can I help you?" His voice echoes over the frosted grass. He has no neighbors. His mother bought this place when land was cheap. Ron's breath hangs in the air.

The man turns away from the car. He is young. Handsome. Leafy brown hair. Good shoes, dressy brown leather with thick rubber soles meant for running. He reminds Ron of something he has not thought of for years, of being a child and seeing a boy and the boy's father. The boy held his father's hands, facing him, and walked up the man's legs. The boy then pushed off his father's body and, still holding his hands, flipped over backward. Ron doesn't know if this man reminds him of the boy or the father.

The man smiles. "This is a nice car," he says. "1997 black Oldsmobile."

"Yeah. So what."

"Are you Ronald Needham?"

Ron tightens his grip on the cane. He has made the wrong choice, coming out here. He thinks of the back door and the field behind it. But the damage is done.

"I'm Detective Victor Amador," the man says. "I have a warrant to search this property."

SAMANTHA

(RUBY)

She is sleeping against the barn door when it slides open and dumps her onto dry grass. She wakes to cool, enameled blue. Arrowing geese. The sun waters her eyes and washes her vision white. She is too slow to scramble. He seizes her and drags her back inside. She arcs like a fish. He has brought a pail. He cuts the bonds at her ankles, drags the jeans off her as she kicks, and seizes one bare foot. "Big feet," he says, "for a girl."

He lifts the pail and turns it over her. She is shocked by the hot, soapy water. Too late, she opens her greedy mouth to drink some. She is naked and wet and finally warm.

"You were filthy," he says. "Now you're a lady." He holds her down. "A princess."

Samantha tries to think of nothing when his hands go to her throat. She thinks of everything. She thinks of Rosie, how worried she must be. Rosie's hair smelled of sweat and vanilla and sun. That day on the beach in the Indiana Dunes, Rosie lay her cheek against Samantha's shoulder and fell asleep. Samantha remembers pebbles and sea glass. A haze on the horizon. Samantha made room for Rosie on her beach towel, the two of them close together, as though the towel were a raft, and Samantha had felt chosen, like they could float away from the world and it wouldn't matter, because she was Rosie's, and Rosie was hers.

Something splinters deep inside Samantha's throat. Memories spray from her. They leave her dripping and empty and gone.

MARYANN

On the flight from Florida, Maryann Lind fell asleep. The plane was oversold. An agent at the gate had asked for passengers willing to take a later flight, which filled Maryann with rage, as though the agent knew her daughter was missing and didn't care. She pushed the ticket stub to the bottom of her coat pocket. Later, after they found Samantha, Maryann discovered the stub inside an unused tissue that smelled like her own perfume. It smelled like a former self. Smelling it felt the way a time-lapse nature show looks, everything rapidly rooting and opening and shaking. She dropped the tissue and the stub to the hotel room floor, then picked them up and crushed them to her face.

Maryann had the window, Geoffrey the middle. The aisle held a woman who had tried to make conversation and, rebuffed, took out her knitting. The needles were beetle green.

Around Maryann's sixtieth birthday, she had begun napping in the breezeway, where the wicker chair crackled like fire beneath her. She had noticed that sleep was different now than it had been. When Samantha was a baby, sleep was so scarce that Maryann sank into it without a trace. Nowadays, she had time for naps, and sometimes, after sleep yet before dreams, suspended in the slow oil of consciousness, she could remember things she had long forgotten.

The plane dipped gently.

Although it was nearly two decades since Maryann had seen Samantha's elementary school, Maryann remembered, as she slept, the nubby
blue carpet of the school's library, the metal hand-pull machines that
dispensed a pack of wide-ruled paper for twenty-five cents, a new pencil
for a nickel. Samantha's homework had been mimeographed. Maryann
remembered the blurry purple math homework and how Samantha
wrote her penciled 4's so that they each looked like a girl with her
hand on her hip. The ditto machine fascinated Samantha. She took her
mother to see it, their matching white huarache sandals echoing down
the green-tiled hall. The inky smell of the ditto machine made Maryann think of cleaning solvent, as if the machine were used to make
something vanish instead of to leave its mark.

She was aware, as sleep deepened, of gratitude. She had forgotten
these things. Now they were returned to her. Geoffrey liked to say that
parents made memories for their children. He said it when they drove,
embattled, through traffic to the city so that Samantha could see *The
Nutcracker*. He said it when she taught Samantha how to make a yellow
cake. We are making memories. But Maryann thought that this was too
simple. It ignored how their memories of Samantha printed over their
own pasts. Maryann had lost the sound of the ring of the first telephone
ever installed in her parents' house, the color of the milkshake maker
at the pharmacy, the names of her childhood best friends. Instead, she
remembered the names of Samantha's friends.

She dreamed that she was on a beach near her home in Jacksonville.
Palms lashed the charcoal sky. A crowd gathered on the dark shore to
wait for swimmers that no one could see in the water. Someone threw
on searchlights, and the beams were so powerful that they bleached
everything. The sky became glass. The people standing on the shore
became translucent, revealing their beating hearts, the red juice in their
veins. Maryann saw insects frozen midair, creatures she had never seen
before, a species of green ladybug. People began to emerge from the
water. She was waiting for her daughter. She was frightened. She looked.
She looked. It hurt to look so hard.

She woke. Geoffrey was awake beside her, his tray table down, his hands folded on top of it. He stared at the shallow circle meant to hold a cup.

Maryann turned toward the window. Her chest rose and fell. During her last conversation with Detective Amador, just before they had driven to the airport, he had mentioned a strip club—casually, as if she already knew, as if its existence in her daughter's life was no more profound than a pack of gum. She had said, You are wrong. This is a mistake. She had felt a gush of hope. If the police had gotten something so fundamentally wrong as this, they must be mistaken about everything. Samantha wasn't missing. She hadn't been in that car with that unfortunate woman. She doesn't work at that kind of place, Maryann told the detective. There was a long pause. Ma'am. His voice was kind and terrible. Maryann hung up.

The stewardess announced that the plane had begun its descent. Maryann's ears closed. She swallowed. There was a prickle in her chest, not a real prickle but an old memory, the feeling of her breasts full of milk, tight with it.

It became important that she make no sound. She looked at the clouds piled creamily into pillars. She thought of mimeographs and cup holders, of ultrasounds, of inventions that display space and presence and intention.

The plane stuttered against the runway. Geoffrey took her hand. It was October 8, 1999. Samantha was found in the Hidden Dells Lake ten days later.

FRANKIE

Frankie bought the night crawlers. Luis wanted minnows, but Frankie knows what bass like best. Frankie can already feel his arm bend under the weight of a fish-heavy net, the thrust of wet life slapping against the side of the canoe. Luis loads the tackle box and poles into the canoe and gets in. Frankie pushes them off with a gritty *whoosh*, hops into the boat, and they paddle out onto the orange lake. Then Luis eases against the gunwale, curly brown head tipped back, and unwraps a weed brownie.

Frankie casts his line. He sees a painter turtle on a log, red-and-yellow neck extended. Another swims nearby, the dome of its shell a glossy black. "You sure your mom doesn't mind me crashing in your basement?"

"My basement is your basement."

"Mi casa, su casa."

"Please," Luis says, chewing, "don't speak Spanish."

"Is it my accent?"

"It's everything."

Frankie doesn't mind that Luis is smarter. He is smarter like Frankie is taller and can jug up a rope faster. Maybe Frankie would have been smarter if he hadn't dropped out when Luis graduated so that they could travel to the best rock climbing sites in the country. Maybe loading his duffel into the trunk of Luis's car was a different kind of smart.

Frankie's bobber dips below the surface and pops back up. He tightens the line. The bobber drops again. He jerks the pole at an angle, feels the line load for an instant and then sail free. He reels it in. The worm is nibbled to a rind. He baits the hook again and casts out, slewing his line over the lake.

Luis lifts his face to the low sun. He is pale enough that sometimes people think he is white like Frankie.

"You gonna fish?" Frankie says.

"I'm watching you fish," Luis says. "Don't worry. My mom thinks you're okay."

Luis's mother is always neatly dressed and keeps her shoes on in the house. When he and Luis arrived in Fremont, she introduced herself with steely politeness and gave a tour of the house. The living room had dark furniture and a painting of a holy lady. Luis's bedroom had been redone by his mother in a way that pretended the space was still his. Framed photographs decorated the freshly painted cream walls: Luis as a baby, Luis in Little League. Luis dropped their bags on his bed.

She led Frankie to the basement and showed him an orange-and-brown plaid couch. "You may sleep here," she told him.

"Mamá," Luis said.

"No tienes vergüenza," his mother said. "Yo no te crié de esta manera. ¿Y explícame, qué hace este tipo aquí?" She was talking about Frankie but kept her gaze on Luis. "Él no es mi hijo. Tú eres mi hijo. Compórtate como tal."

The boat drifted. Maybe Frankie hadn't been careful enough around her. Maybe he had looked at Luis wrong. Maybe it was their bags on Luis's bed. Maybe she knew, not that there was much to know. He says, "Your mom hates me."

"It's not for long." Luis trails a hand in the water. "Just enough to raise cash quick. We put in a few weeks at Best Buy and we're out."

"Red River."

Luis sighs with pleasure. They have driven from mecca to mecca, from Joshua Tree to Bishop to Hueco Tanks, but the Red River Gorge in Kentucky has the sweetest one-pitch sport climbs. Their map in the car is marked with legendary climbs. They blew their savings, though, at Yosemite, despite taking cleaning jobs at a motel that was overrun with squirrels. At Yosemite, they eyed the monolith of El Capitan for days, and instead climbed easier formations. At night, on the ground in the dust of Camp 4, they could see the valley's black shoulders, and Luis said, "I could do this with you forever."

Frankie's happiness was soft and dense. "Me too."

But the morning they finally went up El Cap, Luis looked spooked. A month before, a storm had blown into the valley, pregnant with hail. Climbers on El Cap's Shield route hadn't seen it coming. They had gotten benighted on their third day up the rock. They froze to the cliff and died four hundred feet from the summit.

Maybe Luis was thinking about that as he looked up at the granite cliff. Maybe he was already regretting what he had said in Camp 4.

Frankie took lead up El Cap. His muscles hardened against the weight of a backpack filled with three days of water and food and gear. He did a layback along a pretty easy flake of rock, set the first piece of gear, and clipped the rope in. He felt Luis take the slack. Luis had Frankie too tight, but then he always did.

Frankie guesses they climbed ten hours that first day on El Cap. It was an amnesia of gray rock. There were clear moments: rats crittering in and out of cracks, thrushes zooming past. Belaying as Luis took lead, Frankie watched the wind blow the loose end of the rope up the wall, and would have doubted gravity if gravity didn't make his body hurt so much.

His brain restarted when they reached the last ledge for the day and anchored themselves. Sunset painted the valley. It warmed the wall. Frankie's bagel and peanut butter tasted amazing. His fingers were white with chalk and streaked with blood.

"Jerky?" Luis offered some, but didn't let go when Frankie took it. "Got it?" he said. "Yeah," Frankie said, but saw that it was still hard for Luis to let go. "Luis, I got it." Frankie understood the constant fear of dropping something when doing a big wall, the mandate that everything must be attached to your body at all times or you will never see

it again. On their next day climbing El Cap, they would hear climbers above shout, *"Waterbottlewaterbottlewaterbottle,"* and see a liter of
Gatorade plummet past to explode on a ledge below.

"I'm tapped," Luis said. "Can you bivvy?" So Frankie bivvied, set-
ting up camp on the ledge before night grew over the mountains. Luis
stared up at two thousand feet of bluing rock.

The sky went black. They saw headlamps of other climbers still working the cliffs around them. Their lights slid up the dark.

Luis straightens in the boat. "There's something in the water," he says.

Frankie rubs his hot neck and squints in the direction of Luis's gaze.
"Turtle," he says.

"That's not a turtle."

They finished El Cap on the third day. They topped out, and stood
on the summit's flat ground. The mountains across the valley were dusty
pewter, the sunlight as sheer as water. Luis leaned into him and said,
"That climb was awful." Frankie felt Luis's mouth on the skin of his
neck. Surprise made Frankie pull away, bliss fizzing down his slabbed
arms, the rope kinked in his hands. He immediately wished he hadn't
pulled away because Luis did then, too. Luis said, "I'm so tired," but he
couldn't have been tired, because after they coiled the rope and packed
it, Luis jogged ahead down the trail. He called to Frankie to catch up,
the words pulled thin by the wind.

They gorged themselves on hot dogs blistered over the fire. An apology or plea tried to wriggle out of Frankie, but Luis was acting aggressively normal, which could only mean regret, so Frankie figured that
he should act normal, too.

He stayed by the fire long after Luis zippered himself into his sleeping bag. Eventually, Frankie got into his own, alert with worry and need.
He thought about Luis's mouth against his throat. He thought that he
had been stupid. The solid ground felt foreign beneath him, and even
after he fell asleep the unfamiliarity of it occasionally startled him
awake.

Luis stares at the lake and says, "It's a head."

There is a head in the water. Its hair is slimed with weeds. That log
is not a log. It is a body.

Luis says, "Let's check it out."

Frankie imagines getting closer and seeing the body's face. "Maybe we should let it be."

"We can't let it be."

"But what will we do, after?"

"I don't get what you mean."

If he were the only one in the canoe, Frankie would paddle toward shore. He would call the cops from a phone booth and leave an anonymous tip. He doesn't want to see a body close up. Come on, Lu, he wants to say. Let's head back.

But Luis picks up his oar, so Frankie reels in his line and joins him. Frankie's shoulders are tight as they paddle toward the body. He does a J stroke, curving the boat in the direction Luis wants. He thinks of the map in the car and the cathedral rock of Red River as Luis prods his paddle into the dead woman and tries, unsuccessfully, to turn her face toward the sky.

DETECTIVE HOLLY MEYLIN

Pradko says, "What do we do with this pair of losers?"

Holly casts a glance at the freaked-out kids sitting in steel chairs outside lockup. She has just come from Samantha Lind's autopsy and feels restless, angry. Luis Álvarez and Frank Miller found Lind's body in the Hidden Dells forest preserve lake late yesterday afternoon. Since Holly can keep anyone for any reason for up to twenty-four hours, she ordered that they be held at the station. They looked rumpled and underfed when they got here, cargo pants soaked with lake water. Now they look worse. They probably slept on those chairs. Empty packets of vending machine snacks drift at their feet. Frank Miller, the taller one, has pulled a shoestring from his sneaker and is tying it into tiny, intricate knots. His friend has got a sewing-machine leg, jittering up and down, and keeps looking at Miller for reassurance. Miller studies his shoelace.

"Book them," Holly tells Pradko.

"For what? Being young and dickless?"

"For the weed."

Pradko scrunches his face into an expression of disgusted disbelief.

Holly says, "They had enough in their car to book them with possession and intention to sell."

"Hey, Stalin, it's not their fault they found your girl."

"You heard what I said."

"Da fucking da, baby."

HOLLY LIGHTS A cigarette at her desk. Backyard doesn't care. Pradko, who gets prissy about the new no-smoking policy, looks long and meaningfully at the stairwell, but Pradko can go fuck himself. Amador, mercifully, is still in the archives, wondering what they had done wrong, what they had missed.

They hadn't been fast enough. It's as simple as that.

"Wow," Owen said as he examined Lind's reproductive organs. "Just wow. I've never dissected someone with a chromosomal disorder before." Holly had known the medical examiner would be like this, so she had sent Amador to look in the archives for cases similar to Lind's in the past few years. Holly didn't tell him she blamed herself. She didn't say: I was too slow. I didn't find her in time. Holly didn't explain that since the body was her fault, it was her responsibility to witness the autopsy.

Amador knew it all anyway, without her saying a word. "Hol," he said, and sighed.

"I need you to do this for me," she said, so he did.

Holly took notes during the autopsy so that her eyes would be on her notepad instead of the body. Words formed on the page. Owen estimated that Samantha Lind's body entered the lake sometime between October 6 and October 11. Her left foot had been wrapped in a gallon-sized Ziploc bag duct-taped around the ankle. Her hands weren't bound at the time of discovery but showed signs of previous bondage. The wrists bore grooves, and hemorrhaging in the tissues indicated that the bindings were applied while the victim was alive. The flesh was too decomposed and there was no trace evidence, so it wasn't possible to identify whether the bindings were rope, plastic, or metal. Divots marked the body: the signs of aquatic life. The earlobes were gone. That other pearl earring likely lay in the belly of a fish. Samantha Lind had been beautiful. Holly had never seen her alive but felt as though she had;

she had seen her face so many times, on flyers and in her mind. Holly didn't want to see the body. It was her duty to see the body.

Holly's pen moved swiftly.

Owen found blowfly larvae along the back of the corpse. This was expected, given the body's facedown position in the water and the back's exposure to the air. Younger larvae were also found in other, submerged parts. Estimating the gestation period of the larvae, Owen said that the body had been kept on land, postmortem, for one to two days before submersion. Lind died sometime between October 1 and October 3.

Cause of death was manual asphyxia. The nasal bone was broken, likely the result of pressure applied over the nose and mouth. Contusions marked the neck. The hyoid bone in the throat was fractured.

Lind sustained sexual assault, though no semen was found, or foreign blood or saliva. Any potential trace evidence such as hair or fibers had been washed away during submersion. No samples could be found beneath the victim's fingernails. No DNA. There were no bite marks, which could sometimes be matched to a killer's mouth.

What Holly could never say to Amador, to anyone, was that she would choose this for herself if it meant that Daniel had lived. She would let herself be violated. Bitten. Ruined. It was an awful wish, yet the imagined bargain was as strong as anything she had ever felt: If I could bring him back, what would I not do, not suffer?

The body was found nude except for the freezer bag taped around the left foot. The sole of the left foot, along the medial longitudinal arch, displayed a familiar cut made by a knife: postmortem, made by a steady hand, the depth of the cut an almost unvarying one centimeter.

The crown. Holly sucks the last of her cigarette down to its filter and stubs it out on her metal desk. But it's not the memory of the crown cut into Lind's dead foot that angers Holly most, even though it had been gift-wrapped by the killer, protected from the predations of fish and turtles. What unsettles Holly, what makes her chuck her notebook into the bin by her desk, is what Owen found in Lind's stomach. The contents were mostly undigested, which means she ate the food well after September 26, when she was kidnapped, and sometime soon before time of death five to seven days later. Samantha had been kept alive, maybe for a week. They had had a week to find her. It seems at once a cruelly small window and ample time for Holly to have done her job.

The last thing Samantha had eaten was strawberries.

Holly retrieves her notebook from the bin and flattens the yellow paper's creases with hard fingers. She had been too late to save Samantha. This could not be undone. Nothing done can be undone. But she will find him. She doesn't think the words *murderer* or *culprit*. Only *him*.

GEORGIA
(GIGI)

"Should we go?" Georgia asks.

"No," Morgan says.

"I can't." Rhiannon steps into her slippery blue dress, which glides over her shark-fin hipbones. She leaves the dress halfway up and clinging to her waist as she goes through her bag. She has been to the tanning salon. Her breasts are tan, too. Bella, uncharacteristically quiet, peels a clementine, delicately removing white webs from the flesh.

Georgia pours a dollop of foundation into the well of her palm. I can't either, she wants to say. I have to stay with my mother. A snowy, lonely feeling presses against her chest, almost circular in shape, as though the base of a full cup clinking with ice. She smears foundation over her forehead.

"I have to work," Rhiannon says. One of the beauty bar lights, its bulb practically a bauble, round and thin, is almost out. It goes on and off, epileptic, making a *tink* with each illumination. Georgia catches Bella watching her. Bella splits her clementine in half. Its tart smell mingles with the cigarette Sasha isn't supposed to be smoking. Violet, though on the schedule, is absent.

Angel pumps lotion in a wiggly line up her leg. "It'd be weird." She rubs the lotion into her thigh over a bluish tattoo of kitten paws.

"I'm going," Sasha says.

"The hell you are," says Bella.

"Free country."

Morgan, who is far from stage-ready, cleans her glasses with the tail of her button-down flannel shirt. It is tight across her rigid chest and looks like it belongs to a young boy. "The last thing that Ruby's family needs at her funeral is a bunch of strippers."

Sasha says, "I clean up nice."

Bella throws back her head and howls.

"I used to think you two were more or less the same," Sasha says to Georgia, "but you're okay. *She*"—Bella keeps laughing—"is a nasty-ass skank."

"We are not alike," Georgia says.

Bella's laughter darkens but doesn't stop.

"I just want to pay my respects," Sasha says.

"By showing some whale tail?" Bella says. "How about a graveside pole dance?"

"You won't be welcome," Morgan says.

"You didn't even know her name," Bella says.

"Everybody knows her name," Sasha says. "It's on the news."

Rhiannon dips her fingers into a pot of glitter and galaxies her small breasts, then sprays herself all over with Elizabeth Arden's Sunflowers. "Do you think we'll get more or less business now?"

"More," say Bella and Morgan.

"Where are your hearts?" Sasha says. "Where are your souls?"

Georgia says, "You're making this about you."

"Should we be working here?" Angel runs a brush through her butter-blond hair, which crackles with static. "Are you gonna quit? Aren't you, like, scared?"

"No," Sasha says. "God gave me these tits for a reason."

"Scared won't pay the bills," says Bella. "Speaking of"—she points at Georgia's hand holding the foundation—"what the eff, G? Is your makeup not my métier? Do I not tend to your beauty with the ardor of a well-trained handmaiden?"

"You talk funny," says Angel.

"Pay up," says Bella.

Georgia hands her a twenty. "Angel is not wrong."

Bella opens her kit. "I talk how I talk."

The others have turned their attention to whether Dale should hire more bouncers ("Bouncers are skeevy." "But if you date one, they look after you better." "I am not dating a strip club bouncer. I am on the PTA"). Bella takes the bottle of foundation and dots the cool liquid over Georgia's cheekbones. Bella's small mouth is slightly open. Her brown eyes have flecks of gold. Her citrusy fingers move swiftly over Georgia's face, and that cold sensation from earlier travels up Georgia's back but warms as it goes, like a stethoscope's searching pressure. She likes Bella's hands on her face. It makes her throat tighten, to realize how much she likes it. Bella's hands are firm and focused.

Of course they are. Georgia is paying her to do this.

Georgia's mother touched her face, the last time she recognized Georgia as her daughter. Her dry hand had stammered over Georgia's thick lashes, down her nose. Georgia's eyes sting.

"Hey." Bella pulls sharply back. "Don't you dare." With a short, hard puff, Bella blows into Georgia's eyes. "You'll mess it up." Georgia blinks rapidly. Bella appears satisfied. She lines Georgia's lips with a thin brush, drawing with such precision that Georgia, as if looking into a mirror instead of Bella's face, can almost see the shape of her own mouth. Bella makes an impatient sound in her throat. She abandons the brush and dabs a middle finger into one of the dark reds on her palette. She rubs the color onto Georgia's lower lip. Georgia lets her mouth open beneath Bella's pressure. Georgia thinks, This is different. She thinks, Bella is taking extra care. She wonders why. She has a thought and then smothers it. Georgia is falling into the same trap men at the club fall into. They forget or ignore that they have purchased a woman's attention. Do this for me, and I will give this to you. Quid pro quo is all there ever is, yet some men think they are special. This time, she likes it. This time, she means it. This time, it is more than a transaction. It is for me alone. It's not about the money, they think, and spend more out of worry that they will be proven wrong.

"I didn't know you and Ruby were close," Bella says. "She kept people at arm's length."

We weren't close, Georgia thinks, then remembers retrieving Detective Holly Meylin's card from her locker and calling to give Ronald Needham's full name. She had felt a relieved pride then, a release from obligation. Who *was* close, really, at the club? Georgia looks at Bella. They are not close. Georgia shrugs and says, "We all keep each other at arm's length."

Bella cocks her head. "No. Lacey is godmother to Paris's kid. They go to the Wisconsin Dells together every summer. Skye has boozy brunches. She keeps her cash in a cat-shaped cookie jar with shiny gold eyes."

"Oh."

"No one invites you because they figure you're busy with your mom."

"Yeah. I am."

"So are you going to the funeral or what?"

"I'm on the schedule that day."

Bella huffs. "No, you're not."

GEORGIA'S MOTHER WORKED a series of odd jobs to supplement her main source of income as a lunch lady in the high school cafeteria. Avon was first, supplier of the mauve wallet bought with an employee discount. Avon meant small catalogues that fit in the hand like a prayer book. A mood ring for Georgia who, ten years old, felt envied for the first time when she showed it to the girls at school. They begged to try. ("It's still gray on me," Sarabeth Evans said. "That means you're fickle," Georgia said. "It's not working," Sarabeth said. "It works," Georgia said. "On me it's purple. That means passion." "Maybe," Sarabeth said, "it changes colors for you because you're Black.") Then came Amway, a short-lived experiment because her mother spent more money on the seminar than she made in selling any products, purchased only by Georgia's aunt and uncle.

Georgia's mother often took in sewing, doing alterations for wedding dresses and making simple A-line dresses from patterns. "This is

poplin," she told Georgia, instructing her to stroke the different fab-
rics. "That's batiste. Twill. Organdy. Chambray." Georgia liked organdy
because she could see her hand through it. She had known that cloth
had different textures but not that there were words for their difference. Freshman year, Georgia studied geometry in the evenings in the
kitchen, listening to the whir of the sewing machine in the family room
and the tinkle of dog tags as her stinky poodle, Snowball, waddled over
to lay on Georgia's feet. He was fond of warmth, and could regularly be
found hiding in the dryer atop a pile of towels waiting to be folded. By
senior year, Snowball was gone and Georgia's mother no longer remembered what poplin was.

At fifteen, Georgia's chest swelled. Her body plumped. The button
on her jeans couldn't fasten; she wore sweatpants instead. Although she
had once liked dresses her mother had sewn for her, she now refused
any offers. She didn't want her mother to use the measuring tape, didn't
want the touch of her mother's thimbled thumb against her fleshy hip,
didn't understand how her mother had not noticed, without any objec-
tive measurement, the obvious changing of her daughter's body.

It was during this time that Georgia decided that her virginity was
a burden. It annoyed her to hear girls at school speculate who had lost
hers, who wore a purity ring but was the biggest slut of all because she
would do anything but *that*. She saw the smug ones and the together-
forever ones and the meek and the willing. She felt the planetary pull
of an unfathomable force that would inevitably drag her into its orbit.
Better, she thought, to get it over with. Better, she thought, to set the
terms. She told Tobias, a junior with a white-boy name but whose parents were Peter Pan Cubans, to come over when her mother was at
work. She bought condoms. She told him what he could and couldn't
do. He looked at her with lottery eyes.

She had expected that it would hurt but not the way that it hurt, the
repetitive digging. She had expected it would be awkward but not the
way it was awkward, how, right before, he held his penis like a dowsing
rod to direct it into her. He prodded. He apologized. He couldn't get it in.
When he finally did, they each made sounds that were entirely different.

He left notes in her locker for days. He asked if he could come over again and was confused by her refusal. He called. Although prom was months away, he asked if she would go with him.

"Why?"

"I like you."

"Sorry," she said, and hung up. After that, he left her alone and told everyone that she had "more cushion for the pushin'."

She had expected that it would change her but not the way that it changed her. How when he left and she took a bath, her soapy fingers could reach inside as they could not before. It was as if she had been excavated.

She wanted to tell her mother. She realized that she had done this so that she would be able to tell her mother. I am old enough now, she could say, to know about you and my father. Look at me, she thought, as her mother peeled boiled eggs and then stopped to gaze at her hands in surprise. I'm different.

But it was her mother's difference, unnoticed for too long, that supplanted Georgia's own, that manifested and made meaningful the signs that had accrued for months like a frightening debt: the strange long silences at the sewing machine; the burns on her mother's hands from having grabbed a baking sheet from the oven without mitts; the day that she forgot to check the interior of the dryer to make certain Snowball wasn't inside, and threw a load of wet towels on him, shut the door, and set the machine to permanent press.

IT IS, OF course, a bad idea, but Georgia finds the darkest dress that covers the most skin and goes to the funeral home. In the dim lobby, the carpet creaks underfoot, a muddy blue with a repeating yellow pattern of miniature door knockers.

Georgia takes a seat at the back of the visitation room and sees, also at the back but across the way, Violet. Violet has had her braids taken out, and her shoulder-length hair is straight yet not stiff, with a slight swing. It looks as if it has been straightened with a solid gold hot comb. Sasha is there, too, farther toward the front. Without makeup her face looks tired, and she has a surprisingly accurate idea of Sunday Best.

Her floral dress blends in better than Violet's sharp office skirt suit. Sitting next to Sasha is her daughter, Melody, who glances over her shoulder, sees Georgia, and lifts her hand in an almost-wave. Sasha notices and tracks Melody's gaze to Georgia. Then Violet lifts her chin. The three women look at each other, then look away. It is best not to draw attention to themselves. No one wants to be asked to leave.

Ruby's boyfriend is in the front row, in front of the closed casket with its maple-syrup glow. He is rumpled and big in a too-tight suit. His face, when he glances behind to take in the filling room, has the expression of someone at the scene of an explosion. A little girl sits beside him, blond hair in a crooked braid down her back. My stepdaughter, Ruby said when Georgia glanced into her locker and saw the one photograph taped inside the door. Kind of. Ruby's lock was cut and everything taken by the police. Georgia supposes they have the girl's picture now. Georgia imagines it dusted, the face covered in a veil of fingerprints.

There is an older couple also in the front row, seated slightly away from the boyfriend and his daughter. The man is balding, scalp pink, the woman's gray hair cut short in the way of someone who no longer cares how she looks. Georgia can see little else of them. They are too much huddled into each other.

Parents and kids fill the middle rows. Georgia can tell that the children are about the same age as the boyfriend's daughter. Given the number of them and how friendly they are with each other, plainly made curious by their surroundings, some slightly awed but none sad except for two girls who relish their sadness, they are probably students in the same class at school. Georgia is torn between approval of the parents for bringing their families, and thinking that it is wrong to treat a funeral like a trip to the museum, as though the boyfriend and his daughter and the aging parents are a wax tableaux behind glass, primitive people with no known language, scraping flint for fire.

A priest talks, but Georgia doesn't listen. The balding father tries to speak and can't. The boyfriend, hands flexing against the lectern, mutters so low that she cannot hear him. Then the priest asks if anyone wishes to speak about Samantha. Fear tightens in a band across Georgia's chest. No one will call on her. That's not how funerals work. Yet she feels exposed, as if everyone can see inside her, as if they know that she wants to speak. Samantha had been a good person. Georgia wants to explain that the loneliness inside her is a perfect stone bowl that she must wash again and again in cold water, and that this endeavor takes so much effort that she had never truly seen Samantha, never knew her, never tried, and now she wishes she had.

Samantha's mother stands and walks to the lectern.

Who are you? Georgia's mother said. It was not the first time her mother had asked, but it would be the last time she believed the answer.

I'm Georgia. I'm your daughter. Here. This is me and you, three years ago. You made this dress. And this one. This, when I was little. There are bells sewn into the tulle. Listen.

Her mother touched her cheek. Georgia, she said. I'm sorry.

Georgia, swiftly, silently, leaves through the door at the back of the visitation room before Samantha's mother reaches the lectern and turns to show her face.

Georgia finds a restroom and locks the stall behind her. She lays strips of toilet paper on the seat. Someone else's urine seeps through. She doesn't need to pee anyway, so she leans against the locked door. Poplin, Georgia thinks. Batiste. Twill, organdy, chambray.

She hears someone enter the restroom and turn on the water at the sink. Georgia pulls a ream of toilet paper from the roll and wipes her face with it, then uses the wad of tissue in her hand to sweep the urine-spotted tissue on the toilet seat into the bowl. She flushes.

When she comes out, she sees that the person at the sink is the blond daughter, who shuts off the water and stares in the mirror at Georgia. The girl's face is red, her eyes a steaming turquoise. Her hands drip. "I heard you crying," she tells Georgia.

"I didn't mean to," Georgia says.

The girl wipes her hands dry, balls the rough, brown paper towel, and picks at it, dropping small scraps to the floor.

"Samantha was nice," Georgia says, "even when she didn't have to be. Smart. A hard worker. She had your picture inside her locker. I think she worked hard for you." The girl's expression worsens. Georgia says, "My mom died a year ago."

"What happened to her?"

"She got sick."

Rosie throws the crumpled paper towel into the trash. "That's better."

"I guess."

"Mine got taken by a monster."

Georgia thinks that she is supposed to say that there is no such thing as monsters, but someone knocks on the restroom door. "Rosie?" a man says. "You in there?"

"He called me," Rosie whispers to Georgia. The door opens. The man—the boyfriend—stares at Georgia. "Who are you?" he says.

"Georgia."

Rosie says, "She's Samantha's friend."

The man looks at Georgia more closely. "I see." His expression hardens. "A friend from work, huh?" He reaches for the girl's arm and tugs her, gently, into the hallway. His wide hand still props the door open. When he says nothing more, Georgia feels ashamed, small, and angry for being made to feel small. She realizes that she has forgotten to wash her hands. He lets the restroom door shut with her inside.

She opens the door again and steps into the hallway. He and the girl are gone. Georgia leaves the funeral home. She is the only one walking out to her car, the sound of her low heels on concrete loud. She starts her cold car and leaves it in park for a few minutes while it warms, her breath a fog, the steering wheel a hoop of ice. She decides that it is good that she has left the service early. It is better that she will not go to the internment. She doesn't want to see Samantha lowered into the ground.

HIM

The pearl earring lay in his pocket against his thigh. It felt like a thorned berry. He always took something, but the earring was his favorite thing. The freshest thing always was.

It was dangerous to keep the earring on his person, but he knew and accepted his habits. He let himself enjoy this danger, for a time. Danger felt like being awake when everyone else is asleep.

He had known when he took Ruby which thing of hers he would keep. He had known where he would keep it when he was done with her.

He took the earring from his pocket and lowered his hand into the water. The water magnified the pearl and warped his hand. He hid the earring beneath the rocks, just so.

He could retrieve it whenever he wanted, but he knew that he wouldn't. He never did, with their things. They were now his things, which made them less appealing, and made him eager for more.

DETECTIVE HOLLY MEYLIN

"You're fucked," Pradko told Holly two days after Lind's autopsy. It was Wednesday. The funeral was scheduled for Sunday. She wondered if Amador would go. Amador had informed Lind's parents about her death, and he still didn't seem over it. Pradko folded one of the now-useless flyers bearing Lind's face into a long triangle against his desk, his pale fingers long and narrow and quick. Holly watched Amador watch him do it.

"Better call the FBI," Backyard said.

Annoyed, Holly said, "The murders weren't across state lines. There's no hint of organized crime. This isn't a job for the feds."

"Still," Backyard said, "get a profile."

"Serial killers are all the same." Pradko tipped the wings of his paper airplane. "White guy, mid-thirties, normal IQ, slips it to his mom."

"Like you," Backyard said, "but smarter."

Pradko tossed the plane. It blunted its nose against the floor. Amador watched from his desk, unshaven. Light from the window lay in a blade over his eyes.

"I'm just saying," Pradko said to Holly, "this double homicide's gonna mess with your stats. I do not envy you, baby."

"Don't call her that."

The three of them turned to stare at Amador. He dropped his pencil and pushed back from his desk. The office door sucked itself shut behind him.

"What's up *his* ass?" Pradko said.

"It was the airplane," Holly said.

"It was you," Backyard said.

"Moody little bitch." Pradko sneezed, rubbed his red nose, and cursed his allergies. "What was he telling you, Backyard? That time he had his worried face on. The day patrol found that roached Caddy on the West Side. You got all cozy together in the stairwell."

"Nothing important."

"Got ash all over my suit, working that vehicle. It's like, why you drug dealers gotta burn your cars? Just scratch off the VIN. Be classy, motherfuckers."

"Were you talking about the case?" Holly asked.

"Nah." Backyard lifts his hand and flicks his fingers, dismissive. "Cop stuff. You know."

"I know why Amador's mad," Pradko said. "It's because of Spunk Lord."

"Ronald Needham, mightiest of monarchs."

Holly said, "Jacking off and keeping the proceeds isn't evidence of murder."

"Why jelly jars, is what I want to know," said Pradko. "Why not Hellmann's?"

"Hellmann's would have been appropriate," Backyard agreed.

"That fridge was pretty fucking serial," Pradko said. "Serials *love* collections. They love souvenirs. I guess everyone does. But me, I go to a baseball game and get a hat. They kill a girl and keep her underwear. A collection of cum? I'd be mad, too, if I was Amador. We should have been able to hold that guy."

Ronald Needham kept twenty-two jars in his refrigerator, many filled to the brim with clouded semen. Other jars, labeled with the names of less beloved girls, had a thin layer at the bottom. Ruby had a full pot. There was no Lady Jade jelly jar. Georgia Walker, who had called Holly with Needham's full name a little more than a week before Lind's body was found, was in the fridge, too. Her Gigi jar was doing well in what Pradko called the Spank Bank Challenge. It was unfortunate that the medical examiner hadn't been able to get any DNA off Lind's and Campana's bodies, because Needham's refrigerator was an embarrassment of DNA riches. Techs were working to match his DNA to what they'd grabbed from Campana's mattress at her extended-stay motel.

Unfortunately for Homicide and the techs, Needham's house came up clean aside from the fridge. There'd been no directly incriminating evidence on the premises, including the detached garage and toolshed. They opened an old well. Nothing. Needham admitted, during questioning, that he had been at the club the night of the car wreck, and had bought an hour in the champagne room. "Ruby left. I didn't see her after," he said. "Look, I need my meds. Those are prescription drugs. I want them back." He claimed he went home around 12:30 a.m., slightly earlier than when the two women left, according to Dale Gately, the club owner and manager, and James MacAllister, the bouncer who accompanied them to Lind's car. The women's departure time was corroborated by several dancers. There were no security cameras in the club itself, but Needham showed up on the videotape from the camera in the vestibule. The time stamp showed him leaving at 12:42 a.m.

There was something of Holly's father in Needham: the blunt-cut nails thick as horn, how he sat patiently until the pain crept in. Holly held back the bottle of pills, thinking he might incriminate himself without the relief they gave. This was a strategic error. A tremor hit his hands. Pride slid from his mouth. He asked for a lawyer. He called the union rep who had handled his case two years ago, an injury on an industrial construction site. Then he refused to speak.

Holly's father had neat habits. He carried a clean handkerchief and ate slowly, slicing food with a concrete commitment to the task of rendering it small. He dressed the way men in the local town dressed, buckled jeans and a button-down tucked against a hard waist. He wore a navy baseball cap, seams arching over the stiff fabric that Holly touched, though only while he showered. Water groaned through the pipes. The hat smelled like him. She undid the adjustable band, found the point on its stippled line where it could be made to fit her. She did not put it on. She peeled the band apart again. She pressed it back to her father's size. She thought she had found the right dot on the plastic strip, though had she been more careful, she would have noticed how the dot popped stiffly into its hole, the opening and what filled it new to each other, so rigid in their connection that any fool could feel it, and know it was wrong as her father eventually found it to be wrong. He brought it to her. You have been touching my things.

It was cruel that she remembered him better than her boy. Babies change too much. They transform in your arms. Their hands dimple. They seek. Open and close. She could say: His hair would fall in his eyes now. I would never cut it. She could say: His mouth would look like mine. A freckle will appear beneath his eye, a mote I will brush with one finger, thinking it dirt, dust. It will not go away.

She wondered after the twin of the pearl earring she recovered from the Campana crime scene. Holly didn't like the slippery quality of this case: lost evidence, dead ends, the way Lind's apartment building hadn't yet been properly canvassed. There was always someone not at home, a neighbor they had missed. Zack Antonucci's alibi checked out. Credit card records placed him at the casino around the time the murderer had pulled Campana from the car. She couldn't hold Needham. The evidence against him wasn't even circumstantial. It wasn't enough that he owned a black Oldsmobile; the paint chips collected from the crime scene could fit a number of different models. Later, the lab report would find that his DNA didn't match anything taken from Campana's motel room. Needham lawyered up, and his lawyer submitted a receipt from a Day N' Night about forty-five minutes away from the scene of the crash, and close to the time of it. Needham had bought a bottle of whiskey. The receipt pretty much exonerated him. Meanwhile, nothing connected Lind's boyfriend to the crime scene except his blood in the car, which could have been years old.

Holly thought about her first case. It was on the office shelves somewhere, in a thick white binder, with notes in her neat handwriting, which resembled her father's. The crime scene photographs, thick and sleek, were broad enough to make a rippling sound if fanned in the air. She had done that to one photo she had looked at too long; shook it suddenly, as though it were painted in wet ink and needed to settle and dry. It had shown a dead pregnant woman. She had been naked in her bed, full term, the baby birthed later on the autopsy table, lifted out and weighed as the heart was weighed, the liver, the lungs. In the photograph, the woman's feet were tucked under her body. She had long black hair. An easy case. It had been the husband. Close to home, these things. Too much time around dull knives, a shard of glass whittling around the dishwasher, stuck in its craw. Yet Holly thought not of Lind's boyfriend, but the club: the dancers, the bartender, the deejay, the owner, the bouncers, all come every night to settle into a territory almost like home.

THE LATE-AFTERNOON SUN was glassy. The lot of the Lovely Lady wasn't even half full. Wednesdays were probably the club's slowest days. Holly squinted at the cars, looking for a black one to match the GM models the accident reconstructionist said might have run Lind off the road: Cadillac Brougham (hadn't Pradko bitched about working a roached Caddy on the West Side? Drug dealers. Sure, maybe. But worth looking into), Oldsmobile, Fleetwood sedan, Buick Roadmaster, Chevy Caprice. There was a black Roadmaster in the lot. Holly jotted down the license plate. A wind kicked up. She turned up the collar of her navy peacoat. Leaves scraped across concrete. Her lips were chapped.

She enjoyed entering the club. It reminded her of going into the root cellar of her childhood home: cool, powdery air, wrinkled gray bedrock, preserves on the shelves, a box spring in the corner, the low lid of the ceiling. She left home before she was tall enough to need to stoop. She kept growing during freshman year in college—wasn't she supposed to have already reached her full height? But no: two more inches.

Probably she shouldn't like walking into a strip club. Did other women like it? She supposed that liking the club was a betrayal of women. She knew that it was the dancers' choice to work there, but also that everything about women and men had foreordained this choice. Maybe she shouldn't like the black plastic film on the club's glass door, or the skinny hostess who cast a tired glance at Holly's badge ("You gotta pay just like everyone else"), but the club felt good to her, its snug, carpeted dark. She understood why someone might prefer to come here during the day, when the club was quieter, rather than at night. The club was slow and forgetful, like an eye closed. Most of the strippers weren't even trying to hustle the thin crowd. Holly saw two of them drinking paper-parasol cocktails together at the bar.

The men's attention drifted between the football game and the woman onstage. Holly recognized her from the initial interviews of the strippers, soon after the car wreck was discovered. The dancer was Violet. Her legal name, printed on her Trinidadian passport, was Catherine Francis. "Is this a stork?" Holly had touched the gold-foiled bird. "Ibis," the dancer said, and took the passport back. "They eat lizards." She had offered little else during the interview. When Holly mentioned that the other women had said Violet was a good friend of Samantha's, Violet shrugged. "We dance together sometimes. I'm so Black and she's so white. Men like that."

"I'm here to speak with Mr. Gately," she told the bouncer watching Violet. James MacAllister. On the night of Kim Campana's murder, he had carried her out to Samantha Lind's car and then come straight back into the club to finish his shift—or so he said, and the bartender confirmed. Today he wore a wide red tie. Big, blunt belly. His suit fit, but his shoes were scuffed and dull, laces frayed.

James—Jimmy, the dancers called him—said, "Dale's in his office."

GATELY'S SUIT WAS bespoke and well tailored to his frame, with surgeon's cuffs, the last button on each sleeve undone. He was of average height and had broad shoulders, a broad rib cage, a tapering at the hips. Could he drag an unconscious woman from her car? Yes, if he hadn't been at the club all night, a fact vouchsafed by several employees. A large pane of glass gave a view of the club below. The three plexiglass stages floated in the dark like swimming pools, Stage 2 and Stage 3 round and small, the main stage long and narrow. Behind Dale was a desk clean of papers. Nice wood, the oak the color of pale beer. There were two doors, the one that Holly had passed through, which led to the main floor, and another that Gately said led to the basement, where VIP rooms were under construction. Between the filing cabinets, bookshelf, fancy desk, and aquarium, the office looked like it could have belonged to a lawyer. Holly liked the aquarium, where tiny black mollies and flat angelfish striped silver and black swam back and forth.

"I've spoken with you already," Gately said. During his first interview, he had praised Samantha, who got along well with everybody and was a draw for the club. Men came in specifically to see her. "A good worker. She played by the rules." He had made the club sound like a utopia. "Even when the girls don't get along, they're like sisters. They fight sometimes, but deep down they love each other." There was never anything wrong at his club, not the way he talked. "My dancers trust me. My door is always open. My entertainers can walk in anytime, no need to knock. I'm here to listen if they need me."

Holly said, "We have new information."

"What kind of information?"

"I can't share that with you." True enough, and something she said all the time to people involved in a case, but she felt a tang of failure now to say it. Any information she had amassed so far for this case felt scant, and easily scattered from provisionary little piles of meaning. "It's routine for us to question you again as the case evolves. I might be back here again."

He didn't like that. "How can I help?"

She showed him a photo of Ronald Needham. Needham's Day N' Night receipt made for a good alibi, but she couldn't quite give him up as a suspect. "What do you know about him?"

"Is he a suspect?"

"Answer the question."

"He's a regular."

"Does he spend a lot of time here?"

"Time, yes."

"But not money?"

Gately lightly closed his eyes and lifted his brows, a kind of elegant facial shrug. "He rarely gets champagne."

Holly thought of the jars in Needham's fridge. "Does he spend a lot on the dancers?"

"You'd have to ask them. I don't require my girls to disclose what they make, not like at some other clubs, so I wouldn't know. He liked Ruby, but then, who didn't? She was special. He's with Gigi these days."

Gigi—Georgia—had already been so useful. They wouldn't have found Needham if not for her. Holly wanted to make her useful in other ways, and made a mental note to consider later how best to persuade Georgia to give more information. "Did Ruby ever see men outside the club?"

"Oh, no. She wouldn't do that."

"How can you be sure?"

"It's against the rules. For the girls' safety, of course."

"Don't some girls break the rules?"

"Not Ruby."

"What would you do, if someone broke the rules?"

"It depends. I can't punish every little infraction, or I'd have no dancers left. But I trusted Ruby." The smile he gave Holly was familiar: confiding and self-congratulatory, the air of someone about to give an undeserved gift. Such a smile usually came right before a good bit of information—or information someone thought was good. The smile worked on her. She suppressed the impulse to sit up a little straighter. He said, "Anyway, Ruby wouldn't have dared. Her boyfriend wouldn't have liked it."

"Oh? Do you know Nick Sullivan?"

"Never met him. However, Ruby did say something about him that troubled me. I suppose I should have told you this before. I try not to get involved in my employees' personal lives. That's rare, you know. Many club owners demand sexual favors. They pit girls against each other. That sort of thing doesn't make for good business. It goes against my moral code."

Holly had asked, delicately, during her first interview with him, whether he had any relationships with his dancers outside work.

Affronted, he had denied it, and none of the girls suggested anything to contradict him. In the midst of her eagerness to learn whatever information he was dangling in front of her, Holly noted his return to this topic. Not quite prickly. But stiff. A little rehearsed. Proud.

"Her boyfriend was jealous of her working here," he said. "Some boyfriends are. More than the husbands, even. Ruby called in sick one day, and later she told me that it was because he had hit her. I hate to hear about abuse. It turns my stomach, especially when it concerns my entertainers. But it happens. I was surprised, though, with Ruby. Usually this happens with the lower sort."

"The lower sort?"

"I expect to see this with someone like Sasha. Skye, maybe. There is a type of girl who is drawn to men who do that."

No domestic abuse had been reported. Holly had checked Sullivan's record. "Did this happen often? Did she tell anyone else about this?"

"I don't know. She said she had the situation under control, but that it looked bad enough that she couldn't come in to work that day."

When a subject gives Holly something she knows he wants her to want, she thinks of her mother watching bats blink their wings against a purple sky and explaining to Holly how they roost. When bats lock their feet in place, her mother said, they are relaxing. It's their weight that keeps the feet closed. Talons, Holly corrected her, then felt like her father, which was how she understood that they were talking about her father.

She kept Gately's face in her field of vision, but let her gaze drift and seem inattentive. She watched angelfish slide across the tank. She thought, He does not want me here. He wanted her focus elsewhere. She didn't blame him. Cops weren't great for strip clubs. His very investment in appearing upstanding could mean he'd been sleeping with his dancers or tricking them out. He could be dealing drugs to them. He could be cooking the books and lying to the IRS. He could be using the club as a mob front. Dale Gately could be guilty of a number of things not necessarily related to the case.

She didn't press him. She told him again that she would be back, because it was the last thing he wanted to hear. Downstairs, before leaving the club, she walked around to see whether one could get a good view of the office, and what Dale might be doing in there. From certain angles, a person on the main floor would be able to see him, though only if he stood in front of the office window, as he was then, watching her.

JIMMY

The girls arrived in sweatpants, hair in sloppy buns, faces quiet, no makeup yet, hesitant in a new way that pleased Jimmy. It was a Wednesday, a boring day for a bouncer, so he was going to get the most he could out of their anxiety. They had the look of—what? What's the word for cold, and the thinness of your coat? Jimmy knew the feeling but it felt far away, adrift in the years when he was small, and he was a kid who grew fast.

Changes came to the Lady sure enough after the two dead girls. Change was easy to ignore if you wanted, because the club always changed anyway, girls washing in and out, newbies coming to dance on amateur night. Once in a while he got to see a true professional on amateur night, there for the quick cash grab, her fake rack riding high and solid as the hood of a pickup truck, legs that split wide, bruised from floor and pole work. Those girls ignored Dale's rule against kneeling and crawling onstage. They didn't care about rules. They were there only for the night. They left as soon as they won. Three hundred dollars to the girl who got the loudest applause.

But most girls came to be hired. Auditioning on amateur night was Dale's only requirement for employment, and those once-a-month events were Jimmy's favorites, especially if a dancer got nervous. He loved when she realized she wore the wrong underwear, like a thong. Thongs were sexy, but had to be wiggled down over the spiked hooves of heels. A professional would wear a breakaway V-string that could be undone and dropped like a stray thought.

Jimmy liked to see the shy ones chicken out and leave the stage. He liked to see girls who realized only after they were totally naked that they hadn't actually wanted to do this. Those girls looked startled when they grabbed their discarded dress from the stage. They never won.

He wondered why amateurs never slipped a bouncer a little something in exchange for advice. He would give it. It was only generous. He was a good guy. He was there to protect the girls. Really, he liked their nervousness so that he could say, Hey, you did great. And: You think I'm going to let anyone hurt you?

After Ruby and Lady Jade, Dale cranked things up a few notches, eager for more revenue, and with a good instinct for how to capitalize on new clients who had heard about the club through the free advertisement of the news. He installed a pole. Most girls lazed around it, but others who had previously worked at less classy clubs showed off their skills. Skye took to the pole like a champ, hooking herself upside down, surprisingly spidery despite her wide hips. Dale demanded more shows. Previously a once-in-a-while thing based on whoever had an idea and the will, special acts were now expected of all dancers. There was the standard girl-on-girl fare, which Bella, funnily enough, refused to do. A dyke should be into that, right? He didn't see why Bella got up on her high horse. Might as well get paid for licking pussy. Not that there was any actual licking onstage. Dale would never go for that, though Jimmy would watch, most definitely, and he wasn't the only one. Good moneymaker, really. Dale should live a little. There was a cage show, too, which wasn't half bad. Angel brought her pet snake. Lacey's show he enjoyed best of all: a Michael Jackson routine, complete with a black suit and red bow tie. Seemed kind of odd at first, but Jimmy caught on fast when she opened the white button-down shirt to flash one sweet tit.

It wasn't that he didn't think of Ruby. He just didn't think of her like the girls did. He didn't tell the cops—what was he, stupid?—about that trip to the casino with her and Violet. He remembered it, yes. He thought about it when that lady cop came in to talk to Dale, the collar of her navy coat brushing her short, dark hair. He directed the cop to Dale's office and was glad she didn't stick around to ask him any questions. He straightened his red tie. He kept the memory of Ruby close, unfolding and studying it as he would an old map, creases sueded by use.

He thought about Lady Jade from time to time but didn't think anyone else did. Ruby's funeral would be this weekend, and some of the girls were talking about going. No one had done that for Lady Jade. They had forgotten (if they had ever noticed) her pliancy, that dull face irradiated with a timorous hope you wanted to snuff out before someone else did in an even crueler way.

All kids get into something. For Jimmy it had been whales. It was all so sadly obvious. People were cruel, even to children. When could *fat* become *big*? When could it become a force, a leviathan, a god? He collected polished whale teeth. He interested himself in scrimshaw. He begged for a trip to the Field Museum of Natural History in the city to see an exhibit of colonial art: the tools, the worked ivory, the rib of a whale scrolled with the image of a whale. He still possessed his pin vise with reversible chucks, plus scribing needles. He liked to carve.

People thought he was the luckiest bastard. What man wouldn't want to work at a strip club? He couldn't deny that it beat working at a car dealership, like his brother, or at some soul-sucking office job. But if anyone could see inside Jimmy, they would know how it was to stand for hours half hard, looking at shoals of girls in their slippery skin. They would feel sorry for him. They, too, would think of a maw, a baleen, a net built into the body to suck everything in. He remembered how Ruby handed him a casino token. Its crenellated rim bit his thumb. It did something to him, lit him up like a coin dropped into a slot. He would be understood by anyone who had to listen to Eric gloat over what a great fuck Paris was, his dick between her firm tits. If a scrawny deejay could have a stripper, why not a bouncer, why not him, why couldn't he get some of that?

GEORGIA
(GIGI)

Georgia's cell phone rings for maybe the third time since she bought it. It trills on the kitchen counter. It's a local number, not one she recognizes. She stirs the tomato sauce, wondering if she should answer. It's Thursday, so she has the whole day free until her night shift at the club. She was enjoying the prospect of cooking, uninterrupted, for a few hours. The phone keeps ringing. Maybe it's Kaitlyn, calling from another number. Sudden worry makes Georgia grab the phone.

It's that cop. Holly Meylin. "I'm calling to ask a favor," she says.

Georgia lifts the lid off the pot of boiling water and slides in lasagna noodles. "I already did you a favor. Is Ron guilty?"

"I can't answer that."

"Guess I can't help you, then."

"That's not how this works."

Georgia hangs up. The pot simmers. The phone rings again. Georgia answers. "Yes," she says sweetly.

"What do you want, Georgia?"

"I want to know what's going on."

"How about I tell you as much as I can?"

Georgia looks around her empty apartment. When her mother died and Georgia let the bank foreclose on the house, she worked all the shifts she could to save enough for a deposit on a nice place for one person. She worked so much at the club that the normal world, the world of blue daylight and sidewalks and post offices, felt like a fantasy. When she finally got this apartment, she thought that she would make it a proper home, but it is still almost as bare as when she first moved in. She had left her books in her foreclosed childhood home, had left the posters hanging in her bedroom. They belonged to someone who didn't exist anymore. This new apartment is like a hollow egg. She wants a reason to hang something on the wall. She wants a real life. To be important. Or, at least, to matter. She says, "That's not good enough."

"Okay," Holly says. "I understand."

"You do?"

"That's why I picked you, not one of the other dancers. You're resourceful." Georgia huffs to let Holly know she's not fooled by the flattery. Holly says, "Maybe Ron did it, and we are looking at other people, too. But we can't arrest someone without probable cause."

"Like what?"

"An eyewitness. But the crash took place in the dark on a road near the preserve, so there are no houses nearby with people who might have seen it. If there were other drivers on the road, no one's come forward. Physical evidence would be great, like the perp's hair on the body, or a car that matches what we're looking for. Meanwhile, we gather all the evidence we can. You gave me Ron Needham's name. That was a start."

Georgia drains the noodles.

"I hoped that you would reconsider being my CI," Holly says. "I could pay you."

"How much?"

"Fifty bucks."

"An hour?"

"Per tip."

"That's like fifteen minutes in champagne."

"It's the department's standard pay for CI work."

"Well, your standard pay sucks."

"Maybe," Holly says, "you could do it because the money is beside the point, and it feels good to do something that makes people safer."

"That is some true *Sesame Street* bullshit."

"Do you feel safe, at the club?"

Georgia nearly hangs up again. It's as if the cop is trying to crawl inside her skin. "Sure," she lies.

"He's done this before. He was methodical. Clean. He'll do it again."

"And you want me to snoop around and catch his attention. No thanks."

"I could write you a letter of recommendation."

The sauce on the stove pops meaty bubbles. Georgia turns down the heat. "Recommendation for what?" she says, genuinely confused.

"College."

"I'm not going to college."

"One of the dancers said you wanted to, before your mother got sick."

"Which dancer?" Georgia is going to kill that dancer.

"I looked up your high school transcript," Holly says. "You got good grades."

Steam rises from the boiling noodles. A nervous wish scrabbles around inside Georgia, embarrassing in its need. A rec letter from a detective would be a start, if she managed to get other letters. Holly's offer is tempting less for the letter itself than for what it means: Holly believes that Georgia might be accepted, or at least that Georgia should try. Warily, she says, "How would being your CI work?"

"You pass along anything you observe that is odd or you suspect is related to the case. Sometimes I'll ask you questions. Do you know of anyone who visits or works at the club who drives—or used to drive—a black Cadillac Brougham?"

"I don't pay attention to cars in the lot, unless they stand out, like Skye's yellow Hummer."

"You might not see this Caddy. Not anymore. I think it was roached."

"Roached?"

"Burned to destroy evidence. It's possible that the car is a black Oldsmobile, a Fleetwood sedan, Buick Roadmaster, or Chevy Caprice, but my bet is on the Caddy. You could ask around. See if another dancer knows. They might tell you things they won't tell me."

Georgia drains the noodles. They are cartilaginous, edges frilled like the tentacles of an octopus.

"Will you at least think about it?" Holly says.

Georgia looks through the glass lasagna pan to the speckled countertop below. The open container of ricotta smells like salty rain. She wants to eat it straight out of the tub. She is afraid of missing the one opportunity that could change everything. She is afraid of feeling like a fool. Just a cop trick, maybe. Or worse, it's real, and dangerous. Georgia knows that she is being used; the question is whether the risk of being used is worth the reward. She thinks of Ruby's backless pearl earring in the cop's evidence bag. People at the club barely remember Lady Jade now. It is as if she never existed. That could be Georgia. She should quit dancing.

But the money. "I don't know," Georgia says. "Maybe."

She ends the call, assembles the lasagna, and puts it in the oven. She sets the timer but is nevertheless obsessive about checking the lasagna's progress. She turns on the oven light and peers inside, avoiding her phone on the kitchen counter. But when the lasagna's done and vents its fragrance from where it cools on a cutting board, Georgia looks at the number of the last call received and considers Holly's offer. She thinks, You can't work at the club forever. Forty is the understood age limit. After that, what can a woman's body buy? You have to be something more than beautiful to make a life for yourself that won't end in despair.

She saves the number. She saves it under *Holly*, then feels watched, as though the other dancers are staring over her shoulder. They had all met Holly. Someone might remember the detective's name. Georgia hits the button, backing the letters up into nothing. Quickly, before she can think too much about what it means, she saves the number under *Mom*.

GEORGIA PARKS. HER car smells of tomato and oregano. Just before she left, she had turned on her computer, the gray cube fuzzing as though a flannel layer had grown across the screen. She signed on, listening to the crackling song of the dial-up. Usually she went online to read the news and find recipes and ways to do her hair. Today she looked for Samantha Lind's address. The Web didn't know. In the end, Georgia had to figure out where she'd put the phone book. It lay at the bottom of the bedroom closet beneath a layer of shoes pitched together as though washed up on shore. The phone book pages felt powdery. They sighed beneath her fingers.

She entered Samantha's address into MapQuest. The dot matrix printer was new but still took time, so while the directions printed, she searched for online images of the cars the cop mentioned. Just in case. She wasn't committing to anything. Just looking.

There are no models like that in the parking lot of Samantha's apartment building. Georgia holds the lasagna pan firmly as she approaches the door. The afternoon sky is white. The wind bites. The still-warm pan feels good against her bare palms.

There is no answer when she rings from the lobby. Finally, she follows a white guy inside. He doesn't ask what she's doing here, just holds the door open for her. Maybe she looks like a housekeeper to him, since she's Black and has a foil-covered pan in her hands. Maybe he has let her in simply out of polite habit, or because she doesn't look like a threat even if he knows she doesn't belong here. Sometimes she feels sorry for men, because they are expected to do dangerous things like go to war and fly planes, but then she remembers that men make all the money and have the capacity to hurt her. They could grab her, like someone had done to Ruby and Jolene, and snuff her out of this world. In that light, Georgia's pity appears like simply another means of their dominion.

No one comes to the door of apartment 1B. She hears the cozy sound of a TV laugh track coming from down the hall. A dog barks. The door of 1B is tall and broad, its paint fresh. Georgia is about to set the pan down on the floral doormat when the door opens.

It's Rosie. Her hair is a scraggly yellow mess. "I looked through the peephole," she tells Georgia.

"Good girl."

"I don't like when people call me that."

"Smart girl," Georgia amends. "You should always look through the peephole first. I brought this for you." She offers the pan.

"What is it?"

"Lasagna."

"Why?"

"It's what people do," Georgia says, "when someone dies." Rosie's mouth bundles itself up. Her lower lip disappears. Georgia says, "When my mother died, my aunt and uncle cooked for me, for a little while. Here." The girl accepts the pan but flinches at its warmth. "It won't burn you."

"I don't like lasagna. I like spaghetti and meatballs."

"Maybe I can bring spaghetti and meatballs another day."

"My daddy won't let you. He doesn't like you."

"Okay," says Georgia. "That's okay."

"I was supposed to go to school today." Rosie looks down at the pan, showing the chrysanthemum crown of her head.

"Rosie," Georgia says, "are you home alone?"

"No."

"You're too little for that."

"No, Daddy's sleeping. He's been sleeping all day."

"He's probably sad," Georgia says, "like you."

Rosie straightens. She tips up her chin. The pan wobbles as she gets a better grip on it. "Thank you," she says, her voice cool. She reminds Georgia of Ruby's pearl earring: small and pretty and hard. "A neighbor babysits me sometimes."

Georgia's apartment is dark when she gets home, except for the oven light. It burns in the kitchen, though the oven has long been cold.

RHIANNON QUIT. HER locker has been cleaned out. She gave her stage dresses away and said goodbye before Georgia arrived for her shift.

Dancers quit all the time. But Georgia can tell from the tense quiet in the dressing room that Rhiannon didn't quit for the usual reasons—marriage, a better job, age. "She got scared," Georgia says, "didn't she?"

Bella tidies her makeup caddies. "Someone put a sticker on her locker."

"A coffin," Skye says. Her dyed-black hair hangs down her wide, bare back. "With RIP on it. Like for Halloween."

"Some people can't take a joke," Sasha says.

"Did you put that sticker on her locker?" Georgia asks.

"No."

Violet looks straight at Sasha. "Anyone puts shit like that on my locker, I'll kill them."

Sasha lights a cigarette and blows smoke at the ceiling. "Calm down. Jesus Lord. Everyone needs to chill the fuck out."

GEORGIA HAS A great night. For the first time ever, she clears a thousand. Fewer girls are working and the club is crowded. It is thick with customers despite the rain, or maybe because of it. No one wants to leave. Jimmy told a bachelor party they should book Georgia for champagne, and she got two hundred for the hour, plus the men kept dropping twenties for dances. Then Dale pulled her aside and praised her for being a hard worker. "We need a new star," he said. "I think it could be you." He said he'd tell the deejay to put her on the "special rotation," and sure enough, Eric sends her to the best stages at the right times. Georgia finally understands why Paris is sleeping with him. Georgia doesn't count her money in the locker room after closing, but the wad of dank cash around her garter is thick and heavy and she has kept vague track throughout the night. She banked.

"Hey." A cool hand touches Georgia's shoulder. Georgia startles, but it's just Bella, whose fingers slide away as Georgia, half dressed, turns from her locker to look at her. Bella's makeup is wiped off, and she's wearing jeans and work boots. Her jacket is dark and boyish.

"I'm hungry," Bella says. "Are you hungry?" She shoves her reddish hair out of her face, but it tumbles right back, the ends brushing her jaw and mouth.

"I don't know." Georgia can still feel Bella's touch. It had been an oddly formal gesture. Dancers often touch each other backstage, fixing each other's hair, honking someone's boob out of boredom. Georgia once saw Skye rub a booger off Desirée's cheek. Sasha likes to snap V-strings as she walks by. But Bella never touches anyone unless she's doing makeup.

"Tired?"

"No." Georgia's pulse is bouncy. All that cash stuffed her in purse makes her feel like she's made of sugar. She still can't believe it.

"Wanna go to Denny's?" Bella asks. "I love their Grand Slam Slugger."

Georgia glances down at herself. Her bra is too small. Her breasts spill over the cups. From the locker, she grabs her T-shirt, a really soft one she sometimes sleeps in. It smells like laundry. She inhales its scent as she pulls it over her head, thinking about Bella's offer. She knows that some dancers hang out when they're not at the club. There is a closeness between the other girls, an invisible history.

"No problem, though," Bella says, "if you need to head home." She zips her jacket up to her pale throat.

Even though she has an afternoon shift tomorrow, and should sleep, Georgia doesn't want to go home and is tired of pretending that someone there needs her. She feels like celebrating. She is aware that she is crafting reasons to explain a decision made the moment Bella asked.

"Sure," Georgia says. "Let's go."

Bella's smile is smug and sweet.

"I CAN'T THINK of anyone who comes to the club who drives a black Caddy, but I don't really know cars." Bella licks her knife clean. She asked for peanut butter to go on her pancakes, which she covered in maple syrup. "I get so hungry after work," she says, catching Georgia's look as she folds a strip of bacon into her mouth. Bella has raw-boned wrists and small breasts, and looks even flatter in clothes. "Why are you asking?"

"I might want to buy one."

"Go to a dealership."

"It'll be cheaper to buy from someone I know."

"Jimmy's brother has a dealership. He'll hook you up."

"I don't trust dealers."

Bella tips her head, squinting at Georgia as though she's high up and far away. Silver worms of rain crawl down the windows. Georgia's hoodie is still damp from the downpour that caught them both just before they walked in. Bella says, "You're acting weird."

"No, I'm not."

Bella drinks from her water glass, looking at her over the rim. Georgia thinks Bella might press her, so she asks, "Why do you work there?"

Bella sets down her glass. "My sisters loved makeup. Our parents didn't let them leave the house wearing it, but they would clip style guides out of magazines and paste them into a notebook for me. Do my eyes like this, they'd say. My cheeks like that. I got good at it. I left home early. The Lady was an easy place to land a job. I started maybe a year before you did, just doing makeup at first. But you make more money taking your clothes off, so."

"The Lovely Lady is a dumb name."

"There's a club in Chicago called Keepers. Way better. Nice and simple."

"Could be worse. We could work at a place called the Pink Palace."

"The Playpen."

"Wet."

"The Magic Vag."

"Sluts-R-Us."

Georgia takes a bite of grilled chicken, which tastes like char and salt. She's hungry but hates eating subpar food. Bella's plate is almost empty. "Why did you leave home early?" Georgia asks. It's a nosy question, but Bella can always lie if she doesn't like it.

Bella runs a scrap of toast over her plate, mopping up maple syrup. "My parents are really nice," she says, chewing slowly. "On Christmas, my sisters and I were sent out with plates of cookies to deliver to the whole neighborhood. My mom knew the grocery bagger's name. But my parents didn't like me. It was obvious. The stiffness. I never asked why. Anyway, I knew. All that not-asking got"—Bella makes her hands into an egg she cracks open—"big, solid, like it was real enough to take my place."

Georgia looks over Bella's shoulder at the cashier, who hands a trucker his change. He has a pink face and a brown beard and wears a quilted jacket. He looks solid and fuzzy, like taxidermy. He walks back to his booth, slow and heavy-footed, to slide two quarters next to his empty coffee cup.

"Are you scared?" Georgia asks.

"Nah. Ruby's boyfriend did it. It's always the boyfriend."

"On TV."

"In life! Ruby said he was crazy jealous."

"What if it's not her boyfriend?"

"Whoever it is, he's not going to come back to the club. That'd be pushing his luck. He'll get caught."

"Maybe he wants to get caught."

"No one wants to get caught."

"He's a psycho," Georgia says. "He's not thinking rationally."

"Fine, have it your way, we're all dead."

"I'm just saying we need to keep our eyes open."

"That's why you're being so weird about a black Caddy, isn't it?"

"Well." Georgia finds herself explaining the call with Holly Meylin. When she gets to the part about maybe being a CI, Bella says, "What are you, a naked Nancy Drew?"

"Nancy Drew," says Georgia, "is the whitest white girl."

"Fake little bitch. She was always getting fancy gifts for solving crimes, like a fur coat, then pretending she did it just for fun. Wait, what'll the cop give you? How's the pay?"

Georgia decides that she should tell Bella, so that Bella will laugh and then Georgia can laugh and go home and sleep and never call the detective. "The cop said she'd write me a recommendation letter, for college." The diner light is acidic. Georgia can clearly see the mixed-up colors of Bella's eyes. Georgia says, quickly, "You think it's stupid."

"I don't think it's stupid." Bella's elbows rest on the table on either side of her plate.

It is such a relief that Georgia has to look away. She takes in the streaky amber trapezoids of overhead lights. A pair of quiet men drink coffee in the smoking section, smoke curling up from the ashtray. Their waitress, who also served Bella and Georgia, has blue eyes so pale they look opaque, ceramic. The hostess is a Hispanic girl just out of high school, with a cape of black hair held back by a red ribbon headband. She is pretty, pretty enough to work at the Lady. Bella shifts to rest one long arm along the back of the booth's puffy seat, her eyes on Georgia, her expression curious and secretive in a way that makes Georgia feel warm despite her rain-damp clothes. She asks Bella, "If you could be anyone else here, who would it be?"

"Uh, me."

"You have to choose someone *else*."

"No, I don't."

"Play the game, Bella."

"You," she says. "If I can't be me, I'll be you."

When Georgia asked the question, she pretended it was out of idle curiosity, but Bella's answer goes straight through Georgia's hunger and touches her spine. She asked in hope of this answer. It is what she wanted to hear.

HIM

Sometimes it was like waking from a dream, like his life had been stowed flat in glassine paper. He would realize which girl he wanted and he would slide right out, everything suddenly sharp and full and lucid.

He had never really paid attention to her, not before Ruby. Not before the forgettable girl with Ruby that night, who was just someone to get through. But then, after he had finished with Ruby, he returned to the club. Something whispered at the back of his mind. An eager breeze from a delicate opening in the brain. The crowd got dense. He did not drink. He waited to discover what the whisper wanted. Then he saw Gigi.

She was up onstage, dancing to the Stones, her hips sliding back and forth as though greased. He stayed away from the tip rail, hidden behind taller men. Her smoky hair, deep flesh. Skin the color of wheat. Her stretch marks excited him. He liked that she looked worked upon, already begun, as though her body was an open collaboration waiting for his share.

Need grew on him like an extra limb.

DETECTIVE HOLLY MEYLIN

Holly closed her cell phone and dropped it onto her belly. She was lying on a smelly La-Z-Boy in Major Crash. She had stopped sleeping at home. The Lind case felt too important. The department had a cracked-tile shower when she needed it, and she was okay with sleeping in Major Crash. It was like sleeping on a plane. You never fully drop off. Holly sort of slept, sort of schemed. When she woke up from a bad dream, she dialed Georgia's number. "I'm calling to ask a favor," she had said when the stripper picked up.

Georgia was wary, but had listened. Holly believed that Georgia would help. After all, Georgia had given her information before. Georgia was already a CI, in fact if not in name, and Holly could tell when someone was too curious for her own good.

What would Amador say, if he knew?

He'd say, She's vulnerable.

No one's forcing her, Holly would tell him. We need information.

You're using her.

You want this solved?

You are using her as *bait*.

If Holly had called her father to tell him that Matthew had forgotten

Daniel in the back seat of the car, he would have said, What kind of idiot forgets his own kid?

It could happen to anybody, Holly might have answered, but that would have been a lie. It never would have happened to her. Every day people commit little crimes. They say something cruel. They don't feed the meter. They let the elevator close in someone's face. It's easy for people to look upon their own bad behavior and excuse it, but Holly never let herself forget anything, including the truth of her sins.

Good, she would tell Amador. Let her be bait.

"SOME PISSANT TURD FOIA'd the Lind case," Pradko said when she walked into Homicide.

"A journalist at the *Chicago Tribune*," Backyard said.

The Freedom of Information Act was a pain in Holly's ass. Journalists acted like they deserved to know everything and cops were keeping secrets out of spite.

"Wish *I* got paid to blab shit." Pradko rubbed his red nose. He was allergic to mold. Whenever it rained in the fall, he'd rub his pale face raw and blame the wet dead leaves. A morning mist hung outside the window. The brown and yellow leaves on the ground looked oily, like snakeskin. "Why can't they stick to interviewing Monica Lewinsky? I would definitely blue-dress her. Interviewing her is a bona fide social good. Or go report on Chechnya, I don't give a fuck, just don't salt an open murder case."

"Can you go to the court and block it?" Holly asked Backyard.

"Me?" He widened his eyes. His left eye had a brown freckle in the white, a shade lighter than his dark irises. "Amador would be better. The judge loves Amador."

"Where *is* Amador?"

"Pet project." Pradko sneezed. "He went out to sit alone in his car like a freak. I said, Dude, you can jerk off under your desk here, I don't care, why you gotta go out to your car, but he said he couldn't concentrate. Said he had an *idea*."

Holly didn't bother with her coat. She walked out to the parking lot, the drizzle spitting down in the early gray light. She found Amador's car. He was reading a printout. She rapped on the wet window. He unlocked his doors.

His car was warm and smelled good, like coffee and him. As soon as she got inside, the rain came down hard, static on the roof, bouncing off the hood, rippling down the windshield. Amador handed her the paper with its thin bars of alternating white and pale green. The text showed a news story about the murder of a woman in Hodgkins a month back. "What interests me is how they ID'd her," Amador said.

She read the article. The police ID'd the woman using the serial number of her silicone implants. "You think there's a connection to the Lind case," she said, "but plenty of women have fake breasts, not just strippers."

"I'm not saying the perp is targeting strippers. Not exactly."

"What, then?"

"Maybe he goes after women who don't belong. Who don't fit his idea of what women should be. Serials have rules about who makes good prey."

"You want us to follow this lead."

Amador kept his eyes trained on the view through the windshield as though he were driving, the lines of his face softened by the dim gray light. "Do you trust me?"

He was no longer talking about the case. Holly leaned back in the passenger seat and put her knees against the dash. The rain on the hood sounded nice. "Yes," she said, although she did not trust herself with that trust. Yet it was there, as steady and warm as him. She tipped her head back and let herself rest in this moment only because it would not last. She thought about rain over farmland: a welcome. How it hissed onto the fields, and when it stopped the sky over the corn and apple orchards was an abundant blue that shone like chrome. She missed the south: tractors dusting up the road, grocery stores where baby chicks could be bought along with bread and milk. Amador had this way to him. A quiet dignity in his whiskey eyes. A talent for waiting. He was waiting now. Maybe he was waiting for her to tell him what she missed, what she wanted. Maybe it would be as easy as leaning into him, to feel his hand on her, his mouth. Rain drummed the roof. A pressure mounted within her. He would take away her grief if she let him try, if he could. It would be a kindness. It would be theft.

She said, "Let's give Hodgkins a call, get them to pull the case jacket."

Amador lifted his brows at the rain. "When this lets up."

"Now is good." Holly opened the car door and let the rain fly in.

DENNY'S WAS QUIET. The rain on the windows made the interior dark even though it was early afternoon. Through the windows, Holly heard the hum of cars passing by on the highway. The hostess, who had lip gloss the color of strawberry Jell-O and long, shiny black hair held back by a red ribbon hairband, showed Holly and Amador to a smoking booth. Hodgkins was a tiny department an hour south, with only two guys working investigations, covering homicide and narcotics and everything in between, but Holly got lucky. One of the detectives was in when she called. He said sure, he'd pull the jacket for them. He even had business up their way. We'll buy you lunch, Holly said.

Holly was enjoying her second cigarette and Amador was suffering it when the detective came in, caught their eye, and came their way, without them ever having exchanged much prior about how everyone looked. It was easy to spot another cop. It was how they moved, how they dressed, how they sized up a room.

Ken Roche had deep-set eyes and bags beneath them so pronounced they looked like bluish aprons. He slid into the booth, the shoulders of his coat dark with rain, and lit up, which made Holly feel great. Amador had been silently asking her to stub out her cigarette. He didn't have to say that he hated smoke, or that he worried about her getting cancer. She was glad that she and Ken outnumbered him. She blamed Amador for that moment in the car, for her weakness. It did not matter that he had done nothing. Nothing was enough.

Ken handed Amador a gray binder and ordered fried eggs and sausage. Their waitress had blue eyes like a husky, with milky stars around the pupils. Amador moved the binder to position it between him and Holly and opened it so that she could read it with him, which was his

usual way of responding to how other police—really, most people—
decided that Amador was important and she was his accessory because
he was a man and she was a woman. Sometimes Holly hated his efforts
to smooth things over more than she hated the thing that needed to be
smoothed, but it was such a common occurrence that usually it bored
her.

"I don't got much for you." Ken had a slight downstate drawl, his
voice phlegmy and deep. Amador flipped fast through the binder to get
to the photos. Holly's chest was full of smoke. "Girl wasn't even from
around Hodgkins, just got dumped in my jurisdiction, lucky fucking
me."

Amador's hands slowed. A photo of the body at the scene, a grassy
verge. The body on the examining table. Amador stopped. The body's
foot. The foot's sole. Holly exhaled. Flecks of ash fell on the photo, which
showed a bloody etching, a zigzag, the letter *M* with an extra peak. The
body had decomposed, the flesh shrunken, but the mark was clear
enough. It matched the cuts on Campana's foot, on Lind's.

Amador brushed the ash away. "Rabideaux said it looked like a
crown."

Rabideaux was right. A crown for a king. Holly thought about Nick
Sullivan; she thought about Ronald Needham. She thought about Zack
Antonucci and Dale Gately and even that bouncer, James McAllister,
the last one to see Lind and Campana alive. She wondered who else it
could be, who eluded her, who was far from her roving mind.

RACHEL
(MORGAN)

"Mommy?"

"Mmph."

"There are noises."

"It's an old house, baby." Rachel keeps her eyes closed. It is four in the morning. She worked a night shift at the Lady and had just fallen asleep. "Probably the radiator. Go back to bed."

"I want to be with you."

Rachel pushes hair out of her face and looks at Jake standing beside her bed in the light cast by the streetlamp through the sheer curtains. Without her glasses she sees only shape and color. His belly pokes out from the bottom of the too-small pajama top. His round cheeks are cast in shadow, all yellow light and black lines, like a chubby bumblebee. Four years is the last year he can be a baby. She lifts the blanket, opening its envelope of humid warmth for him to crawl in beside her. She is glad she showered after coming home from the club. Jake nestles against her and pats her cheek. "You are my nice mommy." She puts her arm around him. He says, "I need my sleep water."

Rachel drags herself out of bed and into Jake's room, which glows with a bunny lamp and Christmas lights strung along the wall above his toddler bed. She grabs the bottle and returns, careful not to step on the creaky plank outside Tyler's door.

Jake's head is already thrown back against the pillow, his mouth open, breath small yet heavy.

He sleeps on her hair. He kicks.

She thinks of Ruby, and pulls him closer.

THE CLINKING OF a spoon and bowl drifts up from downstairs. Jake's side of the bed is empty. The lenses of her glasses are greased from last night's mascara, and her feet feel bruised when they touch the floor. "Wide board oak," Tim said. "Rumford fireplace. This is it, babe. Just needs a little love." Never mind that the fireplace coughed billows of black smoke. Tim, of course, never refinished the floors. The boys can't go barefoot without getting splinters.

She hears Jake's melodious chatter and the dry pour of cereal. She is filled with gratitude for Tyler for taking care of his little brother. She will do something nice for Tyler. She will buy the electric guitar he begged for even though he already has an acoustic and can play only one Nirvana song that he sings in a cracked voice. It is not easy for him. She is too hard. Love them while they're little, after that they're gone. His face is already angry with acne, a stranger's face, but he has done what she asked and there seems no greater proof that he is still her child.

Yet the kitchen, when she comes down, is empty save for Jake, who, judging from the confetti of Cheerios all over the table and floor, has poured his own cereal. He has several bowls before him and is spooning guacamole straight out of its plastic tub. A sucked Tootsie Roll Pop lies stuck to the table. "Mommy!" he says. "Good morning hug! Good morning kiss!"

She gives him a hug. She gives him a kiss. "Where's Tyler?"

"I don't know."

They never tell you when you choose a child's name how often you will shout it like profanity. Tyler stumbles up from the basement, hair flopping in his face. "God," he says. "What."

"You gave him a lollipop for breakfast?"

"Uh, no."

"Someone did."

"Maybe he got it himself. Ever think of that?"

"In fact, I *do* think that he has been here all alone, feeding himself crap while you were playing video games."

"A lollipop looks like a planet." Jake pries it off the table. "For except it's on a stick."

"I was doing laundry," Tyler says.

"Laundry?" He never does laundry.

"My sheets," he mumbles. His clear wish to vanish makes her understand what has happened to his sheets. Her anger dissolves into pity. What is it to be a boy, to have your shoulders widen, your body no longer at your command, to stay up late just to be free of family, to sleep and then wake in a jolt of unrequested pleasure, everything wet and warm, then sticky, cold?

"Okay," she says. "Let's just have breakfast."

Jake, sucking the lollipop, catches his mother's eye. Guiltily, he takes it out of his mouth. "I will pause it on the table."

"Oh no you won't." She scoops it from his hand and, when he wails, puts it on a plate and promises he can have it later. She makes a play for the guac, too, but his loud heartbreak makes her relent.

"I love you, guacamole," Jake whispers to his spoon.

"He's like a fake kid," Tyler says.

"Don't tilt your chair," she says. "You might fall."

"It's like you bought him in a box."

"Does the dryer work?"

He shrugs, shoveling cereal into his mouth.

"I asked you a question."

"Yeah," he says. "It works."

The dryer has been fussy lately, narcoleptic, and while it can sometimes soothe itself into a regular cycle, the sounds revealing the hard parts of clothes, the thin *tick* of buttons or a zipper, it can just as easily stop before it's time, or not start at all. More than once, Rachel has been forced to ransack Tyler's closet for something to wear. The dryer isn't even the worst of her house problems. Midsummer, she went downstairs and found the basement awash in glimmering sewage. Tree roots, she was told. They had grown into the pipes, piercing and knotting ("It looks like a dollhouse," Tim said. "Don't you want to live in a dollhouse?").

"Did you feed the chickens?"

Tyler snags a finger onto his black jelly bracelets, pulls them back, and gnaws on them. "Yeah."

The chickens, too, had been Tim's idea ("Fresh eggs every morning!"). The homes in this neighborhood were gabled, with fish scale shingles and gingerbread trim on the porch and eaves, and built with little breathing room between them. She could reach out a window and touch the side of another house. The backyard is barely a backyard and is almost entirely taken up by the chicken coop. The hens have stopped laying. Rachel feeds them for nothing. She should get child support for them as well as the boys. She is stuck with the chickens' strangled cries and mechanical pecking and the filthy shudder of wings. But she has seen Tyler casting grain, his expression akin to hope. Jake named five of the chickens and Tyler one: Big, Little, Pumpkin, Truck, Spaghetti, and Judas Priest. Although Tyler sometimes asks for a chicken dinner, it is only to make Jake cry.

She passes a hand through Jake's tidy hair, which she cut herself. "Chocolate milk?"

"Warmsies, please."

She pops a mug of Nesquik in the microwave.

Tyler says, "How come you never ask me?"

"Do you want chocolate milk?"

"No."

"I need to be at the restaurant by five. I'll be home late. Make sure Jake has his bath."

"Okay." His tone could be defeat or resentment, but it is, regardless, soft, which makes Rachel reach to trace his cheek despite the likelihood that he will duck. He endures her touch, staring at the bowl of his spoon. A fatal clang comes from the open basement door. The dryer.

It smells like singed hair. The sheets inside are wet. She pulls them into a damp bundle and takes them upstairs to the bathroom, where she drapes them over the shower curtain rod.

"They won't dry in time." Tyler is at the bathroom door.

"Sure they will. You go to bed late."

"Not as late as you."

Her glasses have slipped down her nose. His face is a smudge. She rubs the lenses on her shirt, looking down at her hands.

"I just," he says, "want it to work."

So she calls Maytag. Mercifully, they can send someone that day, though late afternoon. The customer service rep insists there must be someone eighteen years or older in the house.

"The repairman better be here on time," Rachel tells the rep.

THE REPAIRMAN IS not on time. The longer she waits the more it seems that he is already here, inside her, parasitic, a tapeworm nourished by her stifled anger, her sense of wanting to run as she once ran cross-country in high school and would run in her neighborhood on weekends. She was quiet and fleet, the streets reptilian after the rain. Her breasts had been mere slips of flesh. The late repairman becomes her house, its rotted shutters. He becomes the house she had wanted instead, the ones she ran past as a teenager: clean, alike, dismissive of style and deferential to the higher purpose of comfort, of needs supplied en suite, of carpeted stairs and air conditioning. Rachel let her husband sweet-talk her out of her ideas and into his, as though love was a way of forgetting oneself. Then the love drained away and she was stranded in a tide pool of her choices. She could not get back to who she used to be. The Maytag repairman is her children, spaced out in front of the TV: Jake enraptured by a purple dinosaur, Tyler slipping between disgust, fascination with his disgust, and bored surrender. When the clock reaches 4 p.m., Rachel has never hated anyone as much as she hates the Maytag Man.

She returns to the kitchen and picks up the phone, a 1950s ("Authentic!") seafoam Bakelite green.

"Yeah," Heidi says.

"It's Morgan."

"Uh-huh."

"I might be late."

"You know," the stage mom says, "I used to be one of you. Then I got too old."

"It's a family emergency."

"Funny how many people have had 'family emergencies' since Ruby and Lady Jade."

"I'm not skipping my shift. I'm not worried about what happened." She is worried, but she also has two kids and a mortgage.

"What are you, thirty-five?" Heidi says. "How about you get here on time and make the most of that pretty face of yours while it lasts. Otherwise I'll schedule you for Tuesday nights and charge you double house fees."

It is unfair. Men get to wrinkle and go gray and make stupid real estate investments and *still* leave their wives for younger women. Meanwhile, Rachel monitors the start of marionette lines above her mouth. She got a boob job not because she wanted larger breasts but because her babies had sucked the life out of hers. Her breasts had looked like a pair of empty change purses. Rachel is angry at Heidi. She is angry at the world. Women are allowed to feel powerful for ten years, and then they turn thirty and men barely look at them again.

"I'll be there," Rachel says.

Heidi hangs up. Rachel is about to call Maytag and scream down the line when she sees that Tyler is sitting at the kitchen table, gaze tick-tocking all over her face, though as she scrambles backward through her end of the conversation, she can think of nothing incriminating he would have heard, save her use of another name, which maybe he did not hear. If he did, she can craft a lie any thirteen-year-old will swallow.

"What will they do to you," Tyler says, "if you're late?"

"I won't be late."

"Like do they dock you, or what?"

"Don't tilt your chair."

"I'm just wondering."

"Another waitress will cover for me until I get there."

"Sure." He leans farther on the chair's back legs. *"Waitress."* His fingers hook into air quotes.

Her stomach bottoms out. Her son is suddenly terrifying. "What's that supposed to mean?"

"Nate's dad saw you."

She gets close. "Saw me where? Saw what?"

"You're not a waitress," he says. "You're a slut."

She cuts her foot under the chair's lifted legs. He tumbles back, eyes flown open wide. His head hits the tiled floor.

"YOU GOTTA SEE this," the repairman calls from the basement. Tyler, a bag of frozen peas pressed to his head, watches her go, eyes reddened. Below the crust of acne, he has his father's skin, pale and delicate. It shows everything. If she swept aside his hair, she'd see the tops of his ears on fire.

The repairman has taken the back off the dryer. Stuffed around the drum are husks of dead sparrows. "Must've flown in through the vent," the man says, "wanting the warmth."

Rachel remembers how Tyler, as a baby, made chirrups of hunger. She used to cut his frail fingernails with her own teeth, she was so afraid of cutting his skin with clippers. She remembers the dear worm of his finger in her mouth, and thinks this is what it means to have a child: to lose him.

SHE MIGHT GET out of this one.

There is no question she was speeding—twenty miles over the limit, and even that hadn't felt fast enough, the anger in her chest like a supplemental power source whose juice could fuel the car's engine—but she knows how to say sorry sweetly. The cop approaches. Red and blue lights splash over his black-and-white patrol car. She will be humble. Adorable. She will be as Tyler said Jake was, as if she had been bought in a box.

She forgets this, however, when the man reaches her window. She recognizes him from the club.

He gives no flicker of recognition. People are conditioned by context, by makeup and murky lighting, and while it is strange to think of being fully naked as a disguise, men at the club never look at the right parts that would let them know her. Except, apparently, Nate Clay's father. Damn her glasses—and Phil Clay. His popped polo collar, his PTA wife with her Rice Krispies Treats, the easiest thing to make, why can't you show a little effort. Nate, too, for being thirteen, for telling Tyler—the whole school, probably.

But she knows this cop, even if he doesn't know her. He is the man who took Ruby and Violet gambling. Rachel is so startled that she says nothing as he writes the ticket. It occurs to her, when he passes the ticket through the open window, that he could be the one who murdered Ruby and Lady Jade. He might be someone to fear. She should have told that woman cop about the casino, about this man. Why hadn't she? How had the club's habit of secrecy grown so powerful as to be invisible, so that Rachel had worried about getting Ruby into trouble even when Ruby was dead, the worry roosting in Rachel's heart with mute weight?

RABIDEAUX, his uniform reads. He has written his badge number on the slip of pink paper.

GEORGIA
(GIGI)

"I can't find my vibrator," Paris says. Georgia watches Bella do Paris's makeup. The dressing room is full, but Morgan is on the schedule and should be here already. Dancers are often late and jam their feet into high heels at the last minute, swiping on deodorant and lipstick, but Morgan is punctual and disdainful of those who aren't.

"You got a dog?" Skye asks Paris. "Mine finds my dildo even when I hide it. Chews it all to hell."

Bella's hair hangs in her eyes as she looks down at Paris and tucks a makeup brush behind her ear. Georgia wonders if Bella will suggest again that they go to Denny's after work. They've done that twice now. The last time, Sasha noticed them leaving together. Don't you know about her? Sasha muttered in Georgia's ear the next day. You do dirty by the Lord, he'll do dirty by you.

Georgia signed up for shifts that she knew Bella worked. There was nothing wrong with that. They were good shifts. But that is not why. It is because she thinks about the cocoon-shaped scar on Bella's shoulder. It is because of how Bella bites a makeup brush between her teeth.

"Maybe your kid took it," Sasha says to Paris.

"She is nine," Paris says.

Lacey raises her hand as though taking an oath. "Electric toothbrush. Age eight."

"But the bristles!"

"I liked the bristles."

"A green glass grape." Bella blends foundation across Paris's cheeks with a triangular sponge. "My parents had two clusters of glass grapes on their mantel, green and red, each grape fastened to its cluster by a wire. I twisted a grape until it came off in my hand, and took it to my bedroom."

The image of this sinks into Georgia and drops to the bottom of her belly.

Violet, who has been listening silently, says, "Pillows."

"Too soft," Lacey says.

Georgia wants to change the conversation, to avoid it turning to her. What do *you* do, Gigi? What do *you* think about? She says, "Who do you think makes more, us or the stage mom?"

"Us!" they say.

"I would never be a stage mom," says Paris. "That is one sad-ass job."

"Heidi doesn't pay house fees," Georgia points out. "She's paid the same amount every night, no matter what. She never goes home in debt, and she gets to wear sneakers."

"You know who really rakes it in," says Lacey. "Dale."

"He is the Bill Gates of boobs," agrees Bella.

"I heard Dale owns a jacuzzi."

"I heard he flies first-class."

"Bitch, where would he go? He never takes a vacation. He *lives* for selling our hot bods."

"I heard his suits cost a thousand bucks each."

"Have you seen his diamond cufflinks? He should marry me. If he had a wife, she would look like a goddamn chandelier."

"Come on," says Georgia.

"I'm serious. Not everyone can pull off big jewels, but I got good bone structure."

"I heard he bought a car right off a movie lot," says Lacey. "A classic Humphrey Bogart–mobile."

"He does not have diamond cufflinks," says Georgia. "No one we know is that rich."

"I should run a strip club," says Sasha. "You could all work for me." They laugh in her face.

Georgia glances at the clock. "Should someone call Morgan?" she asks, and the others chorus *no*—but quickly, resentfully, like Morgan's absence has been on their minds, too, and Georgia has violated a tacit oath by voicing any concern.

Bella glances up from lining Paris's eyes. "Give it a minute." Her voice is gentle. "She'll be here, or she'll call in sick."

"You call in sick all the time," Violet reminds Georgia.

"Yeah," Lacey says. "Your schedule is like a battlefield. There should be a war memorial dedicated to your sick days."

"I bet I gave my vibrator to Goodwill by mistake," Paris says. "I lost it right around the time I filled a bunch of bags to donate." There is some discussion about whether Goodwill would throw it out or price it to sell, and if anyone would buy a used vibrator. Most say no. Lacey disagrees. She would clean it really well, she says. Sasha looks straight at Bella and says she doesn't see what's wrong with good old-fashioned cock.

Georgia focuses on the mirror, dusting anti-shine powder on her nose and cheeks even though Bella already did her makeup perfectly, her fingers light as rain, her mouth close to Georgia's mouth. There is a bottle of wine in Georgia's fridge. She thinks about closing her hand around its cool green neck. A nice one, French. She imagines France. It seems impossible. The Alps serrate the sky and cradle glaciers. Movie stars plunge from rocks into the sea. There is warm bread, fragrant peaches, glassy flakes of salt. Porcelain castles and jade moats. It might as well be Narnia.

She bought beer, too, in case Bella likes that better. This is normal. A good host should offer something a friend likes. Georgia could say, Let's skip Denny's. I hate the food. My place is nearby. There is a dry-aged steak. There are endives and toasted walnuts. Georgia has no friends other than Kaitlyn, and Kaitlyn is family, so that doesn't count. Yes, a friend. Nervousness whistles through her.

Morgan is late. Georgia decides that Morgan's absence is why she feels nervous. Morgan should be here.

And then, suddenly, she is.

Morgan whips into the dressing room and dumps her purse on the beauty bar. "You'll never guess," she announces, "who just pulled me over."

DETECTIVE HOLLY MEYLIN

Holly closes her cell phone. "Patrol Sergeant Tony Rabideaux took Samantha Lind to a casino two Saturdays before the crash."

Amador takes the pencil from his mouth. Pradko winces like he's swallowed sour milk. Backyard looks up from his report, a straightforward domestic violence involving a baseball bat, and does a slow, elaborate blink. Backyard's thick lashes are curled, like a doll's. He exchanges a glance with Amador, who says, "Rabideaux is a known associate of the victim?"

"He brought another stripper, too," Holly says. "Catherine Francis, the one from Trinidad. Her stage name is Violet. He paid her and Lind and a bouncer, James MacAllister, to gamble with him. Lind told one of the other dancers, Rachel Lukehart, that they were going with him. Rachel got a good look at him that night before the four of them left."

"Fuck a foie gras duck," Pradko says.

"Foie gras comes from geese," Backyard tells him.

"We gotta pull in all three witnesses," Pradko says. "Interview those two dancers and the bouncer."

"No," Holly says. "I want to wait. I've got a CI in the club. If we bring the three of them in now, everyone in the club will know that someone is taking information directly to us. Rachel didn't call me. She told my

CI. We'll give it a few days before we talk to the witnesses. The last thing I want is for the CI to be discovered—or for people at the club to keep their mouths shut because they figure someone's listening, even if they don't know who." She glances at Amador, who has been uncomfortably silent. "What's wrong?"

Amador looks like he's about to undergo a deeply unpleasant medical procedure. "There is something I ought to tell you about Rabideaux." He explains how Rabideaux took money from the crime scene and planted some of it in Amador's car to make him complicit. "I never wanted it. My share of the cash is back in evidence."

"Rabideaux is a known associate of the vic *and* he tampered with the crime scene?" Holly says. "And you *knew*?"

Backyard spreads his large hands. "Cops take stray cash all the time."

"You knew, too, I see."

"We didn't know he was going to be a suspect." The room gets eerily quiet. "Is he a suspect?"

Holly can feel the other detectives resist the idea, how it swells against them like an invisible balloon, but she doesn't share their cultish feeling that cops must be loyal to other cops, that they must protect their own. Holly is furious. She sees no reason to defend Rabideaux. "The accident reconstructionist said that the vehicle that ran Lind and Campana off the road could belong to a cop from this department. The driver used a pit maneuver. Any cop knows how to do one of those."

"Or military," Amador reminds her.

Holly ignores him. "Rabideaux was on duty that night, which means he could have been anywhere in or near his section doing whatever he wanted unless he was actually responding to a call. Lind's face has been on flyers all over the department and Rabideaux has said nothing about his association with her. It's possible."

"I disagree," Pradko says. "How would he even know the girls left the club? It makes no sense."

"Unless he was at the club when he was supposed to be on duty."

"Okay, but he *was* on duty. He answered Amador's call for a supervisor on scene. You're telling me he killed Campana, took Lind, *and* came back to the scene?"

"Maybe to control the evidence. He did take the cash."

"Which he wouldn't do," Pradko says, "if he was the perp. Why raise a red flag? Rabideaux is your basic cop who takes money from a crime scene, whatever. Like none of you've been tempted. He's dirty, but not a murderer. And so what about the flyer? Lind has brown hair and no makeup in that picture. Rabideaux probably didn't even recognize her from that flyer. You wanna crucify him for gambling with a stripper."

"Who is dead," Holly says. "We don't know what else he might have taken from the crime scene before the lieutenant arrived."

"I'll pull the dispatch log from that night," Amador says, and his readiness to act after covering Rabideaux's ass does not alleviate her anger. He pretends not to notice. "I'll check the times and locations of any calls Rabideaux responded to before the crash. Maybe there's a window in which he could have gone to the club."

"If he used his patrol car for a pit, you'd see it on his front bumper," Backyard said. "I'll check his car for that or any repair. I'll call the garages in the area, too."

"I'm calling IA," Holly says.

"Aw, shit," Pradko says.

"Internal Affairs needs to know about this. They need to open an investigation into Rabideaux for the stolen money."

"He's gonna get fired," Pradko says. "They're gonna trap him with planted cash."

"He's dirty," Holly says, "if he's nothing else."

"You really like to nail a guy, don't you?"

Pradko means her husband. Holly did everything in her power to make certain no charges were pressed against Matthew, but Pradko's right. Holly saved Matthew in one way and destroyed him in another. She couldn't bear the sight of him. She couldn't smother the rage in her. Pradko doesn't want to believe that a cop could murder someone, but Holly knows that she could. If she had obliterated Matthew's connection to her, if she had been cruel in divorcing him and leaving him alone to carry the weight of what he had done, it was because she feared what she might do to him if he slept in her bed and drank from the cup that had been Daniel's.

An apology crawls over Amador's face.

Earlier, as she napped in Major Crash, Holly dropped in and out of dreams. She stepped into a crowded elevator. Her son was there, hip-high. How had he grown? He had been just a baby when she lost him. She reached for him in joy. The elevator light popped and flashed, and everyone vanished but her. Tiny bone objects littered the floor: a teacup, a vase, a bowl, a jar. She sifted through them, knowing that one of those light bone vessels was Daniel. But which? How could she not know? What kind of mother was she, that she couldn't recognize her own son? Her hand was full of the relics of dead people. To keep Daniel, she must keep them all.

"Yeah," she tells Pradko, but her words are meant for Amador. "I do."

SERGEANT TONY RABIDEAUX

Tony Rabideaux blamed his wife and the washing machine for his unhappiness.

She said she couldn't take it anymore. She said she was tired of being afraid that she had loaded the dishwasher wrong, or that locking the front door when they went to bed at night might enrage him. She never knew what would set him off.

She was too stupid to understand, or too stubborn, even though he had explained many times that if she loved him she would make more of an effort to load the dishwasher so that he didn't have to reorganize everything when he put a plate in. Most husbands didn't even clean up after themselves, but look at him, how he contributed. If she loved him she wouldn't insult him by locking a door before bed. Didn't she feel safe with him? Didn't she realize how insane it was, to lock the door? He stood over their bed, yelling down at her. She got this scared rabbit look. Her face was pathetic. Manipulative. It was so easy to make him happy, if she only tried, and now she was making him feel like *he* was the crazy one.

In the end, it wasn't the gambling that made her leave, or the late nights, or even what she called his blackouts, the times when he couldn't remember what he had said or done. She would remind him. She would say gently, as though he were an idiot, that it was probably because he worked such odd hours and slept whenever he could, often during the day. Oh, she loved having one over on him. But it wasn't that, or the dishwasher, or the lock, or any of her many complaints, why couldn't she ever be happy, why did she have to be such a drag, to act like he was a monster. He loved her. She never smiled. One smile would have meant so much to him.

Last winter she had put a load of laundry in the wash. He had been sleeping. When he heard her cry out, he launched himself out of bed, heart fast, ready to protect her, ready to kick the living shit out of someone. And then this: water sheeting from the closed washer all over the mudroom. Jesus Christ, he said, what did you do. She said, I don't know. I'm sorry, I don't know. He said, You overloaded it, didn't you. He knew he was shouting. He knew she was crying. Why do I always have to fix everything? he said. Why can't you do anything right? He bailed water out of the mudroom onto the outdoor steps, and of course it froze. Of course now there was yet another problem for him to fix. He would have to salt the ice and chip it away so that she wouldn't slip and fall. There was always something. He was always taking care of her, yet she wept as if he had struck her. I guess I must have overloaded it, she said. I didn't think I overloaded it, but I must have.

He turned off the water. He dragged the washer out of place and found, in the drain hose, a chunk of ice. The rage left him. It's not your fault, he reassured her. He was really nice about it. Look, he said, the water had nowhere to go. He said he was sorry. He shouldn't have yelled. She said it was okay, but she was trembling. His tenderness withered. He had made an honest mistake. How could she cringe from him when he was trying to make things right? Why could she never see things from his point of view?

Now his house was empty. He remembered how he would lightly caress her face when she had trouble sleeping, how she'd sigh. He was not a bad man. She had broken his heart. Everything felt surreal without her. He would fall asleep in his patrol car and wake up to classical music on the radio, a starry harpsichord, and think, What the fuck. He couldn't remember turning the radio on. He hated classical music. He went to the strip club—he had to, he was so lonely—and woke up with an empty wallet. He couldn't resist the casino. When he won at roulette, he felt vindicated. When he lost, he was sure next time would be different. She would come back. She would miss him. She would feel bad for having hurt him. She would apologize, and he would forgive her.

He stopped going to the Lovely Lady after those dancers got killed. The club was under scrutiny, and he didn't want to run into anyone he worked with, and certainly didn't want anyone wondering where his cash came from. Cops got paid peanuts. No one liked cops. No one thought about what a hard job it was. No one appreciated him, not even his wife. He was basically a janitor. Constantly cleaning up, getting scum off the streets, making good people safer. He remembered having to pry open the jaws of an old man, like the guy was a dog, to make him cough out the crack he had tried to swallow.

Pocketing cash from a crime scene was a way of evening the scales, but not everyone understood. Some suckers don't know yet that life screws you over. You have got to take what you can get.

Consider that dead girl, Samantha Lind. He had seen the flyer. She had probably had all sorts of plans. She had believed she would get to be happy. He felt sorry for her. Pretty girl. Soft brown hair, soft face. She looked familiar. He must have seen her at the club, in passing, though he probably wouldn't have noticed her much, definitely wouldn't have bought a dance, not when there were strippers like that knockout blonde, Ruby, or that Black chick. Violet. Yes, that was her name. His memory wasn't that bad. It was so simple with Ruby and Violet. He treated them right. They treated him right. It didn't have to be complicated. It was the golden rule: you must treat people as they deserve.

CATHERINE

(VIOLET)

After Morgan made her announcement about that cop, all eyes in the dressing room turned toward Catherine.

"Violet," said Gigi, "did you tell the police about going to the casino?"

Catherine had no patience for Gigi. Gigi had a white voice. Acted white. Like she was fooling anyone. "I don't need to tell anybody anything," Catherine said. Some people didn't know how to keep things to themselves, but Catherine did. For instance, Catherine knew something about Dale that no one else seemed to consider.

Catherine remembered how the woman cop examined her green card. "It's real," Catherine said, then worried she had sounded too aggressive and would be punished for it. But the cop just said, "I know," and thumbed through Catherine's passport. "Is this a stork?" The cop pointed to the ibis, her pink finger right above Trinidad's motto: *Together We Aspire, Together We Achieve.* At home, Catherine saw ibises all the time, their wings like layered slices of paper. They stalked lizards through the green. The cop kept name-switching, calling her Catherine, then Violet. Catherine didn't mind. She didn't care to know the girls' real names. Stage names were more real. They were chosen. They said something about a person. Hers said: she hadn't paid enough attention, growing up, to the violets growing wild in her grandmother's garden, the dense smell of fallen mangoes, the rain on the galvanized roof, how the sound would pat her until she fell asleep.

She had had an idea of what America was. All those bright television shows, snow making people happy, ivy changing color on brick, the candy her mother sent back during the years Catherine lived with her grandmother and great-grandmother. Her mother mailed Snickers and M&Ms, sweeter to her then than the treats she would later miss: Ping Pong, Cheers, Kiss cakes. Then Catherine got here and finally understood that this new country was just another place.

She immigrated first to Iowa. That was years before she moved to Illinois to work at the Lady. Back in Iowa, she lied about her age and got a job doing lap dances. It took a while to get used to it. You kneel on his thighs and bury his face between your breasts. He is supposed to keep his tongue in his mouth but he probably won't. He will wear track pants so his dick can roam free. Sometimes his boner is so big it is like the tiller of a boat.

When Catherine was a child, her world was all she saw. She lived in the south and went to Tobago only for church. She played morale and marble pitch and elastic. She got up early, dawn in neon streaks, to walk the road to school, carrying buss up shut in her lunch. Farmers burned sugar cane in the fields, the smell heavy, nothing sweet, nothing but ash, not like the harvest later, when cut stalks released their juice and the air smelled like caramel.

At school, Catherine sat at a long desk shared with Alice. They wore white shirts and green dresses. Alice's neck was sprinkled with baby powder. Her slender hand wrote neatly on checked paper, her skin the color of a penny, as the sound of passing cars floated in through the school window. Kiskadee birds sang. In Brazil they're called bem-te-vi, Alice whispered. It means, I saw you well.

Catherine didn't care much about Ruby until the day Ruby shared a case of oranges her mother sent from Florida. The dancers ate them backstage until the room actually smelled good. Did you know, Ruby said, that an orange tastes different from all the other oranges on the same tree? It's because each orange gets a different amount of sunlight. Each segment in an orange tastes different, too, because one side of the fruit got more sun than the other. You think, *I am eating an orange*, but really you're eating a whole bunch of little fruits packed inside the same skin.

The other girls teased her. They called her Farm Girl. Catherine, though, was reminded of Alice. Ruby was the sort of person who paid attention.

Which is why it frustrated Catherine that Ruby couldn't see Lady Jade for what she was. The dancers thought Catherine was a traitor because she told on Lady Jade, but they didn't understand that Catherine had been trying to do Ruby a favor. Ruby was too nice. That new girl was trash. Anyone could see Lady Jade was going nowhere fast. That girl will drag you down, Catherine had wanted to tell Ruby, and she had been right.

Everyone else believed Dale had been in the club the entire night it happened, but when Catherine went to tell him that Lady Jade was high, she couldn't find him on the floor. He wasn't in his office. Finally, when she was searching near the kitchen, she saw him coming in through a back door, keys in hand.

The other dancers told the detective Dale never left the club that Saturday night. The bouncers did, too. The deejay, the bartender, the house mom. But they simply assumed this was true because they saw him often enough. And if they didn't see him, they figured he must be somewhere else inside the club. If he wasn't on the floor, he was probably in his office. He could often be seen standing in his office, looking down at the stage, but only if he stood directly in front of the office's interior window. Otherwise, the angle from the club floor made it impossible to look deep into his office. His light was on, so he must be at his desk. If he wasn't at his desk, he was probably talking to the deejay. There were two doors in his office, one to the main floor, the stairs clear plexiglass, and one that led to the basement. He could always be down there, assessing the construction of new VIP rooms. This is what people believed.

Catherine knew better. Dale could come and go as he pleased, with no one else the wiser.

Dale, when he let the door to the parking lot shut behind him, was courteous. "How can I help you, Violet?" he said. She opened her mouth and blabbed. She tattled like she was back in school and wanted Lady Jade's knuckles whacked with a ruler.

A few days after Ruby went missing, Dale called her into his office. "I know you and Ruby were close," he said. "I will waive house fees for you indefinitely. Nothing will make her absence easy to bear, but I want you to have one less thing to worry about." He smiled gently. "Don't mention this to the other entertainers, though, all right? They might get jealous."

Catherine imagined stitching her lips together. If only she had kept her mouth shut. If only she had let Ruby hide Lady Jade in the dressing room until the drug that Catherine had found in Lady Jade's makeup bag and slipped into her drink had worn off. We look like queens, she had once told Ruby, but Catherine didn't feel that way anymore. She felt like nobody.

GEORGIA
(GIGI)

The steak has gone bad. It is slimy and brown. Georgia throws it out and goes in early for her afternoon shift.

The locker room is empty. It's Sunday. Many of the strippers who worked last night will straggle in late, some of them hung over if they couldn't get dances and decided to drink at the bar instead. Georgia's locker door wails on its hinges. She sorts through her outfits. She's working a double shift, so she will need them all. Most dancers consider dresses a necessary investment, but Georgia hates spending money on them. She wishes Cherry, who made dresses and sold them cheap, was still around. Cherry danced even after she got pregnant and smoked joints in the toilet stall between sets to make herself hungry. I gotta eat for the baby, she said. Eventually her bump got too big and Dale made her leave.

Georgia grabs a black latex dress that can unzip from the top or bottom and heads into the dressing room. Violet is the only one there, which is like having no one there. Violet rarely talks to anyone, especially now that Ruby's gone.

Georgia cleans her navel and glitters her breasts. She steps into the dress and is zipping it up when Violet asks, "Are you adopted?"

"Excuse me, what?"

"You heard me."

It's none of Violet's business, but Georgia guesses the question behind the question. It isn't only white people who want to know much Black she is. "My mom raised me. I don't know where my father is. He's got a new family now."

"Is he Black?"

"Yeah."

"So your mom's white."

"You gonna make me take a DNA test?"

"Your dad's light-skinned, I bet."

Georgia shrugs.

"I thought some white Christians adopted you. They say they want to give Black babies a good home, but really they just want to raise them up white. They think it's their calling."

This last word tickles the back of Georgia's brain. At the funeral home, in the bathroom, Rosie had said that Ruby had been taken by a monster. "He called me," Rosie whispered, and Georgia hadn't paid attention. Now she wonders what Rosie meant. Had the girl spoken abstractly, in a kind of kid way? *Jesus called me to be a preacher*, people say. Maybe Rosie meant something like that. If people can imagine a divine voice, they can imagine the devil, too, walking the edges of a nightmare, calling their name.

Or had Rosie meant something simple, ordinary? Had Ruby's killer picked up a telephone and called the girl?

"Look at me, coming in early," Sasha sings, *click-clacking* into the room. "Ready to suck all that money from those limp-dick fools." She peels open a KitKat but doesn't break off a stick, just bites big into the bar. "Today I'm gonna bank, I can feel it."

IT'S ALMOST TIME for the stage lineup when Bella finally comes in, trailed by Skye and Paris, who are snorting with laughter over something Bella must have said. They smell like weed. Paris has her hand on Bella's shoulder, leaning into her. Georgia's chest feels tight.

"Me first!" Lacey drags a chair in front of Bella and tips up her face, eyes closed, as though sunbathing. "Do me fast."

Skye snorts so hard that a spray of snot must hit Paris, who winces and palms her cheeks.

"No," Bella says, her voice sleepy. Her eyes squint as she unbuttons her shirt. "It's Do Your Own Makeup Day." Georgia has seen her naked a million times, but this is different. Bella isn't onstage pretending to be a slut. She isn't even doing what they all do in the dressing room, which is to make their bodies into fuckable props. Bella's expression is vague and dreamy, as though she's alone in her bedroom. She isn't wearing a bra beneath her flannel. She finishes unbuttoning the shirt but seems to forget to take it off. She stands there, her small bare breasts like cream, her belly a long, hard plane.

"We don't have time now to do our own makeup." Georgia's voice is frosty. "We were all waiting for you."

"Well, that's dumb," Bella says. "What if I never came in?"

"We deserve a medal for coming in," Paris says.

"Employees of the Motherfucking Month," Skye says.

"Perfect attendance in the face of force majeure," Bella says.

"You are so stoned," Sasha says.

Bella sighs. "I really wanted to stay home. I got *Four Weddings and a Funeral*. Finally. It's always out at my Blockbuster. I was on a waiting list."

"Hugh Grant." Paris lays a hand over her heart. "So what if a hooker blew him? I would blow him. I would pay to blow him. He is my scrawny prince."

"I like how Kristin Scott Thomas takes flecks of tobacco off her tongue," Bella says.

"Is she the one in the hat?"

"They are all the one in the hat. All of them, always wearing hats."

"You could have let someone know you'd be late," Georgia says, "if you were responsible."

Bella screws her face up. "Responsible?"

"We're not late," Skye says. "We just got fucked up at brunch."

"You skip shifts all the time," Paris reminds Georgia.

"Yes, but no one here is counting on me."

"Counting," Bella repeats. "Am I a boy scout? Have I missed my chance at the Eagle court of honor?"

"I bet your mom's not even sick," Skye tells Georgia. Georgia's lungs spark with pain. "I bet she is fucking fine."

"Just"—Bella lifts one hand—"everyone slap some color on your face and I'll take care of you between sets."

"For free," Sasha says.

"I'm not that stoned."

THE BOUNCERS GIVE the all clear, and everyone walks out to their cars, huddled against the October cold. A faint rain pricks Georgia's cheeks. Paris and Skye, in long down coats like sleeping bags, get into Skye's yellow Hummer. Cars start all around Georgia. Headlights show the rain.

"Hey." It's Bella, whom Georgia has ignored all night, ever since Bella said, Your turn, and Georgia looked at the empty stool backstage, and said, My makeup's fine, and walked away.

Bella's face is sharp in the parking-lot lights. The weed wore off long ago, and Bella's expression, her whole body, is alert with anger. "What's your problem?"

Georgia thinks of the bottle of wine. She thinks of Bella rubbing color onto her mouth with her fingers like it's nothing, like she does it all the time, which she does, with everyone else.

"I don't want to think you're being rude for no reason," Bella says. "What, did I take one of your regulars?"

"No."

The cars drive away.

Bella says, "Sasha said something to you."

"No."

"You are a bad liar."

"That's not it." Anxious, Georgia blurts, "I already knew. What you are."

"You can't even say it."

"But I don't care."

"Wow, how nice."

"I'm mad because you went to brunch."

"Stop dicking around and admit what's wrong. For real."

"I wish." Georgia's voice falters. This is awful. I wish I weren't afraid. I wish I didn't think about you. I wish I weren't jealous, but I am, and hurt, but I am. "I wish that you had invited me."

"You never go anywhere with anyone."

"Except you."

The parking lot is empty. Bella looks away, considering the periphery. From lot lamps, rainy light falls like bolts of glinting fabric. Even the bouncers are gone.

"I bought a steak," Georgia said, "as an excuse to invite you over."

The rain is cold, electric. Bella's gaze returns to Georgia. "So invite me over for steak."

"I threw it out."

"Invite me anyway."

"Will you come over," Georgia says, "for not-steak?"

GEORGIA HAS A hard time with the keys. She fumbles. She thinks what she was thinking throughout the entire silent car ride, Bella next to her, the rain swiping down. What am I doing? I don't know what I'm doing. I have never done this.

Bella closes her hand over Georgia's. Her hand is so warm that Georgia knows her own must be cold. Bella takes the key, fits it into the lock, and opens the apartment door.

Georgia flips on all the lights. Bella looks at her sidelong. "I must have something in the fridge," Georgia says, and moves toward the kitchen.

"Stay."

Georgia stays.

"This is very bright." Bella squints at the ceiling.

Georgia reaches again for the light switch.

"No, I want to see." Bella takes in the sand-colored carpet in the living room, the small brown couch, the one chair at the table. Rain sparks against the window. Georgia hears the wind trying to get in.

Bella says, "I could feel you worrying all the way here."

"I'm not worried."

"You don't have to worry. I'm your friend."

Georgia feels unsteady. She feels like the keys in Bella's hand, swinging in and out of her fist. She closes her fingers around Bella's, which go still. "No, you're not," Georgia says. The ache inside her deepens. She can't seem to say the right thing. She steps closer, so that Bella's fingers are at her waist. They go to the skin beneath her shirt, and she can feel the cool jagged keys, Bella's opening hand, the slide and fall of jingling metal to the floor.

"It's not okay," Bella says softly in her ear, "to let me fuck you just because you're lonely."

I am lonely for you, Georgia wants to say, but can't, so she lifts her mouth to Bella's to show her.

THE RAIN AGAINST the bedroom window has turned to ice. Bella is warm against her, almost sleeping. Georgia's mouth tastes like her. Georgia shifts under the blanket. "So restless," Bella murmurs.

"I can't sleep."

"You work tomorrow." Bella must feel Georgia's surprise, because she says, "I pay attention."

"To everyone."

"To you." Bella says it in a sleepy tease.

"I didn't know."

"I think you did."

"I didn't know what I was doing."

Bella makes a disbelieving noise.

"What's your name?" Georgia asks.

"Bella," says Bella.

"My mother died," Georgia says. "About a year ago."

Bella turns to her, sliding her hand beneath Georgia's pillow. "I know," she says. "I mean, I guessed. I've known for a while."

"You knew, and let me keep lying?"

"It seemed like you needed the lie."

HIM

He watched Gigi and Bella argue in the empty lot. Bella got into Gigi's car. It was obvious what would happen next.

Gigi should have taken his feelings into consideration. She should have thought, Is this not a betrayal? I have shown him my respect, my gratitude, and if I give him no second thought now does that not mean that respect is all pretense, gratitude nothing?

He remembered driving back to the club, the crash glittering, tail-lit, in his rearview mirror. Lady Jade was fresh in his mind, yet already fading. A cheap iris, petals curling the instant the stem was cut. Ruby lay in the trunk of his car, unconscious and bound and gagged. He stayed at the club until it closed, enjoying the thought of her in the trunk's tight darkness. She was waiting for him, and she didn't even know it.

I am not in Gigi's mind, he thought. Not at all. He determined that he would make her know him. He would anchor deep.

DALE

He feeds the fish, tapping a line of orange flakes across the bubbling surface. The club is closed. Everyone's gone. The tank is the only source of light in his office. Fish fan their way to the top.

When the club is empty Dale feels most at peace, even sometimes reluctant to drive home. His home is orderly, his closet full of suits. On the wall hangs a chess set he made himself, pieces carved and sanded and stained: walnut and beech. The board is designed vertically, with little shelves. Each player has its own nook. The king and queen like large insects, their antennae crowns with round-top spokes. The slim slice of the bishop. The sturdy rook. Smart-ass knight. Blank pawn.

If there was a time when he was happy it was in the years he left his father and his father's business for the army. It was a matter of strategy. Stupid kids got sent to the jungle. He enlisted in the National Guard and waited out Vietnam in Texas. *Always Ready, Always There.* He had worked strip clubs even as a kid, helping his father. He would empty the vending machines at each club after hours, restock them, leave half the cash on the bar for the owner and take the other half to his father, who ran the biggest club. The first time Dale—what was he? ten?—came in when the club was closed and saw his father pressing one of his dancers against the stage, thumping into her, his father met his eyes. Like what you see? he said, and kept at it until he slid out. After that he just fucked them and paid Dale no mind. So Dale had good stories. The other men in his squad liked him. He always had a nice word for them. In Combatives they'd have a laugh after they practiced choke holds on each other. He was a likable guy.

An angelfish plucks food from the surface and zips away, its fins like tiny gingko leaves, its body as flat as a shingle. He has had this tank for years. He has run this club since he was young. Ruby questioned whether the VIP rooms were a good idea, but she should have known better. He knew what he was doing.

Dale came home to Illinois. His father made sure of that. He willed his business to Dale. Little prince, his father sneered as he died. There is no chess piece for a prince. Princes wait and take. Like what you see? You smile. You say yes.

GEORGIA
(GIGI)

"Hey."

Georgia smells coffee. The drool on her pillow shines in the late morning light. Her hair is wild. Bella holds out a cup of coffee that smells like grass and bitter chocolate and sunny stone. The first sip is a miracle.

"That is the exact same expression you make when you come," Bella says.

Georgia spills.

"You okay there?" Bella says, extra solicitous, amused, as Georgia coughs and more coffee drips onto the bed.

"Shut the fuck up."

"The mouth on you." Bella leans to kiss her long and deep. Georgia spills again and this time yelps, the coffee burning her fingers. Bella takes the cup from her and places it on the nightstand. Now Bella means it when she asks if Georgia's okay, and yes, she is, she is fine, no thanks to her. Bella brings Georgia's wet fingers to her mouth and licks them clean.

"I have to work," Georgia murmurs.

"Not yet."

"I am a mess."

"You are my mess."

Georgia's mouth opens beneath hers, greedy.

Bella touches her. "Tell me what you want."

Georgia does.

BACKSTAGE IT'S QUIET, a slow, early Monday afternoon. Outside it's clear but cold; the forecast calls for sleet. Georgia is between sets, and since she has a double shift and the secret ace of Dale's special rotation, she is not worried about hitting her number. She has taken a break for lunch: homemade quiche and a pink apple. Bella's not on the schedule ("Will I see you tonight after work?" "You better."). Violet's the only other dancer backstage. The rest have sets or are working the floor. Violet files her nails. Georgia almost admires her, because Violet never seems to care that she's been shunned. Georgia opens her Tupperware and takes a metal fork and knife wrapped in a cloth napkin from her bag.

Earlier that day, after they had finally dragged themselves out of bed, Bella watched Georgia pack lunch and asked warily, "Do you like pizza?"

"It depends."

"Let me guess. Wood-fired, homemade crust. Beef heart tomatoes."

"Well."

"Jesus Christ."

"Can I ask you something?"

"I like Pizza Hut, to be honest."

"What do you think someone means when they say, 'He called me'?"

"This is not a question."

"Do you think it means 'He picked up a phone and called me'?"

"What else?"

Georgia explained what Rosie had said at Ruby's funeral.

Bella said, "You think the monster is the person who killed Ruby. That he called her house and Ruby's kid picked up."

"Maybe."

"So ask the kid what she meant."

Georgia pictured Rosie, her stiff, battle-ready body. My daddy doesn't like you. "Not me."

"Maybe the police could have suspects do, I don't know, a voice lineup. See if the girl recognizes one of them."

"I should call Holly."

"Yeah, okay, call her," Bella said, "but listen: this means that it's not Ruby's boyfriend, and that whoever called knew Ruby's phone number. She gave it to him."

"Or he looked it up in the phone book."

"Then he knew her real name."

Georgia snapped the Tupperware shut.

"Don't go in today," Bella said.

"But the money."

"Fuck the money."

"Are *you* going to quit?"

"Call your cop," Bella said. "Then stop this CI bullshit. Promise me."

"I promise," Georgia lied.

She hasn't called Holly, not yet. She wants to figure this out on her own and give the cop something good, something meaningful.

Violet says, "What's that?"

Georgia has finished her meal and is unwrapping her dessert. She looks down at it. "Shortbread. Sort of. Came out too soft." She's not sure what she did wrong.

"Looks like biscuit cake," Violet says.

"What's biscuit cake?"

"Something from home."

There is a silence. Violet is using the silence to get what she wants without asking for it, which is annoying, but last night and this morning with Bella has made Georgia feel generous, filled to the brim with summery pleasure. "Want some?"

Violet takes a piece. It should break crisply. Instead, it bends. Georgia smells its sweet butter as Violet eats. Violet says, "Everyone's gonna treat me like crap forever. You think it's my fault they died."

"No one said that."

"That's why you hate me."

"We hate you," Georgia says, impatient, because Violet perfectly well knows why, "for telling. Kiss Dale's ass all you want. Everyone does it. But you got Lady Jade fired."

"I do not kiss Dale's ass."

"You kiss his ass so much your lips are chapped."

"Let me tell you something," Violet says. "Let me tell you something about Dale."

DETECTIVE HOLLY MEYLIN

Most of them have decent alibis. Zack Antonucci's credit card placed him at the casino that night. Nick Sullivan was at home with his daughter and had no other car, even if he wanted to sneak out while she was sleeping. Ron Needham, with his jelly jars, looked guilty but had that Day N' Night receipt that proved otherwise. Dale Gately was at the strip club all night. Even Tony Rabideaux checked out. They had pulled the logs for that night and the patrol sergeant had answered enough calls in enough locations that there was no way he could have done it, plus the patrol car he used showed no signs of damage or recent repair. Holly would have his badge, though. Internal Affairs already had proof of him regularly signing out ten minutes early, which doesn't seem like much, but it's stealing time. They assigned someone to follow him. Soon, IA will plant money at a crime scene. He might be careful at first, but people can't help what they are. Once they get away with something, they think they always will. He'll take the bait. Getting Rabideaux fired will be a small victory in the face of her larger failure.

Holly has been living at the station. She vaguely knows that today is chillier than yesterday—outside it's clear but cold; the forecast calls for sleet—but the knowledge is meaningless. She doesn't even go outside to smoke. Her suits smell. She rinses quickly in the scummy shower, cracked tiles painful underfoot. Her father never hit her, after the first time. He didn't need to. She was five when she palmed root beer barrels at the grocery store. Where did you get these? he said. He pulled them out of her pocket. Your mother knows better than to buy sweets. I'm sorry, she said. Sorry isn't good enough. He showed her his hand before he used it. Don't you forget.

It is not the worst thing to fear someone, but it had been bad enough. She needed to please him. Nothing pleased him. Her fear was like being sealed in wax. She became an effigy of herself, a plastic child.

Holly swipes a hand through her wet hair and gets dressed in old clothes.

Pradko is waiting for her outside the bathroom door. "Amador said I'd find you here. He said not to bother you, to wait, but I knew you wouldn't want to wait for this. I am about to become your numero uno, your darling blue-eyed boy. We can close the Campana-Lind case."

"How?"

"I finished canvassing Lind's apartment building. This old lady, Judy Zace, wasn't around because she was visiting her son in Nantucket or Portland or wherever the fuck. Today I finally talked with her. She was friendly with Lind and her boyfriend. Sometimes babysits the boyfriend's kid . . . and lets them use her car. Lind and Sullivan kept a set of keys in their apartment. The make of Judy Zace's car, you ask? A 1993 black Oldsmobile. Better yet, I checked surveillance tapes at the gas station closest to the apartment and found footage of that car, with that license plate, soon after Samantha Lind called home and left a message on the answering machine. Sullivan lied to us. That sneaky bastard wasn't sleeping soundly at home. He left his eight-year-old daughter alone and took Judy Zace's car—a car that is a possible match for the one that ran Campana and Lind off the road. Then he filled up at Amoco and took off down I-55."

In the direction of the club.

GEORGIA
(GIGI)

What if?

The rumor that Dale bought a car off a movie lot had sounded like silly, exaggerated bullshit. A Humphrey Bogart–mobile, Lacey said. A classy, fancy car. Did Dale own the black Caddy Holly was looking for?

Georgia can't ask him. She can ask him nothing. She cannot ever let him think what she is thinking. Surely it can't be him, and if he guesses her suspicion, his offense will be so great that her career at the Lady will be over. How could the thought even occur to you, he would say. I am like a father to you girls.

Maybe this is a trick. Violet got one dancer fired, and she could be trying to get Georgia fired, too, by planting an insane, reckless idea in her head. "I'm not saying he did it," Violet says, "just that he *could* have. He *could* have left the club and come back for payout and closing."

"But how can you work here, if you think that?"

Violet gives her a cool look. "How can *you*?" Violet adjusts her breasts, making sure her nipples are snug inside the thin strips of electric blue fabric that crisscross her chest. "I'm on Stage 2," she says, and leaves. The instant she's gone, Georgia digs out her phone and calls Holly Meylin's cell. The call goes to voice mail. It's almost time for her set, and one of the other dancers could come backstage any minute. This conversation is not something she wants overheard, but she's got a little time and remembers how—long ago, it seems—she slipped the detective's business card into her locker. She fetches the card, finds the Fremont PD's Homicide number on it, and dials.

"Deeetective Mike Pradko," says a man.

"Is Holly there?"

"I am afraid not." He sounds like he's pretending to be a butler.

"When will she be back?"

"Not sure." He has dropped the starched tone. "What's this about?"

What *is* this about? Her pulse yammers in her ears. She's about to say, I think it could be Dale. She's about to say, See if a black Caddy is registered in his name, and then thinks, wouldn't they have already done that, wouldn't they have at least considered him? But *she* hadn't. She opens her mouth, unsure, when the stage mom shouts down the stairs. "Gigi! Are you backstage?"

"Tell Holly to call Georgia back," she says, and hangs up just as Heidi comes into the dressing room.

"Oh no," Heidi says. "Oh no, you are *not* on the phone. You're supposed to be on the main stage! It's empty. Dale is going to have a coronary. Dale is gonna shit all over you *and* me. It's gonna be an Ex-Lax special if you don't get on that stage right the fuck now."

Georgia scrambles, tossing her phone into her locker. She rushes up the stairs, the JLo song getting louder. Is this the first song of Georgia's three-song set? The second?

Maybe the last.

DALE IS WAITING for her when she gets offstage. She is naked except for her heels and the small bills tucked, askew like broken wings, around the garter encircling her upper thigh.

"That was sloppy," he says. "I've been good to you. To be honest, I expected a little more gratitude. A little more professionalism."

Georgia's breath is short from dancing, from fear of getting in trouble, from fear of him. "My mother called. She's sick, you know—"

"Let's discuss this in my office."

"No," she blurts.

His face becomes very still. "No?"

"I mean, that's not necessary. I don't want to take up any more of your time. I'll make up for it. I'll pay double house fees. I don't mind."

A waitress eases around them, balancing beers. She slides Georgia a look. You're gonna get it, her eyes say. Dale says, "I have always been understanding about your mother's illness."

"I know. I'm so grateful."

"I never had a mother, not one to speak of."

"I'm sorry," she says helplessly, and wishes she hadn't lied, because if he knew her mother was dead he might forgive her. She is desperate for his forgiveness.

"Why don't you go home and take care of her," he says gently.

"Thank you, Dale. Thank you so much."

"And stay home. You're fired."

DETECTIVE HOLLY MEYLIN

It's midafternoon, just past two o'clock, and the temperature is already dropping. Holly ashes out the car window. Amador is a human candle, burning in anticipation beside her in the squad car. Her phone rings, but Holly doesn't look at it. Whatever it is can wait.

When they pull into the parking lot of Nick Sullivan's apartment building, Holly sees the black Oldsmobile. Pradko sent a tow truck. They'll bring the car in, process it, and hopefully get something good enough for the judge.

When he answers the door, Sullivan is rumpled, sullen. He's got that befuddled look of someone who's eaten more than his share of sleeping pills. Good. A confession will be easier if he's sleepy and stupid. "What," he says.

They explain, friendly, that they'd like to bring him in for questioning. No, nothing's wrong. Pure routine. No, it can't wait. They are very sorry.

"I've got to leave soon," Sullivan says. "I need to pick my daughter up. School gets out at three."

Not to worry, they assure him. They'll send an officer to the school and have his daughter brought to the station.

He doesn't like getting into the squad car. He's like a horse brought stamping into a trailer, except that Sullivan doesn't want to show that he's afraid.

But he should be.

NICK IS AWAKE for real by the time they reach the station. Holly watches, in the rearview mirror, as he reaches for the car's door handle, but there is no handle, not in a squad car's back seat. His hand slips over the blank plastic side. His eyes are loose in his head, darting all around.

When they walk into the station, Sullivan between her and Amador, he balks, stopping in his tracks in the lobby. "My daughter," he says. "It's nearly three. Someone needs to pick her up."

"We will," Amador says soothingly.

"What the fuck is wrong with you people? Send someone *now*. Call the school *now*. You are not leaving Rose alone at school."

Amador meets Holly's eyes. They know this isn't urgent; people are sometimes late to pick up their kids. Children stay in the school office until someone comes to collect them. Nick has an image in his head that won't exist: Rose standing in an empty, windswept parking lot. But Amador asks dispatch to send an officer to the school, and Holly says, "Okay," and gets out her cell.

There is a missed call from Georgia. She checks voice mail before she does anything else, finger lifted to keep Sullivan patient, but there is no message. So she calls the school office—Sullivan recites the number— speaks with the secretary, and hangs up. "There's no problem," she tells Sullivan. "A family friend already came to pick Rosie up early from school."

"No, that's wrong."

"Mr. Sullivan, I'm beginning to think that you're stalling, that you have something to hide. All we want to do is ask you a few questions."

"Listen to what I'm saying." His face is pale with panic. "There *is* no family friend. No one picks up Rose except me. If someone picked up my fucking child and said they were a fucking family friend, they were lying. Get on that phone and call them back. Find out who has Rose. Do it, or I will kill you."

GEORGIA
(GIGI)

In the car, Georgia stared at the parking lot. The sky had dimmed and the temperature had dropped. It was early afternoon, just after two o'clock. Her shift had barely started, and now it was over. Everything was. She hadn't even bothered to clean out her locker. Jimmy had walked her to her car. "Tough luck, sweetheart."

Georgia called Bella. Her cell battery was getting low and the phone was a hot little brick. Bella didn't have a cell, though, and no one picked up at the number Bella had given her that morning.

She was about to try the police department again when she remembered what Bella had said about getting Rosie to identify the voice of the man who had called her. Either Ruby must have given her number to the man who called, Bella had said, or he knew her real name and looked the number up. Dale knew all their real names. He kept all their phone numbers and home addresses on file.

Georgia glanced again at the time. School would end in about an hour, at three, when Rosie's dad would come to pick her up unless she took the bus. There was only one elementary school in town, and Georgia had gone there as a child, so she knew the way. She started the car.

———

"WHAT'S THE NAME, again?" the school secretary asked. Behind her, the clock showed that it was almost half past two o'clock.

"Rosie Sullivan."

"Teacher?"

"I'm not sure."

The secretary gave her an odd look.

"I'm a family friend," Georgia said. "Her dad asked me to pick her up early."

"Well, he didn't call us. I can't release his daughter to some random person."

"He seemed distracted. He didn't mention a teacher, or say he'd have to call the school. He and Rosie are having a really hard time after what happened to Samantha."

The secretary's mouth pursed knowingly. "Why don't we call Rosie down to the office."

When Rosie appeared, in a denim jumper, pink tights, and white sneakers, beaded pins fastened to each rung on the ladder of her shoelaces, her eyes went wide at the sight of Georgia. "Um, hi?"

"Hi, Rosie," she said brightly.

"Rosie, honey, do you know this woman?"

Rosie looked between them. "Yes," she said finally. "That's Georgia."

"Is she a friend of the family?"

"She's Samantha's friend."

"She says your dad told her to pick you up from school early."

Rosie's eyes were disbelieving, curious. "Okay."

The secretary pushed a spiral notebook toward Georgia. "You have to sign her out."

"YOU CAN'T DO that," Georgia said once they were in her car. She made Rosie get into the back and buckle her seat belt. "You can't let just anyone take you out of school."

"But you wanted me to."

"I could be a bad person!"

"Are you?"

"Listen, didn't you say you have a babysitter who lives in your building?"

"Mrs. Zace."

"We're going to leave you with her. She can call your dad." Georgia drove as quickly as she could while still being safe. When she arrived at the girl's apartment building, she turned around to look into the back seat.

"We can get out now," Rosie said, holding her backpack on her lap.

"Do you remember when you told me that a monster took Samantha? You said that he called you."

Rosie looked smaller, her body tighter. She fiddled with the zipper of her backpack. "No."

"Yes, you do. I want you to help me find him."

Rosie whispered, "I don't want you to find him."

"Will you listen to someone's voice and tell me if that's the person who called you? A recording of his voice. That's all. It won't be him, not really."

"I said I wouldn't tell."

"All you have to do is listen and say yes or no."

"He said he would play with me if I told."

When Rosie said *play*, it held the echo of how the man had said it. Georgia drew a sharp breath. "I won't let him."

"He took Samantha. He can take you, too. Me."

"How about, if it's him, look me in the eyes. If it isn't, look away. Then you're not breaking your promise." She dialed the club on her cell.

Heidi answered. "Lovely Lady."

Georgia hung up. She dialed again.

"Lovely Lady," Heidi said.

Georgia hung up. She dialed again. This time the phone rang and rang. She imagined Heidi muttering about all the creeps who call the club. The answering machine picked up.

"You have reached the Lovely Lady," Dale's voice said, "located at—"

Georgia passed the phone to Rosie, who put it hesitantly to her ear. Rosie looked at Georgia, eyes growing wide and scared. She stared into Georgia's face, unblinking, and did not look away.

DETECTIVE HOLLY MEYLIN

Holly stows her gun and phone in one of the mailbox-sized lockers outside the interview rooms before she steps into the box, where Amador is waiting with Sullivan. The interview room has one skinny window set with safety glass in a wired diamond pattern. Sullivan instantly rises to his feet. Holly holds her right hand out, flat, palm down, and thinks this interview won't end without them cuffing him. "Rosie's fine," Holly says. "I called your home and she answered. She said Judy Zace was there with her."

He looks relieved, yet says, "I didn't ask Judy to pick her up."

Amador says, "Do you know Judy Zace well?"

"Sure, but—"

"Seems like you trust her with your child."

"Yeah." Sullivan starts to speak again, but Amador talks over him. "So you trust her, she trusts you, and you have a nice, neighborly relationship. Borrow a cup of sugar, that sort of thing."

"Yes," Nick says, defensive. "We're good people. We help each other out. That's not my problem. I just don't get why Judy would go to school and pick Rosie up. Something's off."

"I'm sure you can clear all that up when we're done," Amador says.

He places a tape recorder on the desk between him and Sullivan and turns it on.

"You're recording this?" Sullivan says.

"We record every conversation," Amador says.

"You didn't before."

Holly sits and invites Sullivan to do the same. "We did, you just didn't notice it. We want you to notice this time. You need to understand the gravity of your situation."

Sullivan remains standing. "Me, understand? My wife was murdered."

"Girlfriend." It is a true pleasure to nettle him. For a moment it looks like he will strike her. Let him. That and his threat in the lobby will be catnip for a judge.

Sullivan sinks into his chair. "I want a lawyer."

"Do you now," Amador says. "Really?"

"Only guilty people need lawyers," Holly says. "We'll get you one, of course, if you like. If you're guilty. Are you? Should I get one for you?" She must, legally, if he asks, but her questions have made it hard for him to say yes to a lawyer without saying yes to his guilt. If he's clever he'll phrase the right words to work around this, but he is not clever. He is angry and scared. He eyes the tape recorder. "I assume that means we can continue without one," she says. "This shouldn't take long. Right, Amador?"

"Right. Now, you said, Mr. Sullivan, that you were home the night of the crash, that you were sleeping."

"Yes."

"You didn't realize Samantha hadn't come home until an officer showed up at your door."

"Yes."

"You slept through the call she made, and didn't even hear the answering machine's message until the morning."

He hesitates, then says, "Yes. This is ridiculous. It was three in the morning. Of course I was asleep."

"And you kept sleeping. You slept the whole night, soundly, in your bed, at home, with Rosie asleep in the other bedroom."

"How many times do I have to say it? Are you people morons, or what? Sitting around with your thumbs up your asses. Samantha is dead because of you. Investigation? Bullshit. Just the two of you useless pricks asking pointless questions."

"So the answer is yes."

"Yes, the answer's yes."

"You," Holly says, "are a liar."

GEORGIA
(GIGI)

After she left Rosie with Judy Zace, Georgia plugged her dying phone into the car's cigarette lighter, clicked quickly through the four contacts she had saved on her phone—Bella, Kaitlyn, Lady, and Mom— and dialed the last. It rang for a while and went to voice mail. "This is Detective Holly Meylin. Please leave a message." As Georgia drove home, fine rain cut against the windshield in pin-straight lines. The voice mail beeped. Georgia rapidly explained Violet's claim that Dale could leave the club without anyone being aware he'd left. "He called Ruby's house the night of the crash, right after Ruby called. It must have been when she left his office to get Lady Jade's things from her locker. Ruby's kid recognized his voice." It would have been easy for Dale to follow Ruby's car. He knew exactly where she would go, because he would have given her Lady Jade's address, and he would have had slightly more than two hours to get back to the club before it closed and he oversaw payout. As the words rattled out of Georgia's mouth, she knew her suspicion wasn't based on much: a scared child, a phone call, holes in Dale's alibi, the rumor that he had a nice car. None of it was proof.

Georgia turned left when she should have turned right. She did it automatically, the heel of her hand rounding the wheel as she passed the intersection she knew well, the red barn roof of the Dairy Queen, its sign shaped like a painted mouth.

She wasn't driving home. She was driving back to the club.

This was stupid. This was like the girl in the horror movie who goes down into the basement. Bluebeard's wife with a ring of keys. All keys are yours, all doors open to you. Here, the key to my strongboxes, filled with gold and silver. Here, the key to my suite. Yet this one little key you must not use. This one little chamber of mine you must not enter.

"I'm going to the club now. Call me back," Georgia said into her phone, and kept driving.

THE COTTON SKY had darkened by the time Georgia reached the Lady. The lot was half full. The rain had stopped, but gray, solid clouds clotted the horizon, promising more weather. Georgia tried Bella and Holly again, but neither picked up. She grabbed her partially charged phone and her bag.

The door backstage wouldn't be unlocked and manned by a bouncer at this hour, since it wasn't the start of a shift, so Georgia walked through the front door. Heidi, who was at the register, glanced at Georgia in surprise and then pity. "Begging won't work," she said. "Tears won't make him hire you back. And for chrissakes don't offer to blow him. One girl did that and he blacklisted her at all the clubs in the state. I'm lucky he didn't fire *me* for your screwup. Fucking entry-level purgatory here, working the register."

"I forgot to clean out my locker."

Heidi waved her in, flapping an irritated hand.

Georgia skirted the edges of the club, keeping to the darkness below the champagne room. She wove quickly through patrons who gave her a confused look—in sneakers, jeans, and a hoodie, she didn't look like a stripper and she didn't look like the sort of girl who came with her boyfriend or friends to the club, dressed as if on a date, in frilly black dresses and kitten heels and sparkly earrings.

Georgia had walked into the Lady not knowing exactly which dancer she was going to enlist in her plan, but as soon as she saw Sasha take a twenty from a guy and step into her raspberry mesh teddy, pulling it up over her breasts, Georgia decided. "Hey, Sash."

"What's up, you little ho. Heard you got fired. Sucks to be you."

"Can you do me a favor?"

"No."

Georgia took all the cash from her wallet and held it out. "How about now?"

SHE WAITED IN the club's main-floor bathroom, the one for patrons, for about ten minutes as she and Sasha had planned. Georgia had offered no explanations for what she wanted, and Sasha had asked no questions. Sasha promised to get Dale out of his office and keep him backstage. She swore she'd talk his ear off.

Back on the floor, Georgia met eyes with dancers who glanced up from their drinks. Most expressions were no more than a bored good-bye. Lacey blew a kiss. But none of them stopped what they were doing. They sipped from cocktail straws. The ones dancing leaned to whisper into a man's ear. It was the end of a dance. That eerie Beatles song was playing, one with a moody bass and bewildering words. Dresses were puddles on the carpet. The girls were lambent in the darkness, soft fires of skin, their belly chains bright. The dancers did the math in their heads and counted to their nightly number. It was nothing to them that Georgia took the steps to the third floor, up toward the lit window of Dale's empty office.

DETECTIVE HOLLY MEYLIN

"You know what I love about all this?" Holly shows Sullivan a photo of the black Oldsmobile, license plate clear, at the gas station in between his home and the club. Sullivan's face pales. He swallows, his Adam's apple bobbing as though an enormous fish in his gut is biting the line. "You stopped to fill up the tank," Holly says. "To a jury, that shows premeditation. You had time to think about what you were planning to do to Samantha."

"If this had been a crime of passion," Amador says, "murder in the heat of the moment, you'd be jailed until you're an old man. That's a better sentence than what you are going to get, because *you* got out of bed in the middle of the night. You drove to the club. You followed her and Kimberly Campana, and ran them off the road. You raped and killed one woman whom you had never even met, who was disposable to you, like human Kleenex, and then kept Samantha captive. That's cold calculation. That's jail for life."

"The death penalty," Holly says.

"No," Sullivan says, voice hoarse.

"Excuse me?" Amador cups a hand to his ear.

"I didn't do that. You're wrong."

"You're not the murderous type?" Pleasure coils inside Holly. "I thought you threatened to kill me. Guess I imagined that."

"Oh, it happened," Amador says. "I was there."

"That's right, you were. That makes you a witness. Will a judge look kindly on what he said?"

"No."

"What about the rape, binding, and strangulation of Samantha?"

"And the disposal of the body." Amador sets a large photograph of the corpse in front of Sullivan as though it were a placemat. Sullivan makes a thick sound, a tiny cry. "Juries give harsher sentences when a murderer mistreats a body. You cut into her foot. You dumped her into a lake to rot."

"I didn't." Sullivan puts both palms down on the photograph, covering as much as he can. "I would never hurt her."

"Funny you should say that," Holly says. "We have someone who can testify that you *did* hurt Samantha, not long before the night she disappeared."

"I didn't mean to. It was once. She got me so mad. I loved her so much. I love her."

"I bet you were jealous of the men who drooled over her at the club. Of the money, of a whole other life that had nothing to do with you. She chose a strip club friend over coming home to you."

"Listen." Sullivan's big hands are shaking. "I took my neighbor's car, yes. I heard Samantha on the answering machine saying she was going to drive a girl home and I got upset. It sounded like a lie. A stripper she never mentioned before, sick with a stomach bug? No. She was going out with a guy. Some fucking 'patron.' That's what I thought. I know I was wrong. If I could go back . . ."

"What would you do?" Holly asks quietly. They already have him on tape admitting to hurting Lind and taking the neighbor's car. They want nothing less than a full confession. He's already fracturing. All it will take is one good tap to crack him open, to make him flood his murderous goo onto them, the guilt and rage and need for release.

"I didn't know how good I had it," Sullivan whispers. "I had everything."

"We can make this easier on you. Just tell us what you did. Tell us about that night."

"Remorse matters to a jury," Amador encourages.

"I didn't drive all the way to the club," Sullivan says. "I was . . . I don't know what I was going to do. Show up. Make her see me. I'm better than them, you know? All those guys blow their money just to look at naked women. I had something real. She said so. You're not like them, she said. Then, on the drive there, I stopped feeling mad and started feeling dumb. I mean, I didn't even know if she'd still be at the club when I arrived. So I turned the car around and went back home. I got into bed. Then I woke up and my whole life was gone."

The sky outside the window has darkened. The rain has turned to sleet. Ice ticks against glass. Later, Holly will remember the phone in her locker and imagine how it must have buzzed like a frantic locust. She will never forgive herself.

"That's some story," Holly tells Sullivan. "Maybe if you hadn't already lied to us, I'd believe you. I *almost* believe it, though. I almost feel sorry for you."

HIM

He walked the main floor, appraising his world: the new brass pole, a girl twined about it like a merry-go-round animal, his deejay, his bouncers, his clients who would do the very same things he did, take the same things he took, were they not afraid of the consequences.

Gigi looked stricken when he fired her. He liked that. He liked how it hardened his will. She knew better than to beg, which made him want to teach her to beg.

Time was, he could wait awhile for his girl. Time was, he took her farther afield, less close to home. He recognized the risk in choosing one of his own dancers. He even welcomed that risk, with Ruby. He would play safer with Gigi, but playing safe had its pleasures, too: the care he would take as he followed her, the thoughts he would linger over during the long weeks he waited outside her home in one of his cars. Yes, he would move slowly. When she went missing, it would look like she had simply left town. She had gone to work somewhere else, in Chicago, or in some other state. No one would miss her, or remember. She had only her mother, and her mother had early dementia.

A new song began, the sole Beatles song in the club's regular rotation, with a swampy sound, lyrics like a chant. He was returning to his office when Sasha snagged his arm. "Why, hello, Dale." Sasha's tone pretended genteel surprise, as though they had encountered each other at a black-tie fundraiser, or the Kentucky Derby. "Come with me to the dressing room. There is something I simply *must* show you."

GEORGIA
(GIGI)

My door is always open to you, Dale would say, and sure enough the knob turned easily in Georgia's hand. The club's music suddenly softened when she closed the door behind her, the acoustics cushioned, as though the office were a womb with organs thumping all around it. If Georgia hadn't felt so nervous, her hands cold, spine tight, she might have felt sleepy in the old-timey comfort of the room. The polished desk, lustrous as the groomed coat of a bay horse. The emerald light of the library lamp. The chess book. The fish tank's lunar glow. The filing cabinet was made from birdseye maple, its grain patterned with such bubbling swirls that the wood did not look like wood but agitated liquid. She might as well start there, she decided.

The filing cabinet was filled with business records: invoices, accounts paid, ledgers. One file, separate from the rest, contained Xeroxes of the dancers' IDs, home addresses, and telephone numbers, but this wasn't odd or unexpected, as Dale required that information from all his dancers before they began working at the club, in part to make sure they were of age.

Georgia glanced over her shoulder, out the large interior window with its view of the main stage and floor. The plexiglass staircase would let her see anyone coming up to the office, and she was far enough from the window that no one glancing up from below would see her, so long as she stayed away from the fish tank, which was a bit too close. Still, she thought uneasily, if Dale came up the stairs, she would have no ideal exit. She would have to brazen past him on the stairs, or take the door that went down to the VIP rooms under construction in the basement, which she could maybe do if he didn't see her first.

She shut the filing cabinet and went to his desk. Heavy pens, sharpened pencils, new erasers. Mints in a tin. No photographs. No crumpled receipts, no loose change. Everything was catalogue perfect, as though Dale were not the owner and manager of a strip club but someone in charge of set design for a movie about a world-weary politician who finds his moral compass and takes on Washington. She lifted the edges of the Persian carpet on the wooden floor. Nothing, not even dust, lay beneath it.

Georgia glanced at her phone. No missed calls. She slid the phone back into her purse. Relief shimmered through her, and she wondered if she had gotten herself worked up and suspicious only in order to feel the shaky, safe pleasure of having been wrong, or at least not having been proven right. There was nothing amiss in this office, no blood spatter or . . . she didn't even know what. She wasn't sure what she was looking for.

But that wasn't her job, was it? She should leave. She should call Holly again.

And she would have done so, if not for something that caught her eye as she turned toward the door. In the fish tank, beneath the shadow of a suckermouth catfish, amid turquoise gravel, pressed up against the glass, was a glint of gold.

Georgia stepped toward the tank. Dread crept over her flesh, but she pushed up her sleeve. Fish darted, staring with lidless eyes. They drove to the surface for food. She reached into the tank, the water as warm as a glove, past the flurry of hungry fish. Water came up to her armpit, soaking her hoodie, the smell softly rank, like dirty velveteen. She dug into the gravel and pulled the glittering line out of the tank.

It was a frail necklace dangling a pair of ballet slippers. They jerked on their string, dripping water from golden toes.

DETECTIVE HOLLY MEYLIN

Sleet comes down harder, a steady crackle against the window, as Sullivan tries to defend himself, to explain why his blood type was found in Samantha's car. It was his car, too, he says, and yes, he is B positive, but so what if his DNA matched? He doesn't care what the lab report said. He could have cut his finger on something months ago in that car. It was *his* car. Anyway, he didn't give them permission to take his DNA, and they had taken it anyway. That has to be illegal. He knows he refused to give a sample, he just *said* so, but he wasn't hiding anything. He refused to give a sample because he didn't like how they were treating him. He denies ever having gone to Hodgkins, where that other body, Ken Roche's cold case, was found with a crown cut into the foot.

"If you were innocent," Amador says, "you wouldn't have pretended you were home all night. We caught you in one lie. Who's to say you're not lying to us now?"

"I didn't tell you I left home that night because I knew how it would look." Sullivan's voice rises in panic. "Listen to me. I shouldn't have taken the neighbor's car but I didn't *do* anything."

"Why did you take the car?" Holly asks. This is the way to get a confession: to ask question after question, to ask the same question many ways until he slips or breaks.

"I told you, I got a little crazy, but I went back home."

"Tell us again."

Sullivan looks around the little room, at the narrow, dark window. "You can't keep me here forever."

Holly says, "We've got all the time in the world."

GEORGIA
(GIGI)

She found a class ring from 1987 with an aquamarine stone. She raked through the gravel again, stirring silt. Fish swarmed like bees. Water slopped over the side of the tank, running down to the hardwood floor.

A pink barrette. A tarnished silver bangle.

Her throat tight, she lifted a few rocks from the top of a cairn, still believing that she could remedy the mess she had made, that she could put it all back so that no one would notice. Surely these hidden objects held no meaning. Then she saw, nestled below the rocks, a backless pearl earring as white as an eye. Its tiny diamond stud pricked her thumb. She lifted it from the water and brought it close to her face, water leaking down her wrist.

The earring was Ruby's.

HIM

Sasha was determined to show him every filthy corner backstage. The urine-sprinkled toilet seat. Dust on the beauty bar lightbulbs. Glitter on the floor. She walked him past all the lockers marked with dancers' names and smelling of socks and body spray. Gigi's lock still hung from hers.

"Disgusting," Sasha said. "It is a *mess* back here, right?"

"Yes." He meant it but was surprised by her fervency. He encouraged the girls to come to him with their problems, and was pleased by how they trusted him and shared sordid details of their lives. They looked to him for approval, showed affection, faked affection, showed respect, faked respect. Sasha, however, had never been one to seek him out.

"Look at this." She swept her hand to indicate the uncapped deodorant and soiled makeup sponges littering the beauty bar. "Lacey again, I bet. Bella is even worse, that nasty paw box. I pray for her."

Girls began to file into the dressing room to collect T-shirts. It was time for the twofer. Heidi trailed behind, herding them along.

"I will bring this up with the dancers after we close," he told Sasha. "You better get in line."

"What I'm showing you is more important, don't you think?"

"No."

"Dale," Heidi said. "Gigi stopped by."

Sasha went a little stiff, caught him looking at her, then grinned widely in a way he didn't like.

"What for?" he said.

"She had to clean out her locker."

"Did you see Gigi?" he asked Sasha.

"Me? No," Sasha said, but Sasha was a liar.

"Is she still in the club?" he asked Heidi. She shrugged.

He would have suspected nothing, if Sasha hadn't just marched him past the lockers, and if he hadn't noticed that Gigi's still had its lock. If she had cleaned out her locker, why had she left the lock? It wasn't that he knew what was wrong, only that *something* was wrong.

"Heidi, get one of the bouncers," he said. "Tell him to bring the lock cutter."

DETECTIVE HOLLY MEYLIN

They have questioned Sullivan for hours. He keeps saying that he wants to explain, and they're fine with letting him explain as much as he likes, because eventually a suspect gets tired and contradicts himself. Sullivan will screw up, but for now he repeats his story. It has gotten late. The window is black and Holly doesn't know what time it is when someone knocks at the door.

Pradko grins at what must be naked fury on Holly's face. He knows better than to walk in during an interview. "Hi, friends," he says. "Sorry to interrupt, but someone's cell has been ringing inside the lockbox. Maybe one of our fine detectives here wants to check their phone?"

Later, when Holly speeds down slick roads, running her siren, red and blue flung out into the icy night, she will hear Georgia's voice mail repeating in her mind. I'm going to the club now. Call me back. Holly will remember the dropkick to her gut when she saw the missed calls. When this is all over, she will curse her stupidity. How could you miss this? How could you not have known?

HIM

Gigi's locker was stuffed, dresses dripping off hangers, some slumped at the locker's bottom.

"Onstage," he told the girls, who had gathered to see what was going on. "Now."

He went out onto the main floor, hunting for her, and it did not take long. All he needed was to lift his gaze to his office, where she was framed by the interior window, face averted. She stood near the fish tank, staring at the palm of her uplifted hand.

She knew.

A stony anger grew from his belly, filling him like concrete. Steps heavy, he ascended the staircase.

Would she look up? Would she see him coming?

She did, when he had almost reached his office door.

Her face was like a painting, it was so still, her expression rigid and familiar, stunned by fear.

She had two choices. If she was smart, she would open the office door and scream. She would rush toward him and try to go down the stairs into the safety of witnesses. If no one heard her screams above the music, they would see him struggle with her.

If she was stupid, she would turn and open the other door in his office to run down into the basement where the VIP rooms were almost ready.

She did neither. Fumbling with panicked hands, she pulled a cell phone from her purse. Her large eyes on him, she began to dial.

DETECTIVE HOLLY MEYLIN

Later, Holly will lift one of Dale Gately's chess pieces, the king, with a blue-gloved hand and turn it over to see the mark of a crown carved into its base. She will search through his dustless house and see his restrained yet rich style: a chesterfield sofa with buttery leather, suits hanging like rows of splendid dead men, polished silver in drawers, the house wholly his, with no sign of anyone else save for an antique schoolhouse desk sized for a child, its feet black wrought iron filigree. Holly will wonder whether it was a desk for the boy he had been, or a girl he had captured.

He was in the army in the seventies. "Plenty of girls knew that," Sasha will tell Holly. "I bet Ruby knew, too. But you never asked." A 1998 black Cadillac Brougham—and other well-cared-for cars, which he alternated when he drove, so that no stripper was able to identify any particular car as his—was registered under the name of his father, who had died of a supposed heart attack in '78.

Holly will discover that Dale Gately owns property outside of town: a gray clapboard farmhouse surrounded by fallow fields. She will lead a corpse-sniffing dog into the old barn with its dirt floor and furtive birds ducking in and out of the hayloft. The dog will find a corner, lie down, lift its head, and whine.

Amador will flinch when he sees the ballet slippers necklace. He will pull the case file of a girl murdered in the eighties, Jessica Anders. They will study cold cases across the state that go back decades and, for years to come, match ghosts with the other trinkets they had tagged as evidence, a grim lost and found.

When Holly gets a call from a downstate cop who's got a body in an abandoned silo, Holly will drive to the scene and see nothing but bound bones. No evidence. If there was ever a crown carved into the foot, it disappeared long ago.

In a silo, even small sounds echo. Holly will tip her head back, look up into the metal dome, and feel as though she is at the bottom of a waterless well, alone with the unnamed bones. Did you do this? she will think as the sound of her footfalls rap against the curved walls. Is this your doing?

Holly will remember Georgia Walker, and know that while the question is for Dale Gately, it is for herself, too, for the crime of her failure.

HIM

He rushed up the stairs, shoving open the door and shutting it behind him. With a small cry, Gigi backed away. Her sneaker squealed as she slid in a puddle on the wooden floor. In one sharp movement, he knocked the phone from her hand, pushed her into the fall that had already begun, and brought her to the floor.

She was on her side, keening beneath him. He turned her over onto her face, pressing her open mouth against the floor. He worked his right arm around her throat and hugged her to him as he brought his left arm up in a choke hold and palmed the back of her head. He held her tight against his kicking heart. He pressed the sides of her neck as she struggled.

He didn't want her dead, not yet. He wanted to know whom she had told. He would make her say, once the club closed and no one could witness what he did. She slackened in his grip. He felt her sag into her bones.

When he got up from her prone form, he glanced out the window, down into his club.

All was as it ever was. Naked girls danced on the glowing stages. Men smoked, watching the girls, watching the game. Waitresses took orders. People were busy making money, spending money.

No one looked up. No one had noticed anything.

The phone. He reached for the Nokia on the floor. The cell phone's screen showed 9 and 1, but not the final 1. A thrill lit his bones. He had come so close. But he hadn't been caught, and the fact that Gigi was in his office but the police were not, that nothing disturbed his world of the club below, made him think she was here of her own suspicion and had told no one.

The battery was low. He clicked through her last calls. Her phone displayed the last seven dialed calls, their times, and each call's duration. Bella. Lady. Lady. Lady. Mom. Bella. Mom. The first call, to Bella, was earlier that day but no one had answered. Only the calls to the club had been answered, but briefly, and the same was true for one of the calls to Gigi's mother. He pressed and held the voice mail key. Nothing.

He looked down at Gigi. Her hair was a dark cloud. He could not see her face. He was still angry, and he would make her explore his anger. He would make her live inside it. He believed, however, that he was probably safe.

His things lay scattered over the floor. It disturbed him to see them all together, in a shiny, wet pattern like an arcane message, as though the things knew something he did not. He always kept them separate from each other in the tank, and now they looked as though they had been gossiping. Colluding.

He gathered them, small in his hands, easily collected into a fist, and dropped them into his pocket. Then he picked up Georgia's spilled belongings and placed them back into her purse. Hunkering so that he would not be seen through the window from the floor below, he dragged her body toward the door that led down to VIP.

GEORGIA
(GIGI)

It smelled like a forest.

Georgia opened her eyes to icy fluorescent light. Her throat hurt. Her neck felt as though she were wearing an iron collar. She lay on her side, wrists bound behind her, ankles tied.

She was in VIP, in one of the new rooms, the lumber pale, unstained, work lights strung up overhead with orange cords. Raw benches were built into the walls, waiting for leather. VIP was the color of a honeycomb. The door was shut. Her purse sat in the corner, out of reach.

You always think, Don't do this to me, when the awful thing is already done, when it is too late to recall. Georgia tried to cry out, but her voice was almost gone. Maybe that didn't matter. If Dale chose not to gag her, that meant he had locked the door to the basement so that no one would be able to hear her even if she screamed. She tried screaming anyway, and sounded like a baby bird, like air let out of a balloon in sharp bursts.

She didn't know what time it was, whether the club was still open. She imagined dancers strutting the floor above. They sweet-talked men into champagne. Stay that way, she willed. Do it forever. Never close. When the club was closed, Dale would come for her. Down here,

Georgia couldn't hear the club's music. She heard nothing but the work lights' buzz.

Then her phone rang, muffled, inside her purse.

Holly? Georgia was hungry with hope. The phone rang and stopped, rang and stopped. She had chosen her ringtone that day at the mall with Kaitlyn. Was Kaitlyn calling? Her pretty cousin. When they were little, they had worn each other's clothes. Maybe Bella. Tell me what you want, Bella had said. Georgia's lips were wet and tasted of salt.

The phone rang again, then stopped suddenly, mid-ring. Her low battery. The phone was dead. Despair shoveled into her gut.

Georgia strained to hear a ring. It did not come again.

DETECTIVE HOLLY MEYLIN

Holly cuts the sirens as they approach the club. The units she pulled from patrol do the same. The sleet has turned into tiny hail that speckles the hood of the car and stings Holly's face when she and Amador get out and position patrol officers to guard the club's exits. The neon sign over the roof exhales its color into the night, pink as a peony. The sky above is cut from black stone. Cold, and it's going to get colder.

They had no time for a search warrant or a special ops squad, but they can radio for backup if they need it. Amador flags two patrol officers and motions for them to follow Holly and him into the club. The double black doors open and music presses against their bodies as Holly orders one of the patrol officers to go up to the deejay booth and shut down the music. She scans the club for Dale Gately. Amador gets into a bouncer's face, friendly all the while. You don't know where Gately is? Think harder.

Holly sees him at the bar with a glass of water, suit neat, face calm. He is as dapper as a wedding cake topper. He drinks. The water vanishes into his mouth, runs into his body, nourishing it, filtering into each cell. Holly's ribs are a steel barrel filled with treachery. Why do some people get to live? When God told Abraham to sacrifice his son, Abraham didn't say, Take someone who deserves it. He didn't say, Dash the cup of joy from another's lips. He said, Take my only child. Take all my love. It is yours. Holly knows the story ends with a dead ram and the son safe from harm, but that somehow makes God's demand worse. What did the boy do, afterward, knowing his father didn't love him best? Holly would never do that to her son. She would sooner drag God himself to the altar stone.

Gately sees her. He sets down the glass.

She shoves him facedown onto the floor, her knee in his back, her fists in his kidneys. She wrenches his arms behind him and cinches the cuffs.

He tells her this is unnecessary. The music stops midsong. Let me up, he says. He is happy to help with whatever she needs. Yes, Georgia Walker came to the club earlier today. That was some time ago. Holly is welcome to speak with Heidi, the house mom, who saw Georgia arrive to clean out her locker. I fired her. Gigi was upset with me. Sasha will tell you so. Gigi came to my office to beg for her job back. I said no. Detective, these accusations are baseless. She called you? These girls are born liars. It is their job to lie. Gigi is angry, of course, but she broke a rule and I retain the right to run my business as I see fit. Firing some- one isn't against the law. No, I don't know where she is. She left the club hours ago. How am I supposed to know where she is?

"I might," a voice says into the attentive quiet. Holly looks over her shoulder. It is Violet. "I might know where he would keep her," Violet says, "if she's still here."

GEORGIA
(GIGI)

The door to the basement opens, startling Georgia out of a nasty daze. She hadn't been asleep, but almost, exhausted by dread. The room had seemed to grow smaller, the pale walls shrinking. She could almost taste the scent of raw wood. She tricked herself, sometimes, into believing that the walls that confined her also protected her. She fell in and out of this trick, held by it, released. Georgia hears the sound of sharp footfalls, and breaks through her pretense like a stone dropped onto taut paper that splits and exposes the void beneath.

"Georgia?" It is a woman's voice. It is Holly's.

Georgia's voice is too weak to carry. Her numb, bound feet and hands fill with painful static as she bunches her legs beneath her and shifts her body until her sneakers touch wood. She kicks the wall. I'm here. She kicks again, more loudly this time, and the voice changes: excited, closer. Georgia kicks, her ears roaring. Her flesh rushes with urgency. She can barely hear anything other than her hammered thuds.

She's here, the muted voice calls. The locked door jerks in its frame. Someone get an ax.

HOLLY

The lights of the club have been thrown on, and Holly can see the stages and floor the way a cleaning crew would, after hours: the burns in the rust-colored carpet, a tumbleweed of hair drifting down a plexiglass staircase. The club is full of shouting people, and they all want to go home. Backup better get here soon, because every single person, dancers and patrons and bouncers and waitstaff, must be interviewed. For now, Georgia is in the basement, safe from the club's chaos and under the watch of a patrol officer whom Holly instructed to do a vitals check and administer first aid. When Holly and Amador broke through the VIP door, Georgia had been lying on her side like a shot deer, her eyes wide with horror and hope. Holly went to her fast. She cut her ties. Georgia gasped, the sound hoarse, as circulation returned to her hands and feet, and Amador told Georgia that she was okay, that everything was all right, but Holly's chest was stuffed with anger, and she refused to say any such thing.

On the main floor, Amy Tillson—Sasha—her dress pulled up haphazardly, one hot pink strap down at her elbow, argues with a patrol officer by one of the smaller stages. She stabs the man's chest with a pointy painted nail and says she does not care if this is a crime scene, she can't be here all night. Her daughter is home alone. Violet, who led

Holly and Amador to the VIP room, reaches behind the bar for a bottle of bourbon and pours herself a drink, then measures more out for several of the other dancers, who survey the scene with a practical patience not very different from the officers' expressions. The patrons are pissed. They are just beginning to realize how late this evening will go, and that they will have to call their wives.

Dale Gately sits on the ground, handcuffed to the bar's footrail, pale and silent, as though no more human than a snowman. His suit is barely rumpled. His green eyes lift to Holly and then erase her. He has refused to speak since Holly and Amador followed Violet downstairs. Each moment of his silence feels deliberately built, artisanal. Amador had clapped Holly on the shoulder when they came up from the basement, but what was there to feel good about? How is Amador not angry, like Holly is angry?

"Detective Meylin?" says a patrol officer, a curly-haired woman. "Detective Amador wants to see you in the office."

Upstairs, in Gately's office, Amador is on his cell, ordering the evidence team to the scene, telling them that file cabinets need to be seized, the entire club worked over. The floor is wet, the angelfish in the tank frantic. On the desk lie several objects in separate evidence bags. A ring, a bangle, Samantha's pearl earring, each the hardened residue of a life. Outside Holly's childhood home, in the grass yard, the fields of soybeans and corn stretching behind, stood her mother's greenhouse, which had been on the land for generations and was crafted with glass-plate negatives sometime after the Civil War. Many photographs were taken of that war, but after it was over, no one wanted to look at them. The negatives were sold and reused, cheaper than clear glass. By Holly's time, the images used to build the greenhouse had been burned away by the sun. She remembers standing in the greenhouse, air thick with the smell of dirt, her view of the farm split into a foggy graph by the greenhouse's iron frame. She imagined the plants dappled by shapes that the glass-plate negatives once cast, fruits and vegetables ripening in the shadows of people long gone, and of battles over. Holly had saved everything that belonged to Daniel. His things could be on Gately's desk, too, each sealed in a transparent bag. A stranger, maybe, will see them one day—Daniel's cup, his spoon—and they will be no more than things, just as each pane of greenhouse glass had burned clear, the meaning gone.

Amador keeps talking, his voice grim and satisfied—a hero's voice, Holly supposes. He smiles at her. She doesn't want to look at him, so she drops her gaze to the floor and catches a hint of gold tucked beneath the rug's fringe. She pulls on evidence gloves and bends to lift the necklace, its ballet toes dancing.

Amador claps the phone shut. "I know that one," he says, but Holly doesn't ask how. She doesn't have room for his shock, his expression close to wonder. She allows him to take the necklace from her and bag it. He says he thinks that the necklace is connected to a cold case from the eighties, from his childhood. He keeps talking—about pulling old files, contacting the FBI—then takes a better look at her, stops, and says, "Holly. You did good."

"No."

"You saved her."

"Georgia saved herself. She solved this. I put her in danger."

"But she's okay. We got him."

Holly shakes her head. Her fingers tremble. She pats her coat pockets, yet they are empty.

Amador takes a fresh pack, her brand, from his coat and unwraps it. He lights a cigarette, inhaling until it glows. He hands the cigarette to her, although she is too surprised to bring it to her mouth. When he touches her cheek, his fingers smell of tobacco. "You got here in time," he says. "Let that be enough."

It isn't. Yet she leans into his touch, his rough hand. Her anger leaves her. She can't grasp it as it slides away, as he holds her close. She rests her face against his chest. She lets his kindness be enough.

GEORGIA

In the passenger seat of Holly's parked squad car, Georgia tries to plug her dead phone into the lighter, her effort so messy and wayward that Holly eyes her and does it herself.

"I'm sorry," Holly says. Georgia's wrists have bloody grooves.

Outside, the sleet has stopped. The parking lot pavement shines like glass as the snow comes down in fat flakes. The snow disappears into the club's pink neon sign, then reappears over the cars. Everyone—the dancers, the bouncers, the patrons, and Dale—has been kept inside as snow dusts the black parts of police cars and vanishes against the white ones. Snowflakes flare in the red and blue lights.

Holly says she will take Georgia to the hospital and Georgia tries to say that she's fine, but that's too hard to manage, so she just says no.

"I can't make you," Holly says, yet adds that it will be good to photograph what Dale did to her throat and ankles and wrists, and have a doctor's report as evidence for the trial, so Georgia nods. Holly smells of cigarettes. She says that she needs to go inside to talk with her partner, Detective Amador, who is engaged in a witness triage where he has the club under lockdown and has separated everyone for questioning. Dale won't be brought out for arrest until Georgia has left the scene,

Holly promises, and begins to say more, but Georgia's hand jerks up, palm flat, so Holly stops.

"Are you good to be alone for a bit?" the detective asks. Although Georgia nods, Holly points outside to a young officer standing nearby, snow on his shoulders, the one who had shone a light in her eyes in VIP and checked her pulse. Holly says, "He'll keep an eye on you until I get back. I won't be long." Holly reminds Georgia that there's hot coffee right there, in the cup holder, that it's for her and she should drink it. When Georgia's hand closes around the blazing Styrofoam, Holly makes an approving sound and says, "You're okay." Then she opens the door, cold gusting in, snowflakes melting in midair.

Georgia knows a lie when she hears one. She watches Holly walk back toward the club, her short, straight dark hair flicked by the wind, and sees, at the same time, the car window's interior reflection of herself. She stares at her phantom face layered onto the yellow-lit parking lot. The snow shivers. Brass stanchions and red velvet ropes stand in front of the club's entrance to control a line of invisible people. From here, in the warm car, the ropes are mere threads that dip up and down across Georgia's reflection. You are okay. You will never be okay. But you are lucky.

One day Holly Meylin will put a piece of paper in Georgia's hands, the letter of their bargain. The black print will swim in Georgia's eyes and she will remember this moment in the car, how the wind skirled snow across the parking lot, twisting in front of the club's closed blackout doors as she realized that she would never walk into the club again.

Her phone wakes up, ringing. The green screen glows with Bella's name in tall black letters. Georgia answers. Her hoarse whisper makes Bella worry. Anxious questions come. Georgia's cheeks are hot and wet, the cup of coffee a torch in her hand, the cell phone warm against her cheek. The marks on her wrists are the kind that will leave scars. The heartbeat of police lights makes the snow seem alive as it floats over the club, and Georgia imagines that the club is gone, that it was never built. She peels the blacktop away, plucks lot lamps off like birthday candles, and sees this place as it once was, before people. The land is flat here. Nothing interrupts the sky. She sees a field of white unmarked by humanity, the wind lifting the flawless snow's top layer and scattering its lonely salt.

Need pushes into Georgia's chest. She makes everything again as it is. She does not want, after all, a world without people. She does not want to forget how Ruby chose to drive Jolene home. She does not want to forget goodness, how we offer ourselves to one another—that danger, that grace. She remembers Holly's hands at her wrists, her ankles. Holly's bright knife. Georgia watched Holly's hands, which seemed like many hands, quick and steady, cut the ties. Holly could not have carried her. She was not strong enough. But this is what Georgia remembers: being lifted, up and out, and set on the chest of the unsafe world.

"Give me a minute," Georgia says into the phone, "and I will tell you everything."

Living silence fills her ear. Bella is ready, waiting. It feels as good as love.

SAMANTHA

It was a hot day. It was July, the peak of summer, and Samantha had the day off, so she and Nick packed the car with a small cooler of ham sandwiches and Capri Suns and drove with Rosie to the dunes in Indiana. Long grass whispered along the crests of the hills of sand, where pink thistle bloomed, nodding in the light wind. As they walked down to the beach from the parking lot, Samantha pointed out to Rosie how the wind had made ripples along the dunes. There were cottontail rabbits in the grass, Samantha told Rosie, but Rosie didn't care. The sand burned Rosie's feet, even through her flip-flops, and she cried until Nick scooped her up and carried her. Samantha carried the cooler and towels. She was the only one to see the great blue heron rise from the dunes, its gawky shape made elegant by an enormous wingspan, its feathers more gray than blue. Its wings strode into the sky. She called for the others to look, but by the time they did, it was gone.

Lake Michigan was perfect. They immediately went into the water, which was fresh but not cold, and washed away the sweat of the car ride. Nick and Samantha played with Rosie in the shallows, Nick tossing his shrieking daughter into the waves again and again as she begged for more. Then Rosie grew bored of that and pretended to be a sea monster, ducking underwater and bursting through the surface with her hair hanging in front of her face, hands hooked into claws. Samantha pretended to be frightened.

Nick said he wanted to swim beyond the sandbar. The currents could be strong in the lake's deeper waters, so Samantha said she would sunbathe and keep an eye on Rosie, who wanted to collect pebbles on the shore.

Samantha stretched out on her towel. On clear days, Chicago's skyline could be seen across the lake. When she put on her sunglasses, Samantha saw it, just barely. It looked like haze. She lay down, face to the sun, letting the day bake into her body. The club felt far away. It felt like it didn't exist.

Rosie kept running up to show off her latest prize. A smooth, black oval stone. A slightly bigger, smooth, black oval stone. Another. They all held an obvious value to Rosie, who made Samantha examine each one and deposit them in a cairn near the towel. Rosie was going to take them home. Yes, the brown ones, too. And that piece of green glass, its surface softened by time.

Samantha sat up and watched Rosie swim, the child never going deeper into the water than chest high. Beyond her, Nick swam far out, his shoulders dark.

Rosie came out of the water, the lake lapping at her heels, and sprinted up the sand to Samantha. Her teeth chattered, and although Samantha offered to wrap Rosie's towel around her, Rosie didn't want that. She wanted to lie down next to Samantha on Samantha's towel. Rosie said the sun was too bright, so Samantha gave her her sunglasses, which were huge on the girl in a silly, wonderful way. Samantha didn't laugh, although she wanted to. Rosie needed to be taken seriously. She pushed her cold body up against Samantha's, her toes right against Samantha's calf, and shivered until she stopped.

As she lay next to Rosie's warming skin, Samantha imagined that Rosie was her child. Samantha had heard or read that the fetus of a girl already has millions of eggs inside her months before she is born. If I had a normal woman's body, Samantha thought, the egg that would

become Rosie would have been inside me even when I was a baby growing inside my own mother.

Nick was so far out on the lake that Samantha had to squint to see
him, and then she could not see him at all.

"Sam?" Rosie said.

Samantha looked down at Rosie, whose upturned face was half
masked by the sunglasses. Rosie said, as if she knew what Samantha had
been thinking, "I wish you were my real mom."

Samantha pulled Rosie close. The girl's swimsuit was clammy,
her skin as warm as cake. The sky dazzled, washing the world white.
It changed everyone else on the beach into ghosts. The sand became
milk, the lake ice. Rosie, though, was as vivid as ever: the freckles on
her tan nose, the twisted ropes of her hair, the pink ruffles of her swimsuit straps, her worried mouth. Samantha said, "I *am* your real mom."

Rosie smiled. Two new teeth were coming in. One day, Samantha
thought, she would see Rosie's grown smile. Rosie would grow up and
leave her, because that is what children do.

But not yet.

Samantha shifted to sit up and pulled Rosie onto her lap. "Can you
see Chicago?" Samantha pointed. She couldn't see it anymore; the sun
was too bright without her sunglasses. Rosie looked, her hand a visor,
and said, "You mean that sparkly stuff?"

"Yes, on the horizon. It's the skyscrapers."

"But Chicago is so far away."

"I know."

"I can see across the whole lake?"

"You can see across the whole lake."

"Wow."

"Not always," Samantha said. "But sometimes."

The waves pulled away and came back. Rosie dropped her hand to
Samantha's knee. She was heavy and hot on Samantha's lap, and Samantha knew that Rosie would soon grow restless, and break away to run
into the water, and be cranky on the ride home if she did not fall asleep.
Still, this moment was theirs, sure and solid, forever. If Rosie forgot,

Samantha would remind her. Remember when we went to the beach? Remember what we said?

Rosie said, "It looks like a magic land."

"Let's pretend that it is," Samantha said, and held her girl, and was happy.

ACKNOWLEDGMENTS

Thank you to:

My brother, Officer Jonathon Rutkoski, and my sister-in-law, Detective Rosie Rutkoski, for many conversations about police procedure and for putting me in touch with their colleagues.

Detective Sergeant Tizoc Landros, Detective Sergeant Ed Grizzle, and accident reconstructionist Sergeant Phil Stice of the Joliet Police Department, and Detective Keith Flannery of the Manhattan South Homicide Squad, for taking the time to answer all of my questions patiently, thoughtfully, and with good humor.

Mark L. Taff, M.D., former chief medical examiner in Rockland County, New York, for his help regarding forensic pathology.

Dr. Ilene Wong, board member of InterACT: Advocates for Intersex Youth, and Jeanne Nollman, former head of the AIS-DSD (Androgen Insensitivity Syndrome-Disorder of Sex Development) support group. I am grateful for their wisdom and the important work they do.

All those who read drafts or portions of drafts: Marianna Baer, Holly Black, Doireann Fitzgerald, Donna Freitas, Eve Gleichman, Anna Godberson, Drew Gorman-Lewis, Anne Heltzl, Kelly Link, Shannon Luders-Manuel, Sarah Mesle, Neel Mukherjee, Jeanne Nollman, Emily

XR Pan, Becky Rosenthal, Jill Santopolo, Eliot Schrefer, Titania, Robin Wasserman, and Ashley Woodfolk.

Other dear friends who shared advice, perspective, and experience: Renée Ahdieh, Manuel Amador, Akeela Azcuy, Zoraida Córdova, Vinnie Curcio, Joy Daniels, Morgan Fahey, Nelly Lopez, Sarah Maclean, Daniel Matos, Andrew Needham, Carrie Ryan, and Eric Weigeshoff.

Cassandra Clare and Josh Lewis, Adam and Sabina Deaton, Valérie Buffet, Jocelyne Buffet, and Yann Guinard, for their kindness, hospitality, and generosity.

Professor Ellen Tremper, for always supporting me and my career.

The *Harvard Review*, for publishing the chapter "Frankie" as a short story called "El Capitan."

My agent, Alexandra Machinist, for believing in me and having the keenest sense for what is right.

Felicity Blunt, Sophie Baker, Roxane Edouard, Josie Freedman, Ruth Landry, Lindsey Sanderson, and everyone at ICM and Curtis Brown UK.

Everyone at Holt, especially my editor Serena Jones, for her wisdom, and editorial assistant Anita Sheih, Carla Benton, Janel Brown, Kathleen Cook, Karen Horton, Carolyn O'Keefe, Carol Rutan, and Christopher Sergio, as well as the many people who contribute to a book's production. Many thanks, too, to those same counterparts at Tinder (Headline) in the UK, especially my editor Jen Doyle and Alara Delfosse. Serena and Jen masterfully shaped this book into what it is.

Thank you, finally, to my partner, Eve Gleichman. I love you so much.

ABOUT THE AUTHOR

Born in Illinois, MARIE RUTKOSKI is a graduate of the University of Iowa and Harvard University. She is a professor of English literature at Brooklyn College and a *New York Times* bestselling author of books for children and young adults. She lives in Brooklyn with her family.